PRAISE FOR *THE OBL*

Hart's prose is electric and probing, and his scenes stay with you long after you've put the book down. Sweet and brutal in equal measure, *The Oblivion Society* is by turns a bright and bouncy pop song, then as ruthlessly cruel as Celine Dion. Post-apocalyptic survival has never been so much fun!
— Austin McKinley
    Senior Editor, Flying Car Comics

The Oblivion Society [demonstrates] a sly understanding of geek culture. [...] Basically, if you like Christopher Moore, you will like this novel.
— A Betterment Worker
    Working Towards the Betterment of Publishing

What hooked me was the quality of the writing and the ability of the author to tease me on from one page to the next. [...] Literature? That's a hard label to justify, but I think so. [...] I'm glad Marcus Alexander Hart wrote this story. I'm glad that someone still writes books that champion the finer qualities of being human, even if he spills a lot of blood and guts in doing so.
— Glynn Compton Harper
    Author of *A Perfect Peace and Arise Beloved*

This fast-paced novel combines one part sci-fi B-movie adventure, one part foul-mouthed slacker comedy, one part post-apocalyptic road movie, with just a pinch of chick-flick to create an explosive read.
— Alistair Hoel
    nyquil.org

[Check out *The Oblivion Society*] in preference to most of Tom Holt's later efforts, most of Terry Pratchett's later efforts and, despite the comparison, in preference to anything by Robert Rankin. He doesn't beat Douglas Adams but there's no shame in that.
— Leo Stableford
    LeoStableford.com

THE
OBLIVI☢N
SOCIETY

MARCUS ALEXANDER HART

Permuted Press
The formula has been changed...
Shifted .. Altered .. Twisted.
www.permutedpress.com

This book was copy edited by Will DeRooy.
www.WillDeRooy.com

All cover and interior artwork is by Michael Greenholt.
www.MichaelGreenholt.com

The official *Oblivion Society* typeface is "Tom's New Roman" by Tom 7.
fonts.tom7.com

For more apocalyptic fun, visit OblivionSociety.com.

The author may be contacted via email at me@marcusalexanderhart.com.

ACKNOWLEDGMENTS

This book would not exist without Michael Greenholt, Timb Kuder, and Amanda Dague. Mike has inspired me with his *Oblivion* artwork from day one all the way through the final book cover (and then another book cover after that). Timb always found something nice to say about the story, even when it sucked. And the world has Amanda to thank for the fact that this novel no longer contains a chapter based on explosive diarrhea.

This second edition would not exist without Jacob Kier at Permuted Press. You'll notice that there are many words afore the story starts. A foreword if you will. Thanks to David Wong for writing that.

I owe a debt of gratitude to Gary Fixler, Ben Jerred, Austin McKinley, Jer Warren, and Brian Young for their insightful critique. Thanks also to Will DeRooy, for doing such a fantastic job editing my labyrinthine prose into coherent English.

Additional shouts of appreciation and praise go out to—
Mariah Day and Gina Faustino, for promoting ObSoc at Comic-Con;
Irina Gelman, for teaching me to curse in Russian;
Tom Murphy VII, for his generous font licensing;
Sherrie McKinley, for a ghastly suggestion;
the bang. improv family, for making me one of their own;
the LiveJournal community, for answering all of my dumb questions;
Mom and Dad, for understanding;
and all of the other helpers who have been expunged from my memory due to time, age, and cheap beer. You know who you are, and I thank you.

Lastly, and perhaps most importantly, I would like to thank *you* for reading. All of the work that these folks put into this book doesn't mean anything if nobody is reading. So thank you for completing the circle. I hope you enjoy your initiation into *The Oblivion Society*.

— Marcus Alexander Hart
   August 18, 2007

FOREWORD
BY DAVID WONG

I'm not going to lie to you; I love unicorns. Unicorns are mankind's perfect symbol for God: full of grace and beauty, yet equipped with a razor-sharp skull spike that can impale your shit at the slightest provocation.

I love reading about unicorns. I love reading *only* about unicorns. And flamethrowers. These days, I won't pay for a book unless it has the word "unicorn" in the title, and a rendering of a mounted man with a flamethrower on the cover. Life's too short to settle for anything else.

And yet, when I go to my favorite book store and look for the flamethrower shelf in the unicorn section, I find neither. Why? Because, according to the manager who's escorting me roughly from the store, there's no "market" for that genre. As far as the big book chains are concerned, even Vince Wisnewski's superb *Charred Horn* series might as well not even exist.

Now contrast that with *The Audacity of Hope*, the erotic thriller by first-time novelist Barack Obama. A lot of people don't realize that part of Obama's contract stipulated that copies would be sold within five feet of every book chain's entrance, embedded in a life-size cardboard cutout of a naked woman positioned so that two stacks of the book were covering her breasts. If you wanted to see her boobs, you had to buy a copy. It went platinum in a month.

But that kind of promotion costs money. And big publishers only spend that money if they know they can make it back. So, they only spend it on the safe bets. And really, how often do the safe bets make interesting reading?

Of course, you know that already. That's why we're here. The very fact that you're holding this book in your hand proves you know there are alternatives. For every title you see at Waldenbooks, floating around it are the invisible ghosts of a hundred other equally good books that weren't allowed a spot on the shelf. One of these unseen volumes could change your life, if given the chance. But they're by unknown authors who never had the luck, or connections, or didn't blow the right people to stake a claim on the retail landscape. Because of that, it is a statistical certainty that your favorite book of all time is one you've never heard of.

And why? Because The Man didn't want you to hear of it.

But you, you're holding in your hand the tool by which The Man can be slain.* You've tapped into the secret vault of scrolls, the forbidden treasures, the row of fresh milk hidden behind the cartons of expired stuff at the convenience store. This little book is by one of the legions of young, hungry writers with stories to tell, riding onto the literary scene atop their unicorns of cutting edge print-on-demand technology, spewing forth their tales like so much thrown flame.

But guys like Marcus and guys like me, we need you. We don't want to have to beg the corporate hype machine for promotion, compromising the work along the way. And we don't want to have to paint the title of our book onto our bodies and then run naked onto the set of *Good Morning America* to get attention (again). We don't want to have to resort to some cheap-ass *Da Vinci Code* meta fiction hoax to get the word out. (*Wait, did you say sixty* million *copies in print? Hmmm…*)

No, what we need is regular old word of mouth. So if you read *The Oblivion Society* and you like it, tell a friend. If you hate it, tell an enemy you liked it. Just tell *somebody*.

Why? Because books change lives. Don't leave corporations in charge of who reads what.

But enough about that. If you're reading this, it's not because you want to hear about the indie book publishing scene and all the ways we struggle to get noticed. No, the odds are you're here because you heard about The Code.

Now, I'm not going to confirm or deny the rampant rumors about the life-changing secret message that may or may not be hidden in this novel. I'm just going to stick to the facts, as the facts are incredible on their own.

As you've no doubt heard, the "Oblivion Cipher" was discovered by Princeton University cryptologist Isaac Minkov in late 2005. Minkov took one glance at the cover of this tome and knew that it held secrets. He saw that the "**V**" in "Oblivion" was also the Roman numeral for **five**, and "**V**" is the **fifth** letter in the word. Underneath the title, Minkov found the name of the author listed as Marcus Alexander Hart. The "**X**" in "Alexander" is also the Roman numeral for **ten**. It is also the **tenth** letter in the name. **Five** plus ten equals **fifteen**, the exact number of letters in "Oblivion Society."

Minkov knew that to write this off as coincidence would be ludicrous.

No doubt you've already spotted that "Marcus Alexander Hart" is an anagram of "Relax, unearth rad scam." Suspecting that the name was false, a reporter for the New York Times found that it was a pseudonym for underground mathematician Muhammad Weinberg, a top code breaker for the NSA from 1989-1997 who took early retirement after reportedly suffering a

---

* Do not use this book to assault the owner of your local book store. That was a metaphor.

nervous breakdown.

Minkov spent three months with *The Oblivion Society*, decoding sequences within each paragraph to reveal what he called:

"A wondrous new work... perhaps the most important ever written in the English language. Life secrets reveal themselves like gems... fuck. Holy fucking... fuck."

Minkov steadfastly guarded the details of what the book actually revealed, except to say that any common reader could decode it once they knew what to look for, and that the decoding process would require the purchase of no fewer than four copies of the book (with six copies, the text reportedly decodes itself).

What sort of knowledge did *The Oblivion Society* impart that would leave such a profound impression on the man? We may never know. Minkov has since vanished from public view, after accumulating sudden astonishing wealth on the stock market and assembling a harem of some 37 young females. Journalists from all over the world have sought out Minkov, but he rarely leaves his private island in the South Pacific. One witness, a delivery man for an upscale clothing outlet who says Minkov now orders custom trousers that are "extra large in the crotch," says he last saw Minkov racing around the shore on a jet ski made of solid gold, one of his many topless lady friends on back.

I admit I've gone over and over my copy. For instance, in Chapter Eleven (right after Vivian and the gang leave the igloo) I found that by picking every fifteenth letter I could spell the word "fart." That's all I've gotten so far.

And you know what? I don't care. I say just sit back and enjoy the story. And whether you bought the full six copies or could only afford the four, we thank you for your support.

— David Wong
   John Dies at the End

For Amanda,
without whom I could not survive.

On the northern tip of Norway, an obsolete *Wormwood-132* long-range missile pointed into the heavens from the launch pad of the Fimbulvetr Astronomical Institute. Stripped of its atomic warhead and retrofitted with daytime auroral imaging instruments, it was ready for an exploratory voyage deep into the heart of the northern lights.

The nations of the world had commended the institute for repurposing wartime technology for the betterment of mankind on the brink of the new millennium. Or rather, they would have commended the institute, had they bothered to read its launch announcement. But the world's leaders had much more important business to attend to than some dumb Norwegian science experiment.

The president of the United States stuck his nose into his armpit and took a sniff. He recoiled and re-buttoned his navy-blue suit jacket.

"Hoo-boy, Bubba," he thought, *"you smell like the McDonald's fryer at the end of a long day."* He shrugged. *"Well, the coat's not coming off tonight anyway."*

He leaned against a white oak and let his gaze drift through the tree cover and into the Maryland sunset. For a so-called "presidential retreat," Camp Bravo afforded him precious little privacy. It had taken him hours to ditch his Secret Service escort, but now he was finally alone in this secluded corner of the compound.

He smiled as his eyes scaled the unbroken, twelve-foot-tall barrier of chain link and razor wire that protected him from the heathens of the outside world. Unbroken, that is, except for the huge rusted gash directly in front of him.

The Secret Service didn't know about this place.

The first lady didn't know.

The Camp Bravo groundskeepers didn't even know.

Only one other person did.

The president pulled a cigar from his breast pocket and put it in his mouth. He almost never smoked cigars, and when he did, he didn't inhale.

The sun slipped below the horizon, and he looked at his watch eagerly. Perhaps his signal had been too subtle? No, it was fine. Unmistakable. He daydreamed about what he could do with the cigar if he wasn't going to smoke it.

Footsteps pounded through the brush on the other side of the fence, step by weighty step. When the president's anticipation had fully filled out his trousers, a jet-black mound of hair emerged from the foliage, followed by a round, female face.

"Good evening, Mr. President," it purred. "Are you alone?"

The president grinned back at her from his side of the fence.

"It depends on how you define 'alone,'" he said flirtatiously.

The president's relationship with this particular White House intern had become somewhat sticky in recent days, literally before figuratively.

"I see you caught my speech this afternoon," he continued.

"I know you were addressing the entire nation, but I felt like you were speaking only to me," the intern cooed. "I especially liked the part about *breaching the walls* at the *darkest twilight* to meet between the *tall trees*."

The president's impossibly wide grin grew wider.

"Well, if you like trees, come on in and I'll show you the *executive branch*."

With a squeal, the intern shoved her way through the scar in the fence. As the intern's bosom pushed through the decayed steel, it also pushed through the beam of an invisible laser grid, shattering the air of Camp Bravo with an earsplitting security klaxon.

The air was calm in the People's National Strategic Control Centre just outside of Beijing, China. Chairman Qian leafed listlessly through the evening's state-sponsored newspaper. It was full of the same old propaganda touting China as the most powerful nation on Earth. He sighed and took a sip of his oolong tea.

If only it were true.

He looked around the room at the thirty sharply uniformed young men and women working quietly at their computer terminals. Actually, just young men. The chairman couldn't remember the last time he had actually seen a young woman. He sighed again.

One of the officers turned to him with an expression that completely failed to be alarm.

"Mr. Chairman, we've just received an urgent communiqué from one of our operatives in the field. There's been an international incident, sir."

The chairman stood up and smiled hungrily. It was about time. What good was being the leader of the largest standing army in the world if you never got to do anything with it? Finally, this old dragon was going to get a chance to roar! He put down his paper and teacup and issued a terse order.

"Identify."

The officer's short fingers clattered over his keyboard.

"It's from one of our agents in the United States, sir."

The smile dropped from the chairman's face, and he threw himself into his chair petulantly. Of *course* it was the Americans. It was *always* the Americans. He sulked. What good was being the leader of the largest standing army in the world if it was only the *second* most powerful? Contempt dripped from his voice as he issued a second command.

"Clarify."

"The personal fortress of their president has gone to a state of heightened alert, followed by several other military installations in the area. We do not know the reason."

"Classify," the chairman grumbled.

"There seems to be no specific threat, sir, but it would be prudent to raise our own alert level accordingly."

The chairman nodded his head. Sure. Raise the alert level. Just like always. He sighed. He could already see that he was in for another long, dull night of follow the leader.

Two technicians waited out another long, dull shift in the control room of a radar tracking station somewhere in northern Russia. A smattering of faded maps clung to the walls, each depicting the former Soviet Union marked with red pushpins that no longer signified anything at all. The station's gigantic radar dish still scanned the skies twenty-four hours a day, although exactly what it was looking for these days was something of a mystery.

Kurchatov leaned back in his chair and took a swig from a half-empty bottle of vodka. He was bored. Bored bored bored. He took another drink and glanced dully at his co-worker, Sakharov. Sakharov's face was tensed in concentration as he pounded the keyboard of the station's main computer. A bead of sweat welled on his forehead as he chattered to himself anxiously.

"No more of the stupid Zs! Come on, you piece of junk! Give me the long one! The long one!"

Kurchatov stood and glanced over his comrade's shoulder just in time to see him lose yet another game of *Tetris*. Sakharov smashed his fists into the desk in frustration.

"*Govno na palochkee!*" he cried. "I *hate* this stupid game!"

He rammed two fingers into the keyboard, closing the game window and revealing a monochrome screen of green text. In all the years that the station had been in operation, the dish's readout had never changed:

Radar Tracking Station 99

0000 Intercontinental Ballistic Missiles detected.

0000 Submarine Launched Ballistic Missiles detected.

Kurchatov slouched back into his chair.

"If you hate that stupid game so much, why do you sit there and play it all day?"

Sakharov tapped his finger on the desk in an impatient fury for ten full seconds before starting another game.

"The high score is 200,000 points," he muttered. "I'm not quitting until I beat it!"

"Well, how close have you come?"

"199,999.9999899."

"Well, why don't you just round off, *dolboëb?*" Kurchatov snapped. "That's not even a real score! It's just a computer error!"

"*Nyet!* There's nothing wrong with the computer!" Sakharov said, tapping the sticker on the front of its case. "Intel inside. American technology. No mistakes."

Camp Bravo's mistaken sirens smashed into the president's skull like an auditory sledgehammer. Between the trees he could see a distant commotion of soldiers rushing between the buildings, trying to identify and neutralize a threat that did not exist.

He pulled out his cellular phone, punched a speed dial button, and clasped it to his head. Even with his palms crushing down on his ears, he could barely hear the voice on the other end of the line.

"*Camp Bravo Command Center.*"

"Listen, kid! This is the president!"

"*Mr. President?*" the officer gasped. "*There's been a breach of the outer wall, sir! You may be in danger. What is your location?*"

"It's a false alarm!" the president screamed. "Turn off the klaxons!"

"*Yes, sir! Er ... no, sir! I'm sorry, sir, but a trigger of the perimeter alarm automatically puts every base on the East Coast on precautionary alert. I can't just turn—"*

"What do you mean you *can't?* This is the president of the United States giving you a direct order, soldier! Pull whatever plug you have to pull to cut off these damn alarms!"

"B-but, there are procedures, sir," the officer stammered. *"There's no way to just cut them off without completely resetting the emergency CommNet! It would be a huge breach of security, sir!"*

"Lieutenant, I don't care if you have to shut down the whole North American power grid!" the president screamed. "I want those alarms off *now!* Understood?"

"Y-yes, sir!"

Against his better judgment, but on the direct orders of the commander in chief, the officer hammered the security codes into his computer, gaining access to the nation's emergency communications systems. Within a few minutes, he had manually reset every circuit that carried some small part of the security network's data with a blatant and mandated disregard for any other traffic those nodes might have been carrying.

Somewhere deep beneath Cheyenne Mountain, every computer screen at NORAD went blank. Admiral Jack Teller dropped his Big Mac and leapt to his feet.

"What in the corn hell just happened, boys?"

A husky slab of officer poked at his keyboard.

"I don't know, sir. Every base on the East Coast went on alert, and before I could ask about it, all communications were completely cut off."

"What do you mean 'cut off?'" the admiral yelled. "What in the name of Sam Hill is going on out there?"

The top-heavy switchboard operator tapped on her headset and looked at a panel of dark bulbs. She snapped her gum and twisted a finger through her platinum hair.

"We've got like, nothing here, sir. No lines in or out," she reported. "Computers, phones, even the satellite links are like, totally dead."

"Impossible!" the admiral roared. "That's impossible! All this Captain Kirk crap down here is connected to the outside with redundancy out the ying-yang! The only way we've got nothing is if the whole damn comm network is down, and the only thing that could take down that network is a full-scale ..."

A troubled look stormed the admiral's face.

"What was the last thing we got before we lost the world, boys?"

The husky officer reviewed his logs and answered numbly.

"Satellite intelligence says the Chinese military just went on heightened alert, sir."

The admiral glared into the screen for a long moment, angrily cracking his knuckles.

"Scramble my knights of the air," he said. "I want nukes in the bellies of all my bombers, and I want those beautiful bastards ready to fly on my order. You got that?"

"Um, yes sir," the officer coughed, "but if you'll recall what Private Babs just said, we don't have any outgoing communications."

The admiral wrung his massive hands into fists.

"Why, those filthy yellow bastards …"

Kurchatov picked irritably at the filthy yellow upholstery foam crumbling from the arm of his chair. The clucking digital melody of Sakharov's never-ending game of *Tetris* cut through his sanity like a bandsaw. He wrapped his fingers around the neck of his vodka bottle and imagined smashing it over the edge of the desk and letting fate take its course.

His homicidal fantasy was interrupted by a crackling voice.

"Radar Tracking Station 99, come in! Come in, Station 99! This is Moscow!"

Kurchatov's heart hammered against his ribcage as he leapt to his feet. "What the hell was that?!"

Sakharov didn't look up from his game. "The radio. Pick it up."

Kurchatov looked at the buzzing two-way radio and felt very stupid. Right. The radio. It had been a while. He picked up the dusty microphone and wiped it on his shirt.

"This is Station 99," he said. "Go ahead, Moscow."

"The Americans and Chinese are rattling their sabers. Are you picking up anything unusual up there?"

Kurchatov glanced at his comrade, and Sakharov reluctantly minimized his game window, revealing the dish status screen and its usual, burned-in announcement.

Radar Tracking Station 99

0000 Intercontinental Ballistic Missiles detected.

0000.899 Submarine Launched Ballistic Missiles detected.

Sakharov drew a sharp breath.

"What is it, Station 99? What are you reading?"

"Nothing," Kurchatov said. "It's just a computer error."

"It's not a computer error!" Sakharov gasped, grabbing the microphone. "It's a nuclear attack!"

"An attack?! Are you sure?! How many missiles?!"

"Almost one!" Sakharov yelped.

Kurchatov snatched the microphone from his panicked associate.

"Disregard that, Moscow. It's just an error with the—"

"Thank you, Station 99. We'll take it from here."

With that, the radio went dead.

"But it's a false alarm!" Kurchatov repeated. "Moscow? Do you read me? Hello?"

He pounded the microphone on the top of the computer bank in frustration. The ominous digits on the screen flickered and blinked before finally resolving themselves back into four harmless zeros. He crossed his arms and glared daggers at Sakharov as his face turned a furious shade of red.

Chairman Qian lowered his teacup as the standing yellow alert level raised itself to red. His gaze snapped to his second-in-command as if to ask the question his mouth couldn't be bothered to form.

"Russian high command has armed their nuclear missiles, sir. There have been no launches, and no warplanes have taken flight."

The chairman rubbed his hands together hungrily. Russia. Now that was more like it! These days China could occupy Russia without even waking up the reserves. The junior officer continued.

"Sir, all available intelligence suggests a unified Russo-American attack."

The chairman cringed. The Americans. It was *always* the Americans.

"Put the nuclear deterrence on standby alert," he grumbled. "Remind them both that they're not dealing with terra cotta warriors over here."

As the circuits of the American armed forces' communications network cleared their alerts and completed their reset sequences, computer screens and telephone consoles blinked back to life under Cheyenne Mountain. Admiral Teller broke from his frantic pacing and rushed to a bank of reawakened monitors.

"What's happening?" he barked.

"Everything just came back up, sir," the husky officer said. "We've got phones, radar, satellite, everything! It must have been some kind of network glitch."

The admiral breathed a sigh of relief and gave the officer a hearty clap on the back.

"Whew!" he laughed. "That was brown-trouser time for a second there, huh boys? Ha ha ha! Somebody get my wife on the phone—tell her it's a real slow day at the office and I'm coming home early!"

The younger officer didn't return his superior's joviality.

"Um, sir. I think you should see this."

"What's that, Junior?"

"While we were offline the Russians and the Chinese both armed their warheads, sir."

The smile whipped from the admiral's face like a window shade, revealing a countenance of betrayed rage.

"Those Sun-Tzu-reading savages," he seethed. "They knocked out our communications long enough to catch us with our pants down, and now those commie bastards are double-teaming us!"

"Actually, sir," the officer noted, "the Russians aren't commies anymore."

The admiral scowled.

"Dust off the missiles. Go to DEFCON 1. Oh, and somebody get the president on the line."

The wailing alarms fell silent over Camp Bravo, and the president and the intern peeled their sweaty palms from their ears. The only sound that remained was the tinny chirp of a patriotic ringtone coming from the president's pants. The intern clapped her hands to her face and started to cry.

"I'm sorry, Mr. President, I'm sorry!" she squealed. "I never should have come! You shouldn't have either!"

She turned to dart for the fence, but the president grabbed the back of her blue dress.

"Wait! Don't leave!" he shouted.

His cell phone screeched for attention from his front pocket, vibrating provocatively against his already agitated manhood. He yanked the phone from his pants and pitched it into the woods.

"It's alright, it's okay, hon," he continued. "Don't you worry about anything. It was just a little alarm. Absolutely no harm done. You didn't even blow our cover."

The intern wiped her running eyes and smiled impishly.

"Well, sir, to be honest, *our cover* is not what I came here to blow."

The president closed his eyes and grinned smugly as the intern lowered herself to her carpet-burned knees in the wet grass.

"Hail to the chief, baby."

With a great, heaving surge of hot, explosive force, the long, white shaft of a single science rocket slipped from its pad at the Fimbulvetr Astronomical Institute and sailed into the stratosphere.

"Radar Station 99! Confirm your report! Are we under attack or not?"

Kurchatov stared at the computer screen in a wide-eyed panic, his former skepticism replaced with outright terror. The number of missiles detected was suddenly a solid *0001,* and no amount of pounding on the computer would make it change its mind.

"Station 99! Come in! What do you read?"

"I … I think it's a Chinese missile, sir! It's headed straight for Moscow!"

"It appears to be an American missile, sir. It's headed straight for Beijing."

"It's definitely a Russian missile, sir. It's headed straight for Walt Disney World."

"Dear, sweet *Jesus.*"

Admiral Teller marched up to the command center's enormous digital world map and watched the smooth arc of a missile slowly advancing into the sky. As the harsh light of the red alert sirens flashed across his stony features, he took off his hat and saluted the American flag with a broad grin.

"This is what we've waited for. This is it, boys. This is *war!*"

Shortly thereafter, the world came to an abrupt end.

EARLIER THAT DAY...

CHAPTER ONE

The morning was hot, and moist, and thick, and it smelled like a foot. The sun's rays scorched through the atmosphere like a blowtorch, scalding the earth and boiling translucent ripples into the heavy air. This weather was beyond oppressive. It was outright *combative*.

In short, it was a typical summer day in Stillwater, Florida.

Somewhere on Bayshore Boulevard, lost within a creeping armada of tourists' rental cars and retirees' French-vanilla land yachts, was a rattling '83 Volkswagen Rabbit convertible. Years of exposure to the seaside air had turned its gray paint job into a Jackson Pollock of flaking orange rust, and the tattered remains of its canvas top hung from its trunk like Spanish moss.

The driver pulled off her thick, Buddy-Holly-style eyeglasses and ineffectually mopped her perspiring face with her perspiring palms. If she had been a movie star, Vivian Gray would have been crossing the threshold between being typecast as "the nerdy eighteen-year-old high school student" and "the bitter thirty-two-year-old high-school teacher." But Vivian Gray was not a star. Not at all.

Her car radio kicked at her ears with an irritating cacophony of brass and slide-whistles.

"We're *back* and you're *in the middle of another Wacky Wednesday with the Mooker and the Foz Morning Zoo!*"

A doorbell rang, followed by the sound of a bugle, two gunshots, and a mewling cat.

"*Whoops! Bad news for Fluffy, but good news for you! That sound means we're going to be kicking off another twelve-in-a-row megamix …*

(The word "megamix" echoed a dozen times, each iteration deeper and slower than the last.)

"*… of good-time oldies for the Gulf Coast! But first let's check in with Art Anderson over in the WOSU News Center. Hey Artie boy, what's big news in Stillwater?*"

"An oxymoron," Vivian muttered.

A different voice chirped from the radio, speaking in a calm, rehearsed monotone that sounded uneasily out of place among its jabbering companions.

"*State health officials have closed all Stillwater area beaches due to an unusually strong bloom of red tide. Bacteria has been discovered within the bloom that researchers warn cannot be killed by cooking, freezing, or irradiation. A temporary fishing ban has been instated in all coastal waters, and it is imperative that no local seafood be consumed, especially by the elderly."*

"All right, you sexy seniors, you heard Doc Anderson! Lay off the bouillabaisse!"

A sound bite bellowed "No soup for you!" no less than six times.

"Speaking of silver foxes, in today's celebrity birthdays, Shelley Winters turns 79 years young—"

Vivian snapped off the radio and eased her vehicle into a smoldering parking lot. As usual, the lot was populated with an assortment of barge-like seniormobiles, but today there was something different. A collection of tall, impossibly orange bottles lay scattered between the white and chrome street mausoleums like colored eggs on Easter Sunday.

Vivian rattled her car into the first available space, ground the shifter into first gear, and turned off the ignition. She didn't bother to set the parking brake. Much like its roof, the Rabbit's brake had long since rotted into uselessness. As soon as the roar of the engine fell away, Vivian's ears were pummeled with a melody that had recently become all too familiar. The commercial parodies of The Artist Formerly Known as Prince's "1999" had begun the moment Dick Clark dropped the ball in Times Square, and it hadn't let up in the seven and a half months since.

I keep dreamin' of a beverage, forgive me if I go astray,
but your body needs a boost, and your cells are all in disarray ...

Vivian got out of her car. As her sneakers touched the scorching pavement, she could feel their rubber soles liquefying like sticks of butter being shoved into a hot skillet. With a slouch of defeat, she pulled on a powder-blue uniform vest and adjusted her nametag.

Your body needs a tune-up, vitamins are runnin' everywhere.
Time to maximize absorption, and make your food do its share ...

At the end of the parking lot sat a long, dreary fortress of cement blocks that looked like a defunct prison, but without the charm. Across its front, pigeon-infested block letters spelled out the words "Boltzmann's Market."

They say two thousand calories a day is plenty for a slammin' time!
So Fusion Fuel will load and lock you like it's nineteen ninety-nine!

Vivian covered her ears as the jingle thundered through her skull. Rendered in a palette of rough guitar and angsty vocals, the music was grunge, but grunge reduced to a sterile, soulless formula.

It was marketing grunge.

"Oh no," Vivian groaned. "Not another one of these."

Flanking the store's entrance were two huge stacks of speakers bookending an AM General Hummer. The vehicle had an aggressively promotional orange-and-black paint job, making it look like a jack-o'-lantern designed for a combat air drop. Vivian groaned. This happened every time the soft-drink companies introduced some all-new variety of liquid sugar to pour down the nation's gullet. The beverage industry assumed that Americans would unquestioningly drink whatever a pair of pretty faces standing next to an expensive car and an overblown sound system told them to.

If she was lucky, she could make it to the front door before …

"Ring-a-ding-ding! Somebody call the fire department, we've got a red hot redhead burnin' up over here! This grrrrrl needs refreshment, stat!"

Vivian blew a long, resigned breath through her fiercely red bangs as she turned toward the voice. Today's mouthpiece for Big Beverage was fairly typical of the genre. He was a glimmering Adonis, standing six feet tall, with a leanly muscular build and unnaturally blond hair. He wore a complete "extreme sports" ensemble that was to extreme sports what his theme music was to grunge. Although he talked the talk of extreme sports, the salesmodel looked about as hardcore as a spa treatment.

"So where's the other one?" Vivian asked.

"The other what?"

"Usually your kind comes in two-packs," she shrugged. "You know, Ken *and* Barbie."

"It's Nick, actually," he winked. "And I'm gonna single-handedly kick a full-throttle recharge into your tired body battery with a hardcore blast of Fusion Fuel!"

He tossed Vivian a tall, slender club of orange glass with a graphic of a spongy sort of molecule branded in bas relief on its face, identical to the dozens that littered the parking lot. She tossed it back.

"I don't drink energy drinks."

"Energy drinks?" Nick said with disgust. "It's not an *energy drink!* It's so much *more* than that! Fusion Fuel is a diet enhancer that makes your food work harder for *you!* It uses the hidden power of lignite and sulfated castor oil to increase absorption of nutrients by up to 110% for maximum power and stamina on and off the field!"

Vivian smirked.

"I don't drink snake oil either."

A red-faced old woman shuffled past the Hummer. Nick multitasked marks without missing a beat.

"Stop staring—they're free! Haha! Just kidding with ya! Fusion Fuel piledrives vitamins into your hard-working muscles with an intense super-reactive catalyst-altered power punch!"

The way he said "catalyst-altered power punch" seemed to hang a tiny superscripted "TM" in the air. He grabbed a six pack and shoved it into the woman's unreceptive hands.

"Take a sixer to pound down with your whole team! It's an energy absorption explosion!"

Vivian attempted escape into the store, but before she had taken two steps the model was done with the flustered oldster and back on her again.

"Seriously though, Red," he said, "why don't you take this bottle of Fusion Fuel now, and I'll take you out for proper drinks when you get off work. Whaddya say?"

Vivian's cheeks flushed as red as her hair.

"If I say I'll think about it, will you get out of my way?"

"Now that wasn't so hard, was it, Red?" Nick grinned, stepping aside with an overblown sense of chivalry. "I'll be out here all day. Promise you'll come back out and see me later, okay?"

Vivian opened her mouth to make an excuse, but before any words came out, another customer caught Nick's attention. He pounced on the wrinkled old man like a cheetah taking down a Shih-Tzu.

"Fusion Fuel loads up on nutrients and locks them into your hard-working body cells! Load and lock, baby!"

The second Nick's back was turned, Vivian bolted for the entrance. Her feet squeaked onto the worn rubber pad that opened the automatic doors, blasting her with a gale of air conditioning and the acrid stench of red tide.

Vivian covered her nose. *"Ugh! What the ..."*

Adjacent to the front entrance was a pile of soggy wooden crates filled with ice. The makeshift display was populated with a selection of massacred fish, each oozing a pink gravy that reeked of rotting cabbage. Vivian covered her nose and looked at the chalkboard sign hanging over the carnage.

Today's fresh catch - Any 2 for $5!

"Fresh catch," she muttered. "There are parts of the fossil record that are fresher than this."

She closed the first crate's lid, then the second. Before she could close the third, a squeal of feedback preceded a growling voice from the store's public address system.

"Vivian, please come to the office. Vivian, to the office immediately."

Vivian grimaced as she cast her eyes skyward. From the ceiling, a pair of motorized security cameras shook their heads at her disapprovingly. She looked past them and into the dark windows of the enclosed loft that loomed over the store like an Alcatraz watchtower.

She dragged herself up the narrow stairway and pushed open the office door, entering the inner sanctum of the store's owner, Verman Boltzmann. Boltzmann was grotesquely, morbidly obese, and to see his enormous girth packed behind his desk was like looking at a water balloon pinched under a brick.

"God damn it, Vivian! What the hell are you doing to my seafood display?! You come waltzing in here *four minutes late,* and the first thing you do is start messing up the place!"

"*Cleaning* up the place," Vivian corrected. "You're going to have to send that shipment of fish back. The red tide is—"

"Hey! Who the hell do you think you are, coming in here and telling me how to run my own goddamn store?!" Boltzmann wailed. "Don't forget, *you* work for *me*, missy!"

Vivian rolled her eyes. "Only until the county health inspector comes and locks you up."

"Don't you worry your pretty little head about him," Boltzmann said. "That guy'll approve a dogshit casserole for a hundred bucks and a bottle of gin."

Vivian slipped her fingers under her glasses and rubbed her eyes.

"You are a shining paradigm of business ethics, boss."

Boltzmann leaned forward in his chair with a movement like tectonic plates grinding together, shoving a carbon-copy invoice across his desk. Vivian picked up the paper and squinted at its blurry dot-matrix print.

"Listen up, smart-ass," Boltzmann growled. "We just got in another shipment of those bodybuilder vitamins. The Beta Burns. Tag 'em $10.99 and get 'em stocked as fast as your dainty little hands can. For some reason that shit is selling like hotcakes. We can't keep it on the shelves!"

Vivian pointed to a row of smudged numerals on the invoice.

"Well, here's why. That's a six, not a zero. Retail price is supposed to be *$16.99.*"

Boltzmann ripped the paper from Vivian's hands and slapped it face-down on the desk without a glance.

"Just get down there and tag those goddamn pills $10.99. I'm not paying you to stand here and bitch."

"But the price is ..."

Vivian jumped as Boltzmann slammed his fists on his desk like an enraged gorilla.

"Today, Vivian! Move it! Before I bend you over and shove a pink slip up your sweet little ass!"

Vivian leapt out of the office and slammed the door. As she stomped down the stairs, she could hear an altercation brewing at checkstand two.

"Back when I was your age," the customer crackled, "potted meat used to cost ten cents a tin! And the tins were bigger back then!"

"Gee, history is really swell," replied the cashier. "Today it costs $2.99. Same as your suit."

"That's too much. I'll give you a dollar for it."

"Look, this is not Mexico. We do not haggle prices here."

The cashier was Sherri Becquerel, the queen of friendly customer service. Slouched behind the register of checkstand two, Sherri looked about as out of place as a vampire at a beach party.

Although she couldn't have been long out of high school, Sherri's translucent white skin was pulled tightly over her bony skull, making her look as if she had gone through one too many discount facelifts. She was short, flat-chested, and waiflike, and her gaunt figure made her average-sized head appear larger than it really was. Smudges of black eye shadow punched in her oversized eyes, and a smear of black lip gloss blotted out her small narrow mouth. Her appearance and demeanor had earned her the nickname "Scary Sherri" among her co-workers, though nobody dared say it to her face.

For that matter, her co-workers rarely dared to say *anything* to her face.

The enraged senior slowly counted change from his pocket onto the stained rubber of the checkstand's conveyor belt.

"A dollar and fifty cents. A dollar and seventy-five cents. A dollar and seventy ... *six* cents."

Sherri idly brushed some lint from the front of her blood-red *Black Rain* concert tee. Where there should have been a powder-blue uniform vest, Sherri wore a black leather trench coat that was shaped more like a girl than she was.

"Two dollars and eighty-nine cents. Two dollars and ninety-nine cents. There."

The old man grasped the plastic bag and pulled it off the counter.

"Whoa there, Gramps," Sherri said. "Where's the rest?"

The old man's face twisted into a look of distrust.

"You said two dollars and ninety-nine cents!" the old man snapped. "That's two dollars and ninety-nine cents right there. Do you want me to count it again? I can count it again for—"

"Jesus H. Chri ... Sales tax," Sherri interrupted. "It's this new thing you might not have heard of. It was introduced somewhere around the *dawn* of *time*. I need another twenty-eight cents, Methuselah."

The old man looked into Sherri's eyes, and his anger seemed to melt away into troubled indifference. He reached into his heavy, jingling pocket in surrender.

"Three dollars and nine cents. Three dollars and *ten* cents ..."

Sherri slouched behind the counter and dropped her head into her hands. When he had finally piled enough warm, dull coins on the belt to complete his purchase, the old man snapped up his bag of potted meat and turned on Sherri.

"This store is too expensive. I'm never coming here again."

Sherri rolled her eyes.

"Yeah. See you tomorrow, you senile old fart. If you don't die first."

The man looked into Sherri's eyes again, blinked, then shambled away.

Vivian watched with a jealous smile. She had spent long hours wondering what gave Sherri this license to speak her mind without consequence, and she had only been able to come up with one theory. It was because of her eyes. Her dead, expressionless eyes.

CHAPTER ONE

Sherri's eyes were a whispered shade of blue so pale and empty that she looked like an alien, or a heroin addict, or both. Something about them masked any hint of a living soul beyond their glassy surface, and when she insulted you, it felt like the television had just called you a crazy bastard, and to argue would only prove it right.

Sherri leaned back on her register and took a long, hard swig from a half-empty bottle of Fusion Fuel. She noticed Vivian looking at her and gave her a nod.

"I heard the Verminator taking a big hunk out of your ass up there, Powderpuff."

Vivian hated it when Sherri called her "Powderpuff," but she had given up on trying to get her to stop.

"Working here makes me want to slit my wrists," she moaned. "Sherri, you've been in here day in and day out longer than I have, yet you never go homicidal. How do you do it?"

Sherri reached into her coat and pulled out a silver hip flask. She unscrewed the skull-shaped stopper, held it up in silent toast to Vivian, and dumped the remainder of its contents into her already polluted energy drink. Vivian just rolled her eyes and gestured at the leaking fish crates.

"I mean, can you believe that?" she continued. "He's trying to sell the maritime equivalent of roadkill."

Sherri nodded.

"This country is seriously messed up. You can *sell* nasty meat and nobody gives two shits, but you let someone *go down* on your nasty meat and you're public enemy number one."

Vivian opened her mouth, but no words came out. She closed it again and squinted at Sherri. Sherri gestured with her eyebrows.

"It's all over the tabloids."

The checkstand newspaper rack was stuffed with an assortment of wilting tabloids, each sporting its own grainy photograph of the president of the United States embracing a full-figured intern in the White House rose garden. The headlines screamed such off-color remarks as "Oval Office Becomes *Oral* Office! Nation Outraged!"

"Apparently the president has been shoving the little commander in chief into one of his favorite interns' pie holes," Sherri said. "They've got a dress covered in his man gravy and everything."

Vivian winced. "Sherri, have you no filters at all?"

"I can't believe this bullshit is supposed to be *news*," Sherri continued. "It's not like somebody sucking off the president could possibly have any effect on the rest of the world. But the sensationalist press jumps all over this irrelevant shit instead of telling us what a good job he's doing."

Vivian raised an eyebrow.

"So you think the president is doing a good job?" she asked.

Sherri paused.

"How the fuck should I know? The only news I've heard this whole year has been Nostradamus-Y2K-End-of-the-World bullshit. So how about that Hummer?"

"Okay, seriously. Can we just change the subject already?"

Sherri tapped her bottle.

"No, I mean the one in the parking lot. Fascist Fuel, or whatever."

"Oh, that guy," Vivian groaned. "I wouldn't take his stupid energy drink, and then he tried to ask me out."

"So what did you say?"

"Well, what do you think I said? I said no!"

Sherri drained her spiked beverage and wiped her mouth on her sleeve.

"Well, if I were you, I'd fuck him."

"Hey! What's *that* supposed to mean?" Vivian scowled.

"You know. You with your cute little Airwalk sneakers, and your cute little Old Navy capri pants. You two are so *Dharma and Greg*. You could have cute, capitalist children together and you could all sit at home and listen to Len CDs and watch *Third Rock from the Sun*. You're the American fuckin' dream."

Humiliation burned through Vivian's cheeks.

"If you like him so much, why don't *you* go have sex with him?"

Sherri recoiled.

"Oh, shit no. A pretty boy like him couldn't find my G-spot with a flashlight and a copy of *Gray's Anatomy*."

A snarling voice crackled through an interruption in the Muzak.

"This is not a sewing circle, ladies. Quit yakking and get to work!"

Sherri's eyes darted back and forth between the camera enclosures in the ceiling. She spotted the one that was staring her down and extended a pair of bony middle fingers to the lens.

"I saw that, Becquerel! Don't you push me today!"

Sherri held up her hands and wiggled her fingers in the air as if to say, "Ooooh, I'm *shaking*."

Vivian looked into the spying cameras with a dull sigh. She didn't know if there was a God, but she knew that there was always a colossal being watching her every move from on high.

Schlunk.

The glue-encrusted nose of a price gun scraped over the surface of a Beta Burn jar, depositing a sticker marked "$10.99" in its wake. Vivian set the tagged jar on the shelf. She reached into a large plastic-swaddled shipping crate and picked up another jar. She tagged it too with a *schlunk* and set it on the shelf.

Then she repeated the process.

This is how Vivian had spent the bulk of her morning.

"Oooh, look out! Red's got a gun!" a voice boomed. "Put down the gun and step away from the shelf. Don't make me have to get physical, because you *know* I will. Hahaha!"

Vivian's shoulders leapt to her ears as she swiveled toward a perfectly cut statue of marketing-man-meat in the aisle behind her.

"Aren't you supposed to be bothering people *outside?*" she muttered.

"Oh, don't worry about it, foxy," Nick smiled. "I get a ten-minute break every four hours. I just came inside to *feed the rush!*"

He held up a two-liter bottle of SURGE and smiled, and for just a moment he looked exactly like a Coca-Cola-sponsored print ad, but with less personality.

"Listen, Red, on a day like today a girl as hot as you needs a dude who is cool to the core. How about when you get off work I take you for a ride in the HumVee? Give it a try and I think you'll get hooked on cruisin' in one of those bad boys."

Even though they were sheathed behind the reflective gold lenses of his wrap-around sunglasses, Vivian could tell that Nick's elevator eyes were stopped three-quarters of the way to her penthouse. She crossed her arms violently across her modest chest.

"Sorry, I can't tonight. Real busy. You know, washing my hair and whatnot. So … bye."

She bent down and began collecting an armful of jars from the crate with a blunt shove of body language that said, "Move along, folks. Nothing left to see here." Nick caressed her chin in his broad hand and gently pulled her upright, turning her head until their eyes met.

"Washing that beautiful red hair, huh?" he smiled. "That's cool by me. After you're all clean and pretty, why don't you come out with me for dinner? I'm dying to know if you're a natural redhead."

Before Vivian's knee could appropriately respond to Nick's proposal, a barking voice boxed her ears.

"Vivian! What the hell are you doing?!"

A winded Verman Boltzmann waddled heavily into the aisle. In a flash, Nick took his hand from Vivian's face, stuffed it in his pocket, and leaned against the shelves with an innocent grin. Vivian's eyes darted back and forth between the two men as her tongue tried to find its words.

"What am *I*—This guy keeps trying—"

"Shaddup, Vivian," Boltzmann said, waving his hand in her face. "Jesus Christ, I swear you just talk to hear the sound of your own voice."

Vivian's face screwed itself down against her skull as Boltzmann put his beefy hand on Nick's shoulder.

"Is this girl bothering you, son?"

"No sir, not at all," Nick said. "I just came in to slam a SURGE. I always like to shop in the stores where I work. You know, give a little bit back to show my appreciation."

"That's great; that's really great," Boltzmann oozed. "That pop is on the house, just to thank you for coming over here today."

"Hey thanks, Mr. B!" Nick beamed. "Just another perk of being a promo model. I love going to new places and meeting new people like you and Red. And that's what makes me a champion!"

Without warning he balled his hand into a fist and threw it at Vivian's face. "Bam!"

Vivian's shocked recoil was just a second too late, but it didn't matter. Nick's knuckles stopped two inches from the bridge of her glasses, proudly displaying a thick gold ring.

"That's right, I'm solid gold, baby! There's only platinum level above me, and that dude is nailing the boss's daughter, so he doesn't count."

Boltzmann grabbed Nick's fist and pulled it toward his face, squinting at the glimmering ring.

"*Gold Level Sales Champion 1998,*" he read aloud. "That's pretty goddamn impressive! You should be proud of your achievement, son!"

"I am, sir!" Nick gloated, tapping his ring. "This little lady means the world to me. She's not coming off my finger till death do us part."

"Oh, give me a break," Vivian said. "That thing is just a meaningless reward given in lieu of actual compensation."

"You shut your mouth, Vivian," Boltzmann hissed. "Keep up that crap and I promise you you'll *never* be employee of the month!"

Vivian rolled her eyes.

"Whoa, no *way!*" Nick said, noticing the shelf for the first time. "You've got Beta Burn for $10.99?! I'm totally stocking up here! They're charging seventeen bucks for it over at Publix. This stuff is incredible! Feel those guns."

Nick curled the bottle of SURGE as if it were a thirty-pound free weight. Boltzmann squeezed the bulging bicep and nodded enthusiastically, but Nick's gaze was fixed firmly on Vivian, who wasn't watching.

"No shit," Boltzmann said dreamily, not lifting his paw or his eyes from Nick's firmly flexed muscle. "Seventeen bucks, eh? Vivian, what are we charging for these things?"

"$10.99," Vivian muttered.

Boltzmann's voice hardened.

"Speak up, missy."

Schlunk.

Vivian extended the price gun and tagged "$10.99" on the side of Nick's perfect arm in front of Boltzmann's nose. He released Nick and turned on her with a low boil in his eyes.

"Don't you get smart with me," he seethed.

His voice had a forced calmness to it, like a mother who didn't want to beat her own children in front of company. With a gasping effort he bent over, tore the packing slip from the side of the Beta Burn shipping crate, and gave it a once-over.

"God *damn* it, Vivian! It says clear as day that the price on these things is supposed to be *$16.99!* What the hell is wrong with you? Can't you follow simple directions?"

"I *can* follow simple directions," Vivian growled. "And apparently that *is* what's wrong with me."

Boltzmann leaned his glistening face as close to Vivian as his prohibitive circumference would allow.

"Vivian, if you like your job, I suggest you quit your bitching and moaning and start taking a little responsibility for your own screw-ups."

Vivian raised an eyebrow.

"If I *like my job?*"

"Just shut up and retag the goddamn pills $16.99," Boltzmann snarled. "It won't kill you to actually do a little work around here for a change."

Vivian slid her fingertips under her glasses and slowly rubbed her eyes, as if trying to erase reality.

"I gotta get back to work too," Nick said. "So thanks for the SURGE, and—"

"Oh, it's no problem at all," Boltzmann interrupted. "Here, I'll walk you out to your Hummer."

"My *HumVee*," Nick corrected. "The civilian models are called Hummers."

"Oh, yeah yeah. Right, *HumVee*," Boltzmann agreed. "Come on, Vivian, pick up the pace! I'm not paying you to loaf around here ogling boys!"

Boltzmann clapped his porcine hand on Nick's back and escorted him to the end of the aisle and out of the store.

Vivian slowly raised the gun to her head and shot a price tag into her right temple.

Checkstand two was packed four deep with dangerously popular-looking Stillwater High School cheerleaders, and Sherri was price scanning an endless parade of nail polish bottles with an overstated boredom. Each bottle had the name of a different shade printed on its cap, but to the layman they were all indistinguishably "pink."

"Oh my *Gaaaaaawd*," one of the girls mewled. "So, I was talking to Kevin in homeroom, and he was all 'Do you want to go to senior class beach party this weekend?' and I was all like, with *you?* As *if!*"

For reasons that were not readily apparent, all of the girls ripped into a peal of screaming laughter. Sherri didn't give them the courtesy of a sour look. She just kept scanning the bottles and staring blankly into the burning red lasers of her checkstand.

"He's just so *wrong*. Like, *really*," one of the other girls agreed. "Like he's really cute enough for you to like, go swim in the red tide and get like, a bacteria infection or whatever. I'm so sure. But it's not like it would be the first time he ever gave a girl an infection."

The girls burst into laughter again, this time so high-pitched that there were parts only very small dogs could hear. Sherri scanned the final bottle and held out her hand, and one of the girls deposited a wad of perfumed bills in it.

"Oh my *Gaawd!*" the cheerleader gasped, pointing to the bangles on Sherri's arm. "I *luuuuve* that bracelet! The plastic one with the barbed wire stuck in it, right? I have one *exactly* like that!"

Without lifting her eyes from the conveyor belt, Sherri pulled the bracelet from her wrist, held it at arm's length between two fingers like a sitcom bachelor holds a dirty diaper, and dropped it with a heavy plastic *clunk* in the garbage can.

"Ugh, speaking of 'red tide' …" the cheerleader smirked. "God, why do goths always have to be such bitches?"

Sherri's empty eyes snapped up from the belt, locking on to the giggling girls with a glare like a thousand death threats.

"I am not a goth. I am an individual."

The cheerleaders were all suddenly, and perhaps for the first time in their lives, completely silent. After a long moment, one of them finally mumbled a numb rebuttal.

"Well, you're still a bitch."

Sherri handed the girl her change with an unfazed shrug.

"Hey, at least I don't have cottage-cheese thighs, Fatty Fat Pants."

The cheerleaders released a chorus of incensed gasps.

"You … you *bitch!*" the leader screeched. "We're like, *never* shopping here *again* you … you *bitch!*"

The infuriated cheerleaders rushed out the front door in a clucking mass of fair hair and pleats. Sherri smiled wryly.

"Always play to your target audience."

"God damn it, Becquerel! What the hell was that?!"

Boltzmann waddled up to the front of checkstand two like an obese penguin, his jowls slapping furiously against his neck.

"What's the matter with you?!" he bellowed. "That's no way to treat a goddamn customer! You're *fired*, Becquerel! Get out of my goddamn store!"

Sherri slowly pulled a cigarette out of her coat pocket, stuffed it into the corner of her mouth, and lit up.

"Well, it's about time," she said, throwing out a sarcastic salute. "See you in

Hell, motherfuckers."

Without another word she exhaled a long yellow blast of smoke and exited Boltzmann's Market for the last time. A fat purple vein throbbed in Boltzmann's forehead as his gaze fell upon Vivian.

"Vivian!" he barked. "Quit screwing around with those goddamn pills and come work the register! Unless you want to get your ass shitcanned too!"

A thousand sardonic one-liners flashed through Vivian's mind, any one of which would have ensured her permanent liberation from Boltzmann's Market. Before she could stop them, a series of words clinked together like train cars in her mind, racing down the tracks of her central nervous system, through her voice box, and out of her mouth.

"I'll be right there, sir."

"That's what I thought," he said. "Now if you think you can keep your head screwed on straight for five minutes, I'm going back up to the office. *Somebody's* got to actually get some work done around here today."

With that, he executed a turn like the *Queen Elizabeth 2* coming into port and squeezed himself up the creaking staircase to his office. Vivian leaned back against the register, closed her eyes, and thought for a long, hard moment about where exactly she had gone wrong in life.

"Are these the right kind of plugs for this?" an ancient voice croaked.

Vivian blinked twice and tipped her head downward. A hunched old woman barely taller than the checkstand counter was piling D-cell batteries on its belt.

"Plugs, ma'am?" Vivian asked.

"For this machine. Are these the right plugs?"

Vivian looked at the large box filling the woman's shopping cart. Judging by the diagram on the side, it contained some sort of cyclopic robot head. She scanned the single row of English text adrift in a sea of foreign characters.

Hibakusha Electronics 5-in-1 Camping Lantern

"It's for my grandson," the old woman said. "He said he can hook it to his satellite machine and watch the ball games when he's on his class trip."

Vivian felt the need to intervene. She wanted to save everybody the trouble of a return visit.

"Ma'am, I don't think you can watch a ball game on a lantern. I'm pretty sure he was talking about something else. Would you like me to put this back for you?"

The old woman raised a brittle, shaky hand and looked at a crumpled note.

"Five to one camping lantern. That's what he wants. You kids, you all think that all us retired people are all stupid, right?"

"No, ma'am," Vivian said. "I was just trying to—"

The woman looked at her note again. "Five to one camping lantern. It says so right here!"

Vivian sighed.

"All right. Whatever."

She leaned awkwardly over the checkstand and grabbed the heavy box by its corners. With a wrenching of her lower back muscles, she hauled it over the side of the counter and across the price scanner.

BLEEP!

She turned to put down the box, but her hands slipped against the cardboard, dropping the heavy load on the price scanner and jamming its corner harshly into her left breast.

BLEEP!

"Ow! Son of a …" Vivian seethed. "Here, let me take care of that."

She punched the key on the register that would negate the next entry and ran the box over the scanner a third time, neutralizing the errant scan.

BLEEP!

"You did that three times," the old lady said. "Are you trying to rip me off?"

"Not at all, ma'am. I'm sorry, I just made a mistake. It's okay now."

The old woman shrugged.

Vivian scanned all of the batteries. "Your total is $98.73, please."

The woman pawed through her purse and exhumed a one-hundred-dollar bill. When the transaction was completed, the old woman rolled away with an unspoken sense of dissatisfaction.

Vivian glanced at the large clock clicking away all too slowly on the wall above the entrance. There were only fifteen minutes left in her shift. She was in the home stretch now.

She lowered her eyes and peered dreamily through the glass doors and into the outside world.

An elderly woman with a puff of snowy white hair drove a gigantic and equally white Buick into the parking lot. She scrutinized the orange Hummer nervously before turning her attention to Nick and his one-man party.

Sensing the fresh meat, Nick bounced up to the side of the Buick and began rocking out to the corporate grunge music, pointing rhythmically to himself with the index and pinky fingers of both hands and waggling his tongue like a lunatic.

Smoke poured off of the Buick's whitewalls as the terrified woman peeled out of the parking lot and onto Bayshore Boulevard, fleeing for her life in a squealing reverse.

Vivian smiled.

"Well, that's one less for me to deal with," she thought.

"Vivian!" Boltzmann barked.

Vivian jumped out of her skin. How could he always sneak up on her? It was like being snuck up on by a dump truck full of barking dogs.

"Vivian, could you please explain why you charged this nice young woman three times for this camping lantern?"

Behind the enormous bulk of the manager, Vivian could see the old lady with all the batteries glowering with disapproval.

"I didn't," Vivian explained. "I made an accidental scan, then I took one off."

"I can see that," Boltzmann said, waving the receipt in her face. "But there's *three* charges here, each for $79.99. You need to refund her money *twice*. She only bought *one* lantern."

Vivian shook her head.

"No, I'll show you," she said, reaching for the slip. "One is a *negative* scan of $79.99; it's all taken care—"

"Oh no you don't! Don't try to confuse this nice lady by talking nonsense. Just open your drawer and give her back the $159.98 that you ripped off from her. Or should I say, open your *purse*."

"But it's not … I mean, there's the two *positive* scans, and one *negative*. One plus one minus one equals one. It's all taken care of."

"Vivian," Boltzmann said, "I'm going to count to ten, and if you don't …"

"Fine," Vivian boiled, opening her register drawer, "here's the hundred dollars back that she gave me, and here's another sixty just for being so good at math."

"That's more like it," Boltzmann said. "You're lucky she's such a good sport." He snatched the bills from Vivian's hand and gave them to the old woman. "There you go, ma'am. Keep the change. I hope we'll see you in here again real soon."

He turned with a knifelike glare at Vivian.

"I'll be watching you, missy. You watch yourself."

With a humanity that he reserved only for customers, Boltzmann escorted the old woman to the front door before shoehorning himself back into his office.

Vivian slipped her fingers under her glasses and rubbed her tired eyes.

There were only four minutes left in her shift.

Nothing else could possibly happen to her in only four minutes.

"Ripping off old ladies. Ouch, that's a real hit on your karma points, Red."

Vivian pulled her fingers from under her glasses to see Nick leaning raffishly on the end of her checkstand next to four jars of Beta Burn.

"This lane is closed," she said.

Nick's eyes floated to the illuminated sign above the register. Vivian clicked it off.

"Aw, come on now. You know I'm just kidding around. I saw that whole thing go down," Nick said. "Don't sweat it. That fat bastard just ripped off his own store, you know? No skin off your ass."

"There's not a lot left to take," Vivian sighed.

"Okay, so you've had a rough day working point of sale," Nick smiled. "I can definitely help with that. You know what you need to pick you up and get you back to the top of your game?"

"Oh, let me think," Vivian said airily. "Could it possibly, *possibly* be an ice-cold bottle of Fusion Fuel?"

"Is that what you think of me?" Nick asked. He grabbed her hand and cupped it between his own smooth fingers. "You think I'm all work and no play, huh? Well, you've only seen the parts of me that come out when I'm on the job. Let me take you out tonight and show you my private parts."

Vivian blinked.

"I'd rather have the Fusion Fuel."

"You got it, Red!"

Nick plucked a six-pack of Fusion Fuel from the floor at his feet and hung the cardboard handle over Vivian's outstretched fingers.

"Why don't you slam a coupla bottles of Fusion Fuel and then tell me what you think of its extreme blast of citrus flavor over dinner tonight? We can grab some chow around nine. I know a place up in Port Manatee that you'll go totally mental over."

Vivian blew a long breath through her bangs.

"Okay. Nick. Listen. Let me put this into phrases small enough that they can be absorbed through the dense filtration of your frighteningly minute attention span. You are not my type. I am not going out with you tonight. I am not going out with you *ever*. I would not go out with you *if you were the last living man on the planet Earth*. Do you understand?"

Nick nodded.

"So would ten o'clock be better for you? Because I'm totally flexible."

Vivian's throat caught a scream and hammered it back down into her lungs as the clock's minute hand finally pointed to freedom.

"My shift is over," she said calmly. "Goodbye, Nick."

Without another word Vivian stormed out the front door.

Once outside, she was relieved to see that the blistering sun had disappeared behind a cover of thick black clouds. She kicked her way through the debris field of shattered Fusion Fuel samples only to find her tired old Rabbit sagging against the pavement. Jutting from the flaccid heap of a flat driver's-side tire was a jagged shard of orange glass branded with the image of a spongy sort of molecule.

"Well, that's it then," Vivian thought. *"Today officially can't get any worse."*

At that precise moment, the storm clouds overhead tore themselves open, letting fly the kind of Florida thunderstorm that makes God Himself unplug His electronics from the wall socket. The rain was thick and sticky, and it gave off a faint odor of evaporated salt and stale cabbage.

Vivian slouched in utter defeat as the filthy water enveloped her.

"Correction: Things can *always* get worse."

CHAPTER TWO

"Do you think that Obi-Wan Kenobi changed his name to Ben Kenobi out of convenience?" Bobby asked.

"Convenience?" Erik replied.

"Yeah, like can you picture him on the phone trying to order a new droid from QVC or something? He'd be all 'Send that to Obi-Wan Kenobi. No, I'm sorry, not *Joey* Kenobi, *Obi*. Obi-Wan Kenobi. No! Not *Juan* Kenobi! Do I sound Colombian to you? Look, just send it to *Ben,* okay? Ben Kenobi.'"

Erik shook his head.

"Come on. Everyone knows that Obi-Wan changed his name to Ben when he went into hiding after the Clone Wars. It had nothing to do with convenience; it was for security."

"Security?" Bobby laughed. "The man is trying to lay low from the most powerful evil empire the universe has ever known, and he doesn't even bother to *change his last name?*"

"Well, maybe 'Kenobi' was a common last name in their universe," Erik shrugged. "I mean, there's a Captain Antilles and a Wedge Antilles who aren't related, right? Obi-Wan probably didn't change his last name because he knew the rebels would come looking for him someday. Luke would have never told R2-D2 about him if he was 'Old Clark Kent who lives out beyond the Dune Sea.'"

"Wait—so let me get this straight," Bobby argued. "Because he only changed his *first* name, Darth Vader—the meanest, most powerful, most dark-side-of-the-Force-havin' bad-ass in the galaxy—can't find him for twenty years, yet it takes only five seconds for a whiny, dumb-ass teenager to get from 'You belong to Obi-Wan Kenobi?' to 'Oh, you must mean Old Ben'?"

"Uh … yeah," Erik nodded. "Pretty much."

"Okay then. That's officially the most retarded thing that I've ever heard."

Although they'd had their share of differences over the years, there was one thing that Bobby and Erik always had in common.

They were geeks.

Geekhood surrounded them and penetrated them. It bound their galaxy together.

As was typical for a weekday afternoon, the two friends were making themselves at home: lounging on Bobby's couch and watching Bobby's TV in a tiny living room that was not, in fact, Bobby's.

This living room was part of a cluttered one-bedroom apartment. A battered coffee table sat upended with a sweaty *Microsucks* T-shirt and a *Free Kevin* baseball cap hanging from its outstretched legs. Under a dog-eared stack of *Wired* magazines hid a small white TV/VCR combo with a "sad Mac" face drawn on its dusty screen.

While these simple furnishings cowered in the shadows, a titanic wide-screen TV asserted its total dominance over the space, extending out of the living room and into the hallway by a good seven inches. In front of the TV was a makeshift coffee table composed of a life-sized resin cast of Han Solo frozen in carbonite lying across four chipped cinder blocks.

Bobby Gray drained the last foamy remains of his beer and set the empty bottle on Han's forehead. He slowly rolled back his head, tipped open his mouth, and released a low, thundering belch from the deepest regions of his gut.

"BrrrrAAAaaaAaaAaaaAaaaaawwwp!"

"Jeez, Bobby," Erik sighed.

"There is no Bobby, only Zuul," Bobby belched.

Bobby was Vivian's fraternal twin brother, but he had definitely received the short end of the genetic stick. In contrast to Vivian's tall, reedy body, Bobby's physique was comically short and pudgy. He shared his sister's red hair, although his was long, stringy, and perpetually pulled back into a limp ponytail. An orange goatee hung from his chin, looking as if it may have evolved just to hide Cheeto stains. Although they were technically twins, the one thing that made Bobby and Vivian look most alike were their identical Buddy-Holly-style eyeglasses.

"I'm getting another beer," Bobby said, separating his massive backside from the crater it had formed in the couch. "You want one?"

"Boy howdy. Thanks."

"You want a real beer, or another queer beer?"

Erik smirked and clutched his half-finished bottle of Tequiza.

"Shut up. It's real beer," he muttered. "Plus they say it tastes just like going down on a beautiful Mexican *señorita*."

Bobby paused.

"Okay, you know what? Now *that's* officially the most retarded thing I've ever heard."

Erik pouted as Bobby lumbered into the tiny kitchen.

Physically speaking, Erik Sievert was little more than a skeleton accented with bulbous knobs of knee, elbow, and Adam's apple. An Atari-branded polo shirt masked both the humiliating xylophone of a visible ribcage and the doughy pouch of a sedentary midsection. His troubled blue eyes always made him look as if somebody was laughing at him and he had no idea why.

He finished his Tequiza and leaned back on the couch, lethargically watching a string of commercials. A disquieting, rapid-fire disclaimer concluded an ad for menopause drugs, dissolving the scene to a living room decorated in football paraphernalia. A dumpy character actor sat behind a coffee table full of large, empty bowls. Hungry muscleheads closed in all around him, pounding their meaty fists together in a caricature of intimidation.

"It's five … minutes … to the Super Bowl, and all you've … got … are empty bowls!"

The scene cut to an exterior ambulance bay and onto the lumpy countenance of a bad William Shatner impersonator.

"This … is … a Grocery911!"

Erik threw a nervous glance at the kitchen door as he began searching for the remote control.

On the screen, the jocks backed their host into a corner and up against a computer. With something vaguely akin to terror in his eyes, he sat down and began clicking away at a conveniently pre-loaded website.

"When you have … a grocery … emergency, log on to Grocery911.com!"

Erik spotted the oversized remote control and yanked it free of the couch cushions. It was an intimidating rectangle of titanium with a hundred electro-luminescent buttons and a small LCD screen. He stabbed it toward the television and pushed the "channel up" button. The tiny digital screen scrolled the words "INSUFFICIENT ARGUMENTS." He pushed the "channel down" button. The screen replied, "SYNTAX ERROR."

The staccato voice-over continued as the scene cut to an ambulance squealing away from a grocery store.

"Just place your order on the World … Wide … Web … and our Emergency Meal Technicians will … deliver … in thirty minutes or … less! Guaranteed!"

Bobby came back from the kitchen empty-handed.

"We're all out of—"

He stopped dead.

"Change it!" he barked.

"I'm trying!"

On the TV, the ambulance screeched to a stop in front of a suburban house. The driver kicked open the car door, leapt from the vehicle with two full bags of groceries, and bolted for the front porch.

"Oh, now look at that," Bobby said. "I had to go through five levels of firewall to log in, and that idiot just leaves the door open and the keys in the ignition. Talk about a security breach."

Erik sighed.

"Bobby, you *do* realize that this is all staged, right?" he asked. "That guy is just an actor."

"Whatever," Bobby grumbled. "The drivers really do that shit. They're that stupid."

He snatched the remote control away from Erik and continued.

"The only people stupider than the drivers at that company are the suits."

He changed the channel. Erik tried to change the subject.

"Hey, where's the beer?"

"We're all out of beer," Bobby snapped. *"We're having a Grocery911!"*

Before Erik could offer his shopworn consolations, the front door swung open, throwing a hot, moist gust of air swirling through the living room. Vivian stood pathetically in the open doorway, a handful of soggy mail in one fist and a six-pack of Fusion Fuel in the other. She was soaked to the skin, and her face and arms were streaked with black grease and rusty grime.

"Damn, Viv," Bobby said. "You look like you've been making out with the thing that killed Tasha Yar."

"I had a flat tire. In the rain," Vivian muttered. "Thanks for asking."

Her wet skin erupted into goose bumps as she stepped into the air-conditioned apartment. Erik leapt to her side and grabbed the six pack.

"Let me take that off your hands for you, Viv."

"Thanks. That's very consider—"

"Hey, what is this stuff?" Erik whined. "I thought you brought us some beer!"

A drop of cold, dirty water fell from the tip of Vivian's nose.

"Go home, Erik."

Countless repetitions had turned this phrase purely rhetorical to Erik's ears. He slumped back down on the couch and popped open a bottle of Fusion Fuel. Vivian dropped her mail on Han Solo's groin and retreated to her bedroom. Bobby lifted a casual eyebrow toward Erik's drink.

"That stuff any good?"

"No," Erik replied. "It tastes like Ecto Cooler mixed with turpentine."

Bobby nodded.

"Gimme one."

Somewhere the Spirit of Marketing smiled as Erik and Bobby sat there watching commercials and drinking free promotional beverages. A moment later, a toweled-off and pajama-clad Vivian returned and dropped into the only available seat. It was an uncomfortable wicker lawn chair that creaked and pinched at her skin. She leaned forward between Han Solo's toes and retrieved the mail from his lap. It was all junk and bills. She dropped it sleepily in her own lap.

"Oh, man," she yawned. "I am definitely quitting my job. For real this time. You guys don't even want to hear about the day I had today."

Bobby and Erik didn't look away from the television.

"Nope," Bobby agreed. "We don't."

Vivian stared at Bobby for a long, empty minute before returning her tired eyes to the mail. She opened the moist newspaper to the classifieds and smoothed it out over the bills in her lap.

"So, Bob, did you find a job today?" she asked.

Bobby rolled his eyes.

"Man, it's never 'Hey, Bobby, how are you doing?' or 'Did anything interesting happen to you today?' It's always 'Did you find a job today?' Am I right, Erik?"

"Don't look at me," Erik said. "I *have* a job."

Vivian blew a long breath into her damp bangs.

"Hey, Bobby, how are you doing?"

"Can't complain."

"Did anything interesting happen to you today?"

"Not really."

"So did you find a job?"

"Hey, Chatty Patty, can we do this later?" Bobby bristled. "We're trying to watch TV here."

Somewhere deep in her subconscious, Vivian punched Bobby in the mouth. In reality, she pulled a bill from her lap and stuffed it into Han Solo's outstretched fingers between her brother and the television.

"Well, enjoy it while it lasts, sofa spud, because I can't afford to pay your cable bill this month. I'm sorry, but the electricity bill is just too high from you running the AC full-tilt all day, and with your beer tab added in on top of that, I just don't have the money to—"

Bobby grimaced.

"Jeez, Viv, let's stay civilized, alright? You know that it won't be long until I'm payin' the bills with my mad programmin' skills. I mean, this is a wonderful age we're living in. We're almost exactly halfway between *Back to the Future* and *Back to the Future Part II*. The dot-com economy can only get stronger from here."

"Bobby, you've been saying that since last fall!" Vivian snapped. "I thought we had an unspoken agreement since birth that we'd never share a living space that cramped again!"

Bobby picked up the translucent keyboard of a Bondi Blue iMac sitting on an end table next to the couch.

"Relax, Viv. The offers should be pouring in," he said, patting the top of the eggshell lovingly. "I posted my résumé online."

"Oh joy," Vivian deadpanned. "Our troubles are over."

In Bobby's mind, any career worth having could only be found, and executed, via the World Wide Web. His last, and best, job had been in online database management for a little upstart company by the name of Grocery911.com.

The concept behind the business wasn't terribly original. At its core it was little more than another grocery delivery service that had been branded with an "emergency" theme and an ad campaign ripped off from *Rescue 911*. The thing that made Grocery911's system unique was the fact that it was only accessible via the Internet. There were no telephone numbers, no switchboards, and no operators. Just a low-overhead digital network transmitting orders directly from the fingertips of agoraphobic computer nerds to the teamsters at the warehouse.

As the popularity of the website spread, new distribution centers began springing up all along the East Coast. Government auctions were saturated with young entrepreneurs buying up obsolete ambulances and pressing their disintegrating hulks into service as delivery trucks. When Grocery911.com came knocking on the door of Stillwater, Florida, Bobby Gray was there to answer.

After being hired as the chief e-commerce guru of the local distribution "hospital," Bobby soon found himself pulling down an annual paycheck with more trailing zeros than a securely wiped hard drive. He was making big bucks doing a job that he loved in an environment that offered all the free snack food that he could pilfer. It was the perfect job.

Then came the memo.

The memo came down all the way from the CEO, the twenty-two-year-old college dropout who had conceptualized the business while watching reruns of *E/R* and jonesing for munchies at four o'clock in the morning. In the memo, he called the Stillwater office a "financial burnout," noting that it was the only Grocery911 distribution center in the country that was not turning a profit and suggesting that the local team "couldn't sell a dime bag to Tommy Chong at Woodstock."

The executive board launched a demographic research study of the Stillwater area, and discovered that the town contained more collapsible walkers than home computers at a ratio of almost ten to one. Further inquiry showed that eighty-seven percent of the local retirees harbored a fanatical loyalty to the local grocery store, which was peculiar, given that ninety-eight percent found the salespeople there to be "inexplicably rude."

It didn't take long before Stillwater's Grocery911.com distribution center became a brick-and-mortar 404 error.

Soon after the "hospital" had cut off his life support, Bobby and his bleeding-edge electronics were evicted from his beachside bungalow. With nowhere else to turn, he found himself at the door of his sister's unfashionable inland apartment, begging for a place to crash until he could get another job.

Vivian had reluctantly agreed to the temporary arrangement.

That was nine months ago.

Bobby pushed the hockey-puck mouse across the table and clicked open his email.

"Let's see … spam, spam, crap, spam, crap, spam. Ah, here we go. I got an email from a guy I used to work with at 911. 'Subject: FW: Y2K programmers.'

I'll bet that's a job lead right there. See, no need to get your panties all in a bunch."

Vivian looked up from her paper.

"Can you *do* Y2K programming?"

"Sure, how hard can it be," Bobby said. "All you've got to do is look through a bunch of code and find a date."

"Ha!" Erik laughed. "You haven't found a date since the junior prom."

Vivian rolled her eyes.

"Oh, man, this isn't about a job at all. It's just a list of crappy Y2K jokes," Bobby moaned. "Yeah, this is a hoot. Listen: 'Microsoft announced today that the official release date for the new operating system Windows 2000 will be delayed until the second quarter of *1901*.'"

"Oh, that's a *burn!* Bill Gates is gonna be feeling *that* one in the morning," Erik said. "Hey, is that by any chance from the same loser who had that bumper sticker on his car that said 'At Intel, quality is job .9999999998'?"

"Yep," Bobby said. "Same loser."

Erik leaned over to Vivian.

"You see, a few years back, Intel had this defect in some of their chips that would cause rounding errors in their calculations, and so—"

"Oh, hey, Erik," Vivian interrupted. "I don't want to sound like I don't care, but … I've got a headache like you wouldn't believe, and … well, I don't care."

Erik slumped back into the couch and took a swig from his bottle.

"I wonder whatever happened to all of those defective computers," he pondered.

The endless stream of TV commercials was suddenly cut off by a solemn voice.

"We interrupt our regularly scheduled programming to bring you a WGON News special report. Live from the Oval Office, an address by the president of the United States."

The graphic of the presidential seal slid off the screen like a squeegee, wiping away swirls of patriotic graphics to reveal the commander in chief sitting at his desk in the Oval Office. He wore the sharp navy-blue suit and powerful red tie that were requisite for a serious televised address. His eyes expressed the kind of guilt that comes not from breaking the rules, but from getting caught doing it.

"Good evening, my fellow Americans. This afternoon, in this room, in this chair, I stand before you accused of engaging in inappropriate relations with a certain White House intern. In response to these allegations, I issue this solemn promise to the American people: I did not make contact with that woman with the intent to arouse or gratify her sexually. Legally speaking, I did not have sex with that woman."

"So, to recap the conclusions of our nation's finest legal minds," Bobby noted, *"gaggin' ain't shaggin'."*

"Turn it off," Vivian groaned. "If I wanted to hear lame excuses for infidelity I'd get myself a boyfriend."

Erik picked up the remote control and clicked a button, but the TV failed to respond.

"Your remote control sucks."

"Nope," Bobby said, "that remote is top of the line."

"Then why can't I work it?"

"Because *you* suck."

Erik sighed.

"That being said," the president continued, *"indeed, I did have a relationship with that woman that may not have been entirely appropriate. In fact, some of my critics have gone so far as to call it* inappropriate. *I am sorry that these people feel this way, and I vow to attempt to refrain from engaging in this behavior in the future."*

Bobby shook his head.

"I'll bet that intern is under the desk giving him oral sex right now."

"Cut it out," Vivian snapped. "I got enough of that today from Sherri."

"Oral sex?!" Erik choked.

Before Vivian could issue her standard reply, the room was filled with a shrill, ululating battle call. It was the ring of Bobby's princess phone. His *Xena: Warrior Princess* phone.

The phone consisted of a plastic cliff face with the warrior princess straddling a numeric touch pad. Vivian grasped the life-sized chakram throwing disc embedded in the stone, detaching the half of its circumference that served as a receiver.

"Hello? Oh, hey, Sherri. Speak of the devil, and she calls you."

"This matter is between me, the two people I love most—my wife and our daughter—and our God," the president continued. *"I must put it right, and I am prepared to do whatever it takes to do so. Tonight my family and I will retire to our private retreat at Camp Bravo to begin the process of healing as a family."*

With these words, the president's eyes almost seemed to grin to themselves. He blinked, and the brief sparkle was extinguished. He made a conspicuous adjustment of his necktie and continued.

"Together in this darkest twilight *of our interpersonal lives, we will* breach the walls *of blame and meet one another* between the tall trees *of forgiveness and pity."*

"Man, he gets caught committing adultery and all of the sudden he thinks he's a Successory," Erik quipped.

He tossed the remote control to Bobby and spoke in a high, crackly screech.

"Change it, Butt-head!"

"Sherri, I'd love to help you celebrate your liberation," Vivian said, "but nothing on Earth or in Heaven is keeping me from getting to bed early tonight. Why? Because *I* still have to get up and go to work in the morning!"

"I am honored to lead the American people in this time of great peace and security," the president said. *"And I ask you to turn away from this spectacle and return the nation's attention to the challenges and promises of the next millennium."*

"So help me," Bobby groaned, "if he says 'Because as a nation, we're gonna party like it's nineteen ninety-nine …'"

He flicked a button and replaced the image of the Oval Office with the digital cable system's menu grid.

"I'm hanging up now, Sherri," Vivian said firmly. "I'm hanging up. I'll see you at wor … uh … I'll see you around."

Vivian hung up the phone and creaked back into her chair.

"What was that all about?" Erik asked.

"Hide your virgins," Vivian replied. "Sherri's going downtown to drink her last paycheck tonight."

She returned her gaze to the classifieds page and ran her finger down the columns.

"Hey, this one actually sounds good," she said. "'Bluestone Books is hiring full-time staff. Flexible hours. Competitive salary. Must be well read and knowledgeable about literature.' Hey, that's got 'me' written all over it."

She pulled a length of knotted phone cable from behind the couch, grabbed Xena around her waist, and headed for the kitchen.

"I'm going to call about this ad," she said. "Bobby, turn off the TV and get a job."

"You got it, chief!" Bobby chirped, grabbing his keyboard eagerly.

As soon as Vivian had disappeared into the kitchen, Bobby dropped his keyboard and picked up the remote control and whirled through the channel previews.

"Crap, crap, commercial, crap, infomercial, crap. Ah ha! Score!"

The cable menu flicked away, leaving the screen filled with Mel Gibson in *Mad Max: Beyond Thunderdome*.

Erik grinned. "I used to know this movie by heart, but I haven't seen it in years."

"Bueno, dijiste una pelea limpia. ¿Qué propones?"

"Como manda la ley."

"El Thunderdome."

Erik blinked.

"Somehow it's not exactly how I remember it."

Bobby nodded.

"Spanish channel."

He took a long drink from his Fusion Fuel.

"It's still the best thing on."

"Dos hombres, mano a mano, sin jurado, sin apelar, sin escape. Entran dos pero sale uno."

"Haha! I got that!" Erik said. "'Two men enter, one man leaves.'"

Bobby chuckled.

"I wonder how you say 'Bust a deal and face the wheel.'"

"Bartertown has the most awesome constitution," Erik said. "All of its laws are like bad song lyrics."

"Well, what do you expect when Tina Turner is your mayor?"

Erik shrugged.

"She's cool in this movie, but I never understood her nickname. I mean, 'Master Blaster' I can wrap my head around. It sounds bad-ass, like the old Amiga game. But 'Aunty Entity' I just don't get. Is it supposed to be like 'anti-entity,' like she's *not* an entity? Or that she's *opposed* to entities? It's meaningless. They could have come up with something better. *I* could have come up with something better."

"You think so?" Bobby challenged. "Okay, Harlan Ellison, if you were living in post-apocalypse Australia, what would your nickname be?"

"Well, let's see. It would have to be something that sounded tough, so that nobody would want to mess with me. Something like … Erik the Barbaric."

"Ha!" Bobby snorted. "You're about as barbaric as Bob Saget."

Vivian returned from the kitchen with gloom hanging from her face. She set the phone down, picked her paper up, and came to rest in the prickly grip of the wicker chair.

"No luck?" Erik asked.

"They said that I was under-qualified," she frowned. "Apparently their definition of 'knowledgeable about literature' is 'Can name the last ten books by Danielle Steel.'"

She noticed the TV.

"Are you two actually sitting here watching a movie that you've already seen a hundred times, in a language that you can't even understand? I wouldn't ordinarily make this kind of a demand, but seriously, you two, get a *life*."

"Ooh, you better watch yourself," Bobby said. "You don't want to enrage *Erik the Barbaric!*"

"Alright, smart guy," Erik snapped. "If you're so clever, what's *your* post-apocalypse name?"

"Okay, brace yourself for this," Bobby grinned. "In the world of the post-nuclear holocaust … I would be known as … *Atomic Bob!*"

Erik shook his head.

"That is *so* lame. Did you actually *think* of that, or did it come *directly* out of your ass?"

Bobby smirked and turned to Vivian.

"What about you, Viv?" he asked. "After society has collapsed and humanity has been wiped off the face of the planet, what would they call you?"

"Grateful."

"That's worse than Aunty Entity," Erik muttered.

"Oh, come on, you're not even trying," Bobby said. "You'll never survive unless you come up with a name that's scary enough to intimidate a horde of savage bikers. Think tough."

"Bobby, I'm busy!" Vivian roared, slamming down her paper. "I don't want to play this game! In fact, *you* don't want to play this game. You want to get off your lazy butt and find a job already!"

She yanked a page of damp classifieds out of her paper and thrust it at Bobby.

"Here! Just call a number!"

"Bah. Number," Bobby said, brushing her away. "You're so twentieth century."

He picked up his keyboard and toggled off his *Matrix*-inspired screen saver.

"How about this: If you can come up with an end-of-the-world nickname better than the ones we've come up with, I'll get on an online job board right now and apply for as many jobs as you do, one to one. Deal?"

Vivian rubbed her eyes with her palms.

"Do you *promise?*" she said bitterly.

"Cross my heart," Bobby grinned.

Vivian looked at the ceiling and sighed.

"Okay, how about … Vivian Oblivion?"

Bobby's eyes grew wide. Then he squinted.

"Not too shabby," he conceded.

"Not too shabby?!" Erik squeaked. "Oh, come *on!* 'Vivian Oblivion' kicks your sorry ass, *Atomic Bob.*"

"Alright, alright. Fine."

Bobby clicked defeatedly through the online job listings.

"Crap, crap, scam, crap. Okay, here we go. 'Major technology firm seeks qualified candidate for chief executive officer. Minimum five years experience in a similar position.' There. Consider me applied."

"That's great," Vivian said dryly. "I think perhaps you are not taking this seriously."

"That's not true," Bobby said. "If we don't aim high, we'll never know what we're capable of achieving, right?"

"Very inspiring," Vivian muttered. "Would you mind aiming a little lower with your next application? You could try to aim for—oh, I don't know—a job that you could actually get on this plane of reality."

She picked up her newspaper and tapped her finger on the page.

"Like this one, for example. 'Waffle House seeks graveyard shift waitress. Competitive wages. Uniform provided.'"

"Wow, that sucks," Bobby said.

"Reality sucks," Vivian snapped.

She gathered up the phone and retreated to the kitchen.

"Why do you always do that to her?" Erik asked.

"Do what?"

"You do everything you can to avoid getting a job, and you don't show your sister any appreciation for what she's done for you."

"Oh, jeez," Bobby moaned. "When did you turn into our mom? Next you'll be telling me not to sit so close to the TV and to finish my peas."

Erik took a sip of his drink and pointed his bottle at Bobby.

"All I'm saying is, I think this R2 unit has a bad motivator."

"Look, Erik, you've got it all wrong," Bobby sighed. "It's not that I'm lazy, or that I don't appreciate Vivian letting me crash here, or whatever. It's just that she's so … I don't know, *inexperienced.*"

Erik raised an eyebrow. Bobby continued.

"I mean, she's just gone from one meaningless, thankless job to another her whole life. She's been doing it so long that she forgets that there is actually something better out there. A career is like a parking garage with those 'severe tire damage' strips all through it. Once you advance up a level, you can never go back to a lower one again."

Erik squinted at Bobby and crossed his arms.

"Okay, look, it's like this," Bobby explained. "Remember the first time you used a 56K modem after years of using a 28.8? It seemed like Buckaroo Banzai's jet car by comparison. But now that we've got DSL, 56K is intolerably slow. Once you've tasted broadband, you can never be happy going back to your old modem. It's the same thing with jobs. I've had the T1 line of employment yanked away from me, and now she expects me to just go back to 9600 baud. It's not that I don't want a job. As soon as I find the right one, I'll be on it like Pepé Le Pew on a striped cat, but in the meantime, I can't be expected to degrade myself by flipping burgers or pumping gas for tourists, right?"

Erik clapped quietly.

"Nice reading. Very spontaneous and non-rehearsed. So what did Vivian say when you laid that on her?"

Bobby sighed.

"She said she wouldn't pay my Internet bill anymore."

Vivian shuffled back into the room and dropped the phone, spilling its receiver across the carpet. She fell into her chair with a *crunch*.

"They said I was under-qualified when I admitted I didn't know what was meant by the phrase 'scattered, smothered, and covered,'" she said. "They actually told me that I was *under-qualified* to be a *Waffle House waitress*. That's like being under-qualified to be a car accident victim."

She shook her head and turned to Bobby as he clattered away at his keyboard.

"What did you find, Bob?"

"'Wanted: volunteer video game testers for new next-generation console,'" Bobby said. "That sounds awesome. I just sent in my résumé."

Vivian looked at him with disbelief.

"Bobby, you do realize that 'volunteer' means that you don't get paid, right?"

Bobby squinted at his screen.

"Hmm, well, it looks like the job was in Tokyo anyway."

Vivian shook her head.

"Okay, Bobby, how about a 'safety' application, just in case the CEO thing doesn't work out. Could you apply for something lowly and *possible,* like janitorial or food service, please? Just to humor me?"

"Alright, alright," Bobby griped.

Vivian returned to her paper, scanning the columns with an increasing sense of despair.

"This city is an employment wasteland," she said. "There's not a single worthwhile job within twenty miles of here."

"Hey Viv," Erik said, "if you're already resigned to working as a waitress anyway, you might as well apply at the Hooters out on Songbird Key. It's right on the other side of the bridge, and I've heard that those girls make tons of money in tips, plus they have full benefits."

"Oh, right," Vivian snorted. "Can you picture me in little orange hot pants with my breasts all bunched up in a tight tank top like some Lamborghini poster girl from 1985?"

Erik stared blankly through Vivian's abdomen as a smile spread dreamily across his face. Vivian scowled.

"Go home, Erik."

Erik's face flushed red. Vivian crumpled her newspaper and threw it at him.

"All right, I give up. I'm just going to apply over at Publix," she said. "Sure, it's a lateral move into the same lousy job, but at least their seafood doesn't require a garnish of antibiotics."

She picked up Xena and shuffled off to the kitchen, dragging the beeping receiver across the carpet behind her. The boys turned their slothful attention back to the dubbed film on TV.

"You know, there's something that I've never understood about this movie," Bobby said. "If everybody in Bartertown is drinking water laced with radioactive fallout, how come they're not all zombies?"

"Well, that's because radiation doesn't cause zombies," Erik explained. "Zombies are always caused by toxic waste or some sinister biological agent that the military accidentally unleashes on the general public."

"I call bullshit on that," Bobby countered. "In *Night of the Living Dead* the zombies rose from the grave because of radiation coming off of a space probe."

"They *allegedly* rose from the dead because of radiation coming off of a space probe," Erik corrected. "They never give a definitive explanation for what happened. It's like the writer knew that his science was crap, so instead of giving concrete facts he just let the characters take batshit guesses as to what was going on."

Vivian came back into the room, set Xena on the coffee table, and numbly dropped into her chair.

"Well, what about *The Hills Have Eyes* then?" Bobby continued. "The radiation from a nuclear test site spawns a bunch of whacked-out cannibalistic mutants."

"Well sure. But that's *mutants,* not *zombies,*" Erik said dismissively. "Apples and oranges. Zombies and mutants are completely different things."

"Oh, they are *not,*" Bobby said. "They're all the same genre of irradiated, flesh-eating freaks."

"No they're not! There's a world of difference! Zombies are nothing but rotting, reanimated corpses! They have no thought processes! All they do is shamble through the night, infecting people and eating brains. They're *always* an evil menace and a threat to humanity. A mutant *can* be evil, but it doesn't *have* to be. Look at the Teenage Mutant Ninja Turtles, or the X-Men, or the Fantastic Four, or even the Toxic Avenger! All mutants! All heroes!"

Vivian ground her palms into her throbbing forehead.

"God, Erik! Shut ... *up!*" she snapped. "You sit here blathering on and on in these endless tirades of B-movie nonsense as if anybody *cares!* None of that is real! It's just fanboy gibberish!"

Erik's soft eyes took on an abused puppy-dog quality.

"Oh, come on, Vivian. We're talking about *mutants* and *zombies* here. Outside of 'fanboy gibberish,' what else is there to know?"

Vivian took a deep breath.

"Well, Haitian legend says that a zombie is created when a *bokor* performs a voodoo ritual upon a person, turning him into a mindless slave. According to scientific studies, however, the 'zombie' trance is actually a psychological state caused by a combination of tetrodotoxin powder and various hallucinogens. Voodoo zombies do not eat human flesh. Mutants, on the other hand, come from damaged DNA strands improperly spreading their genetic code into newly forming cells. An extreme dose of radiation can cause grotesque mutation but, more often than not, it also causes early death. It *never* causes super powers. And for the record, mutants *also* do not eat human flesh."

Erik's lips pursed into a pout.

"Oh *yeah?* Well, what about mutant *sharks?*"

Vivian closed her eyes.

"Go home, Erik."

Bobby nodded toward the phone.

"So I'm gonna guess by your showers of sunshine that you did *not* get the grocery job?"

Vivian sighed.

"After my years of tireless service at Boltzmann's Market, the good folks at

Publix consider me vastly *over*-qualified for employment. Bobby, please tell me that you've applied for something reasonable."

"We're three for three," he said, pounding the Enter key. "I applied in food service, just like you asked."

"Thanks, Bob. I appreciate that. What's the job?"

"Waitress at the Hooters out on Songbird Key," he said. "I've heard I can make tons of money in tips, plus I'd get full benefits."

Vivian pulled off her glasses and pressed her palms over her eyes.

"I give up," she moaned. "I just give up."

She dropped her head and fell quiet. Erik scowled at Bobby, who was now clicking through online galleries of Hooters waitresses. He reached out consolingly for Vivian's knee, but when his hand was halfway there, he thought better of the idea and pulled it back.

"Hey, it's not all that bad, Viv. Seriously," he said. "Listen, it's not the end of the world. Okay, so you've got a crappy job that you hate, but you've got a lot of good stuff going on in your life too, right? It's like I always say: Life is like a box of Smilex."

"Don't give me that *Up With People* crap," Vivian grumbled. "I'm not in the mood for smiling."

"No no," Erik said. "Not smiling, *Smilex*. You remember. The chemical from *Batman*."

Vivian looked up and glared at Erik in disbelief.

"Please tell me that you're not actually trying to cheer me up with your bogus movie pseudo-science."

"Just listen," Erik said. "In that movie the Joker terrorized Gotham City by putting toxic Smilex into the city's cosmetics and toiletries."

"So nobody could wear eye shadow? Oh, the humanity."

"No, you could wear eye shadow, if you were *lucky*," Erik corrected. "No single item contained the entire formula. There might be elements of Smilex in your eye shadow, and some in your lipstick, and some in your soap. If you used any single one of those you'd be fine, but use all three together and they form Smilex, and you become one very happy corpse."

"Erik, I'm begging you," Vivian moaned. "Either make a point or stop talking."

"My point is that life is like a box of Smilex," Erik repeated. "It'll only kill you if the right combination of your life's toiletries are bad. I mean, sure your job sucks, but without it you'd switch to 'Unemployed' brand toothpaste, 'Homeless' brand hairspray, and 'Starving' brand shampoo. Next thing you know Batman is finding your bloated, grinning corpse floating in the Gotham River."

Vivian sighed.

"You're right. You sure took the scenic route to get there, but you're right. It could be worse. I guess as long as I'm working, we'll be all right."

"That's right, stay positive," Erik beamed. "And hey, you never know when the phone is going to ring with a job offer."

As if on cue, the warrior princess erupted in her ululating ring. Vivian grabbed the receiver.

"Hello. Vivian Gray speaking," she said hopefully.

"Vivian!" a guttural voice screamed. *"What are you trying to pull?"*

"Mr. Boltzmann? I—I don't know what you mean."

"I don't know what you mean," Boltzmann squeaked in mocking imitation. *"Don't try to play innocent with me, missy. You're not that good an actress."*

Vivian didn't know where to go from there.

"I'm sorry?"

"You'd better be sorry! Your drawer came up a hundred and sixty dollars short today. Did you think I wouldn't notice? Do you think I'm stupid?"

Vivian suddenly understood.

"No, I don't think you're stupid," she lied. "Listen, there was a misunderstanding with the refund that I gave to that woman with the camping lantern. You see, it cost eighty dollars, but you made me refund her twice, so she got one hundred and sixty back. That's where the missing—"

"So what you're trying to tell me is that the woman paid you for the lantern three times, so you had an extra two hundred and forty dollars, and then somehow when you refunded one-sixty, your drawer came up one-sixty short?"

Vivian put her hand on her pounding forehead.

"That's *not* what I'm saying at *all*. Listen to me—I'll go through it *very slowly* so you can understand."

"Oh, I understand! I understand your little scheme just fine!" Boltzmann screamed. *"You charged that woman for the lantern three times and pocketed the extra one-sixty for yourself. Then, when you got caught, you took another one-sixty from the register to cover what you had already stolen!"*

Vivian's head spun with the pure mathematical illogic of it all.

"Listen, tomorrow when I come in I'll explain the whole thing, using diagrams," she said. "Puppets if necessary."

"Shaddup, Vivian!" Boltzmann wailed. *"You're done explaining. And don't bother coming in tomorrow. You're* fired*!"*

Vivian's throat closed up.

"W—what?!"

"And I'm taking the three hundred and twenty bucks that you stole out of your last paycheck, smart-ass!"

With a harsh *click*, the phone went dead. Vivian's mouth continued to work at forming words, but only a dial tone remained to hear whatever she would come up with.

"Is that so?!" she finally yelled. "Well, you can't fire me, because I *quit!*"

She slammed the phone down in its cradle. Bobby and Erik stared at her in quiet disbelief.

"Vivian, I'm all for telling the Man where to shove it," Bobby said, "but didn't you just totally Smilex our asses?"

Vivian glared at him.

"I hope you saved the box that television came in, because as of the end of the month, we're both going to be living in it."

A long, tense silence fell over the apartment. Erik looked at Bobby, then at Vivian. His eyes had a faint glimmer, as if his mind was pulling together the words of wisdom that would make everything all right.

Finally he broke the silence.

"Well," he announced, "I'm gonna go home."

"Right behind you," Bobby agreed.

In the blink of an eye the boys had vanished, punctuating their disappearance with a slamming door.

Vivian sat alone in the darkness. The stack of unpaid bills on the table seemed taller than it had just a moment before. After considering all other possible courses of action, she grabbed a long loop of phone cable and considered wrapping it around her neck.

Before she could take action against her own windpipe, the phone released its warbling ring.

"Hello?" she answered weakly.

"Hiya, Red! It's me, Nick. We met here at the store today."

Vivian closed her eyes tightly and started hammering her head with the earpiece.

"How did you get my number?" she croaked.

"Easy! I got it out of your employee file when ol' Verm pitched it in the trash. Man, you sure pissed him off something fierce. I'm not even going to tell *you the things he said about you after he hung up! It was totally* obscene!*"*

Vivian's hands rolled into fists, then slowly relaxed.

"Well, I'm glad you enjoyed the show. Now I have to hang up and see if I can find a job cleaning bedpans at some senior assisted-living home. Goodbye."

"Hoo, harsh," Nick laughed. *"Hey, before you do that, why don't we see if I can get Verm to give you your job back? I could totally do it. That guy loves me. Plus I saw the whole thing with the old lady go down. I'll explain it to him man-to-man."*

Vivian thought the proposition over. As sad and twisted as it was, it could actually work.

"That's ... well, that's very nice of you. I'd actually appreciate that a lot."

"It's no problem," Nick said. *"No problem at all."*

"Well, okay then," Vivian smiled. "Thanks, Nick! Thanks a lot. I'll see you at the store tomorrow."

"Actually, I was thinking you'd see me tonight. *On that date that we talked about."*

A chill streaked down Vivian's spine.

"Oh … I, um … I'm really not available tonight for a date. I'm … going out with a friend," she stammered.

"Aw, that's too bad," Nick said. *"I was going to talk to Mr. B about all this in the morning, but it looks like I might be scheduled at a store over on Songbird Key tomorrow …"*

Vivian frowned.

"I see—so this is about extortion. In that case, forget it. I'm not the kind of girl who trades evening companionship for career advancement."

"I know you're not," Nick agreed. *"You're the kind of girl who cleans bedpans in assisted-living homes. Come on, Red! Am I worse than that?"*

In her mind, Vivian flicked through all of the cards in her hand, weighed her options, and decided to fold.

"Okay, okay, fine," she conceded. "You know what? I'll go out with you tonight. *If*, and *only* if, you can get Boltzmann to give me my job back. Deal?"

"You got it, lady," Nick said. *"I've already got us reservations at the Banyan Terrace for nine o'clock."*

"And let me make this abundantly clear right now," Vivian added. "I am only agreeing to dinner, and that's only for the sake of my job. This is not an all access pass. Understood?"

"Don't worry, I won't hurt you," Nick laughed. *"I only want you to have some fun!"*

CHAPTER THREE

Missile after missile streaked through the sky in impossible numbers toward the oblivious cities below. In response, a single antiballistic missile blazed up from the ground, intercepting three of the incoming warheads and vaporizing them in a ball of yellow light. Seconds later another ABM managed to eliminate two more attackers, but even with the missile defense operating at full speed, saving one city invariably meant sacrificing all the others.

"God damn it, there's just too many of them!"

"Make every shot count! Use some strategy!"

"I am! They're too fast! And this stupid joystick sucks ass!"

With the sound of a gravelly digital explosion, the TV screen flashed through a cycle of apocalyptic 8-bit color. Bobby threw down the Atari 2600 joystick in defeat.

"*Missile Command* sucks," he barked. "Frickin' Reagan-era, SDI bullshit."

Erik was working his usual night shift at the Planet Packrat Collectibles Emporium, and Bobby was keeping him company in the sparsely trafficked junk shop.

Within its cracked walls, Planet Packrat held the remains of a thousand forgotten childhoods. Hundreds of mismatched toys and tchotchkes haunted its dusty shelves like ghosts of an era not long passed. Abraded *Star Wars* action figures gathered in heaps in shallow plastic bins. Two Voltron robots looked down from a shelf behind the counter, one complete, one missing the yellow lion that would have formed its left leg. In the corner of the front window sat a stuffed Mogwi with a plastic knife and fork rubber-banded to his hands, propped up against a cardboard sign reading "Open Till Midnight."

Erik sat on a stool behind the checkout counter. He was holding a butterscotch-colored alley cat, stroking her matted fur like a cut-rate James Bond villain. The cat thrashed her tail back and forth angrily.

"Who's the good kitty? I think you're the good kitty! Such a good kitty kitty," Erik cooed. "*Be-de-be-de-be-de!* How's it goin', Twiki?"

Twiki's attention was fixed on a mouse scurrying toward a hole in the worm-eaten baseboard. She made a desperate leap for the floor, but Erik caught her in mid-leap and continued to cuddle her lovingly.

"Oh no you don't!" he scolded, raising a finger to the cat's face. "No more killing mice! It's a filthy habit! Do you understand me?"

Twiki answered by sinking ten claws into Erik's forearm. He dropped her with a pained squeak and she darted away, disappearing under a shelf of *Jem and the Holograms* dolls.

"I don't see why you don't just let her go ahead and exterminate the place," Bobby said. "I wouldn't be surprised if there's worse things than mice living in this shitbox building."

Erik shook his head.

"Don't you know how dangerous it is for cats to chase mice? Haven't you ever seen a *Tom and Jerry* cartoon?"

Their exchange was cut short by the roar of an ill-maintained engine pulling up outside. It belonged to a rusted-out Ford Aerostar sporting a bumper sticker proclaiming, "I still miss my ex … *but my aim is improving!*"

"Oh no. No no no," Erik stammered. "Not again. Not tonight."

In the passenger seat of the minivan was a woman oozing an aura of spent sexuality through a thick screen of exhaustion and ennui. She adjusted her sagging breasts in her worn halter-top and took a long, sultry-cum-suicidal drag on an unfiltered cigarette.

But Erik didn't notice her.

The driver of the Aerostar was a rugged, sun-beaten man whose hair seemed locked in a struggle between "Young Elvis" and "NASCAR enthusiast." The rawhide of his cheeks stretched tightly across his jawbone as his teeth worked over a mashed toothpick.

Erik didn't notice him either.

No, Erik's glare was focused on the minivan's rear door as it slid open to reveal two grimy, doe-eyed children.

"Well, gotta go," Bobby said. "It's beer o'clock!"

"No!" Erik chirped. "Come on, Bobby, don't leave me alone with them again!"

Although he had never actually met Richard Stokes, he had become all too familiar with the children of his failed marriage. As an ostensible toy store, Planet Packrat served as Stokes's primary child-care facility as he introduced himself to every lady of the night south of the Mason-Dixon line.

"Don't go! Please, Bobby!" Erik pleaded. "I can't take another night alone with the gruesome twosome! I'm begging you. As your best friend. *Please.*"

Bobby looked out the window, then back at Erik. Finally he let out a long sigh.

"Okay, I'll stay," he said stoically. "After all, you *are* my best friend. I would never leave you when the goin' gets tough."

A relieved smile spread across Erik's face. "Really?"

"Nah, I was just messin' with ya."

With that, Bobby yanked open the front door, allowing the two abandoned children to scamper inside. He threw a salute at Erik and slid into the street.

"Catch you tomorrow, chump. Have fun baby-sitting."

Erik fumed as his alleged best friend bobbed past the front window and off into the sunset. He was now alone.

Alone with Debbie and Harry.

As a connoisseur of '80s music, Erik had initially found their names amusing. That was before he had discovered that one way or another they were going to get him. To get him, get him, get him, get him.

Harry Stokes was a five-year-old kleptomaniac, perpetually wrapped in an oversized Army jacket full of hungry pockets. Debbie Stokes was twelve. She was the kind of girl who said things like "girls are made of sugar and spice and everything nice" to cover up the fact that she was, in fact, completely horrid.

They strolled into the store as if casing the joint. Debbie immediately spotted her favorite thing in the store.

"The kitty!" she yelled. "I see you, kitty kitty! I'm gonna get you!"

Twiki seized up in terror before scrambling for safety. Debbie pursued with a giggling squeal, and the two of them disappeared into the shadowy fringes of the store. Harry toddled over to a shelf of *FernGully: The Last Rainforest* toys and picked up a Batty Koda doll.

"Ooooo, cuuuuuwl! Lookada cwazy bat!" he jabbered. "I wannda havea cwazy bat!"

Erik watched Harry stuff the doll into his coat pocket. He sighed. He knew that as long as Harry Stokes was in the store, its inventory was in jeopardy.

The monolithic screen of Bobby's TV flickered a game of *Jeopardy!* in front of Vivian's half-lidded eyes. She sat in a deep slouch on the sofa with her feet on the makeshift coffee table, jabbing Han Solo in the gut with her bare heels. Her chin pressed drowsily into her horizontal chest, and her limp arms sprawled out across the cushions. To look at her, one might imagine that Vivian had been relieved of her entire underlying bone structure.

Although she had already cleared most of the board, Vivian's mind wasn't really in the game. She couldn't stop thinking about Nick. Or rather, her date with Nick. Or more specifically, how to *get out of* her date with Nick.

"Instead of spark plugs," Alex Trebek droned, *"a diesel engine ignites its fuel mechanically by using* this *to create heat through the properties of Charles's law."*

How had she gotten herself into this situation? All she wanted to do was go to work, come home, and go to bed. She didn't need this kind of stress. She didn't need this kind of …

"Pressure," she said.

"What is pressure?" the television contestant answered.

"That is correct."

"I'll take 'To Your Health' for three hundred, Alex."

"As esophageal cancer cells multiply at an uncontrolled rate, they pose a threat to their host organism through this *unrelated biological process."*

Maybe she just wouldn't show up. After all, what was the worst that could happen to her if she lost her stupid job?

"Starvation," she grumbled.

"Starvation is correct," Alex Trebek confirmed. *"Potentially leading to death."*

Vivian crossed her arms and glowered as her stomach let out a low, rolling growl. Reluctantly, she grabbed the only edible thing within her reach.

A warm bottle of Fusion Fuel.

She pulled out her Swiss Army Knife, pried off its cap, and took a hesitant sip. The flavor was overbearing and foul, which she found somehow poetic, as she felt the same way about the person who had given it to her.

"I'll take 'Basic Instincts' for one hundred, Alex."

"Contrary to popular belief, this *colorblind mammal is compelled to charge by erratic motion, not by crimson hues."*

Even if she *wanted* to go on this date, she couldn't. She was too tired to get off the couch, let alone drive all the way up to Port Manatee. Plus she didn't have the right kind of clothes for a fancy restaurant. And she hated wearing makeup.

"Bull," she sighed.

"Absolutely," Alex Trebek agreed. *"It is 'bull.'"*

Vivian raised an eyebrow, then shrugged. All right, she conceded this point: Her excuses were complete bull. She just didn't want to go. She didn't need to justify herself to Alex Trebek.

She took another hardy swig from her bottle and realized that she had finished it. She smacked her lips. Huh. Fusion Fuel actually wasn't too bad if you just gave it a chance. Her nose wrinkled.

Oh, was this supposed to be symbolic or something?

Nahh. It was just another stupid coincidence.

"All right, Alex Trebek, you've got all the answers," she said sarcastically. "What do you think? Should I go on this stupid date or not?"

"This three-word slogan has been used by Nike since 1988."

Vivian poked a button on the remote control and the gigantic screen went black.

"Okay, okay, fine. I'll go on the date," she surrendered. "At least he's not taking me to one of those crummy tropical-themed places downtown."

The setting sun blazed in the shuttered shop windows of downtown as

CHAPTER THREE

Bobby made his way down the abandoned sidewalk. Unfortunately, Stillwater's businesses catered to the "Early to bed, early to rise" sleep schedule of the elderly. The faint melody of a lousy reggae cover of "1999" led him to the only thing outside of Planet Packrat still open at this hour: the Bikini Martini.

The Bikini Martini was an overdone theme bar designed to draw in the kind of tourist who was not aware that Florida was not a Polynesian island. The open-air building was made of logs bolted together and cosmetically tied with coarse rope, like *Gilligan's Island* with a building safety code. The bar itself was a freestanding island of bamboo poles and thatched palm fronds, but the surrounding tables were white plastic patio furniture sprouting Budweiser umbrellas. Behind the wood-planked barroom was a large outdoor lot filled with white sand and errant cigarette butts.

On one side of the "beach" was a cabana stage where lousy bands played, and more tables where people who hated themselves could sit to listen. On the other side was a submarine the size of a short bus with its keel buried in the sand. The sub wore a peeling coat of cheery yellow paint, complete with cartoonish blue waves permanently cresting along its sides. A carved wooden plaque identified the vessel as the *Stillwater Sawfish,* but decades of erosion had rendered the rest of its history unreadable. Not that anyone seemed to care.

Bobby sat down on a creaking bamboo barstool. A girl behind the bar slid up to get him a drink.

"Heya, Bobby," she smiled.

Sunny Sasaki was the kind of bartender who knew every person on the continent on a first-name basis. She had a genuine, easy-going charm that made you feel as if she was an old friend even upon first meeting. But her personality was only half of the reason she was the highest tipped bartender in Stillwater County.

"I'm glad you came in here tonight," she said. "I've got something that's going to get you all hot and bothered."

"You seem to think I haven't already noticed," Bobby grinned.

Sunny was, to put it mildly, an Asian goddess. Her perfect feminine curves were wrapped in nothing more than a green bikini top and a sarong slung low across her inviting hips. Regardless of one's gender or sexual preference, it was a challenge to look at Sunny and not immediately picture her naked.

"I've never seen anything so beautiful," Bobby swooned. "When did you get it?"

Sunny smiled into Bobby's captivated eyes, which were staring straight over her shoulder.

"We just got it installed this afternoon," she said. "It gets over three hundred channels in perfect digital clarity."

She pulled a remote control from beneath the bar and turned her gaze to match Bobby's. Attached to the corner pillar of the bar, above a TV showing some boring Norwegian rocket launch, a tiny satellite dish pointed into the clear night sky.

"What happened to the *big* dish?" Bobby asked.

"The big dish is yesterday's news. Analog. Crap," Sunny said. "This digital service carries all kinds of obscure stuff like this, and you don't ever have to rotate the dish to find different satellites."

"That's all true, but the big dish isn't subscription based. It can pick up all the wild feeds of newscasters picking their noses and yelling at their cameramen. I mean, you just can't put a price on that kind of entertainment."

"Well, you've got me there," Sunny nodded, pulling a mug of beer. "The big dish is in the Dumpster out back. You can always fish it out and take it home with you if you need to see newsies farming nose goblins."

"You know, I might just do that. It looks like I'm about to get my cable cut off next month, and I'm sure as hell not using rabbit ears."

Sunny laughed and touched Bobby's hand as she slipped him his drink.

"You've always got a scheme cooking, Bobby Gray. And that's why I love you."

Bobby knew this declaration of love was just a part of Sunny's routine chatter, but he made a mental note to leave her a big tip nonetheless.

"Well, I've got to get back to work," she continued, sticking out her pinky and her thumb. "Hang loose, channel surfer."

She slid the remote across the bar to Bobby and disappeared toward the thirsty mouths on the other side of the bar.

As Bobby annoyed the other patrons with his incessant channel-flipping, a new face slipped through the thatched doorway behind him. The dark stranger pitched a set of rental-car keys to the valet and strutted toward the bar.

The man's skin was a nondescript shade of mocha, and his unusual features could have passed him off as a member of any race on the planet without taxing the imagination. Over his broad chest he wore a wifebeater covered with a silk rockabilly shirt—black with blue flames licking their way up its sides. With his greasy black hair, his sculptured sideburns, and a beaming smile of hubcap-sized teeth, the guy looked like the poor sap who didn't get the callback for a GAP commercial. He swaggered up to the bar and leaned across it.

"Excuse me, miss?" he called.

Sunny turned, sending a wave through her onyx hair that seemed to linger in a sensual slow motion. Her eyes danced over the new guy's face as she approached.

"Heya, stranger," she said. "I don't think I've seen you around here before."

"You haven't," the newcomer smiled. "The good Lord only cast me in a cameo in this tiny town. I fly back to Los Angeles first thing in the a.m."

He said "Los Angeles" in the same tone of voice that someone might use to casually name-drop the Queen of England. To his obvious disappointment, neither Sunny nor Bobby looked the slightest bit impressed. He lowered his voice confidentially and continued.

"I'm just in town for a bit of *personal enhancement.* Tracked down the same guy who did Affleck. For real. Sometimes you gotta get down with the small town to get the job done right, you know?"

He waggled his eyebrows and gazed into Sunny's almond eyes with a grin as broad and toothy as a great white shark's. Again, whatever impression of awe that he was trying to create completely failed to congeal.

"Well, good for you, tiger," Sunny said noncommittally. "What can I get you to drink tonight?"

The stranger leaned in and raised an eyebrow.

"Girl, if you'd get me some milk, I'd pour it over you and make you a part of my complete breakfast."

Bobby burst out laughing, spitting beer on the bar.

"Very subtle, Casanova," he said, wiping his chin.

"We don't serve milk here," Sunny noted coolly. "How about I get you a beer?"

"How about you get me your name?" the stranger smiled, patting a gold cross hanging from his neck. "So I know what to write on the thank-you card I send to God."

Sunny rolled her eyes.

"It's Sun, but everybody calls me Sunny."

"And I can see why," the stranger nodded. "You light up this whole place with your radiance."

Bobby turned and drew an invisible line on an invisible tote board on the side of the bar.

"'I can see why, you light up the place' gets another point," he said dully. "Now it's only three behind 'They must call you Sunny because you have a heavenly body.'"

"Damn, look at Mr. Smart Guy over here," said the smooth talker. "If he was any more nosy, we'd have to call him Pinocchio. Why don't you keep it to yourself, homes?"

"I'm sorry, maestro," Bobby conceded. "Go on with your work."

"So what do they call you, slick?" Sunny asked, feigning interest for the sake of a bigger tip.

"The name is Terence Trent DeLaRosa, meaning 'of the rose,'" he said, rolling the R with a flourish. "My friends call me Trent, but you can call me whatever you like."

"How about Terence Trent DeLaMerde?" Bobby suggested. "Meaning 'of the bullshit.'"

Terence Trent DeLaRosa's eyes narrowed.

"Look, friend," he said, planting a heavy hand on Bobby's shoulder, "I don't need you making a running commentary over here and disturbing this lovely young lady."

Bobby stiffened and spoke in a low, threatening tone.

"I think that you should take your hand off of me now."

"And why is that, dawg?" Trent said, puffing out his chest.

"Because it's really starting to turn me on."

Trent let go of Bobby and turned back toward Sunny.

"What a comedian this guy is," he said to the empty air.

Sunny had long since left the two bickering egos in favor of a cuter guy on the other side of the bar.

"Keep it up, Romeo," Bobby said. "I think she really likes you."

Without a word, Trent sat down and stared at Sunny's perfect, apple-shaped bottom, imagining exactly what he would like to do to it.

The rigid hose slipped into the snug opening and began vigorously pumping away.

At a twilit gas station just off of Stillwater Bay, Vivian was filling her Rabbit's tank. Through the magic of a long shower and a short reconnaissance mission into the back of her closet, she had metamorphosed from a weary wage slave into a budding wallflower.

A black polyester cocktail dress hugged her long, minimal curves, terminating two conservative inches below her knees. The gown's neckline hovered above her modest chest in a manner that would have been suitable for a funeral. She was waiting until she got to the restaurant to put on her high heels—the Rabbit's clutch was difficult enough to operate as it was. In the meantime she wore her sneakers. Her hair was pulled up in a knot impaled with a pair of take-out chopsticks.

There were many things that Vivian Gray could do well. Dressing with flair was not among them.

She leaned on the fender and waited while the gas pump chugged away. The sun had finally disappeared behind the horizon, making the temperature balmy and comfortable for the first time that day. She had a secret place where she liked to go to be alone on nights like this. Unfortunately, tonight she would not have the opportunity to enjoy solitude.

She pulled a backpack-style purse from the back seat of her perpetually open convertible. After a moment of fruitless rummaging within, she pulled out a tiny flashlight and shined it inside. In the deepest, darkest depths of the purse she finally found what she was looking for: a dried-out tube of lipstick.

She twisted out a crumbling pink shaft and applied it to her lips with a clumsy, unpracticed stroke. This face-painting was just to fit in at the Banyan Terrace, she reminded herself. It was all just a part of the blackmail process. It was to get her job back. It was not to impress Nick.

"I hope you don't have to go too far with that fella tonight."

Vivian jumped and spun around guiltily. The voice belonged to an avuncular man fueling up an age-beaten Winnebago with Pennsylvania license plates.

"Excuse me?" Vivian asked, wiping an errant streak of pink off her chin.

The man ambled over and pointed to the Rabbit's comically undersized spare tire. "That fella there. The donut. I hope you don't have to go too far with it," he repeated. "You better get that replaced or it'll blow at the worst possible time. Believe me, I know what I'm talkin' about when it comes to cars."

"Oh, right. Thanks," Vivian said. "I know. Don't worry, I won't go too far. Ever."

The man nodded.

"If I were you I'd never go too far neither. Every time we come down to Florida the wife gets to wantin' to close up the farm and move here permanent. Stillwater is just like paradise, ain't it?"

Vivian flashed an insincere smile and nodded. She didn't want to get into it. The man looked her up and down with a twinkle in his eye like a proud father on his daughter's wedding day.

"You're all dressed up mighty purdy, if you don't mind me sayin' so," he said. "You goin' someplace fancy with your fella?"

"I'm going on a date with a guy that I don't like in order to save a job that I don't want so that I can afford to pay bills that aren't mine."

The man let out a long, low whistle and leaned up against the Rabbit next to Vivian. Apparently he was in as much of a hurry to get back to his motor home as he was to get back to his farm.

"Well, that don't seem fair, does it?" he said. "Listen, I figger I can help you out a little."

He wrestled a misshapen old wallet from the back pocket of his shorts.

"Oh, no no. I'm okay, really," Vivian said. "I couldn't take your mon—"

Before Vivian could complete her protest the man pulled a wrinkled photograph from his wallet and shoved it under her nose.

"What do you think of that?" he said reverently. "Ain't she a *beaut?*"

Vivian struggled to focus her eyes on the picture hovering inches from her glasses. It depicted a bright yellow classic convertible with the man behind the wheel wearing a leather jacket and smiling from ear to ear.

"That there's a 1953 Cadillac Eldorado," he said proudly. "Beautiful, beautiful machine. I restored her myself."

"That's ... nice?" Vivian ventured.

"She's more than nice! She's an absolute gem!" the man said, stabbing his finger into the photo. "*That's* the kind of car you drive to paradise!"

He sighed and tucked the picture back into his wallet before continuing.

"But the wife, Lord love 'er, she don't like to stay in hotels. Says she don't like Bernice sleepin' on unfamiliar beddin'. Not that there's much of a chance of that happening, if you know whut I mean."

He shook his head heavily and looked at the dilapidated motor home. Through its windshield, Vivian could see a lanky, underweight teenage girl with dirty blond hair and the most homely face that she'd ever had the misfortune of laying eyes upon. The girl's mouth hung open like the leaf trap on a motel swimming pool, displaying two rows of teeth that seemed to be arguing about directions. She had a nose like an overripe radish and her eyes were neither the same size nor color. Vivian suppressed a horrified gasp, which collapsed into a feeling of overwhelming shame in her stomach.

"It's like I always say," the man said solemnly, "some people are the Caddy, and some are the motor home. Do ya see what I'm sayin' here?"

"I uh … I think so," Vivian stammered. Her pump had clicked off ages ago.

"Let me explain myself. On the one hand you've got people like the '53 Eldorado. They're flashy and slick, and everybody wants a piece of them just because they're so damned beautiful. But a lot of these classic cars are all chrome and polish with nothin' under the hood. All glitter and no horsepower, right? Then on the other hand you've got folks like the ol' mobile homestead here."

He threw a glance at the motor home, though his mournful eyes were obviously focused on its passenger seat.

"Sure, the motor home here ain't a looker, but it's real reliable. It's got all the comforts of home on the inside, so it don't have to be beautiful on the outside. Smart people know better than to just buy the Caddy because of its looks. They think about what's really important and hold out for the real deal. Anyone would be damned lucky to get a solid, down-to-earth motor home like that instead of some flashy, troublesome Caddy. Damned lucky. Do you see what I'm sayin'?"

"I think I may have picked up your deftly woven subtext," Vivian muttered. "It's what's on the inside that counts."

"That's right," the man nodded. "So don't you go turning this boy of yours away just because he's the motor home and not the Cadillac."

Vivian blinked.

"Oh, no, you misunderstood. This boy *is* the Cadillac."

The man's eyes widened, and he took Vivian by the shoulder with a confidential whisper.

"Shoot, missy! If you've got the goods to get yourself a Cadillac, quit yer whinin' and go ride it to paradise!"

A vision of paradise jiggled in front of Trent and Bobby's eyes as they waited for their third round of drinks. Sunny vigorously shook a silver cocktail shaker, causing her physique to bounce in the most pleasing way imaginable. Trent continued trying to talk her out of her sarong.

"Girl, it's a sin seeing an angelic creature like you all penned up behind that bar. You should be out dancing under the stars from which God dropped you. How about after you close down this dive you and I hit the beach, yo?"

"I'd really love to," Sunny lied. "But after work the only thing I'm going to be hitting is the books. I've got a lot of studying to do if I intend to pass the summer term."

"Oh, so you're a little schoolgirl, eh?" Trent said. "What institution of higher learning would be so cruel as to keep a sassy little co-ed like yourself all cooped up in the school house all summer long?"

"It's just community college," Sunny said. "I've been taking classes to become a nurse."

"In that case, I'd be more than happy to help you with your homework," Trent grinned. "What do you say you come back to my hotel and we play doctor for a while, girl?"

"Well, with my grades, *playing* doctor is about the best I can do. I'm thinking about quitting school and just working the Martini full time. After all, I'd still be giving shots—I'd just be trading in needles for glasses."

She poured her shaker into a pair of shot glasses and pushed them across the bar toward Trent and Bobby. Before she could retrieve her hand, Trent took it in his own and spoke reassuringly.

"Don't give up on your dreams so easily, girl. If you're half as smart as you are sexy, I guarantee you're gonna be the best doctor in the world before you know it. For real."

Sunny returned Trent's hand to the bar.

"Well thanks, but a *whole lot* of doctors are going to have to die before I can claim that title."

With a glimmer of sadness in her eye, Sunny excused herself to the other end of the room. Bobby's gaze drifted past her and onto the disgustingly familiar scene unfolding near the submarine. A stout frat boy with a red face staggered toward the sub, escorting a drunken co-ed who had lost the ability to stand unsupported. A table full of his Greek brothers were cranking their arms in the air, barking and making deeply unintelligible catcalls.

The frat boy slipped a wad of sweaty bills to the bouncer stationed beside the sub, and he pulled open the watertight hatch. The frattie swung his date inside and then stepped in behind her, making one last bellowing call to his friends before the bouncer closed the door. As the portal clanged shut, yellow siren lights on the sub flashed weakly, and crackly speakers emitted a fake diving klaxon mixed with a sound bite of Steven Tyler crooning, *"Gooooooiiiiiing dooooooown."*

The fraternity brothers exploded into testosterone-charged hollering. Bobby shook his head and returned to his unfinished beer.

"Hey, B-Dawg," Trent said, apparently addressing Bobby. "See that fly honey over there?"

Bobby looked across the bar and spotted a full-figured vixen in a red leather dress. She was making a good show of herself, despite the fact that she was obviously in denial about her actual age.

"The burned-out Loni Anderson chick?" Bobby asked.

"Yeah. I bet you twenty bucks I can get her phone number before you do."

Bobby burst out laughing.

"Why would I want her phone number? She looks like Brett Butler in a porno movie!"

"Older women just have more experience in *knockin' da boots!*" Trent said, leaning back and banging the chunky heels of his wingtips together in the air.

"Okay, you're on. I could use your twenty bucks to buy some better drinking buddies."

"I'll use *your* twenty to buy that hoochie some breakfast!"

Trent jumped off his stool and strutted over to the woman. She noticed him coming and smiled. Trent returned her smile and oozed an introduction.

"Damn, girl, is your daddy a thief?"

"No, why?" asked the woman, sounding suspiciously as if she was trying to hide something.

"Because I just wanted to know who stole the stars from God and put them in your eyes."

The woman laughed the hoarse cackle of a seasoned smoker.

"That's cute; I like that," she said, running her fingernails up Trent's neck and around the back of his head. "But you know what I would like more?"

"A bottle of fine merlot, my hotel suite, and a 'do not disturb' sign?" Trent offered.

The woman grabbed his ear and slammed his head down on the bar with an empty *thud*.

"I was thinking more along the lines of four steel shackles, my fourteen-inch strap-on, a tube of Astroglide, and your sweet virgin ass," she growled, flicking her tongue stud against her teeth. "But we can forgo the lube if you like, slave."

From the other end of the bar, Bobby could see the color drain from Trent's face as he wriggled free of the savage grip and hurried back to his stool.

"So where's her number, hotshot?" Bobby asked.

"I don't want none a' dat ass!" Trent said, staring blankly into the bar.

"I didn't want any either, but you wanted to make the stupid bet. Pay up."

"I don't think so, home-dawg! I don't have to give you nothin' if you can't get the digits."

"Alright, alright. I'll be right back."

Bobby's barstool creaked a sigh of relief as he stood up. Trent watched in anxious anticipation as his rival strolled with casual indifference toward his fate. From this end of the bar, he couldn't hear what the two of them were saying, but he could see every move that they made.

Bobby tapped the woman on the shoulder and said something, thumbing at the door. The woman nodded and looked slightly alarmed. Bobby made a comforting gesture and continued. The dominatrix pulled out a pen, which she promptly used on a cocktail napkin.

Trent's jaw dropped to the bar. Not only had the husky loser managed to get her phone number, but he didn't look at all alarmed about the unholy reaming that would ensue when he used it.

When the woman was done writing her number, Bobby apparently wrote his number on a napkin and gave it to her in return. The woman left the bar, and Bobby returned to his weary stool.

"Here's her number," he said, tossing the napkin in front of Trent. "Knock yourself out … or let her do it for you."

"Daaaaaamn, B-Slice! How did you work that so fast?"

"I told her that I ran into her car and we should exchange numbers so my insurance company could pay for the damage."

"Oh, shit no, dawg! That's not cool! You tricked her! You didn't convince her that she wanted to blast off on your love rocket!"

"The bet I made was twenty dollars for a phone number," Bobby shrugged. "You'll have to raise the stakes if you want to go medieval on my ass."

"Whoooa, cuuuuwl swowrd!"

Erik turned to Harry Stokes to see him hauling a theatrical sword out of a *Superman III* garbage can. This bin contained an assortment of wooden and plastic costume weapons, but Harry's discriminating eye had gone straight for the only steel blade in the bunch.

"Izaawesome! I'ma Powa Waynja! I'ma Powa Waynja!"

"Harry, no! Put that down!" Erik squealed.

Harry bolted across the store, brandishing his heavy blade in a lurching, off-balance swing. He teetered down an aisle, coming to a stop next to his sister's upturned backside. Debbie was on all fours with her head stuffed under an eight-foot-tall shelving unit.

"Don't be scared, kitty! I'll get you out!" she called. "Come here, kitty! I love you!"

The shelves teetered menacingly as Debbie attempted to cram her tiny body underneath them. Rows of ancient Looney Tunes and *The Great Muppet Caper* drinking glasses tipped over and rolled in bouncing arcs, but a mewling hiss stabbing from beneath the shelves suggested that Debbie was in greater danger from feline-related injuries than from falling glass.

Erik leapt between the siblings and threw a skinny hand on each of them.

"Harry! Give me that!" he snapped, yanking the sword out of Harry's fist. "Debbie! Get out of there before you kill yourself!"

He grabbed Debbie by the belt of her little pink jeans, hauled her out from under the shelf, and dropped her on the carpet.

"Alright, you little mother fu—"

He took a deep breath.

"Alright, you little *monsters,*" he revised. "This is a place of business. This is not *Romper Room.* You can't just hang around here all night and play with Do Bee and wait for me to look at you in my magic mirror!"

The children looked at each other quizzically. Erik continued.

"So either buy something or get—"

He noticed that Debbie was clutching a tiny object to her chest.

"Debbie, what's that?"

"Nothing."

"Give it to me."

"No!" Debbie snapped. "It's mine!"

"Whatever it is, it's not yours," Erik argued. "Now give it to me."

"No!"

Erik thrust out his hand.

"Debbie Stokes, you give that to me *now!*"

"Fine!" Debbie screamed. "Take my baby away! See if I care!"

She unclasped her hands and slapped a dead mouse into Erik's outstretched palm. His face bleached white as the mangled rodent's blood leaked through his fingers.

"Eeeaugh!" he screamed, dropping the carcass with a tiny, wet *splat.*

He grabbed a box of tissues and frantically wiped his palm. He continued to wipe long after the blood had been cleaned, as if trying to erase the stain from his mind.

"Ew, ew, God," he chattered. "Oh God, ew. Ew."

When he had exhausted the entire box, Erik turned on Debbie.

"Debbie, what's the *matter* with you? Where did you get that?"

"The kitty gave it to me!" Debbie cried. "The kitty gives me presents because she loves me!"

"Twiki gave this to you? Well, she's a bad kitty!"

He reached his long arm under the shelves and grabbed Twiki by the scruff of her neck, pulling her out and thrusting a finger at her bloody mouth.

"Twiki!" he snapped. "I told you to stop killing mice! It's disgusting! No more dead mice, Twiki! Do you understand? No. More. Dead. Mice!"

In a flash of feline muscle, all of Twiki's front claws were once again planted in Erik's forearm. He dropped her with a yelp, and she darted away, closely pursued by a giggling, bloodstained Debbie.

"Man, I've gotta stop doing that," Erik whimpered.

"You can't stop doing that, can you, baby?" Trent grinned, making goo-goo eyes across the barroom. "That business-suit beauty can't stop checking out the T-man's goods."

Bobby glanced over at a bony, straitlaced woman perched like a crane behind a nearby table. She noticed the boys staring at her and turned away with a fierce scowl.

"Ally McBeal with PMS?" Bobby asked. "Yeah, go get her, stud boy."

"Oh, I'll get a piece of that," Trent nodded. "But first how about another friendly wager? Double or nothing you can't get her phone number."

Bobby squinted at Trent.

"You don't even have my twenty, do you?"

"Don't be dissin' my greenbacks, Heavy B! I got the dollars if you got the digits."

"Alright, alright," Bobby sighed. "Let's do it."

"None a dat insurance scam bullshit this time, yo. She has to give you her phone number because she wants to do a little naked bed wrestling. Are you down?"

"Yeah, yeah. You want to try first again, Mr. Smooth?"

"Damn straight, and this time your sorry ass isn't going to *get* a turn!"

Trent strutted across the room, approaching his mark from behind. He leaned in over her shoulder and trickled a hot, moist whisper into her ear.

"Did it hurt?"

The woman recoiled, choking on a sip of her drink. She twisted in her chair and sized him up furiously.

"Did *what* hurt?" she snapped.

"Did it hurt when you fell down from Heaven?"

The girl gave him a fiery scowl.

"*That's* not the direction that I came from. Get lost, asshole."

She crossed her legs tightly and returned her stare to the bar.

"Oooh, feisty!" Trent said. "I love the women down here in Florida. Y'all keep it real, yo. I hate it when people try to act fake and pretend they're something they're not, you know?"

"Bullshit," the woman spat. "You're the stereotypical fake asshole poseur male. Look at yourself. You're a mess. Your skin is a fake bottle-bronze, your fake gold jewelry looks like it's out of a box of Cracker Jacks—even your big, fake, shit-eating grin looks like it's made out of toilet-bowl porcelain."

Trent covered his conspicuously white teeth with a conspicuously bronze hand.

"Damn, baby, why so harsh?" he said, investigating her cocktail. "You must be drinkin' the Haterade! I came here to get myself enhanced, not beat down!"

"Well, I came for the view," the girl snarled. "Not to get harassed by every asshole tourist looking to show off his newly enhanced fake dick."

"Oh no, I assure you, little Moses is all natural," Trent said, adjusting the lump in the front of his trousers. "And he's ready to raise his staff and divide your Red Sea, girl!"

From across the bar, Bobby saw Trent take a whiskey sour square in the face. Dampened and downtrodden, he returned to his loser stool at the bar.

"You must have really scored that time!" Bobby said. "She bought you a drink!"

"Shut up," Trent growled. "You're not gettin' none a' dat. She's got da itch wit' da capital B."

"Well, at least she's already spent her ammo on you."

Bobby set down his mug and waddled off toward the boiling feminist. Trent called after him in a forced whisper.

"Remember, the number has to be for *sex!*"

"Yeah, yeah ..."

Bobby approached the girl's table, and she gave him a look that suggested she was ready to smash her tumbler on the table and ram a shard of glass through his throat. As if completely oblivious, Bobby just sat down and started talking. Trent was impressed: If nothing else, his adversary had balls. It was a shame this chick was about to tear them off.

He took another sip of his drink and glanced at the submarine. To chaotic applause, another frat boy climbed out of the hatch and held aloft a pair of red satin panties as if they were the Holy Grail. Trent looked back at Bobby just in time to see the skinny girl grinning from ear to ear and handing him a folded napkin. She continued to beam as Bobby returned to the bar.

"Oh you are so bullshit," Trent snapped. "Quit frontin'. I said that the number had to be for *sex!*"

"It is! I don't know how you didn't catch the vibes she was throwing off, but that girl is horny as hell. I assure you, this number is for sex."

"You're lying!" Trent bawled. "You're such a big liar they call you Simba the lyin' king! If it's for sex, then prove it, fat boy!"

"Alright, alright. Keep your shorts on."

He gestured over the bar to Sunny.

"What's up, Bobby?" she asked.

"I don't know how open you are to experimentation," he said, pushing the napkin across the bar, "but that girl with the bad attitude over there *really* wants to get up your skirt."

Vivian's Rabbit skirted the ornate fountain that stood in the center of the traffic circle, welcoming her to Port Manatee. Although she was only ten miles north of Stillwater on the map, she was a million miles away financially. There were no roadside tourist traps in Port Manatee, no cut-rate rental cars or seedy hotels. There were only seaside manors, private beaches, and a harbor full of yachts so sprawlingly gargantuan that they threatened the very laws of hydrodynamics.

She turned off of the main street and onto a white concrete driveway that swerved between rows of perfectly manicured miniature palms. With a lingering press on the brake, the Rabbit scraped to a halt in front of the valet counter at the Banyan Terrace.

A green-vested valet rushed up with smug look pulled tightly across his pimply teenage face. He glowered at the disintegrating Rabbit as if it were a pile of freshly skinned kittens.

"I'm sorry, ma'am," he said curtly. "The Banyan Terrace's parking structure is full to capacity this evening. You'll have to park your ... *vehicle* someplace else."

His mouth and tongue formed the word "vehicle," but his voice clearly said "piece of shit, unworthy of our accommodation." A second valet pulled a long black Mercedes around the rattling convertible and into the garage, as if to literally drive this point home.

"Perhaps you could check again," Vivian said, digging into her purse. "I think there may be a space you've overlooked."

The valet held out his hand knowingly, and Vivian slipped him the contents of her wallet. Three dollars and a losing lottery ticket. The oil on the valet's face rippled with insult.

"Oh, come on," Vivian pleaded. "I'm already half an hour late for my reservation. Work with me here."

The valet looked at the row of impatient luxury sedans queuing in the acrid smokescreen pouring from the Rabbit's back end. After a long pause, he stuffed his tip into his pocket and opened Vivian's door.

"All right," he muttered. "I might be able to squeeze it in under a ramp somewhere, but I can't guarantee that it won't get scratched."

"That's fine," Vivian sighed. "Just leave it in gear when you park it. The hand brake doesn't work."

"I would expect nothing less," the valet sneered.

Vivian wrenched her sneakers from her feet and replaced them with heels of a timeless design that any generation would have found bland. She started to toss her ragged sneakers in the back seat but then thought better of the idea and set them on the dashboard instead.

When the valet slipped behind the wheel, he found himself face-to-face with two mangled tongues effusing a foot odor so noxious its use in warfare would have been banned by the Geneva Convention. Vivian gave him an innocent smile as he covered his nose, put the car in gear, and wrestled it up the driveway and into the parking garage.

Vivian proceeded up the sidewalk toward the restaurant. Her awkward, stumbling steps betrayed how long it had been since she had been given an opportunity to wear high heels. Even so, the scenery made up for her inconvenience.

The Banyan Terrace was straight from the pages of a fairy tale. The hanging root systems of a pair of two-hundred-year-old banyan trees had been carefully braided over a series of arches for generations, forming a knotty wooden tunnel that led to the green glass front of the building. When Vivian reached the end of the path, a doorman greeted her wobbling stride with restrained doubt and ushered her through the entrance.

The main foyer of the Banyan Terrace was nothing short of spectacular. A rock face towered the full height of the two-story interior, spilling a champagne-like waterfall into a serene goldfish pool below. The whole room smelled of fresh bread and clean linens.

Maybe this wasn't going to be so bad after all.

"May I help you, miss?"

Vivian looked to her right and saw a narrow, balding maitre'd posted behind a lectern.

"Yes, I'm supposed to be meeting with a friend," she said, turning the word over in her mouth as if trying to make it sound true.

"The gentleman's name, please."

"It's um … Nick."

"The gentleman's *last* name?"

"I, uh … I guess I don't know his last name," Vivian admitted.

The maitre'd gave her a glare that made the way the valet had looked at her car seem like true love.

"If you don't have a reservation, miss, I'm afraid I'm going to have to ask you to—"

"Check under Aspen. Nick Aspen."

Vivian turned to find Nick standing behind her, grinning at the annoyed maitre'd and holding a drink in each hand. A spectacularly tailored suit had transformed his image from faux extreme to actual class. His green eyes caught Vivian's, delivering a friendly wink. Despite all efforts to the contrary, she blushed.

"C'mon," he said, gesturing with a broad shoulder. "We've already got a table over here."

Vivian shot a victorious glance at the maitre'd before falling off of her heel, bumping into Nick, and splashing his drinks onto the carpet. The maitre'd put his fingers to his forehead in a gesture that screamed, "There goes the neighborhood."

Nick led Vivian to a table overlooking the outside gardens. A tall white candle stood in its center, flickering its light as if to demand that romance transpire in its presence. He set down his beverages and escorted her into her seat before taking his own.

"Where you been, Red?" he smiled. "I've been here for like, an hour. I just hit the bar and picked up some drinks while I was waiting for you to show up."

He pulled a tall glass of light beer toward himself and pushed the other glass toward Vivian. It was a stemmed fishbowl the size of her head, filled with a frosty pink beverage and ornamented with a fat strawberry. He continued.

"I got you a strawberry daiquiri to match those beautiful strawberry locks of yours, Red."

"All right, stop calling me Red," Vivian snapped. "My name isn't Red—it's Gray. Vivian Gray."

"Vivian Gray," Nick said dreamily. "Vivian Gray. That's a pretty name."

"No it isn't. It sounds like one of the suspects from *Clue*."

Nick smiled and raised an eyebrow.

"Well, with a tight little body like yours, I'm sure that you could get away with murder."

He threw her a wink and magnificent grin. Vivian rolled her eyes.

"So, have you talked to Boltzmann about my job yet?"

"That's no way to be, Vivian Gray!" Nick laughed. "You're in the most expensive restaurant in Port Manatee! And just look at the rockin' dude you've got on your arm! That bogus McJob of yours should be the last thing on your mind right now. You need to loosen up for a while."

He took a sip of his beer, smiled his centerfold-perfect smile, and put his hand on her knee. She politely removed it.

"So, shall I assume then that you have *not* yet talked to Boltzmann about my job?"

Nick's smile faded.

"Alright, you got me. I haven't," he admitted. "And, to be totally honest, I was never really going to."

"Oh, come on! Extortion is a very simple process! I go on a date with you; you get me my job back. What part of this transaction don't you understand?"

"The part I don't understand is why you're so anxious to get that heinous job back when you could be doing something so much more intense with your life!"

"Oh right," Vivian huffed. "Like what? Selling Fusion Fuel like you?"

"I was thinking more like selling Fusion Fuel *with* me," Nick said. "Vivian, I want you to ditch that grocery store job and come join my modeling agency. That's the real reason I wanted to take you out tonight."

Vivian burst out in sour laughter.

"I can't believe I wore lipstick for this," she grumbled, wiping her lips on a napkin. "If I'd have known that you had no intention of getting my job back I never would have come here."

"Seriously! I *know!* For some reason you're so dead set on living at the bottom of the retail food chain you won't even give a dude a chance when he wants to kick your career up a level! I could make it so that the next time you walk into Boltzmann's Market that fat bastard would be kissing your ass instead of the other way around. Doesn't that interest you at *all?*"

Vivian's scowl softened as the thought poured through her mind. She took a long, contemplative pull from her daiquiri before speaking.

"All right, I came all the way out here for this; I may as well hear the pitch."

"Rockin' cool! That's the way to be!" Nick grinned. "I've had my eye on you ever since I saw that fiery hair of yours this morning, Red … er, Vivian. I'm tellin' ya, you could be the Angie Everhart of the Gulf Coast if you just joined up with my agency. Nobody can ignore a natural redhead! You'd get the top-dollar jobs just banging down your door!"

Vivian peered over her glasses.

"I see. So you're just looking to make sure that I exploit my follicles to the fullest? I suppose there's nothing in it for you?"

Nick's smile wilted as his eyes shifted to his drink and lingered there for a long moment.

"Well, I guess you *would* need somebody to show you the ropes," he said. "And, you know, I guess I *do* need to find myself a top-shelf partner if I'm ever going to make platinum level …"

Vivian nodded.

"Ahh, yes. Perhaps I should take this opportunity to remind you that I'm not the boss's daughter," she said, drawing finger quotes in the air. " '*Nailing*' me isn't going to provide you with anything but disappointment."

Nick shook his head defensively.

"It's not like that. The boss's daughter isn't just *sleeping* with Mr. Platinum, she's also *working* with him. They're a promo modeling team. No, that's not even fair—they're a promo modeling *force.* But you and me, Vivian, if we teamed up we could totally kick their asses, hardcore!"

"Oh, we could *not.* Have you even bothered to look below my scalp, Nick? I'm not exactly supermodel material here. I'm just a tall, skinny goon with no fashion sense. I'm not even pretty!"

Nick tipped his head and a smile blossomed across his face. He put his hand on top of Vivian's and spoke in a voice like warm honey.

"You are so pretty, Vivian. I know you've got the soul of a model. All you have to do is let down your hair and take off your glasses."

He gently grasped Vivian's glasses and pulled them from her face. Her eyes turned toward each other, leaving her staring at her own nose in a blind, cross-eyed goggle.

"Okay," Nick conceded. "So maybe just let the hair down then."

Vivian snatched her glasses and planted them back on her face, straightening out her vision with a series of quick blinks.

"Just forget it, Nick. Nothing you can do or say is going to make me want to be your partner. End of discussion."

Nick sighed and picked up a tall green menu. Vivian did likewise.

"Alright, you win," he said. "I guess I'm on my own for this tour. I just thought you might like to get out of Stillwater for a while."

Vivian's eyes flicked over the top of her menu curiously.

"What do you mean, 'get out of Stillwater'?"

"Oh, you know. New York, Chicago, San Francisco, wherever," Nick said matter-of-factly. "The Fusion Fuel promo blitz is gonna hit all of the big metro areas."

Vivian blinked.

"Wait, wait. Do you mean to tell me that they send you all around the country just to be obnoxious and peddle your quack remedies?"

"Oh sure," Nick shrugged. "My agency is the big time, baby. We only take national-level gigs. You didn't honestly think that I just worked Stillwater, did you? None of us models are ever in Florida for more than a few days a year."

Vivian took a long, quiet sip of her daiquiri.

"So," she said casually, "tell me more about this agency of yours."

"I've never earned so much money for such easy work," Bobby said. "Do you want to just fork over the forty you owe me, or shall we go for eighty?"

"Okay, B, we've had our fun. What do you say I just buy the next round and we call it even?" Trent said. "Let us not forget what the Bible says: 'Money is the route to all evil.'"

Bobby snorted.

"Well, the Bible's never seen my sister when the rent is due. Pay up, sucker."

The amiable smile on Trent's face collapsed into a scowl.

"Whatever, homes. You been scammin' all night," he muttered, gesturing at Sunny. "Hey beautiful barmaid, you gonna let this punk straight-up rob your customers right under your fine little nose?"

"Oh no, don't drag me into this," Sunny said. "I have a strict policy of non-involvement in bar bets. You two work this out yourselves."

Their conversation was interrupted by another chorus of frat-boy cheers as the bouncer pulled open the submarine's hatch. A jock in a crushed cowboy hat stepped from the vessel, still fastening the oversized buckle of his belt. He strode into the swarm of his brothers, and they greeted him with a thunderous round of congratulatory slaps delivered to his thick back and arms.

"Hey, Sunshine," Trent said, gesturing to the sub. "What's that all about?"

"Some bars have a mechanical bull. Some bars have karaoke. This bar has a lawsuit waiting to happen," Sunny sighed. "The guy who owns the Martini picked up the *Sawfish* at auction when the Stillwater Oceanographic Institute lost its funding back in the '70s. Since then it's gone from 'deep sea' to *Deep Throat*."

When the crowd's focus had long since left the darkened sub, a narrow co-ed stumbled from its door, rubbing a nosebleed on her limp forearm.

"So it's like some kind of make-out room?" Trent asked.

"Wow, nothing gets past you, eh Sherlock?" Bobby grumbled, sliding off his stool. "Okay, it's been real. Time to cash out, big shot. My work here is done."

Trent put his hand on Bobby's shoulder and pushed him back onto his stool.

"Whoa whoa, hold up, homes. What do you say we make one more friendly wager? Go for an even hundred bucks."

Bobby sighed.

"You're lucky I need the money. Alright, whose number do you want this time, Valentino?"

"Uh uh—when you play for the big bucks it's high stakes," Trent said. "For the Benjamin, you have to get a girl into that sub."

"Oh, screw you!" Bobby spat. "If I wanted to sit in a puddle of frat-boy spooge, I'd go to a House of Pain concert."

"S'cool with me, bro. S'cool. I respect a man who knows his limits," Trent gloated. "Scamming numbers is one thing, but there ain't no way a butterball like you could get something sweet down on his meat."

Bobby's freckly cheeks prickled into redness. He settled back on his stool and cracked his knuckles.

"Alright, smart-ass, any girl in the bar. Pick one."

Trent turned back to the barroom and profiled the few remaining beauties. He picked apart every shapely young girl in the room, trying to anticipate any loopholes his unscrupulous competitor might exploit. He needed to find a girl who would humiliate Bobby as badly as Bobby had been humiliating him ever since he walked through that bamboo doorway.

And then in that same doorway she appeared. A drunken savage stumbled into the bar on bony legs wrapped in torn fishnets. One hand clutched a forty-ounce malt liquor in a wet paper bag, the other an unfiltered cigarette, belching out black fumes like a '73 Plymouth Duster.

"Right there," Trent said. "There's your girlfriend, B. Go get her."

Bobby glanced at the newcomer.

"Forget it. A hundred bucks isn't worth it."

"Bullshit," Trent said. "You just don't have the goods."

Bobby looked the girl up and down.

"A hundred bucks?" he confirmed.

"Yep."

"To get her in the sub."

"Right."

"And you've got the money?"

"Right here," Trent said, patting the bulge in his back pocket.

Bobby chugged the remaining half of his beer.

"Alright," he said, wiping his mouth on his forearm. "You're on."

He creaked off his barstool and met his mark halfway across the planked floor. Smoke blasted from the girl's pierced nostrils like steam from the pits of Hell. She stared Bobby down with scalding menace.

But it's hard to intimidate somebody after you've bagged his groceries.

"Hey, Scary Sherri," Bobby said. "You look more like a corpse tonight than usual."

"Pissh off, Gray. I'm schelebrating," Sherri slurred through an almost visible haze of alcohol. "If you like your teshticles where they are, I suggesht you step out from between me andza booze."

She threw a pill into the back of her throat and washed it down with a nip from her bottle.

"Look, this is going to sound strange, but I promise my intentions are pure," Bobby said, holding up his right hand. "There's fifty bucks in it for you if you'll just sit in the sub with me for five minutes. No sex."

Sherri rolled her eyes skyward and tapped on her lips.

"Hmmmm, innsheresting offer, but I think I'm going to go with *'Fuck you!'*"

She resumed stomping unsteadily toward the bar.

"Fair enough, fair enough," Bobby said, blocking her path. "But what if I told you that this simple task would not only earn you fifty bucks but would also completely humiliate that smarmy *Swingers*-lookin' asshole at the bar?"

Sherri glanced over Bobby's shoulder.

"Cheshire cat with sideburns?"

"That's the guy."

Sherri blinked and took a long, hard swig out of her forty-ounce.

From across the bar, Trent's stomach plunged into his empty wallet as he saw Sherri take Bobby by the hand and lead him down the boardwalk to the submarine. He looked at Sunny with desperation.

"How? How did he? How *could* he?"

Sunny looked at Sherri and Bobby climbing into the sub and shrugged.

"You know what they say," she mused. "Nobody can ignore a natural redhead."

Vivian raised her hand and drew in a breath, but before she could push it through her vocal cords yet another waiter had swept past her table without so much as a curious glance. He slid a silver tray of exotic coffees onto a neighboring table to the delight of a sexy young Latina with a high giggle and a low décolletage. Vivian dropped her extended hand on the table next to a fishbowl containing nothing but a shallow pink froth and a nibbled strawberry stem. Her head wobbled across her shoulders, and she propped it up on her elbow.

"Did you see that? That's the fifth waiter who's totally ignored me," she muttered. "How many waiters does Charo need over there? At this rate we'll starve before we even place an order."

Nick laughed.

"You can't give up that easy. If you want to be a promotional model, you're going to have to learn to get people's attention."

"By doing what?" Vivian said. "Wearing a low-cut dress and giggling vapidly? I'd rather starve."

Nick waved a dismissive hand.

"You're looking at it all wrong. You just see a girl busting out of her dress over there. I see a girl using what she's got to command every waiter in this restaurant. I'll totally bet she's not even getting charged for that coffee. I'm telling you, Vivian, if you ever want to succeed you've got to learn to use your assets."

"I *do* use my assets," Vivian snapped. "The assets I choose to use are right here."

She tapped her index finger on her cranium.

"Well, in a perfect world that might actually get you somewhere," Nick said. "But in reality, you'd get a lot farther in life if you just got yourself a low-cut dress and a push-up bra."

Vivian's eyes went narrow with disgust.

"Spoken like a true model. How can you even *suggest* that physical beauty is more important than intellect?"

"I guess there's a time and a place for everything," Nick shrugged. "But if brains are really more important than looks, then how come Miss Teen South America over there has five waiters and you have a big round zero? I'm tellin' ya, Vivian, you just need to find the self-confidence to use your sweet little body to your advantage for once. Smarts are all fine and good, but there's no way in a million years you're gonna out-flash a girl with assets like hers using nothing but your big brain."

Vivian's eyes blazed.

"You want flash?" she snarled. "Just watch me, pretty boy."

She leaned over to the giggling Latina's extravagant coffee set and gestured at the sugar and creamer.

"May I?"

The girl gave an affronted nod as if Vivian was a vagrant who had just climbed out of the sewer and asked for her underpants. Vivian leaned back over to her own table and tore open five purloined packets of non-dairy creamer, pouring them into her slender palm.

"So what, you're just going to start begging for food?" Nick laughed. "That's the best plan your big brain can come up with?"

Without warning, Vivian blew the powder through the candle's flame, producing an enormous flash of fire. A cacophony of falling silver and china cascaded through the room as every waiter dropped what he was doing and whirled toward the scorched air. Even the spicy Latina stopped her giggling to pay homage to what had, if only for a second, eclipsed her as the hottest thing in the room.

"Whoa! That was *intense!*" Nick gasped. "What did you put in that?!"

"Just science," Vivian smiled. "The entire surface area of each granule is exposed to oxygen, so it burns quickly and spreads the flame to its neighbors exponentially."

Nick's gaping mouth twisted into a grin. Vivian continued.

"I'd like to see you out-flash *that* with a Wonderbra."

Before Nick could reply, the maitre'd rushed across the room, surrounded by a gaggle of whispering waiters. He stepped up to the table and cleared his throat.

"As you may or may not be aware, the Port Manatee fire codes expressly forbid pyrotechnic displays in places of business."

"Sorry, I was just trying to get your attention," Vivian said. "We're ready to order."

"The Banyan Terrace does not oblige take-out orders," the maitre'd replied.

"Oh, we're not leaving," Nick smiled.

"Yes," the maitre'd said, "I'm afraid that you are."

The watertight door of the *Sawfish* slammed shut with a harsh, rattling *clank,* blotting out the sound of the fake klaxons and whooping fratties outside and leaving Bobby and Sherri in a dark, stale silence. Although the sub was the size of a short bus on the outside, its thick walls gave it the same interior dimensions as a Ford Festiva. A string of Christmas lights threw a light wash of illumination over a squalid chamber containing nothing but a graffiti-tagged wooden bench bolted to the wall. Sherri dropped heavily onto it and took a drag of her cigarette, making the claustrophobic interior of the sub that much more unpleasant.

"Judging from the condition of the floor," Bobby observed, "it looks like this thing has seen more 'spit' than 'swallow.'"

Sherri pulled her legs onto the bench, pressing her knees against her chest and leaning her back against the entry hatch. Bobby plopped down on the other end of the bench, making a conscious effort not to make contact with Sherri's boot-clad toes. She popped another pair of pills into her mouth and drowned them in malt liquor.

"What's the matter?" Bobby asked. "Got a headache?"

"I don't *get* headaches," Sherri said, "I *give* headaches. Ish Special K. I scored it offa shum guy over at the Gator Club."

Bobby looked at her skeptically.

"Isn't Special K a liquid?"

"Yeah, when ish raw. You gotta evaporate it into powder."

"Okay. Sure. Those are *pills*."

Sherri fumbled another pill between her numbed fingers.

"The dealer saysh he presshes the powder into capsules."

"Even if that was possible, which it isn't, you would have taken enough by now to kill a rhino."

"Who are you, McGruff the fucking crime dog? Shudda fuck up."

She threw the pill at Bobby, and it bounced off his belly and landed in his lap. He held it up the to the light and then burst out laughing.

"What'sh so funny?"

"You might want to see your dealer about a refund. I think you've been ripped off."

"Tell me about it. This schhit is *weak*. I've taken like, twenty of theesh bitches and I'm not even gettin' a buzz—I just feel like …"

"A natural woman?"

"Huh?"

Bobby held the pill in front of Sherri's empty eyes.

"These aren't Special K. They're those estrogen pills for old ladies. I've seen the commercial on TV. *Don't treat menopause like a lady* …"

"Bullschhit."

"Look, the name is printed right on there. *Menoplay*."

"Aw fuck *me*," Sherri moaned. "That asshole told me it was hard-ass street talk! 'Me no play.' You know, like it's hardcore shit that doesn't fuck around."

"*Me no play?!*" Bobby laughed. "Who's your dealer? Tickle Me Elmo?"

Erik sat behind the counter, thumbing ticklishly through a dog-eared 1968 copy of *Criswell Predicts Your Future From Now to the Year 2000!*

"Oh Criswell, you loon," he smiled, "none of these predictions were even *close*."

He glanced up from his book to see Debbie squeezing and hugging the Batty Koda doll. What had formerly been a mint-condition collectible now hung from her arms in a limp and mangled heap. Erik sighed as he approached her.

"Alright, Debbie, give me that before you completely ruin it."

"No," Debbie sulked. "It's my baby."

"It's not your baby. It's the physical embodiment of a spastic Robin

Williams voice-over."

"It's my baby!" Debbie shrieked.

Erik shoved his palm under her nose.

"It's not your baby until you pay for it! Now hand it over!"

"I hate you!" Debbie screamed. "You never let me have anything the kitty gives me!"

She reared back and clapped her baby into Erik's palm, and a pair of limp membrane wings unfurled, revealing the mangled body of a dead bat. Erik's blood-spattered arm spasmed involuntarily, sending the deceased on a final flight across the room.

"Ew! Ew, God! No," he stammered, wiping his hand on the carpet. "Where did you get that?!"

"The kitty gave it to me!"

Erik looked past the tip of Debbie's pointing finger to see Twiki darting away, leaving a trail of red paw prints in her wake. His eyes followed her past Harry, who was trying to stuff an Inspector Gadget doll in his coat pocket.

Erik shook his head heavily and looked at his wristwatch. The arms of a cartoon Mr. T indicated quarter to midnight.

"Look, your dad is going to be here any minute," he sighed. "Why don't you kids just go wait outside so that I can lock up? I'm too tired to play *Charles in Charge* any more."

"Okay! I'mago ouside!" Harry said, running for the door.

Erik dropped a hand on his shoulder.

"Whoa whoa, not so fast, Captain Kleptoroo."

He turned Harry around and began patting down his coat, relieving it of its misbegotten treasures.

"Oh look, it's Optimus Prime," Erik said, pulling the robot from a bulging pocket. "And who's this playing backup? Why, it's the California Raisins!"

Debbie stepped up behind Erik and spoke sweetly.

"Can I go wait outside?"

"Yeah, sure," Erik said, pulling a handful of pink M.U.S.C.L.E. figures from Harry's pocket. "Your brother will be out in a second."

The bells on the front door gave a jingle as Erik continued his inventory control.

"Leonardo, Donatello, Raphael, and *two* Michelangelos."

Erik sighed and searched Harry's innocent-looking little eyes.

"Why do you do this, Harry?" he asked. "Why are you constantly trying to steal stuff?"

Harry shrugged.

"Debbie ses I godda beeda virgin."

Erik blinked uncomfortably.

"Well. That's a 'very special episode' that I'm not going to get into tonight."

He stood up and pushed open the front door.

"Alright, get out of here. Your dad oughta be showing up any minute."

Harry shuffled out the door and Erik closed it behind him. As he glanced out the window, he saw Twiki spinning around and swinging back and forth like a disoriented feline pendulum in Debbie's loving arms.

"Debbie!" Erik snapped. "How did she get Twiki out of—"

He smacked himself on the forehead as everything suddenly became clear.

"A *diversion*. Harry was a *diversion!*"

The bells on the shop door chimed wildly as Erik exploded into the street, shouting at the top of his lungs.

"Debbie Stokes, you give me back my cat!"

"You can't have her!" Debbie wailed. "She loves me! The kitty loves *me!* Don't you, kitty?!"

Pleased to add her two cents to the debate, Twiki lashed out her claws and drew a long red gouge across Debbie's cheek. With an earsplitting scream, Debbie dropped her stolen pet and planted both hands on her wounded face. Twiki landed dizzily on her feet, took two reeling steps, and fell down the mouth of a curbside storm drain.

"Let me see your face!" Erik squeaked, dropping to his knees. "Are you okay?"

"My kitty!" Debbie wailed. "Harry, catch my kitty!"

"Owigh, Debbie!"

Erik stumbled to his feet.

"Harry, no!"

But it was too late. Erik's eyes had barely focused on the narrow drain by the time Harry Stokes had disappeared down its throat with a scream and a shallow splash. Erik ran over and peered into the eight-inch-tall opening.

"Harry! Harry, are you all right?"

Somewhere in the blackness below, Harry was crying.

"Aaaaah! No! No! I don' wanngo swimmies. I don' wanna, I don' wanna. I wanngo home. I don' wanngo swimmies, I wanngo home."

"Hold on! I'll be right down!"

Erik impotently scrabbled his fingernails around the edge of the manhole cover above the drain, trying to pry it loose. Debbie stuck her head into the opening and shouted.

"Harry! Stop crying and find my—"

Before she could finish, Erik yanked her out of the drain and dropped her on the curb with a furious impatience.

"Stop it! Leave him alone! You just sit here and be quiet, or else!"

"Or else *what?*" Debbie said petulantly.

"Or else! Or else ..." Erik raised a bony finger as a long string of nothing ran through his head. "Or else you don't even want to *know*, okay?! Now just sit still for five seconds!"

With that, he tore off across the street and back into the shop. The second Erik was out of her field of vision, Debbie was back on her hands and knees in front of the grate.

"Find her, Harry! Find my kitty!"

"Debbie Stokes!" Erik bellowed. "What did I just tell you?!"

Debbie looked over her shoulder and screamed in terror. Erik loomed over her with the blade of the heavy sword hoisted above his head.

"Move it!" he barked. "Or *else!*"

Debbie scrambled over the top of the drain and pressed herself against the nearest building. Erik jammed the point of the sword under the manhole's lid and pried it up and onto the sidewalk. He dropped the blade and gave Debbie a stern look.

"You stay here and don't move, you understand? I'm going to go save your brother."

Debbie nodded nervously.

"Please, just find my kitty."

Erik climbed down the short ladder of iron bars that protruded from the wall of the cement cube. The floor appeared solid and slick, but as he jumped off the ladder he realized the bottom of the chamber was shin-deep in murky water.

"Ack! Jesus," he hissed, pulling his waterlogged sneaker out of the muck.

"I … I don' wanna finda kitty. I don'. I don' wanna. I wanngo home."

Erik's eyes quickly adjusted to the dim light, picking out Harry's shivering form hunched in a corner. He was soaking wet and nearly paralyzed with shock, but otherwise he appeared to be unharmed.

"You're okay," Erik said. "Come on, let's get you out of here."

He pulled Harry to his feet and helped him climb the wet, slimy ladder. When Harry was safely on the street, Erik squinted into the corrugated steel tunnels that branched off from the chamber.

"Twiki? You in there?" he called. "Here kitty kitty."

A pair of reflective eyes peered at him from the shadows. He grasped his lost pet by the scruff of her neck and lifted her up.

"That's a good kitty kityaaaAAGH!"

As soon as Erik pulled the creature into the dim moonlight he realized that it wasn't his cat at all, but the fattest, most virulent-looking sewer rat that he had ever seen. He screamed like a girl, dropped the rat, and tumbled backward into the tunnel on the opposite side of the cube. He splashed himself back onto his feet, wiped his rat-dirtied fingers on his runoff-dirtied pants, then wiped his pant-dirtied hand on the wall.

"Ew! Ew! Gross! Gross! Gross!"

His jabbering was interrupted by the sound of an Aerostar pulling up on the street above, followed by a slamming door and a furious shout.

"Holy Christ, Debbie! You're bleeding! What happened to your face?!" a burly voice hollered. "Harry! You're soakin' wet! And you're dirty as shit! What in hell is going on around here?! Where's that toy geek at?! I'm gonna drive a fist up his pansy ass!"

"It was just *one strawberry daiquiri*," Vivian moaned. "I still think I'm okay for drive."

"You're okay for drive?" Nick asked skeptically.

"I'm okay *to* drive," Vivian corrected. "I'm okay for *driving*."

"Lady, I don't think you're either one," Nick smiled. "Look, we're already halfway there, so there's really no point in arguing about it anymore. Just give it up and relax for once in your life. I'll have you home in like, five minutes."

Vivian crossed her arms and pressed herself into the passenger seat of the Fusion Fuel Hummer. Although Nick was in the driver's seat, the two of them were separated by a two-foot-wide tower of steel that housed the vehicle's elevated drivetrain. The car customizers had attempted to hide this barrier beneath black leather upholstery and a plethora of Fusion Fuel bottle holders, but it still divided the Hummer's east and west sides as subtly as the Berlin Wall. This was just fine with Vivian, as she was in no mood to be any closer to Nick than she had to be.

"Well, how am I supposed to get my car tomorrow?" she asked.

"Don't sweat it. I'll swing by and pick you up."

"I don't doubt it," Vivian grumbled. "You haven't stopped trying to pick me up since we met."

Nick shook his head with a long, patient sigh.

"Tell me, Vivian Gray, what are you going to do when we get back to your apartment?"

"Go to bed. Alone."

"And that's going to make you happy, is it?"

"Well, I'll be happy to have this day over with, that's for sure. It's been nothing but miserable from start to finish."

Nick threw her a sideways glance.

"I had a really good time with you tonight too."

His disappointed tone cut through her.

"I'm sorry, Nick," she backpedaled. "I didn't mean it like that. The date was fine. I'm really sorry that I got us kicked out of the restaurant. I was having a really good time."

"No you weren't."

"No," Vivian admitted, "I wasn't. Everyone in that restaurant treated me like dirt just because I didn't drive the right car or wear the right clothes. They judged me entirely by my appearance."

Nick nodded.

"And you wanted them to look past all that and just appreciate you for your mind?"

"Yes. Exactly."

"And so you tried to use your mind to blow up their restaurant?"

Vivian sank in her seat.

"Touché."

She looked out the window and down the shallow bluff toward the bayside below. A shadow of longing passed over the back of her mind.

"So taking you to the Banyan Terrace wasn't exactly your kind of scene," Nick acknowledged. "But what exactly is your scene, Vivian?"

"What do you mean?"

"I mean, if you didn't go out with me tonight, where would you have gone?"

Vivian glanced at Nick, then back toward the moonlit beach. She bit her lip.

"Are you speaking hypothetically for the sake of conversation, or do you actually want to know?"

"I actually want to know."

"Then make a right turn up here."

Nick squinted.

"Um … do you mean *left?* There's no road to the right."

"Yes there is," Vivian said. "It's not paved, but if my little Rabbit can handle it, your big Hummer certainly can."

Nick slowed down and peered into the periphery of his headlights.

"It's a HumVee," he said distractedly. "The civilian models are called Hummers."

"I hate to break it to you, Nick, but you *are* a civilian model."

She pointed into the darkness off the side of the road.

"Here. Pull off at the break in the guard rail."

Nick turned the wheel and coaxed the behemoth off the shoulder of the paved road. Its broad wheelbase was wider than the two strips of packed dirt that ran down the bluff, and its studded tires flattened the grass all the way to the white sand below. He parked on the beach and silenced the brutish engine.

"You'd rather be *here* than the Banyan Terrace?" he asked skeptically. "What is this place?"

He leaned toward the windshield and looked at the colossal hulks of steel and concrete that loomed out of the darkness. The Hummer was parked under the mainland end of the Skyshine Causeway Bridge, the titanic elevated thoroughfare that linked Stillwater to its island neighbor. A broad black swatch of humming asphalt soared above them in a graceful arc that traversed the bay and touched down on the end of Songbird Key. From this vantage point, the lights of the distant luxury condominiums and premium hotels of the key were putting on a better show than the architecturally blotted heavens above.

"This used to be a construction road years ago when they were building the bridge," Vivian said. "Sometimes I come down here to be alone. The tourists never come this far down the beach."

"I can see why. Is there some kinda sewage plant nearby or something?"

Vivian looked through the Hummer's headlights and into the gently rolling waves. The water was as lumpy and pink as her Banyan Terrace daiquiri, but instead of strawberries it was garnished with clusters of dead, rotting fish. Nick looked at her and spoke soulfully.

"How can you possibly be happy in a place like this, Vivian?"

"It's not usually like this. This freak red tide just rolled in a few days ago."

Nick shook his head.

"No, I mean here in Stillwater. How can you actually be happy living in this bogus little corner of Heaven's waiting room?"

Vivian frowned and stared into the filthy surf.

"Oh, I'm far from happy here. Some days I can barely get out of bed knowing that it's just going to mean facing another identical, humiliating day in this dead-end town."

"Well then why won't you team up with me? You could get out of this place and never look back."

Vivian sighed.

"Thanks for the offer, really, but … I *can't* be a model."

"Don't kick your own ass like that! You *can* be a model!" Nick argued. "You just need to start believing in yourself and put your assets to work for you. I've known it since the moment I saw you."

"Oh, get real, Nick!" Vivian snapped, tugging on her copper bangs. "You wouldn't have even given me a second look if it wasn't for a potentially lucrative genetic quirk in my sixteenth chromosome. Believe it or not, my head holds more valuable assets than red hair."

"I never said that it didn't! But you're so intent on getting everyone to bow down before your big brain that you totally shut out every other good thing that you've got going for you. And there's a lot of them. I mean, look at these beautiful assets right here."

Nick leaned over and gestured to Vivian's bosom like a spokesmodel on *The Price is Right* romanticizing a blender. Vivian crossed her arms and started to voice a syllable of indignity, which Nick silenced with a manicured finger over her lips.

"Don't get all embarrassed; I'm just speaking professionally," he said pleasantly. "You're obviously unhappy with the size of the twins, but let me tell ya, reedy girls like you are the hottest thing right now. The days of the double-D melons are history. Even Pamela Anderson just got her implants taken out. Don't you see? You're sitting here thinking you're *soooo* ugly while one of the most successful models in the world is trying to make herself look *more like you.*"

Vivian rolled her eyes and took a breath, but Nick interrupted her before she could protest.

"And of course there's the asset that gets you fired up so easily," he said, tucking a stray lock of red hair over Vivian's ear. "You know the redhead Spice Girl? The alleged 'Ginger Spice'? You know that hot chick from *Will & Grace?* Both out of a bottle. How can you not believe that you're beautiful when top-shelf hotties are doing dye jobs just to look more like you do straight from the factory? You can cry about your looks all day and night, but your physical assets aren't what's holding you back, Vivian."

"So, in your expert opinion," Vivian glowered, "what, pray tell, *is* holding me back?"

Nick leaned over the drivetrain wall and tapped his fingertip on her forehead.

"You think your big brain is so great, but it's the one and only thing you've got working *against* you. For some reason you think that something terrible is going to happen if you let down your hair just one time. If you would just believe in yourself long enough to take a chance, this could be the last night that you ever spend in Stillwater. You and me and this HumVee could be heading out across the country in search of extreme fun and adventure tomorrow morning. Don't let your big brain talk you out of it."

Nick stretched his arm over the wall and took Vivian's hand.

"Nobody in this town can see that you're platinum level, Vivian," he whispered. "Not even you."

Vivian felt the warmth of Nick's hand running through her fingers as his words absorbed into her tipsy brain. Promotional modeling wasn't exactly her dream career, but neither was Boltzmann's Market. She was being offered a real opportunity to change her life, and the only thing keeping her from taking it was her own self-doubt. After all, she reasoned, she had been failing to get out of Stillwater by using her brain for her entire life. Maybe it *was* time to use, as Nick said, all of the assets at her disposal.

"Okay," she said. "I'll try it. I'll join your agency and tour the country with you. I'll be your partner."

A smile passed over Nick's face that was so glitteringly perfect it could have stood twenty stories high on a Times Square toothpaste ad. His enthusiasm pounded off of his body in glowing waves, evaporating Vivian's skepticism and pushing the corners of her mouth into a reluctant grin.

"You see? Nothing but good things happen when you just believe in yourself!" he cheered. "We're gonna be the new platinum team, baby! Platinum! You've made the right choice teaming up with me, Vivian Gray! C'mere and sign the papers!"

He twisted in his seat and leaned toward Vivian, closing his dazzling eyes and putting his lips into a pucker so beautiful that it seemed sinful to describe it with a word as ridiculous as "pucker." The drivetrain pressed numbly into his side as he craned his neck and continued to lean over, thrusting out his inviting, pouty lips. Vivian looked at the uncompleted kiss hanging in the air in front of her.

"Ah, what the heck," she shrugged.

She leaned over the barrier, stretching her long neck to give Nick a tiny peck on the lips. Vivian dropped back into her seat and bit her lip. Guilt trickled through her brain. Her body, for once, told her brain where to stick it.

"See, now that wasn't so bad, was it?" Nick smiled.

"No, the kiss was okay," Vivian admitted reluctantly. "I'm not keen on the hump though."

"Oh, come on, I wasn't even going to try to go there on the first date," Nick said defensively.

Vivian shook her head and tapped her fingers on the hump of the drivetrain. "The hump," she clarified.

"Oh, right, right, the hump. Well, there's not a lot I can do about that."

"No, I guess not," Vivian agreed.

"Luckily there's plenty of room for both of us on your side!" Nick grinned. "Don't move a muscle, partner. I'll be right over!"

Before Vivian could argue, Nick threw open the driver's-side door and leapt into the powdery sand. A fetid, overpowering stench of rotting cabbage and decaying fish rolled off the churning bay and into the car. Nick took a reeling step backward and covered his nose before slamming the door and prancing around the back of the vehicle.

Vivian's heart pounded in her chest; her mind was racing a mile a minute. What just happened? Yes, she was excited for the opportunity to get out of Stillwater, but this was very unlike her—she didn't kiss boys in cars—she could barely remember the last time she kissed boys at all, yet she couldn't say that she didn't enjoy the kiss, and she certainly couldn't say that she wouldn't like another. What was she going to do?

She caught a glimpse of Nick in the rearview mirror and turned to face it, seeing her own reflection. She angled the glass toward her anxious face and gave herself a long, hard look. Two chopsticks stuck out of her messy librarian's bun perpendicular to each other, like two street signs bolted together at a crossroads. Vivian recognized that she was at a sort of crossroads herself. One road led an intellectual introvert back to a wasted life in Stillwater, the other led a physical extrovert on to a life of adventure.

In one decisive movement, she grasped the chopsticks with both hands and unsheathed them like a pair of swords, dropping a wrinkled cascade of fiery red hair around her head. She shook it out and took a deep breath.

"Nothing terrible is going to happen if you let down your hair just one time."

She bent over to stuff the chopsticks into her purse, but before she could reach it the Hummer was blasted with a flash of hot white light. Two seconds later Vivian was knocked unconscious by seven tons of steel rising to meet her forehead.

"Menopause pills?" Sherri raged. "Shit! If you tell *anyone* about this, I swear to God you'll be dead in a—"

"Hot flash?"

Before Sherri could wallop Bobby in his smart mouth, the bouncer swung open the door of the sub, flooding the cabin with a blast of barroom noise and fresh air. Sherri had been leaning against the door, and when it suddenly went missing she tumbled out of the sub and onto the boardwalk. The gathering of frat boys began their ceremonial round of catcalls and dog barking, and Sherri threw off her coat and raised her bony fists with a snarl.

"Okay, that's it! None of you fuckers are leaving this room alive!"

Bobby started to exit the sub in a more traditional fashion, only to be stopped short by a wall of teeth. Trent shoved him back into the sub and slid into Sherri's vacated spot on the bench.

"Oh no you don't," Bobby said. "I don't care how much you want to bet, I'm not letting you go down on me."

"No no, the T don't swing that way," Trent chattered, glancing back over his shoulder. "Hey, no shit now, did that pretty little kitty with the itty bitty titties just make a withdrawal from your sperm bank?" His eyes flitted around the cabin as if looking for some evidence of the dirty deed.

"A gentleman doesn't kiss and tell," Bobby smirked. "You draw your own conclusions."

He made another move for the door. Trent pushed him back down, took another glance outside, and whispered.

"Do you think she'd do me next?"

Before Bobby could answer, the bar was bathed in a fiery blast of light. The Bikini Martini was well distanced from ground zero, but the flash was still hot enough to make the fraternity brothers release their bellowing screams one last time.

Blinded by the flash, Sherri staggered backward toward the sub, flailing her bare, sizzling arms. Her wrist connected with the open door, catching its interior handle on her bracelets. The heel of her boot caught the edge of the hatchway and she tumbled inside with Trent and Bobby, the weight of her body slamming the watertight door behind her.

"Hey! Toy freak!" Richard Stokes bellowed. "Quit dickin' around down there! Hiding out in the sewer ain't gonna save you now!"

At that moment, a shaft of sparking blue light blasted through the manhole. A few brief, chaotic seconds later, a thunderous shockwave rolled through the street above, buckling the tunnel and knocking Erik unconscious on his back in the shallow, dirty water.

CHAPTER FOUR

Consciousness trickled into Vivian's body, giving her a dull awareness of being crushed. She peeled open her eyelids and found herself upside-down on the floor of the Fusion Fuel Hummer. She righted herself with a groan, pushing her rear end back into the passenger seat. The strain on her compressed lungs immediately lifted, and her groggy head began to clear.

The Hummer's windows were opaque with spidery fractures, and tiny shafts of pink light sliced through its interior like swords stabbed through a magician's basket. Vivian found her glasses and put them on, splitting her vision into slices. She blinked twice and realized that her left lens had cracked from top to bottom.

"Oh my God," she thought. *"What happened?"*

Her head throbbed. She could remember that she was on a date with Nick, and that they had come to her secret place, but after that it went fuzzy. She remembered an empty daiquiri glass the size of a birdbath.

"Nick? Nick, are you there?"

She pulled on the door handle, but the door didn't open. She shoved and pounded it to no avail. Finally she leaned back against the drivetrain hump and kicked both heels into the orange leather trim. A seal of fused paint gave way, throwing open the door and filling the vehicle with a cloud of reeking pink fog.

Vivian winced against its sting as she staggered to her feet on the beach. When she opened her eyes, she found herself in the middle of a surreal, nightmarish parody of the beach she once knew. The words tumbled from her slack jaw.

"Well. This can't be good."

Tentacles of black smoke twisted from the ruined city of Stillwater into the churning gray sky, forming a charcoal cloud that scraped every point of the horizon. Large, powdery flakes of ash fluttered from the doomsday cloud, gathering like snow in the battered Hummer's crevices.

Vivian took a few stumbling steps in the sand, too overwhelmed to realize that she had broken the heel off of one of her shoes. She ran her eyes along the first mainland span of the Skyshine Causeway bridge overhead. A hundred feet from shore it terminated against the empty sky in a claw of smashed concrete and twisted steel. Its broken trajectory stabbed through the fog and into an empty void where Songbird Key should have been.

Songbird Key was gone, replaced by a bank of dense pink fog rolling off the sizzling bay. The acrid, cabbagey odor of red tide, airborne in millions of gallons of vaporized seawater, burned Vivian's eyes and nasal passages.

"How did ... How ... how can this be?"

Her knees went weak, and she turned and hobbled back to the Hummer. Smashed against a bridge abutment, it had been reduced to little more than a mass of bent steel and smoldering orange logos. Vivian didn't know what was going on, but two things had become abundantly clear.

One: This vehicle *was,* in fact, a fully armored, military-surplus HumVee.

Two: She and Nick would *not* be driving it across the country.

"Nick?" she called. "Nick, are you there?"

There was no reply.

"Is anybody out there?"

Erik shivered in his sleep. He rolled over to grab a blanket and dunked his face in four inches of murky street runoff. With a spluttering gasp, he rolled over onto his hands and knees.

"Bllghg! Ack! What the—"

He leapt to his feet, bashed his head into the tunnel's low ceiling, and fell back into the puddle. Bright white flashes of pain seared the backs of his eyeballs.

"Agh! Gaaah dammit!"

He climbed to his feet, cautiously this time, and blinked his tingling eyes up and down the cramped drainage pipe in which he had been knocked unconscious. In one direction was nothing but a velvety blackness. In the other, a whisper of light spilled over a mountain of pulverized earth and pavement that had collapsed into the drain.

Erik held his watch up to the faint light to find Mr. T's arms pointing at nine minutes to twelve. Noon?

He looked back at the sliver of light pouring over the debris. An eerie pink fog rolled through the opening, like a mug of Pepto-Bismol filled with dry ice. Erik climbed onto the pile shouted through the crack and into the street.

"Hello?" he called. "Hey?! Hey!"

He clawed at the hole.

"Hey, what's going on?! Is anybody there?!"

His mind raced as he dug frantically at the debris. What had happened to the Stokes family? Were they still there? Did they go for help? Help for *what?*

Several frenzied minutes and two broken nails later Erik stopped digging and fell into a panting slouch. He couldn't have cleared this heap of rebar-laden concrete with a bulldozer, let alone with his soft, girlish hands. Given no other options, he reluctantly rolled up his pant legs and waded into the shin-deep water in search of another way out.

A distant splash echoed out of the darkness, followed by a dull crackling, like stalks of celery being ever so slowly bent in half. Then another splash, and a flat, shallow breathing.

Erik suddenly realized that he was not alone.

"Hello? Debbie? Harry? Hey! Who's there?"

As he waded down the pipe, the sparse pink light tucked itself away between the ribs of the corrugated steel walls and disappeared. Soon he was splashing through the low tunnel in complete darkness.

"Hel ... hello?" he called.

He held one arm in front of him and shuffled cautiously through the murky water. The splash of his own feet echoed back and forth between the metal walls, drowning out all other sound. He stopped. When the ripples of his own footsteps had faded into silence, he again heard the strange crackling sound. It was getting louder. Closer. His heart pounded in his throat.

"Is ... is somebody there?"

He slapped himself on the forehead. *Is somebody there?!* Did he really just say that? This was suicide! Never in his life had he seen someone tiptoe into the dark unknown shouting "Is somebody there?" and live to tell the tale. If he were watching this from the safety of his couch, he would be *furious* with himself.

What was he supposed to do now? To keep walking would be to deliver himself straight into the arms of a psycho, that much was certain. But he couldn't turn back either. No, the second he got too scared to move forward and turned around, the killer would be right behind him. One nerve-shattering orchestral blast later, he'd be nothing but a red slick in the water.

His eyes pooled as his lip quivered helplessly. There were only two possible outcomes to this situation, and neither would see him live another day. The echo of the approaching splash grew deafening. The hideous crackle reverberated back and forth, louder and louder until it sounded like bacon frying in his skull. He peered into the darkness, trying desperately to see, but he could see nothing. But something was there!

This was it. This was the end. There were no other options.

"No, wait!" he remembered. *"There is a third option!"*

Just when the tension is cranked up to the highest level possible, just when killer is certain to spring machete-first out of the shadows, what leaps out of the darkness with a howling screech?

As soon as the idea had crossed his mind, Erik felt a familiar texture brush against his exposed and trembling leg. It was rough, wet fur. He felt a clawed foot step on his own. He relaxed and let out a relieved breath.

"Twiki! You scared me to death, you little creep! Come here!"

She made a leaping attempt at escape, but Erik's experienced hands grabbed her in the utter darkness. He picked her up and hugged her tightly against his chest.

"Oh, you had me so scared!" he sobbed. "I thought you were going to kill me!"

Erik's furry captive thrashed against his embrace, but he didn't care. He was used to her playing hard to get. But as he struggled to contain her, Erik realized that Twiki was not only heavier than he remembered, but also much stronger.

"Twiki? Twiki, stop it!" he chirped. "Hey! Hey, what's got into—"

His question broke into a piercing shriek as two paws' worth of claws dug deeply into his sides.

"Aaaaaauuugh! Stop! Stop it!"

Fueled by adrenalin, Erik ripped the attacker from his shredded body, inadvertently slamming it into the low ceiling of the pipe. He heard a *crack* and felt a blast of hot blood on his face.

"Ugggh! Oh God!"

The body went limp and slipped from Erik's agony-weakened hands with a heavy splash. The jagged rips in his sides burned with a ferocious intensity, like canals of boiling, scalding grease. He clutched his wounds, drawing strangled breaths through clenched teeth.

"Twiki!" he seethed. *"Bad kitty!"*

Blood gushed through his fingers as his eyes fell upon the carcass lying in the polluted water. All he could see was a pointed jawful of teeth pushing a soft blue glow against the blackness, as if grinning at him from the afterlife.

Erik slid down the wall, collapsed into a heap, and closed his tearful eyes.

Bobby opened his eyes. He closed them again. Then he opened them.

There was no difference either way. Open or closed, his eyes could discern nothing but one flat shade of black inside the tiny submarine. He turned to his other senses for backup.

Smell reported a stench of stale nicotine and bad breath. Hearing came back with the sounds of shallow respiration.

Touch told him that he was lying on his back with varying loads of dead weight crushing his body, the most egregious being a sharp elbow digging painfully into his chest. He grabbed the elbow to push it away, and his thumb sank into a hot, fleshy wound. Before he could recoil, the gash slammed shut, crushing his thumb between hard, bony plates!

"Aaaaaaaaargh!" he screamed.

He yanked back his hand and the grip on his thumb released, followed by a sputtering cough and gasping breath.

"Blaagh! What did you put in my mouth, dawg?! I thought I told you, T-Money don't swing that way, yo!"

Bobby shoved Trent off of his lap and sat up.

"Relax, dumb-ass. It was just my thumb. Your heterosexuality is still intact."

Trent shifted in the darkness.

"Hey B, I don't mean to be insensitive to those of alternate lifestyles, but I just want to make it clear that I personally don't—"

"Oh shut up," Bobby snapped. "It was an accident. I thought your chin was an elbow."

"Sure sure, okay. No harm, no foul. But seriously, now, hands off the family jewels."

"What the hell are you talking about?"

"Look, I told you, homes. The T don't play this game."

Trent grabbed an offending hand from his lap, finding it wet and hot to the touch. The second he made contact it slipped out of his grasp, and a pained shriek and unbridled string of obscenity flooded the cabin.

"Aaaaaaaugh! Fuck! Fuck! Jesus H. Fuck! Fuckerall Fuckington McFuckerberry!"

Trent and Bobby scrambled blindly into the walls as Sherri's thrashing fury wound to a sobbing conclusion.

"Jesus Harold Christ, what did you just do? Burn me with a fucking cigar?" she whimpered. "Try that when I'm not asleep and see how funny it is when I shove that shit up your ass, motherfucker!"

In the perfect darkness of the *Sawfish,* Bobby and Trent exchanged uncertain glances.

"I … I'm sorry—my bad," Trent stammered. "I apologize if my tender touch is too hot for you to handle, love, but—"

"Wait, wait, where am I?" Sherri spat. "Who the fuck is that?"

"It's just little ol' me, Terence Trent DeLaRosa. We're in the submarine of love."

There was a tense silence.

"Holy shit," Sherri whispered. "You and me didn't—"

"Don't worry," Bobby said. "You didn't."

"What the … Bobby Gray, are you in here too?"

"Yeah. Hi Sherri."

"Shit, you and me didn't—"

"No, no," Bobby said. "Relax, you didn't do it to anybody."

A long moment passed before Sherri spoke again.

"So did the two of you—"

"No!" Bobby and Trent barked in unison.

Sherri blinked.

"Holy shit, I'm fucking blind!" she gasped, waving her hand in front of her eyes. "How much did I drink last night?"

"Last night?" Trent laughed. "Do you think they just closed up and left us in here or something? 'If the sub is a-rockin' don't come a-knockin'' only goes so far, right?"

"Okay, so my memory is a little cloudy," Sherri admitted, "but the last thing I knew I was shitfaced on Schlitz, and now I wake up and I've got the mother of all hangovers. You do the math, Pythagoras."

"You're not blind. The lights just burnt out," Bobby said. "Look, I'm not drunk enough for this much fun. Trent, gimme my hundred bucks. I'm outta here."

Bobby found the door and pushed it open, flooding the tiny chamber with cold, moist air.

"Ain't no way I'm payin' out, dawg!" Trent argued. "You just said that she didn't do it to *anybody!* The bet was—"

"To get her in the submarine; nothing else," Bobby interrupted, bending over and stepping through the low hatch. "Look, I'm done with this stupid bet if you are, but for what it's worth, I still beat your sorry—"

Bobby stopped dead, his giant backside framed in the narrow doorway.

"Uh uh, no way, homes," Trent argued, shoving Bobby out of the way. "It was implied! There was an explicit implication for explicit content, and once again you holy Jesus, Mary, and Joseph ..."

Trent choked on the same apocalyptic nightmare that had frozen Bobby in his tracks. The Bikini Martini had all but evaporated around them, replaced with steaming bamboo poles and the empty, smoking hulls of the surrounding buildings. Where the barroom had once stood there was now nothing but a brittle framework of blackened beams and bent plumbing, offering an unobstructed view of the fire-gutted cars in the street beyond. And all of it was blanketed in a damp cloud of pink fog, reeking like a mountain of rancid sauerkraut.

"What ... what did ..." Trent stammered. "I mean, seriously, I'm supposed to be on *vacation* here, dawg! I ... I'm just here for a little bit of personal enhancement! I mean, has this ever happened here before?!"

"Shhh," Bobby whispered. "No. Shut up."

They stepped out of the sub into a field of random, broken souvenirs of humanity. A bent filing cabinet leaned against the curb, transforming once-important documents into meaningless debris as it released them gently into the breeze. A refrigerator door lay in the street, followed by a toaster and half a dozen smashed television sets. The gutter was littered with *Planet of the Apes* toys and a stuffed Mogwi with a knife and fork rubber-banded to its hands.

"Whoa, your face!" Trent gasped. "You got your burn on, homes! For real!"

Bobby rubbed his hands across his cheeks. On the right he felt nothing but a night's accumulation of skin oil and stubble, but the left triggered a hot, tight

CHAPTER FOUR

burning. He looked at his arms. The right was of its usual couch-potato pastiness, but the left was glowing with an angry red sunburn. He glanced back at Trent.

"Looks like you got a piece of that too. The back of your neck and arms have gone all Red Lobster."

Trent's eyes widened as he gently probed the back of his blistering neck.

"Wait, I remember now!" he said. "I was talking to you in the sub and some asshole threw a pot of hot coffee down my back! Next thing I know, I'm in the dark and homeboy's violating me!"

"No, no, you've got it all wrong," Bobby said. "Number one, it wasn't coffee. I remember now. There was an explosion. That explains the sunburns and the, well …"

He gestured around at the neighborhood of smoking carnage.

"And number two," he continued, "I didn't violate you. Shut up about it already."

Bobby bent down to investigate the remains of the heavy plank boardwalk. The wood was imprinted with a series of stains that looked almost human in a Rorshachian way. A scrap of fabric was pinched between the boards in the center of a long hourglass of char. He picked it up and immediately recognized the pattern from Sunny's sarong.

"Well, all I know is that somebody *up there* must have been looking out for us," Trent said, flicking his finger skyward. "We got off lucky, homes. If we weren't in that sub when this shit went down, we'd have been royally messed up, right?"

Bobby didn't answer. He was staring over Trent's shoulder, agape.

"Right? Hey, B-Dawg. What are you looking at over oh *daaaaamn!*"

The boys stared with horror at Sherri clinging limply to the side of the sub's hatch, looking like she was ready for the grave … or had just returned from it. Whereas the submarine had shielded Bobby and Trent from the flash, Sherri's pale, unprotected skin had taken it full-on.

Like a decade of damaging sunlight focused into the blink of an eye, the flash had faded Sherri's burgundy skirt and blood-red T-shirt to flaccid shades of pink. It bleached her coarse black hair to a wispy mass of white. In that instant, the milky white pallor of Sherri's skin had been scorched into a crispy palette of reds and purples.

"I … I didn't think it was possible," Bobby stammered, "but your eyes are more horrible now than they were before!"

Sherri blinked and turned toward the sound of Bobby's voice. Her ghostly blue eyes had vanished, replaced with two bloodstained spheres of a deep, visceral red. Her pupils were completely lost in a sea of ruptured capillaries, giving her the unfocused gaze of something not of this Earth. As if to punctuate the ghastliness of it all, long sanguineous tearstains ran down her cheeks.

"Is it nighttime?" she whispered.

"No," Trent said. "You were right. It's morning."

Sherri blinked slowly, glaring into blank infinity.

"Shit! I *told* you I was fucking blind!"

She slowly lowered herself to the ground and leaned her charred body up against the doorframe.

"*Sssssst!* Owww!" she winced. "Jesus, somebody get me a drink and explain what the fuck just happened to me."

The boys looked on with shock, not quite knowing how to respond.

"Judgment Day happened," Trent said dramatically. "Revelations 7:12. I looked and behold there was a great earthquake, and the sun became as black as sackcloth, the moon like blood."

"Okay, *you* shut up. You're useless," Sherri said. "Bobby, get me a drink and tell me what's happening."

"I don't really know," Bobby admitted. "But I'm placing my money on Y2K."

"My options are a wrathful God or Y2K?! That's the best you've got?" Sherri spat. "Considering that it's the middle of August and God is a fictional character meant to scare you out of casual sex, I'd say you've both been spoon-fed paranoid bullshit so long you can't even form your own thoughts anymore."

"No no, seriously," Bobby said. "I know that the Y2K bug isn't supposed to take the world by the nuts until January, but that's why they're testing the crap out of everything right now. I don't know if it was the power grid, or a gas line, or what, but I'm betting the Stillwater DWP just scored an 'F' on their Y2K readiness exams."

"That's exactly what I'm saying," Trent agreed. "Matthew 13:40. Just as the weeds are gathered and burned with fire, so will it be at the end of the age."

Bobby squinted at Trent.

"And?"

"The end of the age *is* Y2K! The millennium! This is what Matthew was talking about, dawg! Judgment Day! We're in agreement here, B!"

"We are *not* in agreement, you idiot! Just because downtown Stillwater burned down it doesn't mean that we're facing a doomsday of biblical proportions!"

"Oh yeah?" Trent challenged. "If it's just some little thang, then where are all the people? Where's John Law at? Huh? Where's the rescue crews?"

"And the booze! Where's the fucking booze?" Sherri hissed, lifting a smoldering arm. "Come on, people, I'm dying here!"

Bobby scratched his beard thoughtfully.

"There must have been an evacuation."

He looked at the scrap of green sarong in his hand and nodded.

"Yes. There had to be an evacuation," he continued. "I'll bet there was some kind of chemical spill or something. I mean, smell that nasty-ass air! We probably shouldn't be breathing this shit. God knows what it is."

"Yes," Trent nodded, "He does."

"Okay, seriously now," Sherri said, "who do I have to fuck to get some booze around here?"

Trent sat down next to Sherri and spoke softly.

"Chill, baby. That's what we're trying to tell you. There is no booze. There is no *anything*."

"We don't know what happened," Bobby said, "and we've got no way to find out."

Sherri turned toward his voice and blinked.

"When the shit goes down, the mass media and their corporate sponsors are never far behind to market their fear-mongering onto the public. Why don't you just turn on the TV and see what the talking head on the news says?"

"That's what we're trying to tell you, girl!" Trent repeated. "There is no news! There's no TV!"

"There's always TV," Sherri said coolly. "This is America."

Bobby shrugged.

"She does have a point. So the TV is gone. We've got to be able to find a radio or *something* around here. We live in the golden age of telecommunication. There's no way we're completely out of touch with the rest of the world."

Vivian touched the broken piece of her heel to the spot where it had detached from the bottom of her shoe, then pitched it into the sand with a smirk. For lack of a better option, she jammed her remaining heel between the body frame and the open door of the HumVee and bent it back until it snapped off. She then slipped her shoes back on and stood up on flat feet, although her toes pointed into the air like she was one of Santa's elves.

A noise came from the depths of the ominous silence. She pricked up her ears. Footsteps! The sound was definitely footsteps plodding through the crushed shells of the beach toward the wrecked HumVee.

"Oh my God, Nick!" she gasped, rushing around to the front of the vehicle. "Nick, where have you been? I was so—"

Her words lodged in her throat as a hunched, moaning creature reached out at her. With a flash of adrenalin, Vivian's fist flew from her shoulder, connecting sharply with a grimy forehead. Her would-be assailant dropped flat on his back in the sand.

"Don't hurt me!" he wailed, rolling into a pathetic ball. "I'm harmless! I'm not a looter!"

Vivian gasped.

"Oh my God! Erik?!"

She dropped to her knees and pulled him across her lap, clutching him around his damp, filthy shoulders.

"Please! Don't hurt me!" Erik whimpered. "I … I was just … what the … *Vivian?*"

"Erik, I'm so happy to see you!"

Vivian gave Erik a relieved hug, but he was too busy rubbing his throbbing forehead to return the embrace.

"Ow! Hey, why did you just go all *Mike Tyson's Punch-Out!!* on me?!"

"I'm sorry! I'm so sorry," Vivian chattered, shaking out her smashed fingers. "You scared me to death! You're bleeding! What happened to you?!"

"Twiki attacked me!"

Erik pulled up his shredded shirt, revealing two massive clusters of wounds torn in his sides. Thanks to Vivian, a layer of white sand and broken shells now clung to the gooey surface of coagulating blood.

"Twiki, your *cat?*" Vivian said. "Are you sure?"

"I … I think so," Erik murmured. "It was dark. The hurricane blocked all the storm drains. I had to go all the way to the end to get out of the pipe."

He pointed at four giant drainage pipes extending from the bluff and hanging gape-mouthed over the bay. This reply created a whole new slate of questions in Vivian's mind, but none of them seemed important enough to actually ask.

"This wasn't a hurricane," she said quietly. She looked at the pillars of smoke and flame licking the sky up and down the coast. "I think this was something much, much worse."

Erik gagged as the thick pink vapor rolled into his sinuses.

"Well, I don't care what it was," he coughed. "I just want to get to the hospital before I run out of blood."

His struggle to stand pushed a fresh wave of pain through his wounds and a tight groan from his throat. He fell back into Vivian's arms, and she laid him gently in the sand.

"We'll get you to a hospital," she said. "But first things first."

She stood up and grabbed the ripped edge of her skirt, tearing off the fabric in a long, jagged line a few inches above her knees.

"Oh, that's swell," Erik moaned. "I'm dying here and all you're concerned about is this season's hemline. Who are you—Mr. Blackwell?"

Vivian rolled her eyes.

"We'll get you to a doctor; we just need to get that bleeding under control first."

A little nursing and a lot of whining later, Erik's wounds were dressed in a six-inch-wide bandage of black polyester torn from the hem of Vivian's cocktail dress.

"That's not exactly sterile," she said, "but at least it'll keep you together until we can get you to the hospital."

Erik lifted his shirt and looked at the neatly tied bandages.

"Thanks, Viv. Come on, let's get the hell out of here."

He began struggling toward the bluff, shouting over his shoulder.

"Let's try to find where they set up the hurricane shelter."

Vivian rubbed her eyes.

"Erik, there's not going to *be* a hurricane shelter. I'm telling you, this wasn't a hurricane!"

"Why do you keep saying that?" Erik shouted. "Look at this destruction!"

"Exactly!" Vivian said. "Look at *this* destruction! Hurricanes cause flood damage! Wind damage! Not fire damage!"

She slammed the HumVee's door with a harsh metallic *crash.*

"Look at this car, Erik! Have you ever seen a hurricane do this?!"

She threw out her arms toward the scorched vehicle. Erik wasn't looking at her, but past her, at the smoldering door.

"I've never seen a hurricane do that," he admitted.

Vivian squinted at him, then turned to see what he was looking at.

Etched in the door's peeling black and orange paint was a steaming human silhouette, its ghostly arm terminating in a tiny reflective glint. Permanently welded into the steel of the door handle was a ring inscribed *"Gold Level Sales Champion 1998."*

"Come on, champ."

Bobby turned the key in the ignition of a smashed Oldsmobile, but the electrical accessories failed to power on.

"Come on, champ. Let's go. Come on, come on, come on …"

The key clicked back and forth in the tumbler but had no effect. He pulled it from the steering column and threw it onto the dashboard.

"Damn it! Another dud. You having any luck over there, Trent?"

Trent tried the key of a New Beetle, but the round little car wouldn't cooperate either. He removed the key and put it on the warped dashboard.

"Uh uh," he answered. "I got no tunes here either."

"Man, this is *unbelievable,*" Bobby grumbled. "These cars are all obviously too toasted to drive, but I thought we could at *least* get a radio working!"

He waddled over and plucked another key from the smashed valet box lying on the sidewalk. It was for a Honda. He compared it to the remaining wrecks in the street and made his way toward a Civic crushed under a utility pole.

Blinded and unable to help with the radio-finding effort, Sherri sat limply on the singed back seat of a nearby station wagon. The side of the vehicle was marked with soapy letters reading "Alpha Beta Gamma Summer Break '99: Fort

Lauderdale or Bust!" Sherri rested her head on the edge of the doorframe, and her blood-red eyes stared emotionlessly into the middle distance. Her central nervous system had saturated itself with pain-relieving endorphins, downgrading her agony to a subdued throbbing. She wrapped her arms around her bony chest and shivered.

"Man, it's as cold as a witch's clit out here. If you can't give me any liquor, could you at least give me my coat?"

"Doubtful," Bobby said. "Judging by what ended up landing *here,* I'd say your coat is probably in Port Manatee by now."

Trent kicked aside some debris, uncovering a thrashed leather collar.

"Au contraire," he said. "I think you may be in luck, my little chilly filly."

He grabbed the collar and pulled it from the wreckage, but the rest of Sherri's coat had been reduced to a shredded mass of black leather.

"Strike that," he said. "This thing got the beat-down, for real."

"Wait," Sherri said, "did you find it?"

"Yeah, but you can't wear it; it's all—"

"Gimme it."

Trent shrugged and handed what was left of the coat to Sherri. She worked over the tangle of burnt cowhide, producing her skull-capped whiskey flask. A quick examination with her fingertips revealed a jagged hole and a dry interior.

"Shit," she muttered. "There really *is* no booze left."

She threw the flask and heard it clatter away somewhere in her personal darkness.

"Shhh!" Bobby said. "Did you guys hear that?"

"What?" Trent asked. "The flask?"

"No no," Bobby said. "There's something else. I think there's somebody there!"

Sherri and Trent stopped breathing and listened. There was no sound at all. Then suddenly, something! A *clank* of tumbling debris, followed by an odd crackling noise.

"Hey! Is someone there?" Bobby yelled. "Heeeey! Hey! Over here!"

"We've got an injured girl over here!" Trent added. "Let's get some help on, yo! Send a doctor!"

"Fuck the doctor!" Sherri shouted. "Send Jim Beam!"

Their voices echoed off the remains of the buildings and then evaporated into a whispery silence. Trent scrambled onto the roof of a demolished SUV and turned all the way around, scanning the urban rubble of downtown.

"Do you see anything?" Bobby asked.

"No. Nothing but fog," Trent said. "There's nothing out … whoa! Check it out, homes!"

"What? What do you see?"

Trent set his feet apart and rubbed his hands together.

"By my right of victory! By my blood!"

He grabbed hold of a metal handle jutting from the scraped roof and, with a dramatic thrust of his body, drew Planet Packrat's theatrical sword from where it had been jammed into the wreckage. He held the blade aloft and bellowed.

"Give me the power!"

Bobby glared at Trent. "What the hell are you trying to do, turn into He-Man?"

Trent swished the heavy blade through the air.

"He-Man? Oh, come on, B. Have you no sense of higher culture? That was *Excalibur.* I saw that film, like, fifty times. The hot chick gets 'em out in the first twenty minutes, yo."

Bobby rolled his eyes. Trent continued.

"I just pulled the sword from the stone. That makes me king of England."

"That's not a stone," Bobby sighed. "It's an SUV."

"Fair enough," Trent nodded. "That makes me king of Detroit."

"Well, that's very special," Bobby said. "Would you mind coming back down here and trying another key, your majesty?"

"You're just jealous," Trent smiled, climbing to the ground. "You know the king always bags the fairest maiden in the land."

"Oh please, God," Sherri moaned. "Don't let him be talking about me."

She slid her shoulder off of the doorframe and fell on her back across the seat, her boots sprawling out onto the pavement. The second she landed, a tongue of pain licked down her back.

"*Ahhhh!* Ouuuuch!!" she hissed.

The sting of her burns slipped her mind as her head rolled into a cold puddle on the seat. A puddle with a stale yet recognizable odor. She sat up and patted the puddle with her fingers, trying to scout out its edges and origins.

Bobby pushed through the cloud of pink vapor toward the Civic. The door had gone missing, so he just plopped into the driver's seat and punched the key into the ignition.

"Come on, champ; come on, champ ..."

He cranked the key and nothing happened. Not so much as a flicker.

"Damn it! They're *all* hosed? This is statistically impossible."

He jammed the key into the soft, melted plastic of the dashboard and grumbled. His nose stung from the pungent air. With a roaring snort, he gathered and released a huge, wet loogie into the passenger seat. The syrupy mass was an unnatural shade of pink.

"Aww, nasty," he grumbled. "It's like Barbie snot."

He heard a noise. It was the crackling again, but this time it was louder. Closer.

He glanced out the shattered windshield and saw a dirty old Army-surplus backpack fly out of the Alpha Beta Gamma station wagon. It was followed by seven dirty socks, a chain of condoms, four rolls of toilet paper, and three issues of *Hustler*.

Sherri's ransacking of the frat boys' car did not produce any crackling.

Bobby hopped out of the Civic and met Trent next to the valet box.

"Hey!" Bobby whispered. "Do you hear that?"

"Hear what?"

"Shh! The crackling. Listen!"

Trent strained his ears gamely for Bobby's alleged crackle. He could hear the fluttering of papers. A loose door creaking on ravaged hinges. Somewhere the breeze whistled eerily through a lonely window screen. The overarching theme of his auditory picture, however, was silence.

Pure, thick, pink silence.

"BBBBRRAAAAAAAAAAWWWWWP!"

Bobby leapt in the air like a startled housecat.

"Waaaaah! What the hell was that?!"

"Pardon me," Sherri said dryly.

She was sitting on a large box in front of the station wagon, chugging a can of beer and wearing the remains of her shredded coat as if in protest of the whole situation.

"Whoa!" Bobby said. "What is that?"

"It's beer, lame-ass," Sherri said triumphantly. She jabbed a thumb toward the station wagon. "There was a whole cooler full of it in the way-back. I told you there was booze—you guys are just too brainwashed by the rules of society to think outside of your narrow—"

"No, shut up," Bobby said. "I meant, what is that you're sitting on?"

Sherri looked down and blinked.

"How the hell should I know? I'm fucking blind, remember?"

Bobby shuffled over and shooed Sherri from her perch. He picked up the box and read it.

"Hibakusha Electronics 5-in-1 Camping Lantern. Where did this come from?"

Vivian and Erik plodded through the abandoned streets of Stillwater with directionless ambition. They didn't know exactly what they were looking for, but they each had a sense that they'd know it when they found it.

The pulverized road was dotted with vehicles reduced to charred husks and broken glass. Vivian didn't look directly at them as she trudged by. She knew that within each makeshift crematorium was a driver who had met with a terrible fate, but a fierce sense of denial kept her eyes pinned to the ground.

She couldn't get her mind off of Nick. He was dead. Vaporized. His life had been snuffed out against the side of his precious HumVee, and a feeling of deep mourning gnawed at her mind.

Or rather, its absence did.

As she looked over each ruined element of her demolished town, she felt no heightened emotion for Nick whatsoever, and that fact disturbed her. It was as if he was just another wrecked building or another crumbled street. Set within the epic scale of her loss, Nick's last shadow was nothing more than another gray, cold cog of Armageddon imagery that meshed in the machine of her numbed mind. She could hardly describe the ache that was churning her gut.

"I'm hungry," Erik said.

Vivian jumped at the sound of his voice. As she processed the words, she realized that her own stomach was cramping into an empty knot.

"I … yeah, I guess I am too," she said. "Maybe it's time for … breakfast?"

She looked at the unyielding black clouds above. Erik looked at his watch.

"More like lunch," he said. "It's already … 11:51? Still?"

"What do you mean, 'still'?" Vivian asked.

Erik shook his wrist and listened for ticking.

"I think my watch stopped," he said. "It was 11:51 when I looked at it like, two hours ago."

Vivian shrugged.

"Maybe the water killed it when you were in the drain."

Erik shook his head.

"I doubt it. It's supposed to be waterproof up to a hundred feet."

"Well, maybe you just smashed it into something."

"Doesn't look like it," Erik said, rubbing his finger on the dial. "It doesn't have a scratch on it."

"You probably just forgot to wind it."

"Uh uh, it's got a battery. I may be retro-chic, but I'm not a primate."

"Look, Erik, forget about your stupid watch, okay?" Vivian said irritably. "Let's just find some food."

She looked around at the crumbling neighborhood. Ordinarily she would have known exactly where she was, but looking through the surreal lens of the post-apocalypse, Vivian found herself lost. She scanned the area, trying to find some small kernel of familiarity.

An expanse of empty blacktop. A corner of white concrete.

It meant nothing to her.

A section of collapsed blue roof. A giant "B." An overturned … wait.

The meaningless details snapped together in her mind's eye and rippled outward from the "B," forming a complete picture that overlaid the desolation.

"Oh my God," she whispered. "It's Boltzmann's Market."

The ruins before them were, in fact, all that remained of Boltzmann's Market. The shockwave had beaten the store's concrete shell from an elongated cube into a pathetic, slanted heap. The left side of the store still stood more or less intact, dangling its "B" over the dusty parking lot, but from there the roofline plunged through a pile of collapsed debris until it touched the ground on the right.

Vivian stood petrified, covering her mouth in silent shock. Erik looked at the building, then at her.

"Hey, isn't this that sucky place where you work?"

Vivian nodded grimly. Erik continued.

"Wow. Be careful what you wish for, eh?"

In the crushingly bleak absurdity of it all, Vivian choked out a guilty laugh.

"Come on," she said. "There'll be food in there."

They walked across the parking lot and up to the front door. Vivian had repeated this trek a thousand times under the blazing oppression of the Florida sun. Today she shivered under the shadow of a massive, lazy whirlpool of smoke and scorched stratosphere.

When they reached the door, they found only bent metal frames holding teeth of shattered glass. Erik made a motion to step through the opening and into the darkness, but Vivian put her hand on his shoulder.

"Wait; hold on," she said. "I've got a light."

She unslung her purse from her back and pulled out her flashlight. She clicked the switch, but it didn't light. She tried again, then pounded it against her palm and tried again.

"What's the matter?" Erik asked. "Batteries dead?"

"No, they're fine. I just used this yesterday."

"Huh. First my watch and now your flashlight," Erik shrugged. "I guess it's just a bad day for electronics."

Vivian's forehead wrinkled as she pondered how both devices could have failed at once. She shook her head as if to keep her paranoid hypothesis from jelling. It was probably just a coincidence.

"Forget it. It's not even that dark in there," Erik said. "Let's just go."

"I'm not going into a collapsing building in the dark," Vivian said firmly. "It's too dangerous."

"Oh, it'll just be for a minute. Come on, I'm too hungry to be afraid of the dark today."

He bent down and climbed through the shattered doorway.

"Erik, wait!"

But it was too late. Erik had disappeared into the darkened bowels of Boltzmann's Market. Vivian frowned. There was no way she was just walking blindly into a demolished building, no matter how hungry she was. She snapped the switch of her deceased flashlight on and off impotently.

"Find another way," she muttered to herself.

She dropped the flashlight back into her purse and looked around the parking lot. An uprooted palm tree lay across a scorched blue sedan with tiny flames still nibbling at the last of its upholstery. She snapped off a frond and held its leafy end to the flame until it caught. This makeshift torch would have a short lifespan, but at least it would cut through the darkness long enough for her to safely gather some provisions from the store.

She returned to the blasted door and stepped through it cautiously. From within a cloud of pink and gray smoke she could hear a wet, muffled crunching.

"Erik? Where are you?"

"Mmnn!" he replied through a full mouth. "M'mover here! D'ritos!"

Vivian stepped gingerly toward Erik's voice. A fire had gutted a good portion of the store before shrinking into a handful of flickering embers. The air smelled of burnt sugar, with undertones of barbecued meat and brine.

The tiled floor was both slippery and sticky at the same time. Vivian held her torch low and saw a river of stagnating cola, marbled with artificial purples and oranges. Apparently the collapsing roof had crushed the soft-drink aisle. She kicked a bottle of gin out of her path and turned her gaze back into the smoky darkness.

"Erik? Come on, where are you?"

"Over here," he called.

"Where?!"

Vivian raised her torch and squinted into the fog. She picked out a silhouette examining the warped shelves.

"There you are. Come on, let's just grab some stuff and get out," she said, lifting her torch toward the shadow. "This place is freaking me—"

Her thought was disrupted by her own bloodcurdling scream. The figure wasn't Erik, but an unfortunate county health inspector who had been in the wrong place at a very wrong time. The buckling shelves had sent a metal strut springing out like a harpoon, impaling him through the chest and holding him up to the ensuing blaze like a marshmallow over a campfire. One entire side of his body had been charred to a charcoal-black mass of carbon, and a wisp of silvery smoke vented from his empty eye socket. His remaining eye was opened wide and fixed unblinkingly on Vivian.

At the sound of her screams, Erik came sprinting from the next aisle, clutching a half-eaten bag of Doritos 3Ds.

"What?! What's going aaaugh!"

As his feet hit the slick of spilt soda, Erik's sneakers kicked out from under him and dropped him flat on his back. He slid across the aisle, knocking out Vivian's legs and slamming into the corpse's dangling ankles. With the force of the impact, the metal spear made a crumbling slice through its ashy flesh, dropping the remains on top of Erik.

"Aaaaugh! Shit! Holy shit! Get it off! Get it off!"

Erik flailed under the torched cadaver, tearing its limbs from its body in his frantic struggle. Vivian clambered to her feet, slipping and sliding in a breathless panic. She grabbed the disintegrating health inspector and threw him off of Erik's spastic body. In the dim torchlight, Erik's cheese-powder-stained face was as white as hotel linens.

"Let's get the hell out of here!" he shrieked.

Their appetites effectively ruined, the two terrified survivors bolted out of the aisle and toward the front of the store.

"Where's the door?" Erik panicked. "It's too dark! I can't find the front door!"

"It's over here," Vivian said, holding up her torch. "Come on! And watch your ste—"

Vivian's foot caught the cable of a fallen fluorescent light, yanked itself out from under her body, and sent her smashing down again on the cracked tile. Her torch flew out of her hand and skidded across the floor, bouncing to a stop against the remains of checkstand two. Its flames licked at an intact heap of paper grocery bags, quickly igniting the whole pile.

Vivian pulled her face from the puddled floor and began wringing the slime from her hair. It flowed from her red locks with an unnerving, clotty sort of warmth. She froze in the slowly increasing firelight. Erik slipped to her side and grabbed her by the elbow.

"Oh God, are you okay, Viv?! You went down hard and—oh shit, you're bleeding!"

"No," Vivian said numbly, looking at her stained hands. "I'm not."

Her eyes rolled toward the blaze enveloping the checkstand, landing upon the ghastly white flesh of Verman Boltzmann's drained carcass. The blubbery heap of his earthly remains was draped over the conveyor belt like a whale beached on a breakwater. His skin was riddled with a network of gruesome splits and tears, as if the blast had finally given his substantial innards license to rupture his overstuffed hide. As the flames licked his body, stinking yellow rivulets of molten fat oozed from his lacerations like lava from a volcano that really needed to work out more often.

Erik's legs went weak and buckled beneath him. Before he landed on his knees he had already thrown up half a bag of nacho chips.

Vivian just stared. Frozen. The warm blood of her late boss dripping from her chin.

"Come on! Let's go!" Erik screamed, staggering back to his feet. "Dead things, Vivian! Dead things!"

He grabbed her by the arm and yanked her toward the foggy pink glow of the door as the fire quickly spread through the remaining debris. They stumbled out into the parking lot and collapsed on the dusty pavement, forcing the smoke and nausea out of their bodies with sharp, phlegmy coughs. After a long moment, they fell silent. Vivian watched black smoke pour from the building as the flame consumed the remains of Boltzmann's, and Boltzmann's remains.

"All right," she whispered. "Let's not *ever* do that again."

"Alright, let's do it again," Bobby said dismally. "Turn it right. Right. Right. Stop! No, left, leeeeft. Stop! Come on! Baby steps!"

The 5-in-1 camping lantern sat on the roof of the Alpha Beta Gamma station wagon, surrounded by the broken plastic of several D-cell battery packages. Bobby fiddled with the on-screen menu of the five-inch television built into the lantern's face. Sherri lounged across the back seat of the vehicle, nursing her third beer.

"This is bullshit, yo," Trent said. "Why don't you just use the antenna?"

"I did use the antenna, genius," Bobby said. "I tried the TV and radio bands. It doesn't pick up anything on AM, FM, UHF, or VHF. It's just a cheap-ass camping lantern; it's not Ted Turner's limo. I'm amazed this piece of shit actually has a built-in satellite receiver. Now turn the dish to the left, *slowly*."

Trent grumbled and shuffled in tiny steps, scraping the edge of a ketchup stained satellite dish into the pavement. The Bikini Martini's new digital mini-dish had been blown to atoms with the rest of the bar, but its obsolete one-and-a-half-meter analog forebear had survived inside the steel Dumpster. Trent was now struggling to hold its awkward girth up to the southern horizon.

The black and white screen crackled to life as the signal bar leapt to maximum strength.

"Stop! Stop!" Bobby ordered. "We got something!"

"So come on with us now, and discover the wonder of youuuuuu! Welcome to Zoobilee Zoo!"

"God damn it!" he barked. "Zoobles again. Turn right."

"No way. Uh uh. I'm done," Trent said, leaning the heavy dish against the Dumpster. "I've gone all the way around seven times and you ain't found nothin' but that kiddie show. Are you sure you're working that thing right, B?"

Bobby flipped through the thin instruction book.

"Yeah, yeah, I'm sure. I don't get it. Even if we can only find one satellite through this shitty cloud cover, we should be able to get more than one non-subscription feed off of it. This TV sucks ass."

He threw the book back into the box and slumped against the wagon's fender. Trent squinted at Mayor Ben's face chirping on the tiny screen.

"Hello, my little Zoobaroos! It's zoo-pendous to see you again for another zoo-riffic adventure!"

"Does he actually talk like that for the whole show?" Trent asked.

"Shhh!" Bobby hissed. "Turn that off!"

"For real," Trent agreed. "This guy is as irritating as underwear with a zipper."

"No no, listen!" Bobby said. "I hear it again! The crackling! Listen!"

"Ah shit, not this again," Sherri muttered.

Trent turned down the volume and once again listened to the thick, heaving silence. Somewhere a piece of metal banged against another, echoing dimly across the distance. Then nothing.

"Hello out there!" Bobby yelled. "Hey! Is anybody there? Sunny?"

His words echoed off of the buildings and evaporated into quiet.

"Give it up," Sherri said, curling up in the back seat of the wagon. "There's nobody coming for us but the reaper."

"Stop it! I'm serious!" Bobby snapped. "There's something out there!"

He stood up and yelled into the pink fog.

"Hey! I know you're out there! I can hear you! Say something!"

His words decayed and died in the air. He cupped his hand to his ear and concentrated, but there was nothing. Nothing. It must have been his imagination after all. He drew a breath to say as much but was interrupted by a tiny voice.

"Bobby? Oh my God—Bobby!"

Bobby blinked in surprise, then whirled around and ran into the fog. He barely recognized the voice, as he wasn't accustomed to it sounding happy to see him.

"Holy shit!" he yelped. "Vivian?!"

The blood-and-soda-streaked forms of Vivian and Erik emerged from the obscurity of the vapor, both running to meet Bobby in the open street. The two redheaded siblings caught each other in a tight embrace.

"Oh Bobby!" Vivian sobbed. "Oh God! I'm so glad you're alive!"

A tear formed in the corner of Bobby's beady eye.

"Right back atcha. After all, I do still need a place to crash."

Vivian choked a laugh through her sobs and punched her brother in the arm.

"What the hell have you been doing to Erik?" Bobby continued. "He looks like shit."

"Oh, ha ha," Erik said, pointing at Bobby's sunburned face. "You're not looking so great yourself. You've got a whole 'Let That Be Your Last Battlefield' thing going on there."

Trent stepped in front of Erik and bowed ceremoniously to Vivian, planting a kiss on her hand.

"And who is this lovely creature that has graced us with her presence?"

"This is Vivian. My *sister*," Bobby said menacingly. "So whatever you're thinking, just stop."

"Enchanted to meet you, Vivian," Trent oozed. "Thank the good Lord. I was beginning to think that the last woman on Earth was an angry little goth girl."

"Hey!" Sherri snapped. "When you label me you negate me, you preppie fuckwad!"

"Sherri?" Vivian gasped. "Oh my God, Sherri, is that you?"

She ran to the side of the station wagon, leaned down, and poked her head through the back door. Although she managed to squelch the first words that her brain threw out, her gasp at the sight of Sherri's sunburnt flesh was quite audible.

"Go ahead and stare," Sherri shrugged. "Doesn't bother me. I'm fuckin' blind."

"Oh, Sherri. I … I'm so sorry," Vivian stammered. "I mean, you … your skin is all …"

"Yeah, the sun's a bitch. Lucky I was wearing SPF 90."

Vivian bit her lip. Blinded or not, being captured in Sherri's bloody gaze was unnerving. She stood up and pulled her head from the doorway, coming face-to-face with the camping lantern on the roof. Her brow wrinkled.

"So we meet again. Haven't you caused me enough trouble already?"

"What is that thing?" Erik asked.

"5-in-1 camping lantern," Bobby said. "Radio, TV, satellite receiver, flashlight, and lantern. All the conveniences of home in a smaller, shittier package."

"You're such an addict," Erik sighed. "You can't even stop watching TV for five minutes in the middle of a disaster."

"Hey, get offa me," Bobby grumbled. "We were just trying to find some news. We couldn't get a single radio working in any of these shitmobiles. Every last one is dead."

Vivian's face clouded as she looked up and down the street.

"So do you guys know what the hell happened last night?" Sherri asked.

"We got our asses kicked by a hurricane," Erik said.

"Okay, so we've got Y2K in August, wrath of an angry God, or a hurricane that made an unannounced, one-night-only appearance," Sherri muttered. "For fuck's sake, you people couldn't identify your own asses if somebody didn't give you a hint."

"It wasn't any of those things," Vivian said. "I think …"

Her throat closed against the words, as if saying them would make them true. "I think …"

"Oh, just spill it, Powderpuff," Sherri snapped. "What do you think it was?"

"I think it was a nuclear bomb."

The group fell silent for a long moment. Everyone who was able looked at everyone else, trying to discern some sense of whether Vivian was serious and, if so, whether she was right. Finally Bobby broke the tension with a fit of derisive laughter.

"Oh, come on, live in the now, Viv! This is 1999! The Cold War is over. We won. There are no nukes anymore."

"Be serious!" Vivian said. "All of the signs point to a nuclear explosion."

"Alright, girl. I'd buy the bomb if we were someplace that mattered, like Hollywood," Trent said. "But do you think somebody would actually waste their big badda-boom on a Podunk whistle-stop like *Stillwater, Florida?*"

"They didn't bomb Stillwater," Vivian snapped. "They bombed Songbird Key."

Sherri shook her head.

"Ohhh, of course," she said sarcastically. "Everyone knows that commies hate condos."

Vivian rubbed her eyes.

"Okay, I can't explain the *whys*. But if you apply Occam's Razor, the only reasonable *how* is a nuclear detonation."

"Apply the octo*what?*" Trent asked.

"Occam's Razor," Vivian repeated. "It's methodological reductionism. It basically states that for any given problem the simplest solution tends to be the best solution."

"If I had Occam's Razor, I'd apply it to my throat," Sherri said wistfully.

"Just look at the facts," Vivian continued. "Songbird Key is gone."

"What do you mean, 'gone'?" Bobby snuffed. "Everything I've seen all day is gone."

"No no. I don't mean 'burned up' gone," Vivian said. "I mean 'underwater crater' gone. This wasteland of fire damage we're standing in would be consistent with a blast at that range. And what about this?"

She yanked the flashlight out of her purse and rapidly clicked its non-functional switch on and off.

"So what?" Trent said. "Homegirl's got some dead batteries."

"It's not dead batteries," Vivian corrected. "The EMP did this."

"This is all because of a fucking ambulance driver?!" Sherri shouted.

"No, the EMP. Electromagnetic pulse. Nuclear detonations temporarily electrify the atmosphere and wreak havoc with electronics," Vivian explained, pointing up and down the street. "Don't you see? Electric ignitions. That's why you couldn't start any of these cars!"

She grabbed Erik's arm and wrenched him around, showing his watch to the others.

"That's why Erik's watch is stopped. Look, it's stopped dead at nine minutes to midnight. That's got to be the exact time the bomb went off!"

Vivian's explanation echoed into cold silence. Everyone's memories of the previous night eerily validated her last point.

"Alright, Vivian, I don't mean to interrupt your '50s-era duck-and-cover flashback," Bobby said, gesturing with his thumb, "but I think Mayor Ben here would disagree with your batshit EMP theories."

Vivian looked at the picture on the lantern's screen.

"Where did that come from?" she asked.

"Right here," Bobby said, kicking the cardboard box. "It was in the frattiewagon there."

Vivian bent down and looked at the packaging. Inside the shipping foam was a static-protection bag made of shiny metallic foil.

"Well, this explains it," she said, holding up the bag. "It was encased in metal. Anything completely shielded by metal would be protected from the pulse."

"But what about the satellite dish, yo?" Trent said. "It came out of the Dumpster."

Vivian crossed the street and knocked on the metal top of the solid steel Dumpster.

"And the Dumpster is made of *whaaaat?*" she asked rhetorically.

The wheels of rebuttal spun frantically in the minds of Vivian's companions. Some of them wanted to be right for the sake of being right, others for the sake of proving Vivian wrong, others just out of a refusal to accept the horror of her increasingly convincing argument. But in the end, nobody could contest her hypothesis, and by the virtue of Occam's Razor, it became a chilling fact.

"It's just like I said," Trent nodded. "God is cleansing the earth with fire."

Erik shook his head and gently crossed his arms over his slashed midsection.

"The apocalypse isn't nearly as much fun as *Hell Comes to Frogtown* led me to believe it would be."

"So, what now?" Sherri asked.

"We've got to get out of here," Vivian said. "This place has got to be buzzing with radiation right now. We need to get as far away from ground zero as possible, ASAP."

"Whoa, whoa, not so fast," Bobby said. "We've got to search for other survivors first!"

He pulled the bloodstained scrap of sarong from his pocket and squeezed it sadly. Vivian understood.

"I'm sorry, Bobby," she said softly. "There are no other survivors in Stillwater. Believe me."

She reached into her purse and pulled out a gold ring fused to a broken door handle. Bobby had never met Nick, but as Vivian mournfully rubbed her thumb over the scorched ring, he understood. She continued.

"Nobody is leaving this town but us."

She dropped the handle on the ground and patted her brother on the back.

"There's nothing we can do here," she said. "We've got to go."

"But how?" Trent asked. "We told you, girl. None of these cars work. What are we supposed to do?"

"Well, the way I see it we have two choices," Vivian said.

She kicked off her broken shoes and pulled a pair of a deceased frat boy's tube socks onto her blistered feet.

"We walk, or we die."

Erik's oversized Adam's apple twitched as he swallowed hard.

"You say that as if it can't be both," he whimpered.

"For real," Trent said. "If the Almighty is layin' down the smack, there ain't nowhere to run."

"No, Vivian's right," Bobby admitted. "We need to grab our shit and get the hell out of here before we all end up like …"

He dropped the scrap of sarong and watched the breeze carry it away. "We just need to get out of here while we can."

With muttered agreements, the five survivors gathered anything of potential use from the debris. Bobby unhooked the camping lantern from its cable and slung it over his back by its shoulder strap. He grabbed the edge of the dish and hefted it toward Erik.

"Give me a hand with this, man."

"Oh, come on, Bobby. I don't care how addicted to TV you are. I am *not* carrying that."

"I know it's a load, but we've got to take it," Bobby argued. "We're bound to pick up a news feed if we keep scanning the satellites. Plus once we get back to civilization … hey, free Skinemax."

Vivian picked up the discarded Army backpack and began stuffing it with the loose rolls of toilet paper.

"What's up with that?" Trent asked. "You gonna get revenge on your math teacher on the way out of town?"

"I don't know how long it'll be before we find safety," Vivian said. "And I, for one, don't want to be without this when we need it."

"Good thinking, Vivi," he grinned, picking up the chain of condoms. "And in the spirit of preparedness …"

Vivian pulled the bag's drawstring tightly shut.

Erik helped Sherri out of the station wagon, holding her hand gingerly and guiding her blinded steps. Vivian stuffed her purse into the Army backpack and then hung it over her slender shoulders. She looked at her brother, and he gave her a nod.

"All right, ramblers," Bobby said. "Let's get ramblin'."

With that, the tiny caravan of unlikely survivors left the ruins of the Bikini Martini and set off down the long and lonely road out of Stillwater.

Five minutes later, another set of feet quietly crackled through the abandoned street.

CHAPTER FIVE

The five survivors trudged down the road in an exhausted caravan. It had been hours since they had left Stillwater's city limits, yet the noxious pink vapor still covered the earth in ethereal sheets.

Vivian walked awkwardly in her broken shoes. With the high heels severed their stiff toes curled upward, making each step a conscious exercise in balance. Even so, in these streets full of broken glass and crushed gravel, they were better than nothing. Her lingering hangover and the reek of the fog squashed together nauseously in her belly. She yearned to step outside of reality for a minute, if for nothing else than to get a breath of fresh air.

Trent walked just in front of her, carrying his found sword with masculine authority. He flung the tip of the sword into an alley with a dramatic leap.

"Who goes there?" he demanded.

He glanced at Vivian out of the corner of his eye. She wasn't paying any attention. He continued anyway.

"Yeah, you best not be there. Don't be messin' with my ladies unless you're looking for a beat-down from Big T. I protect my girls 24/7, yo."

He glanced back at Sherri. She also wasn't paying any attention to him. He pranced ahead and continued his protective posturing.

Sherri's bleached-white hair and shredded coat fluttered in the breeze, making her look like a shipwrecked ghost. Her damaged nerve endings had now fully surrendered, leaving her charred flesh bathed in a pleasant numbness.

"Hey, Powderpuff," she whispered, "do you hear that?"

"Yeah, don't worry," Vivian said. "It's just that guy Trent acting like a freak."

"No, not that. Believe me, I've heard enough of that to be able to identify it. It's like this weird crackling."

Vivian listened. All she could hear were five sets of feet crunching on wrecked pavement.

"I don't hear it," she shrugged. "I'm sure it's nothing to be concerned about."

Behind the girls, Bobby and Erik struggled to carry the burdensome load of the satellite dish. They each had their hands hooked under the lip of the parabola; Bobby in the rear, Erik in the front. After his morning of torture, Erik was moving slower than Bobby could tolerate, and he was reminded of this fact regularly by none-too-subtle jabs of the dish into the small of his back.

"Ow! Jesus, Bobby," Erik whined. "Take it easy back there, will ya?"

"Well, pick up the pace already. You're slower than a Kermit download."

Erik stopped walking and dropped his end of the dish with a *clang.*

"Oh, well excuse the shit out of me! I don't need a *break* or anything! After all, I *did* get a good night's sleep and a complete breakfast! Oh wait, I'm doing that thing again where I confuse eating Cap'n Crunch with *bleeding to death from a near-fatal mutant attack!*"

"Mutant attack?" Bobby said. "Erik, what the hell are you talking about?"

"In the storm drain! I got attacked by some kind of mutant!"

"You said you got scratched by your cat!"

"I thought it was my cat, but now I know better!" Erik chirped. "Vivian was right, this was an atomic bomb! I was attacked by a radioactive mutant!"

Bobby let out a single, derisive laugh.

"You're imagining things," he said. "This is exactly like when we were kids and you saw *Poltergeist* for the first time. Remember that? That same night you thought a ghost was attacking you in your bedroom."

"That was totally different. I was just—"

"Remind me, how many stitches did your grandma end up getting that night?"

"Look, shut up about that, okay?! This was totally different!"

"There were no ghosts then, and there are no radioactive mutants now," Bobby said calmly. "It's just your overactive, movie-freaked imagination."

"My imagination?!" Erik yelped. "My imagination?! Oh, I suppose *these* are my imagination too?!"

He grabbed the bottom of his shirt and yanked it up over his chest. The skin surrounding his injuries had become ghoulishly swollen and inflamed, and unidentified protrusions pressed against the back of his soiled dressings.

"That's messed up," Bobby said. "It looks like you're smuggling Klingon foreheads under there."

"I'm going to die! I just know it!" Erik panicked. "I had a mid-life crisis when I was thirteen years old!"

Vivian looked at Erik's sides with a diagnostic squint.

"I'm sure you just need some antibiotics. You'll be fine as soon as we find an emergency shelter. In the meantime, we need to just sit down for a while and rehydrate ourselves. I see a fountain up ahead."

"Good thinkin', Vivi," Trent agreed. "Sit your weary body down and let the T soothe your parched throat with some cool, gentle water."

He bounded up to the fountain and sprung lightly onto its sea-foam green edge. Not long ago it had been a beautiful work of art, but today it was only a knee-high ring of concrete and cracked tile about ten feet in diameter. The nub of a fluted column extended abortively from its center, terminating in a mass of bent pipe. Trent looked into the pool and winced.

"On second thought, maybe we best keep moving until we find some cocktails."

He probed the tip of his blade into the water and swirled it around. It was thick with fallout dust and rainbowed swirls of oily condensation. Vivian limped over to the fountain and sat on its edge.

"Okay, so forget the rehydration," she muttered. "How about we just sit down long enough for some skin to grow back on the soles of my feet?"

She pulled off her shoes and rubbed her swollen feet. Trent knelt in front of her and brushed her hands away, taking her blistered foot in his fingers and massaging it gently.

"Hey Vivi, those pretty little shoes aren't really appropriate for walking this kind of long haul."

Vivian glared at him with an expression that said, "No shit, Sherlock."

Trent continued. "So what do you say you let Big T carry you on his back for a while?"

"I don't think so. Just give me a minute. I'll be fine."

"Come on, girl, just spread those long legs and jump on," Trent grinned, breaking into song. *"Come on, ride the Trent! Hey ride it! Wooo-wooooo!"*

He turned his back to her and pointed his sunburnt arms at his swinging backside. Vivian raised an eyebrow.

"Let me explain something to you right now," she said. "I wouldn't 'ride the Trent' if he was the last lifeboat on the *Titanic,* all right?"

"Aww, it's not like that, sweetness," Trent said, putting his hand over his heart. "It's my duty as a good Christian to give you the piggyback, girl. It's right in the Bible. 'During your times of trial and suffering, when you see only one set of footprints in the sand, it was then that I carried you.'"

"Hey Mr. Pious Playa," Erik said. "If you're so anxious to carry something, why don't you carry this freakin' dish for a while? Bobby's having a contest to see what he can kill first: the batteries in the TV or me."

"Oh, quit being such a drama queen," Bobby muttered. "You'll thank me when this TV finds the emergency broadcast that ends up saving your ass. I'm gonna give it another try."

He leaned the satellite dish against the fountain and hooked it up to the camping lantern. Erik slumped on the ground and did his best to look miserable. Sherri plopped down on the edge of the fountain and hung her head nauseously between her bony knees.

"Man, I am still hung over as shit," she moaned. "I didn't drink enough last night to still be feeling this bitch."

"I hear that," Bobby agreed. "Usually I can just sleep it off, but my guts are all a-tingle today. The puke has been burning up and down the pipe all day like a barf barometer."

"Me too," Erik said. "I wasn't even drinking last night and I *still* feel like I'm gonna hurl. It's like the air is just *crawling* in my *stomach*."

"Okay, I don't know what y'all are talking about," Trent said proudly. "I drank responsibly, and I feel right as rain. Nothing is sexier than somebody who knows when to say when, right Vivi?"

Vivian didn't hear him. She was still preoccupied with what Erik had said, because she had been feeling the same thing all morning. This awful pink air was *crawling* in her stomach. And in her lungs and bladder. In her toes and fingertips. She knew this feeling could only be one thing, and it wasn't a hangover.

It had to be radiation poisoning.

"Vivi?" Trent repeated. "You okay, sweetness? You look like you're about to give greetings and salutations to your old friend Ralph."

Vivian clutched her tingling abdomen. There was no point in telling them what was really making them sick. It was better they didn't know. There was nothing they could do about it even if they did. As helplessness wrenched down on her stomach, Vivian realized that Trent's assessment of her expression was about to become accurate.

"No no, I'm okay. I feel fine," she lied. "I just have to um … go to the bathroom or something."

Trent swished his sword into the air and offered her his arm.

"Please, allow me to escort you to a discreet location. I shall be honored to be your humble bodyguard whilst you take care of business."

"Ha!" Sherri laughed. "Or with the bullshit filter on, 'The thought of peeping on you squatting with your panties around your ankles gives me a hard-on.'"

Vivian glanced at Trent. He looked about as innocent as a barbecue at Jeffrey Dahmer's house.

"I think I can keep an eye on myself," she said. "Could somebody else please keep an eye on Trent?"

"Oh, that's cold," Trent muttered. "A guy tries to look out for a lady, and look what happens. That's just cold."

Vivian limped around the back of the nearest building in search of some modicum of privacy in which to lose her lunch. All detail had been ripped from the face of the structure, leaving nothing but a monolithic stack of concrete slabs five stories high.

She leaned against the cracked wall and felt her body rolling in a cold boil. It was like thousands of insects were running across the inside of her skin. Scuttling around her limbs, scurrying up her back, burrowing into her face. Her stomach convulsed and her mouth jerked open, but it produced nothing. Not even a gag or cough. Just nothing. She wrapped her arms around her trembling body and slouched against the building.

Through her cracked glasses she could see a grim automobile graveyard. To her right, half a BMW leered at her through its broken grille. To her left, a Lexus was driven hood-first into the earth, its rear tires slowly rolling against the stale air. The pink vapor oozed over the derelict automobiles, seeping through their broken windows and pouring from their bent tailpipes. Slowly. Sickeningly. She could almost hear it breathing: inhaling and exhaling in a heavy stroke, crackling like a bonfire.

A jingle of broken glass against cement roused her from her trance. In a flash she had retrieved her senses and launched to her feet. She turned in place, her eyes stabbing into the fog.

"Trent? Damn it, Trent. Leave me alone! Give me some privacy for a minute!"

She closed her eyes and listened. The heavy breath was coming from behind the vertical Lexus. With a sudden fury she rushed around the automotive wall, her own footsteps eclipsed by the heavy pounding of the retreating voyeur.

"Yeah, you better run, you pervert! Is it too much to ask for you to just leave me alone for a minute so I can—"

Vivian stopped short and her words fell into empty air. There was nothing on the other side of the car but a broad, yawning hole in the side of the concrete monolith.

"I found something!" Bobby said. "Turn left ... left ... stop! We got it!"

With Erik rotating the dish, Bobby had finally managed to get a picture on the lantern's TV. The crackle of the tiny speaker drew the boys into a huddle around it. Even Sherri leaned in with casual interest.

The screen showed a simple animation rendered in watercolors. It depicted an ape-like man shambling across an empty white screen, holding a blunt rock. The hominid froze at the left of the frame, and a stout, upright-walking *Homo erectus* emerged from behind it wielding a crude hand axe. After two steps, the primitive man froze, and a caveman in animal skins emerged holding a sharpened spear, and so on until the screen contained a simplified representation of the evolution of Man. The lineage culminated in the thin, tall form of modern man, *Homo sapiens sapiens,* holding a glowing, oversized atom in his outstretched hand. A soft voice echoed the text that faded onto the bottom of the screen.

"Realize your potential. WOPR - Liberty Valley, Pennsylvania."

"Hey!" Trent said. "That's not the Zoo Crew! You found something else!"

"Naah. It's the Zoobles all right," Bobby grumbled. "This is just a network identification bumper at the beginning of the show. I saw it this morning too."

As soon as he said the words, the promo dissolved into the upbeat opening theme of *Zoobilee Zoo*. Bobby punched the "scan" button and watched with diluted optimism as the screen rolled through channel after empty channel.

"Wait, wait," Erik said. "Are you telling me that with this big dish and all the satellites on the horizon, all you can pick up on this thing is *one station?*"

"So far," Bobby said.

"And that one station is playing a *Zoobilee Zoo* marathon?"

"Not exactly a marathon," Bobby said. "It's the same episode. At the end it goes to black for about two minutes, then bars and tone, the bumper, and then back to the start. The tape must be stuck in a loop."

"Hello, my little Zoobaroos!" Mayor Ben cackled. *"It's zoo-pendous to see you again for another zoo-riffic adventure!"*

Erik rubbed his forehead with his fingertips.

"That's it. Forget it. I'm not going to carry this heavy-ass dish another inch just so that I can bask in the nightmarish glow of Ben Vereen in cat makeup."

Sherri shrugged.

"When I was a kid I always thought that makeup was kinda hot. There's something sexy about a dude with animal parts."

"Okay, fine," Erik muttered. "From now on, let's make the furvert carry the dish."

"Hey!" Sherri snapped. "I'm not a furvert just because I'd fuck Mayor Ben!"

"Perhaps not," Bobby said. "But that fact *does* open up a whole new slate of potential psychological problems."

"Oh, fuck you and your satellite dish," Sherri grumbled. "What do I need TV for? I'm fucking blind."

"Jeez, what is with you people?" Bobby huffed. "I can't believe you just want to just abandon our only chance of ever seeing an emergency broadcast!"

"It's not that we don't want to keep scanning for news," Erik said. "We just can't keep carrying that two-ton dish on our backs! We'd all be totally gung-ho about keeping it if we had a car!"

"And if 'ifs' and 'buts' were fruits and nuts, every day would be Christmas," Bobby smirked. "Fine, just forget it then. We're never gonna find a working car in this wasteland."

From out of the fog, Vivian ran up to the fountain and slid to a dusty stop in a pair of ruby-red sneakers.

"Good news, everybody," she said. "I just found our ride out of here."

"This way! In here! Come on!"

Holding aloft the camping lantern, Vivian urged her companions through the garage-door-sized hole in the concrete cube. A ramp within stabbed upward into the heart of what had previously been the parking garage of the Banyan

Terrace.

The garage had buckled against its own framework, shearing the floors from their moorings and piling them in sedimentary layers. Ruined upper levels sagged over massive support pylons, forming a broad, straight tunnel through the center of the wreckage. The remains of luxury cars lay smashed within the collapsed walls, forming narrow, shadowy cavities between their fenders like tunnels in an ant farm. After about a hundred feet, the ramp terminated in a chamber of dark, stale air twenty feet wide. The building groaned under its own unsteady weight, dusting the five survivors with powdered concrete as they marched up the ramp. Erik shuffled up to Vivian's side and whispered.

"Vivian, are you crazy?! I thought we were going to stay out of condemned buildings from now on! What are we doing here?!"

"We're here to get the Rabbit out of its burrow."

Vivian lifted her lantern, throwing its light over the nose of her rusted convertible. It was nearly buried in fallen architecture, but apparently unharmed.

"You've *got* to be kidding me," Bobby sighed.

"Damn, Vivi," Trent said. "God may have given women all the sugar and spice, but he sure didn't give y'all any skillz when it comes to parking an automobile."

"*I* didn't park it," Vivian muttered. "I gave the valet my life savings for this exclusive VIP space."

In the strictest sense of the term, the space where Vivian's Rabbit was parked was not a space at all. For those to whom this was not readily apparent, the floor had been marked with a series of tight, parallel lines and stenciled letters reading "NO PARKING!"

The convertible had been backed, as the valet had promised, under the ramp to the next level of the garage. To each side of the vehicle stood a titanic pair of concrete pylons straining to hold the collapsed floors above. Their buckling weight had come to rest against the fenders of the Rabbit, barring access to its doors and, in fact, making it impossible to get around its sides at all.

The diminishing slope of the ceiling ran parallel to the length of car's windshield, pressed harshly on its rollbar, and continued downward to meet the ground ten feet behind its rear bumper. The collapse had left only one access point to the Rabbit's interior: an eight-inch gap between the crumbling ceiling and the top of the windshield.

"What are we supposed to do with *that?!*" Erik said. "It's crushed! Let's get out of here before we are too!"

"It's not crushed; it's just trapped," Vivian said. "And it's the only car in the whole building that's still intact. All we need to do is pull it out of there."

"Uh uh. No way, Viv," Bobby said. "That car is probably the only thing holding up the roof. And even if we do get it out, it's not like we could start it."

"Come on, Bobby," Vivian pleaded. "The keys are right there in the ignition!"

"It doesn't matter," Trent said. "We punched a key into every car at the bar and we didn't even get as much as an alarm to go off, yo."

"It's the EMP—you said it yourself," Erik agreed. "The ignition circuits are gonna be fried. Keys or not, we'll never get that little car running. It wasn't shielded with metal."

"Yes, that might be true," Vivian said. "It wasn't *completely enclosed* in metal, but there sure was a lot of metal trapped in the *hundreds of tons of automobile-laced concrete* that it *was* enclosed in!"

"Yeah, exactly," Erik said. "The same hundreds of tons of automobile-laced concrete that are going to crush us to death as soon as we start messing with it! Let's just get out of here already!"

"So that's it? We're not even going to try?" Vivian pleaded. "It's not even worth the *chance?*"

"The chance of *what?*" Sherri said. "Of getting our asses killed trying to save a car that barely ran *before* the apocalypse?"

Vivian pushed up her glasses and rubbed her eyes as a low crackle ripped from the overstrained walls.

"Fine. You can all just leave. I'll pull that car out all by myself if I have to."

"Oh, come on, Vivian," Erik said. "Be reasonable."

"I tried being reasonable," Vivian growled. "Reason says that the ceiling will collapse if we disturb the car. Reason says that the EMP destroyed the ignition. I'm not getting anywhere using reason."

"So what are you going to do?" Bobby asked.

"I'm going to believe in myself," Vivian said. "And I'm going to drive that car out of here."

With that, she set down the lantern and sprang onto the hood of her car. She squeezed her arms and shoulders through the gap and came to a struggling stop, her body pinned between the windshield and the deteriorating ceiling above. This was exactly how far she had managed to get in her previous attempt when she had snatched her sneakers from the dashboard. She couldn't even reach the keys from here, let alone the shifter or pedals. Yet she clawed her feet into the hood, trying to shove herself through the opening as bits of gravel flaked off of the ceiling and rolled down her back.

Bobby and Erik exchanged glances. Sherri stared blindly into the sound of the scuffle. Trent just gazed hungrily at Vivian's wriggling backside. Finally he turned on the group and spoke with the authority of a man who changed the course of history, as portrayed by a washed-up actor in a made-for-TV movie.

"Gentlemen, gentlemen. What kind of pathetic creatures are we? For real, yo? Whilst we stand here all scaredy-catted up, that woman is risking her fine neck to score some wheels for us cowering and lowly wretches. Listen up, dawgs: If the lady wants her car, we shall help the lady get her car. It is our duty

CHAPTER FIVE

as men to fulfill our women's every wish."

"I wish you'd decide if you're a poseur intellectual or a poseur gangsta," Sherri muttered.

"We're not leaving without Vivian," Erik frowned. "And I guess Vivian's not leaving without her car."

"So by transitive axiom," Bobby sighed, "we're not leaving without Vivian's car."

"Now that's what I'm talkin' about!" Trent beamed. "Come on, let's give the lovely lady a hand."

He leapt to the Rabbit's fender and slid his hand down Vivian's long calf. She kicked at him distractedly.

"What's the word in there, Vivi?" he asked. "You all good?"

"I'm stuck," Vivian replied. "The gap is too narrow. My chest won't fit through it."

"Here, let me help," Trent said, stepping forward. "If I hold down your girlie bits all Janet-Jackson-style, you'll be able to—"

Bobby put a heavy hand on Trent's shoulder and shook his head scornfully.

"Damn, homes, don't be like that," Trent grumbled. "I'm just trying to look out for the greater good here, yo."

Vivian wrestled back through the gap, slid down the hood, and hopped down to the floor.

"I can't reach the ignition," she muttered. "I'm just too big."

"Aw, Vivi, don't be all down on yourself," Trent said. "You're not too big. You're the perfect size. Everyone knows a woman with a few curves is far sexier than one that's all skin and bones."

"Well, it's my 'curves' that are the problem," Vivian blushed, crossing her arms over her chest. "I could have fit in there if I was all skin and bones like …"

She stopped before she had completed her thought, but nobody seemed to notice. Their heads all turned in unison to the same place.

"You're all staring at me, aren't you?" Sherri scowled. "Forget it. I can't drive stick."

"You don't have to," Vivian said. "All you have to do is see if it'll start."

"And we *have* established that I'm fucking blind?" Sherri continued.

"Okay, I know the situation is somewhat less than ideal," Vivian said. "But you're the only one here thinner than I am."

"Or, alternately," Erik suggested, "we could take this as a sign that we should just give up and get the hell out of here right now."

Vivian turned her back to Erik and put her hand on Sherri's crispy shoulder.

"Please, Sherri. You're our only hope."

Sherri rolled her ruddy eyes.

"Alright, alright, I'll do it," she said. "Don't get all melodramatic about it."

With a broad smile, Vivian helped Sherri onto Rabbit's hood and up to its windshield. Sherri easily slid both arms through the tiny gap, grabbed the front seats, and pulled her narrow body through. She dropped into the car, landing on her head and tumbling over.

"Ow! Shit!"

Vivian took the camping lantern and held it to the windshield. She could see Sherri lying face-down, her hips stuffed between the front seats, her knees planted in the faded upholstery of the back. The rusted lever of the defunct parking brake jabbed into her blistered stomach.

"Are you all right?" Vivian asked.

"Do I look all right?" Sherri bitched. "I've been in fetish beds more comfortable than this!"

"Well, can you reach the ignition?"

Sherri could see nothing but a maroon-hued darkness. She groped around the wheel and down the steering column until she located the dangling keychain.

"Got it," she said. "Let's burn some dead dinosaurs."

"Wait! Wait!" Vivian said. "It's still in gear! Push in the clutch first or it'll stall."

"Oh, fuck you. It's not going to start anyway!"

"Come on, Sherri," Vivian begged.

"God, you're so needy."

Sherri swept her left hand over the floor until it connected with the clutch pedal. With the sum of her meager upper-body strength she shoved it to the floor.

"Unuung! Now what?"

"Turn the key and hope for the best," Vivian said, crossing her fingers.

While struggling to keep the clutch pushed in with her left hand, Sherri awkwardly reached her right hand over her shoulder and caught hold of the key. With a breathless groan she gave it the most violent crank she could muster.

The key pushed against the sides of the tumbler.

The tumbler turned with a click.

The engine returned nothing but a cold, blue silence.

Not a rev of the starter. Not a flash of accessory lights.

Nothing.

Gasping air into her strained lungs, Sherri let go of the key and collapsed with her chest hanging over the edge of the driver's seat and her forehead resting on the floor.

"It's totally dead," she wheezed. "Just like us."

Her words floated out of the crevice, slapping the optimism clean off of Vivian's face.

"I told you it wasn't going to work," Bobby said.

"It must feel great to always be so right," Vivian scowled. "Fine. Let's get out of here before you're right about the roof collapsing too."

"Yes! Yes, let's do that!" Erik agreed. "Come on, Sherri! Time to move out!"

A scrambling commotion came from inside the car, quickly increasing in intensity and then falling into silence.

"God *damn* it," Sherri barked.

"What is it now?" Vivian sighed.

"I can't get up. My sleeve is stuck on something."

In the darkness under the dashboard, the mangled cuff of Sherri's sleeve had looped around the clutch pedal. Vivian held the lantern up to the windshield and squinted at Sherri's prone form.

"Well, if your sleeve is stuck, just take your coat off."

Sherri thrashed against the stringy remains of her coat, which only served to pull them tighter around her captured body.

"I can't get it off!"

As the Rabbit swayed angrily on its loose suspension, knots of crushed cement broke free of the ceiling, tumbling down the ramp and clattering off of crushed cars. Everyone threw their arms over their heads and ducked for cover as the support pylons let out a moan like whales on honeymoon.

"Stop! Sherri, stop!" Vivian screamed. "Don't move! Stop moving!"

Sherri's struggle broke off into coughing and strangled breath, and the Rabbit stopped grinding against the walls. Even as the debris temporarily stopped falling, a loud, splintering crackle issued threateningly from the walls.

"God damn it!" Sherri snarled. "I'm stuck like a dick in a duck in here!"

"Oh no, no no," Erik mumbled. "Now what do we do?!"

"Don't panic," Vivian said. "Just calm down and don't touch *anything*. You got it?"

"Got it," Bobby nodded.

"You know I got it, girl," Trent agreed.

A thunderous sound of snapping timber rang out from Erik's direction, sending a shower of gravel cascading into Vivian's hair.

"Erik! I said don't *touch* anything!"

"I didn't!" Erik yelped. "The wall just—oh my G-God …"

Erik's grimy complexion paled as he gazed into the crevice between the two demolished vehicles behind him. Trent brandished his sword.

"Aww, what's got you spooked, Little E? Man, you need to work up some testicular fortitude and quit being such a little …"

He took two bold steps before freezing in his tracks.

"… pussy!"

Trent was right. In the dim light of the lantern, all available evidence suggested that the creature before him was indeed a pussycat. It had the reflective yellow eyes, the pointed ears, the clawed feet. But this pussycat stood just over three feet tall at the shoulder.

Erik tried valiantly to form a sentence.

"What the … I … I mean … this … it … it's *Twiki!*"

"I thought you said you killed Twiki!" Bobby hissed.

"I did!"

"Well, apparently she didn't get the memo!"

Twiki was not dead, but she did not look at all well as she emerged onto the concrete ramp. Her mangled butterscotch hide stretched horrifically over a skeleton suitable for a Saint Bernard. Yellow bones ruptured through her fur at the overstressed joints of her knees and scapulas. Her teeth curled from her head in great crooked rows, jutting out like broken glass jammed into her black gums. Massive, blood-soaked claws extended from her toes, scratching horribly against the cement floor. As she stepped out of the shadows, her body crackled like an overstuffed barrel on the verge of eruption.

"That crackle!" Bobby hissed. "That's what I've been hearing all day!"

Erik gasped. "She must have followed us here!"

Erik, Bobby, and Trent all pressed themselves against the walls as Twiki stepped forward, letting out a piercing hiss. Vivian slowly pushed her palms and heels into the Rabbit's hood, crab-walking herself to the windshield and pressing her back against it. Four sets of eyes frantically flashed back and forth as they tried to work out a non-verbal plan of action, but none of them understood anything any of the others tried to convey. All they understood was that any plan for retreat was foiled by one tiny detail.

"Hellooo, assholes? I'm still stuck in here!" Sherri yelled. "Hey, what's going on out there?"

Twiki's head snapped toward the sound, locking her huge golden eyes upon the redhead pressed against the Rabbit's windshield. Vivian leaned her head toward the gap and hissed out of the corner of her mouth.

"*Sssh!* Not now, Sherri!"

"Don't *sssh* me! What's that noise? It sounds like Snap, Crackle, and Pop are having a three-way out there!"

"Sherri, shut *up!*" Vivian bristled.

Twiki's eyes narrowed as she turned her hulking body toward the convertible.

"Okay, Trent, it's showtime," Bobby whispered. "Get in there and do your thing!"

The hilt of Trent's sword trembled violently in his fist.

"I … I … w-w-what's that now?" he chattered.

"You protect your girls 24/7, remember?" Bobby coached. "This is what you've been waiting for all day, tough guy. Make us proud!"

Bobby put his doughy hand on Trent's back and shoved him into action. Trent took several stumbling steps and came to a stop directly between Vivian and the mutant feline. Twiki rocked back on her crackling haunches and hissed as Trent raised his sword with two blanched hands. He stood completely frozen in his wingtips, too terrified to even blink.

"S-st-s-st-stay b-b-back," he stammered. "I ain't p-p-pl-playin'.'"

With Twiki momentarily distracted, Vivian didn't waste a second in returning to Sherri's rescue. She thrust her head and shoulders into the gap, once again wedging to an abrupt stop at her chest.

"Sherri!" she hissed. "Get out of there! Now!"

"I *can't!* What part of 'stuck like a dick in a duck' didn't you understand?"

Vivian pushed her feet against the hood and struggled, but she was just too big for the gap.

Or was the gap just too *small* for her?

"Sherri! Can you still reach the clutch pedal?"

"Hellooo? I'm *tied* to it!"

"Push it in!"

With a grunt and a thrust of her tiny bicep, Sherri drove the clutch to the ground.

"Now what?"

"Just hold it there!"

Sherri wedged her elbow under the front seat, pinning down the pedal with the bones of her own forearm. Vivian wrestled herself free and threw a glance over her shoulder. Trent still stood with his back to the car and his sword in the air, not having moved a millimeter in any direction since the last time she had seen him.

"Y-y-y-you d-d-don't wanna m-mess with m-m-me," he yammered. "I'll m-m-mess you up! For r-r-real!"

"Keep it up, Trent!" Vivian hissed. "Just keep her occupied for one more minute!"

She whirled around, squatted against the hood, and planted her palms shoulder-width apart on the sloping ceiling. She took a deep breath and coordinated every muscle in her body for one concentrated push. With a sad, rusty *creak,* the car began, ever so slowly, to roll forward. Vivian could feel a stream of fine debris flaking off of the ceiling and funneling down her back. Her skull pounded from the exertion, but the gap was growing ever larger as the angled ceiling crept farther and farther from the windshield.

"Just believe in yourself," she thought. *"Like Nick said. You can do this!"*

Behind Vivian's back, a wet, throaty hiss slithered around Twiki's jagged teeth. Her gaze was fixed on Trent's chattering teeth as her weight shifted back on the tensed muscles of her legs.

"Y-y-you d-d-don't want to g-g-get all violent," Trent choked. "D-d-do you, g-girl?"

The yellow slits of Twiki's eyes narrowed as she released a cry like a hundred babies being thrown into boiling water. Trent could see each individual claw dig into the pavement in slow motion as Twiki's powerful hind legs launched her payload of teeth toward his soft flesh.

It was time for Trent to make his big move.

His sword clanged noisily to the concrete as he dove to the ground, shielding his head with his arms. Twiki sailed over his prone form, landing claws-first in Vivian's back. Her chest cracked the windshield as the monster's full weight slammed down on her unprepared body, and a piercing scream squeezed from her lungs as oversized claws sunk into her flesh and clattered down her ribcage.

"Shit! Vivian!" Sherri screamed. "What in the name of fuck is going on out there?!"

Twiki ripped her claws out of Vivian's back and turned on the hood, slipping on the bloodied pads of her paws. She didn't care about Vivian. Vivian was just collateral damage. Her real prey was escaping.

As Bobby and Erik scrambled to Vivian's aid, Trent was running in exactly the opposite direction. With a deafening screech, Twiki launched off of the Rabbit and darted after him. Trent changed direction and dove into a tiny space between the remains of two parked cars jutting from the tunnel wall. The crush of the collapsed garage had compressed the wrecks into nothing more than rectangles of oily steel, but there was still enough space for Trent to shimmy between them. His craven screams were muffled by Twiki's sinewy mass as she wriggled into the narrow crevice behind him.

Bobby and Erik grabbed Vivian's limp body and turned her over on the Rabbit's hood. Her naked green eyes stared blankly into the darkness.

"Oh my God, oh my God," Erik chattered. "Please don't be dead! Don't be dead!"

Bobby picked up Vivian's glasses and slipped them over her empty eyes. Tiny movements of air and spittle whistled between her teeth as she struggled to remain conscious.

"Bobby, we've got to get her out of here!" Erik squeaked.

Erik grabbed Vivian's wrists, but Bobby shoved him away.

"I'll take care of Vivian!"

He squatted down, grabbed his sister around the waist, and hauled her over his shoulder.

"You work on Sherri! I'll be right back!"

Without waiting for a reply, Bobby turned and ran down the ramp toward the only way out. His heart pounding in his throat, Erik scrambled onto the hood of the car. The garage wailed as tombstone-sized chunks of concrete smashed down like bombs along the corridor. Before Erik could wonder what triggered the collapse, a small gap between two nearby wrecks vomited out a bucketful of gravel, followed by a scrambling Trent. Apparently there were still pockets of space within these fallen walls large enough for him to claw his way through. Almost before he hit the floor, the fleeing hipster was back on his feet and sprinting for the exit. Erik grabbed Trent's sunburnt arm and stumbled along behind him like an ineffectual anchor.

"Trent! Stop! Get over here and help me!"

"Get offa me!" Trent wailed, shoving Erik away. "She's after me! That bitch is gonna kill me!"

A groaning ripple ran through the ceiling, knocking off a hail of skull-sized debris. From the same gap from which Trent had emerged, a gouged, dust-covered Twiki was clawing her way to freedom. Trent knocked Erik to the ground and took off running.

"Trent!" Erik screamed. "Get back here, you wuss!"

Trent was already halfway to the exit before Twiki pushed herself free of the scar in the wall. Erik leapt to his feet, grabbed the discarded sword, and pointed it at his ex-pet. Twiki's fierce, gurgling breath rolled into an earsplitting screech as the fur on her back rose into angry spikes.

"I tried to tell you that killing is wrong," Erik said, "but I guess you'll have to learn the hard way!"

With all the grace of a man who had never played an organized sport in his life, Erik leapt forward and swung the sword in a clumsy, girlish arc. The blade not only failed to hit Twiki by a wide margin, but also slipped out of his hands and sailed through the air in a helicopter-like spin, clipping the sloped ceiling and dropping hilt-first into the Rabbit.

"Ow! What the hell?!" Sherri screamed. "Quit throwing shit at me, asshole!"

Erik's shoulders bunched.

"Sorry!"

He turned back to his former cat with a nervous smile.

"Ah, yeah, so about that whole 'trying to kill you' thing. I was just—"

Without a second glance, Twiki plowed past Erik and down the ramp. Trent was still a good thirty feet from the end of the tunnel when she caught up with him. He dove between two ravaged automobiles and back into the catacombs of the groaning walls. A second later, Twiki disappeared into the opening behind him.

Erik climbed onto the Rabbit's hood and thrust his hands into the ceiling, trying to push the car out of its grave as Vivian had tried before. He slipped in a puddle of her blood and slammed his jaw into the top of the windshield, sending a shockwave through his skull. Fist-sized clods of jagged concrete pounded down upon Sherri.

"Ow! Ow! Shit!" she thrashed. "Will somebody get me out of here already?!"

"Shut up! I'm trying!" Erik wailed. "I can't move the car!"

"Well, stop throwing shit at me!"

"I'm not! The ceiling is coming down!"

"The ceiling is *what?!*"

Erik didn't have to explain. At that very moment the building let out a groan like a constipated elephant, dropping the thousand-ton ceiling. With a shower of debris, the sloped roof came down, starting from its fulcrum ten feet behind the Rabbit. The concrete slab fell in a cascading wave, pinching the back end of the trapped vehicle and launching it out of its cell like an unwilling Tiddly Wink.

"Shit, we're moving!" Sherri yelped. "Where's the brake?!"

Erik threw out his arms and grabbed the corners of the windshield as gravity yanked the suddenly liberated Rabbit down the ramp.

"Don't hit the brake!" he screamed.

Not known as one who worked well with others, Sherri punched her free hand into the brake pedal. She pumped it furiously, yet the car just kept picking up speed. Had she retained the gift of sight, Sherri would have realized that she was actually pumping the accelerator.

"The brake is broken!" she wailed.

"Don't hit the brake!" Erik repeated.

Sherri lifted her hand from the gas pedal, but before it had moved an inch it came to an abrupt halt. In her frenzy, the shreds of her right sleeve had become entwined around it.

"You've got to be shittin' me," she groaned.

As tons of tumbling steel and concrete squeezed in all around him, Erik looked at the single point of light in the distance and suddenly understood what it felt like to be toothpaste. The Rabbit sailed down the ramp with building speed, but the walls were coming down faster than the dead hulk could accelerate. The last thing that Erik would ever see would be the light of the approaching exit snuffed out by the same toppling concrete that would crush him into a wet meat pancake.

"Fuckshit O'Fuckery!" Sherri cursed.

Her constrained arms thrashed madly against their bonds. Clutch, gas. Clutch clutch, gas.

From the other side of the windshield, Erik couldn't hear Sherri's curses over the squeaking of the pedals, the thunder of the splintering garage, and the roar of the Rabbit's engine as it sprang to life.

Before Sherri realized that her full weight was shoved against the gas pedal, the tires squealed madly against the floor. The Rabbit bucked forward with a blast of speed, tearing down the ramp and through the exit just as the last remaining supports came down, blasting an eruption of dust and gravel against its rear fenders.

Sherri ground her back into the steering wheel as she struggled to push herself off the floor, throwing the Rabbit into a mad, careening arc around the side of the building.

"Bobby!" Erik screamed. "Look out!"

Under the weight of his sister, Bobby lurched out of the runaway Rabbit's path as it tore past him.

"Brakes, Sherri! Brakes!" Erik wailed. "*Now* you can hit the brakes!"

Sherri's left arm was now tightly bound to the clutch, her right to the gas. There was only one thing to do.

"Hold on to your ass!" she screamed.

With a lurch of her neck, she slammed her sunburnt forehead down on the brake pedal, locking the Rabbit in a squealing spin. The bald tires skidded across the fallout-dusted pavement, not coming to a full stop until the front bumper rammed the side of the fountain. Erik slipped off of the slick hood like a puck on an air hockey table, splashing down in the filthy water. Having served its purpose, the Rabbit's engine shuddered, wheezed, and stalled itself out.

Erik scrambled out of the water and dropped with a wet *plop* onto the dusty sidewalk. An out-of-breath Bobby arrived and gently set Vivian down on the fountain's edge.

"Erik, you okay, dude?" he puffed.

"I'm okay," Erik nodded. "You?"

"Yeah, I'm okay," Bobby said, touching his bloody shirt. "None of this is mine."

"I'm okay, you're okay, everybody is fucking okay!" barked Sherri. "Now will somebody fucking get me the fuck out of this car for fuck's sake?!"

Bobby waddled to the side of the convertible and pulled open the door. Sherri's narrow hips were still wedged in between the front seats, her legs thrown across the back, both arms tied down to the pedals. Bobby grabbed the sword from where it lay across her back.

"Stay still for a second," he ordered.

With a few sawing thrusts of the blade he cut the knotted strands of leather from Sherri's wrists. He dropped the sword in the street, then pulled Sherri's thrashing body out of the vehicle.

"Sherri, you started the car!" Erik squealed. "How did you do that?"

"I don't know—it was rolling and I just mashed all the pedals," Sherri said. "I told you I don't know how to drive stick."

"She did a push start," Vivian mumbled.

"She did what?" Erik asked.

"It's a trick to turn over an engine with a bad starter," Vivian whispered. "You just get it rolling and pop the clutch."

Erik snapped his fingers.

"That's right! Just like in *The Karate Kid!* Remember, Viv? Daniel's mom's car would never start, so they always had to pop the clutch, and when he went on that date with the rich girl—"

"Erik," Vivian murmured, "not now."

Vivian's face had turned a pale, floury white as two streams of blood leaked down her back and into the squalid water of the fountain. Erik's face collapsed. He sat by Vivian's side and gently took her hand.

"I'm sorry, Viv. You were right: The car works. We're going to find a hospital. We're going to be safe. All five of us."

Bobby's eyes popped open.

"Holy crap," he gasped. "What happened to that other idiot?"

Erik looked at what was left of the garage. It no longer retained the shape of a cube, but had fallen into a classic heap. The pulverized cement dust hung heavily in the moist pink vapor, threatening to reconstitute itself into a statue of a cloud.

"He didn't make it," he said softly.

Vivian and Bobby looked reverently at the slabbed pile. Sherri shrugged.

"Serves him right," she said. "Cowardly prick bastard."

Erik scowled at her. It was wrong to speak ill of the dead, even if they had it coming.

"He *technically* saved our lives in there," he said. "Sherri and I probably wouldn't have made it out alive if he hadn't been … distracting Twiki. He may have had his shortcomings, but we have to at least thank him for that."

The others nodded and grunted.

"Compliment accepted," a smarmy voice said. "Now y'all know, when the goin' gets tough, you best step back and leave the heroics to the T!"

Four heads snapped toward two rows of gleaming white teeth emerging from the cloud.

"So he's alive then," Sherri sighed. "Gee, that's swell."

"Alive and kickin, yo! That wild pussy was all up on me, but the Lord guided me to safety just before the walls came a-tumblin' down."

Bobby looked at Trent skeptically.

"Yet you *somehow* managed to get out without so much as a scratch."

"Not hardly, Big B," Trent said. "That escape was tight, yo. I'm talkin' 'door hit my ass on the way out' tight."

He turned and stuck out his hip, gesturing over his shoulder at a single, miniscule slash of blood that cut across the back of his khaki trousers. Erik leapt to his feet and shot out a finger.

"You cowardly prick bastard! We could have all died in there because of you!"

"Little E, you're straight flippin' like a dolphin at Sea World," Trent said. "I saved all y'all and you know it. You had nothin' but good things to say about the T a minute ago."

"That was because I thought you were dead!" Erik snapped.

Trent shook his head.

"You thought the cat was dead too. It's a good thing you're not a medical professional, Dr. Gravedigger."

"Look, I killed whatever attacked me in that sewer!" Erik said. "So maybe it *wasn't* Twiki after all!"

Trent waved his hand dismissively.

"That's right, E. You best change your story. Only one man had the stones to kill that savage beast, and it was yours truly, Terence Trent DeLaRosa. I used my mad skillz to mess that girl up, yo."

"She's not the only girl you messed up!" Erik screamed. "You almost got Vivian killed!"

Trent brushed Erik aside and knelt down next to Vivian's hunched, bloodied form.

"Vivi girl, I offer you my humblest and most sincere apologies. You know that I wasn't jumpin' out the way up in there! I was tryin' to lure that foul creature away from you. How was I to know it would be too dumb to take the bait?"

Vivian pushed Trent away and wobbled to her feet, making her way to her brother and leaning heavily against him.

"Leave her alone, Trent," Bobby growled, gently embracing his sister. "I saw your distraction technique, and it looked to me like the only thing you were trying to save was your own ass."

"Save my ass? Save my ass?"

Trent turned and thrust out his backside, pointing to his scrape.

"Hello? I tore myself a new asshole trying to save you ungrateful clowns. For real! Vivi, you know I'm bein' straight with y'all! I was just tryin' to get that thing away from you so that I could properly dismantle it without soiling your pretty green eyes with the spectacle."

Vivian turned her clouded head away from him and rested it on Bobby's shoulder. Trent continued.

"Come on, girl! I killed that monster! I killed it for you! Once I knew you were safe I ripped that bitch apart, yo! With my bare hands! I was all smashin' in its grill like 'Bam! This one is for my homegirl, Vivi!' I ain't lyin', girl! And you know what? If that freaky freak was here now, I'd do it all again just so you could see it. For real. That's the gospel truth, y'all."

Just as Trent raised his right hand and unsheathed his winning smile, a crackling sound ripped from the settling cloud. The particulate-laden vapor curled away from the monstrous, screeching form of Twiki as she came barreling into the street at full speed. Torn to shreds by the collapsing walls, the ragged net of her fur barely contained a spill of pulsating organs, their moist surfaces coated with pulverized concrete.

Trent turned to run, but his heels knocked against the fountain. There was no time to consider another direction. There was no time to even scream. Everything in his universe disappeared as Twiki launched off of the ground, reducing his entire world to two flying rows of blood-slicked fangs.

The next thing Trent felt was a whoosh of steel through air and a face full of hot, stinging viscera. Before he knew what hit him, the full weight of a flying, headless feline connected with his chest, splattering him with liberated organs and knocking him backward into the fountain.

The tip of the sword smashed into the sidewalk, completing a whistling arc that had sliced through Twiki's neck like a guillotine blade. Through the blood-red midnight of her vision, Sherri had cleanly decapitated the monster in mid-air with one mighty swing.

Trent thrashed his way out from under the draining carcass and flopped with a gruesome, soggy *splat* onto the sidewalk.

"I … I … you … you …" he gasped. "You … you …"

"Yeah, yeah, shut the fuck up," Sherri said. "I know what I did. I'm regretting it already."

She drove the tip of the blade into the sidewalk inches from Trent's ear.

"Now could you all stop freaking the fuck out for a second and tell me exactly what it is that I just saved your asses from?"

"It was my cat!" Erik squealed. "She mutated into an atomic monster! It's the radiation from the bomb!"

"Erik, you're *insane*," Vivian muttered. "Radiation doesn't turn house pets into monsters!"

"Vivian, for cryin' out loud, look at it!" Erik chirped, pointing toward the fountain. "It's glowing like something Homer Simpson brought home from work!"

Everyone glared at the decapitated remains of the beast resting on the bottom of the fountain. The murky water obscured its form, but they could still make out the shapes of claws and teeth radiating an eerie blue glow from the pool. Erik continued.

"Whatever attacked me in the sewer did the exact same thing after I smashed its head. These things glow when you kill them! Now tell me *that's* not a classic indication of a radioactive monster!"

Bobby scratched his chin.

"I suppose it's not *impossible*," he said. "I mean, after the Chernobyl meltdown they had all kinds of freakish mutant animals being born with too many heads and not enough anuses."

"That's the key word," Vivian said, "*born*. Radiation is not a toggle between 'normal' and 'B-movie.' Those mutants had their DNA damaged while their cells were still forming."

"Who are you—Mr. Fucking Wizard? Who the fuck cares?!" Sherri yelped. "Cats are turning into hellspawn here! Does it really matter what *caused* it?"

"You're right. It could have been anything," Erik said nervously. "Who knows what kind of atomized toxins we've been exposed to today. Asbestos, mercury, olestra! I mean, just smell that air, for Christ's sake!"

With those words, everyone's acclimated nostrils were suddenly reminded of the stinking pink vapor. Trent blinked with sudden realization.

"Hold up; hold up. We've been huffin' on that air all day too. If that's what turned pretty kitty into a stone-cold killer, why isn't it happening to us?"

"Who says that it's not?" Bobby said. "Maybe it *is* happening to us. Maybe it just hasn't started to take effect yet because we're so much bigger than Twiki is. Er ... *was*."

A long moment of silence passed.

"Well, it's not going to happen to me," Sherri said.

"How can you be so sure?" Trent asked.

Sherri whipped the sword from the ground and set it against her neck.

"Because I'll kill myself first."

Everyone stared at Sherri as her words splattered against their ears.

"Oh, that's such a poseur goth answer," Erik smirked. "*I'm* not going to mutate, *I'm* just going to commit *suicide*. I'm so *dark* and *tragic*. Why don't you just kill all of us too, while you're at it?"

"Who says I won't, smart-ass?"

Sherri's bloody eyes rolled over the shadows of her friends. She stabbed a blistered finger toward the fountain and spoke with menace.

"Whatever happened to that cat is probably happening to every one of us. I say we make a pact right here and now that as soon as one of us starts to go all *Food of the Gods* like that, the rest of us swear to take the motherfucker down."

She made a fist and thrust it into the center of the group.

"Who's with me?"

"Oh jeez, Sherri," Erik sighed. "Kill me if I turn into one of them? That's a little *From Dusk Till Dawn*ian, isn't it?"

Trent put his hand on Sherri's and gave it a lecherous squeeze.

"No no, she's right, E. Don't get me wrong, I consider it an honor and a privilege to know all of you fine people, but if you come at me like that big pussy at the fountain, I'll send any one of you to the next world in a heartbeat. That's a promise."

"Oh, please," Erik said. "The last guy I saw who dealt with monsters as effectively as you had a goatee and a box of Scooby Snacks."

Bobby clapped his hand nonchalantly on top of Trent's.

"I'm in."

"What?!" Erik squeaked.

"Seriously, *look* at that thing," Bobby said. "Take a good look at it, Erik. It's not Twiki. It's not even a *cat* anymore. That thing had an unrecoverable system error on a genetic level. If that shit happens to me, I hope that one of you will have the balls to put an end to it. I'd do it for you. That's all I'm sayin'."

"That is so messed up!" Erik argued. "Bobby, I'm your best friend! Vivian is your own sister! Are you telling me that you could just take that sword and *murder* one of us? Well, we wouldn't murder you! Right, Viv?"

He threw a hopeful look at Vivian. She turned her eyes to the ground and dropped her bloody hand on top of Bobby's.

"I would," she whispered. "It's the right thing to do under the circumstances."

"Under the circumstances?!" Erik squealed. "*Under the circumstances?!* This is crazy! And illegal! Under no circumstances do the laws of civilized society allow friends to murder each other!"

"We're not in civilized society," Vivian said darkly. "And until we are, the only laws we have are our own. Everything else has been lost to oblivion."

She looked at the glowing remains in the fountain.

"We're now part of the oblivion society."

CHAPTER SIX

The push-started Rabbit's three bald radials hummed a hypnotic bass note over Interstate 67 northbound, accompanied by the uneasy guest tenor of the temporary spare. The wind sang a shrill aria as it rushed over the surface of the satellite dish, lashed to the hood with a scavenged rope of colorful, triangular flags, which contributed a continuous round of flappy-slappy applause.

The air was like an arctic wind in the open convertible. Vivian sat shivering in the driver's seat, peering over the top of the dish through her fractured glasses and windshield. Logic dictated that someone less injured should drive, but after being attacked by a giant housecat, Vivian was not on speaking terms with logic. In its place, she had fallen back on habit. Her car was all that was left of the world as she knew it, and she was going to drive it. Period.

She hunched over the steering wheel in order to keep her weight off her lacerated back. For lack of any better options, the survivors of Twiki's final catfight had bandaged themselves up with the only fabric on hand: the moldy canvas of the Rabbit's convertible top. The thick, coarse canvas was completely inappropriate for medical dressings, but it was better than nothing, and nothing was the only other thing they had.

Trent had mummified Vivian's entire torso in a stiff, unyielding wrap. He blathered all the while about stopping the blood flow and the principle of the tourniquet, but when he was done with his handiwork it was obvious that he had been trying to improvise a cleavage-enhancing corset. In this endeavor, he had been quite successful.

Erik was slumped unconscious in the passenger seat, arms crossed, palms pressed to the soiled bandages of his own injuries. The others were wedged into the tiny back seat. Although removing the convertible's top had provided a few inches of extra elbow room, the back seat would have been cramped for two passengers, let alone the three it was now forced to accommodate.

Bobby was behind his sister, with his head tipped over the back of his seat, snoring loudly into the wind. Trent was on the opposite side. Between them, Sherri's slumbering face was buried in Trent's chest, depositing a puddle of drool on his shirt. Trent slept with one arm around her shoulders, one hand on her narrow thigh, and his cheek resting softly on the top of her head. Judging by the grin on his face, even in his dreams, he could feel the nubs of her hitherto unknown breasts pressing pertly against his side.

Nobody could say how long it had been since they'd left the ruins of the Banyan Terrace parking garage, but it had been long enough to make Vivian uneasy that they had not yet reached a destination. Any destination at all. Her dusty eyes scraped against her eyelids as they rolled to the instrument panel. Again, not out of logic, but habit. She knew that no matter how many times she looked at the dashboard clock, its arms would remain seized at exactly nine minutes to midnight.

Vivian started to nod off, then jerked into a caricature of alertness. She was exhausted beyond the point of conscious thought, yet she dared not stop. In the quiet of the desolate highway, she could hear Sherri's words repeating in a haunting echo.

"Whatever happened to that cat is probably happening to every one of us right now."

This was the fear that had driven a wedge between Vivian and logic. What *did* happen to that cat? What if it *did* happen to one of her friends? What if it happened to *her*? In her sleep-deprived psyche, her fear of the mutant cat became one with the fear of the unknown.

She had driven out of the cloud of pink vapor that shrouded Stillwater County ages ago. It wouldn't be much longer until they were out from under this canopy of churning black atmosphere and basking in blue sky and hot Georgian sun. If she just kept driving she'd find civilization, and somebody would give her a simple, logical explanation as to what had happened.

Everything would be okay. She just needed to keep driving.

Her feverish thoughts were interrupted by a long finger of smoke touching the horizon. She squinted into the distance, and her heart began to beat hard in anticipation. The black column slid over the landscape, ever closer, ever larger in her field of view. She flicked her eyes to her unconscious companions, but none of them stirred. Her breathing quickened, crushing her lungs against the sides of their canvas prison with each constricted pant. Then, as suddenly as it had appeared, the shape was upon her, hurling itself at her front bumper. It was a cat the size of a pickup truck, its coat burning with a hellish red flame. The monster's metallic eye sockets were five feet apart and devoid of flesh. Vivian jerked the wheel and her car swerved, missing the demon's blazing grimace by mere inches.

The Rabbit's sleeping passengers launched into abrupt consciousness as it fishtailed across the empty lanes with a heart-stopping squeal.

"Jesus Christ, Vivian!" Bobby roared. "What the hell?!"

"Bobby!" Vivian gasped. "It ... it was a—"

She threw a terrified glance into the rearview mirror and saw nothing but a burning pickup truck lying in the center of the road. The smoldering wreck was completely bereft of life, feline or otherwise. Vivian rubbed the residue of the hallucination out of her eyes with her palm.

"I'm sorry. I thought it … I mean, the headlights looked like … never mind."

"Whoa, where are we?" Erik asked groggily. "How long have I been asleep?"

"I don't know. A long time," Vivian said. "I think we're getting close to the state line."

"Well, don't you think we should switch drivers for a while?" Erik asked pointedly.

"No," Vivian yawned. "I'm fine."

Before Erik could attempt an appeal, the sound of bony fists pounding into flesh splattered from the back seat.

"Hey! What the fuck are you doing?" Sherri shrieked. "Get off of me, you assbag!"

"Ow! Hey! Watch the sunburn!" Trent yelped. "We're all friends here!"

He let go of the thrashing girl and held his blistered arms above his head in surrender. Sherri gave him one last elbow in the chest.

"Don't you ever fucking touch me again, diaper boy!"

"Ha! Diaper boy," Bobby laughed. "Classic."

Trent scowled. The slash in his hindquarters necessitated a unique bandage configuration, and a corseted Vivian had taken her passive-aggressive revenge. Over his khakis, Trent now wore what could only be described as a comically oversized diaper of canvas bandages. He looked at Sherri and smiled innocently.

"You don't have to be so aggressive, girl," he said. "These quarters are cramped and you're chilled all the way to your fine little bones. Why don't you just snuggle up and enjoy the generous body heat that the T is serving up? My guns are hot, and your honey-barbecued skin is so, so cold. It's more comfortable for everybody if we get them together, sweetness."

Sherri's eyes narrowed.

"Touch me while I'm asleep again, and I'll tear your arm off and shove it down your throat until you punch yourself in the balls from the inside."

Trent fidgeted in his diaper, wrapping his arms around himself and pulling as far away from Sherri as possible.

"Alright, look, I respect and admire this whole 'punk rock' thing that you play so delightfully, but you're going to have to let down this hostile curtain sooner or later for the sake of humanity."

"What the fuck is *that* supposed to mean?!" Sherri spat.

"I think you know. 'Be fruitful, and multiply. Replenish the earth, and subdue it.'"

Bobby let out a snort.

"Dude, I think the earth is about as subdued as it's going to get."

"Plus," Sherri added, "I don't care what your bullshit mythology says, there is no chance of me ever having sex with you. *Ever.*"

"Seriously, dude, give it a rest," Bobby said. "For all we know, we're all ten seconds from turning into bloodthirsty mutant monsters, and you still can't wrap your head around anything bigger than your own wang. You're pathetic."

"On the contrary," Trent said smugly. "I am comfortable expressing my healthy affection for the fairer sex because I know we're all safe. I've figured out the secret."

"Alright, I'll bite," Bobby said. "What's the secret, professor?"

"I've been trying to think—what protected us? What makes us so special?" Trent said. "What was flowing through each and every one of us that was *not* in that creature that attacked us? Then it hit me. It's all about the spirits."

"Hmm … spirits," Bobby pondered. "You know, that's actually a pretty good theory!"

"But of course," Trent gloated.

"What if it *is* the spirits? Alcohol is a powerful disinfectant, and we were all sauced to the gills last night," Bobby continued. "You and me were going into about round eleven, and Sherri must have had at least twice her body weight in malt liquor."

"Wait, hold up," Trent said.

"And I had a daiquiri the size of a beach ball," Vivian nodded. "Maybe all of the alcohol in our bloodstreams killed whatever caused Twiki to mutate!"

"Then I'm gonna be fine," Sherri said. "I've been pissed since I was fourteen years old."

"No no, listen!" Trent said irritably. "I'm not talking distilled spirits, I'm talking the *Holy Spirit*, yo. I'm talking *souls*."

"Nah, I like Bobby's answer better," Sherri said. "I don't have a soul."

"You *do* have a soul," Trent argued. "God created man in His image and endowed us each with a soul. Animals don't have souls. That's why that little kitty cat turned into a demon!"

"Oh, shut up, Trent," Erik said. "My cat had just as much of a soul as I do. Cats are people too!"

"Cats are *not* people," Trent said. "Starting today, cats aren't even cats. They're the minions of Beelzebub himself. The only thing standing between our warm bodies and his cold puppet strings is that little impervious suit of armor called the everlasting soul, yo. Besides, Little E wasn't even drinking last night, were you?"

"Shut up," Erik grumbled.

"That's right," Vivian said. "Erik, you *weren't* drinking last night."

"Well, no, not last *night*," Erik replied sheepishly. "But I did have a bunch of Tequizas over at your place before work yesterday afternoon. So, you know, I'm alright. Don't nobody worry 'bout me."

His eyes rolled to his swollen bandage and lingered for a long moment before returning to the gray scenery.

"Alright, I don't care what y'all choose to believe. It will all become clear when *He* wants it to be clear," Trent said, pointing skyward. "Vivi, my love, could we please pull over and take a little rest break? If I have to endure this sandpaper seat against my sunburn for another minute, I'm going to go insane in the membrane, for real. Are you with me here, Lobster B?"

"Nah, my sunburn's fine," Bobby said, rubbing the flaking side of his face. "But I'd still like to take a break from Sherri's bony-ass elbows digging into my side for a while."

"Oh, and let me tell you, it's a real picnic having your fat gut all blubbering on me like a horny walrus," Sherri snarled. "Can somebody explain to me one more time why I'm stuck back here with fat-ass and the perv while you two beanpoles get to sprawl out all over the front seat?"

"It's sort of like triage," Erik said. "Vivian and I shouldn't be physically traumatized right now. We have the most severe wounds."

"Where the fuck was *I* when we took this vote?!" Sherri shouted. "Because last time I checked, you two pussies had some little scratches and I had a full body sunburn and eyeballs full of my own blood! What makes you think you're so goddamn fragile, Sievert?"

"Never mind," Erik said.

"Fuck you, never mind! Get your narrow ass back here; I'm riding in the front."

Erik looked at the floor sullenly.

"Okay, okay. I didn't want to show you this, but I guess it's only fair."

He slowly unbuckled his seat belt, turned, and stood on his knees to face the back seat. He moved with an unnatural stiffness in his torso, as if unable to bend anything from his distended waist upwards. His hair thrashed around his skull as his head cleared the protection of the cracked windshield.

"Believe it or not," he said, "there are worse things than having to sit next to Trent."

He pulled up his shirt, revealing purple and black swells of infected flesh rolling from the top and bottom of his bandages. Behind the wrappings, clusters of knobby flesh thrust from the center of each wound, some remaining contained within the soiled fabric, others poking bony points through its surface.

"Oh, *hell* no!" Trent squeaked, putting up a wall of palms between himself and the seething scabs. "That shit is messed up. Seriously, homes, you need to get those filthy-ass bandages changed, and you need to do it yesterday!"

Vivian gasped. She had never seen living tissue swell up so quickly. That is, outside of Twiki. Her vision went hazy as she watched Erik gingerly slide his fingers under his bandages and yank them apart with a furious thrust. The wrappings disintegrated, and a hail of blood and meat exploded from his destroyed midsection, revealing Twiki's gore-streaked face screaming through his shredded organs!

"No freakin' way," Erik said gloomily. "There is no way this bandage is coming off until there's a doctor around."

Vivian blinked hard and shook her head. Erik's bandages were still intact around his bloated wounds. She pounded her palm against her forehead as a shiver of relief and residual hallucinogenic terror flushed through her body. All other eyes remained fixed on Erik's gruesome belly.

"Hey, what's the big deal? What are we looking at?" Sherri squinted. "C'mere, let me touch it."

Her finger shot out and poked into the bandage. As she touched it, the bony mounds within seemed to close in around her hand. Erik slapped her away with a gasp.

"Holeeeeeeey shit," Bobby said. "Did that feel as bad as it looked?"

"It didn't, actually," Erik shrugged. "She just surprised me. It … it actually doesn't hurt at all."

He poked his own finger at the numb scars.

"In fact, it doesn't feel like *anything*. It's not even warm. It's like—"

"It's like a cadaver's flesh," Sherri said, rubbing her fingers with fascination.

Erik's expression agreed, then tried to deny agreement, then settled on regret for bringing it up at all. He turned and slumped back into his seat without another word.

"Your body's dying," Sherri said. "Pay no attention."

Vivian's face wrinkled at this suggestion, though Erik's words troubled her more than Sherri's did. She knew that the human body released chemical responses to deal with pain, but she couldn't believe that anyone could sustain injuries as severe as Erik's and feel absolutely *nothing*. It wasn't natural. It wasn't right.

It made her wonder about herself.

With the biggest breath that she could accommodate, she straightened her arms against the wheel and pressed her slashed back firmly against the seat. Two streaks of searing pain raced down the parallel gashes in her flesh and up her spine, hitting the bottom of her brain with a flat, heavy punch. She leaned forward, sucking air through clenched teeth and taking small comfort in the lingering burn. Never had she imagined that she'd be so thankful to feel pain.

Sherri pulled her frozen knees to her chest and rolled herself into a tight ball. Her boots on the seat further cramped Trent and Bobby into the walls, but they each silently conceded their space in hopes that it might keep her quiet for a while.

"It's colder than the ninth circle out here," she moaned. "Seriously, Powderpuff, will you pull over already? What's your deal? Are we in bat country or something?"

"For real," Trent agreed. "Either stop the car, or kill me."

"Does it have to be one or the other?" Bobby quipped.

"We can't stop," Vivian said. "I'm sorry that you're all uncomfortable, but until we find safety, nothing short of an act of God will stop this car."

Almost before the words had left her lips, the Rabbit's engine began to convulse under the hood.

"Oh no," Vivian muttered. "Come on, little car. Not now. Not now!"

She furiously pumped the gas pedal, but the engine chugged a rattling death throe and fell silent. The lifeless Rabbit rolled a few hundred feet to a placid stop in the middle of the road.

"What happened?" Erik whimpered. "Why did the car stop?"

"Who cares why it stopped?" Sherri said, stomping on Trent's lap and vaulting out of the vehicle. "As long as we get to get out of the car for a while."

"It's out of gas," Vivian groaned. "I'm sorry. I didn't know. The gauges are all dead. I mean, I knew the fuel wouldn't last forever, but I just filled up last night, and I was hoping that it would last until we got to ... you know ... *something.*"

"Don't sweat it, Vivi," Trent smiled. "You said yourself that only an act of God would stop this car. Maybe we were supposed to stop here. Maybe He's trying to give us some kind of sign."

"Yeah, I'm sure that's it," Sherri said, stretching out her legs with long, ambling steps. "We just drove three hundred miles non-stop in an overloaded beater, and somehow through the majesty and spectacle of God's will we managed to run out of gas. That's it. I'm converted."

Vivian slid out of the car and carefully stretched her weary back and shoulders.

"What do we do now?" Erik said.

"There's only one thing *to* do," Vivian replied. "We're going to have to walk to the next gas station and bring back as much fuel as we can."

"Why do you think the next gas station is within walking distance?" Bobby asked.

Vivian slung the Army backpack over her shoulder.

"Because it has to be."

Hours passed, and the sky slowly cooled from a dismal gray to an earnest black as the five survivors trudged down the derelict highway. In the distance, an enormous rectangle of fluorescent yellow peered through the haze of the encroaching night. An unspoken hope united them all in the idea that this shape was a gas station.

Bobby led the pack, followed by Trent. Sherri followed the cranberry-colored blob of their combined silhouettes in her vision. Erik walked stiffly behind her, his shoulders slumped, his eyes barely focused on the back of her boots. His bloated torso lurched from side to side with each plodding step.

Vivian followed, watching his labored gait and trying to ignore the fact that he looked like something out of *Night of the Living Dead.*

She shook her head to clear the zombie imagery before it could form, throwing herself against a wave of lightheadedness. She breathed in through her nose and out through her mouth, concentrating on pulling the oxygen through her constricted lungs.

"We've been walking for hours," Erik moaned. "If we don't find something soon, somebody's going to have to carry me."

"S'no problem, eh!" Bobby said.

"Really? Cool. I was expecting a little more resistance than that."

"No. *S'no problem,*" Bobby repeated. "Look."

Erik lifted his gaze from Sherri's boots and looked to the side of the road, and his entire field of vision was filled with a blinding shade of Day-Glo lemon. The structure that they had been hiking toward was not a building at all, but a billboard of disgustingly gratuitous proportions.

From the left side of the sign, a cartoon Canadian Mountie towered thirty feet into the air, chest deep in snow and holding aloft a shovel. Despite his hypothermic predicament, the grin on his face and the twinkle in his Pac-Man-shaped eyes betrayed no fear of death. To the right was a field of hot-pink text in block letters three feet tall. Trent read them aloud.

"Pierre sez, 'S'no problem, eh!' North of the Border - 363 miles."

"S'no problem my *ass,*" Sherri griped. "I'm tired, I'm blind, and my butt crack is frozen shut. I'm done."

Her bony legs crumpled, dropping her body into a lethargic sprawl across the pavement.

"When you get the car started, come back and run me the fuck over."

"I'm with Sherri," Bobby said. "I'm beat, and it's getting dark. Well, *darker.* Looks like it's time to stop for the night."

"What do you mean, 'stop for the night'?!" Erik squeaked. "What are we supposed to do? Just lay down here by the side of the highway and go to sleep like a bunch of rail-riding hobos? Are you insane?!"

"I'm sorry, Erik," Bobby sighed. "All of the five-star places were booked up tonight."

"No, I agree with Erik," Vivian said. "We have to keep moving. We have to find some shelter before it gets dark. It's not safe here."

"Look, we've been walking for hours and we haven't seen jack shit," Bobby said. "I'm sorry, but we're on the interstate in the middle of nowhere. It's safer to just stay put until morning. We don't want to be wandering around once it turns blacker than Darth Vader's codpiece out here."

Vivian's panicked breath surged against her bandages, yet her lungs refused to accept the air. They couldn't just stay here in the open. It was illogical. It was dangerous! Her corset suddenly felt tight enough to splinter her ribs. In desperation, she turned to the one person who was guaranteed to go along with anything she said.

"What do you think, Trent? We should keep going until we find shelter, right?"

"Sorry Vivi, consider me with Heavy B," Trent said. "My dogs are barkin', yo. It's time to bed down and get some serious sleep on. But there's no need for unease, girl. We're all safe here."

Vivian's eyebrows arched in disbelief.

"Safe? What makes you think that?"

"That's the sign. The sign from God," Trent said, pointing at the billboard. "He wanted to tell us that there's no problem. We're safe here."

"That is *not* a sign from God!" Erik argued. "It's barely even a sign for some crappy North Carolina tourist trap! It's just a bad pun and a rip-off of Dudley Do-Right!"

"That's two for, two against," Bobby said. "Sherri, you're the tiebreaker. Whaddya say?"

Sherri rolled over and pressed her cheek into the pavement.

"Put me down for whatever says I don't have to get up."

"That's it then," Bobby said, collapsing into the grass. "We're down for the night."

"But … but!" Vivian stammered. "But, you guys, seriously! We've got no protection!"

"You've got all the protection you need right here, baby," Trent said, holding out his arms. "Come on over here and get enveloped in a field of securi-T."

"You guys, this is serious," Vivian pleaded. "If we're going to stay here, we need to at least build a fire before it gets any colder."

"Ix-nay on the ire-fay," Trent said. "Don't go messing with the equation, Vivi. We're safe now. A fire might just attract those things that go bump in the night. Besides, you've got all the warmth you need right here, my little frost bunny."

With a broad grin, Trent again held out his arms. Vivian ignored him and began searching through the tall grass for sticks.

"Bobby, come and help me with this, please?"

The heap of her brother returned nothing but a resounding snore from the very base of his sinuses.

"Great," Vivian muttered. "Thanks a lot, Bob."

She could feel her face prickle with hot frustration. Why wouldn't anyone just help her?

"I'll help you," Erik said.

He smiled and took a stiff, lurching step toward her. Vivian stared into the bloated wounds peeking from beneath his shirt.

"Oh, uh … thanks, Erik. But you shouldn't exert yourself with your … I mean … you really don't have to—"

"Yeah, quit being such a kiss-ass, Little E," Trent sneered, holding out his arms. "She can stay plenty warm tonight without your help."

"He's right," Vivian said.

Her face crunched in revulsion.

"I mean, he's *not* right, but you're all … I mean … Look, you're in no condition to—"

"I'm okay," Erik said, squatting laboriously to pick up a stick. "I want to help you get a fire going."

"Of course you do," Trent grumbled. "Lousy cock block."

"Trent, are you going to help us or not?" Vivian snapped.

"I *am* helping! I tell you, this fire is not meant to be, Vivi," Trent yawned, slouching down against the front of the sign. "When you get tired of your little fire idea, my offer, and my arms, stay open all night, girl."

He put his hands behind his head, kicked his legs apart on the ground, and closed his eyes smugly.

Vivian took a shallow breath, unclenched her jaw, and went back to gathering sticks. Although crippled by his wounds, Erik worked diligently with only minor grunts of complaint. In about ten minutes they had gathered a decent stack of kindling by the shoulder of the road. They squatted next to it, surrounded by a silence broken only by three points of faint snoring nearby.

"Thanks for your help," Vivian said.

"Eh, I had to," Erik shrugged. "If it gets any colder out here, *I'm* gonna take Trent up on his offer."

Vivian smiled weakly. She picked up two of the larger sticks and started rubbing them together.

"Oh no," Erik said. "What are you doing?"

"What does it look like I'm doing? I'm starting the fire. Of all people, surely *you* have seen somebody do this in a movie."

"No, I haven't! Have *you?*" Erik moaned. "Oh man, I thought you had a lighter in your purse! This will never work."

Vivian lowered her sticks.

"Why not?"

"Because it's just a cheap plot device. Have you ever noticed that every time a civilized person in a movie tries to make a fire, he says 'I saw this once in a movie,' then he rubs the sticks for an hour but never gets it to work? Only faithful Indian guides and crafty indigenous aliens can actually pull off that trick. It's how the screenwriter teaches the jaded urban protagonist to appreciate a simpler way of life."

"Don't be ridiculous," Vivian said. "It's just simple physics. Friction makes heat; heat makes fire."

"I'm sorry, Vivian," Erik frowned. "We probably would have had better luck using your glasses to focus the sunlight. That one always works."

He looked at the blackened sky.

"Well … when there's sunlight."

Vivian continued her stick-rubbing.

"Well, this isn't a movie," she muttered. "Trust me, this will work."

She rubbed her sticks furiously. She had laid down dry brush for kindling. There was sufficient airflow around the friction surfaces. She knew what she was doing, and she was doing everything right. Yet after many long minutes of increasingly sloppy strokes, she dropped the cold sticks and resigned to a gasping defeat.

"Damn it!" she wheezed, tugging at her constricting bandages. "This … should … work …"

"Oh Viv, I'm so sorry," Erik said, putting his hand on her icy shoulder. "I'm not trying to be a jerk or anything; I was just telling it like it is. The stick thing just doesn't work. Ever. We may as well just go to sleep."

Vivian leaned dizzily into Erik's chest as she struggled for air. A stagnant aroma of skin oil and rotten cabbage wafted from her hair into his nose, but he didn't mind. He put his arm around her, gently squeezing her against his gnarled midsection. As his scars pressed against her, Vivian gasped and shoved herself away from him. Her cheeks blushed as her eyes flicked guiltily to the ground.

"Right, uh … yeah," she said with forced nonchalance. "So, okay. No fire then."

Erik knew what she was thinking.

"It's okay, Viv. I'm going to be all right. I promise I'm not going to hur—"

He stopped and shook his head.

"Not going to *let anything* hurt you."

He put his hands over his scars and stared silently into the night. Vivian lay down in the rough grass. Although there was no light at all, she could swear that she could see a blue glow coming from behind Erik's bandages. She tried to blink her eyes and realized that they were already closed. A minute later, she was lost in a black and dreamless sleep.

Erik watched Vivian's exposed, vulnerable body shivering against the ground, and an idea congealed within his muddled head.

CHAPTER SEVEN

Vivian lurched into consciousness with a gasping breath. Her lungs felt as if a set of encyclopedias had been stacked on her chest. She sat up and found herself swaddled in a blanket of Day-Glo yellow Mylar emblazoned with an enormous pink "3." She blinked hard, letting her poorly rested eyes soak up her surroundings.

Directly to her side was the pile of sticks that she and Erik had collected, still intact, still unburned. In the dim gray light of this perversion of morning, the pile looked exactly as it had in twilight. Exactly the same, except for the shredded bark.

And the blood.

Her mind reeled as she kicked her way out of her impromptu sleeping bag and stumbled to her feet. Once the blanket was off, she realized that it too was smeared with broad swaths of dried blood.

She quickly examined herself as her heart hammered against her compressed lungs. The blood wasn't hers. Her eyes flashed around the sketchy campsite.

Bobby and Trent were exactly where she had left them the night before, unconscious and vigorously snoring. Sherri lay on her back in the middle of the road with her limbs splayed like Da Vinci's Vitruvian Man. They were all unharmed.

A blanket-sized hole had been torn in the face of the billboard, truncating the distance to North of the Border to only 36 miles. Vivian's panicked eyes darted so quickly that she passed over what she was looking for three full times before she spotted it in the billboard's shadow: Erik's body, showing no apparent signs of life.

"Erik?" she squeaked. "Are you okay?"

She scrambled over to where he lay, and her hand clapped to her mouth to stifle a scream. His chest was soaked in dried blood, covered with the palm of his limp hand.

"Erik?" she gasped, dropping to her knees. "Erik!"

She pulled his hand off of his bloody chest and let out a relieved breath.

There was no massive chest wound. There wasn't even a rip in his shirt. But the blood?

She turned his hand over to find his slender palm fringed with ragged skin. His other hand was wrapped around her Swiss Army Knife, soaked in the blood of another mangled palm and tangled with fibers of yellow plastic. With Vivian yanking at his arms, Erik roused groggily.

"Erik!" she cried. "What happened?"

Erik blinked dimly.

"Rubbin' sticks didden work," he mumbled. "Made a blanket insead."

With that, he closed his eyes and slumped wearily into the dirt. The previous night unraveled in Vivian's mind. He must have rubbed those sticks for *hours* before giving up and devising a Plan B.

"Oh Erik, why did you do this to yourse—"

She squatted down next to Erik's collapsed body, but before she could right him, she noticed something beyond the edge of the billboard. She blinked hard to clear the mirage, but it remained steadfast, not a hundred yards behind the tower of tourist trap advertising. Nestled off the highway, on a loop of blacktop that could only be called an offramp in the most liberal of definitions, sat a sleepy little mom-and-pop gas station surrounded by a platoon of Jeeps in various states of decomposition.

Vivian grabbed Erik by the shoulders and shook him from his dozing.

"Erik, you found it!"

"Wha? Whadd I find?"

Vivian stood up and turned toward the others with glee.

"You guys! Wake up! Wake up and come here!"

She heard the sounds of interrupted snoring, muffled stirring, and coughed obscenities coming from the other side of the massive sign. A moment later, Bobby, Trent, and Sherri had assembled at her side.

"A gas station!" Vivian pointed. "Look! Erik found it!"

"Little E didn't find anything, oh ye of little faith," Trent grumbled. "It was the sign, yo. The *sign* led to our salvation. Just like the T told you it would."

"Yeah, nice work," Bobby said sarcastically. "We could have slept inside that building last night if God hadn't put this giant comforting sign in our way."

"Or we could have walked past it in the dark and never found it at all," Trent countered.

Sherri interrupted with a rasping, trachea-blistering cough.

"You gonna live?" Bobby asked.

"Yeah, yeah," Sherri croaked. "I just need my wake-up smoke. Man, I'd give anything for a cigarette right now."

"A lot of good it would do ya," Erik said, raising his shredded palms. "Even if you had one, you couldn't light it."

Sherri turned to him with incomprehension.

"Why not?"

She whipped out a Zippo lighter and produced two inches of yellow-blue flame with a snap of her finger against the flintwheel. Erik folded his clotting palms under his arms with a scowl.

"Never mind."

"Well, I don't know about you good folks, but I'm starvin' like Lee Marvin," Trent said, thrusting out a genteel elbow. "I know we skipped the step that traditionally comes before, but could I escort you to breakfast anyway, Vivi?"

"Go to Hell, Trent," Vivian growled.

"I'd go anywhere for you," Trent said. "But I won't go there."

"Jesus, I've only been awake for five seconds, and you people are already annoying the piss out of me," Sherri said. "Let me at that gas station already. I need a pack of cancer sticks."

Following Sherri's lead, the group stretched the remaining sleep out of their bodies and headed for the nearby filling station.

The gas station was what some would describe as "antebellum quaint." A Confederate flag fluttered limply in the breeze from a flagpole jutting from the side of the building, and over the door hung a weathered sign bearing the words "The South will rise again!"

The weed-infested Jeeps that crouched near the building leaked various noxious fluids into the dry dirt. Whoever had accumulated these derelicts had obviously been trying to cobble their remains into one working specimen, and had obviously failed.

In the driveway sat two gas pumps from a time in history somewhere after "antique" but before "modern," just skirting the edge of "obsolete." The building's front porch was haunted by a wooden rocking chair and a chunky red cooler with a white swoosh.

"All right!" Erik cheered. "The pause that refreshes!"

He scrambled onto the porch and yanked open the antique cooler. He pulled out a bottle, wrenched off the top, and dumped the whole thing down his dry throat without coming up for air.

"Ahhh," he said with a satisfied belch. "Can't beat the real thing."

"It's about time," Sherri said, stomping onto the porch and sticking out her hand. "Gimme one!"

Erik popped open another bottle and slipped it into her fingers.

"Catch the wave," he smiled.

Sherri plugged the bottle into her lips, took an impressively long swig, and then spat out the soda like a carbonated volcano.

"Aaaugh! This isn't beer!" she gasped, foam dripping from her chin. "Why didn't you say this was Coke?"

"Didn't I?" Erik asked.

"This is bullshit," Sherri declared. "I'm going to find some real food."

"I'm with you," Bobby agreed. "Let's eat already. I feel like somebody did an 'rm star' on my stomach."

He grabbed the handle of the sagging front door and wrenched it open, and an overwhelming stench of putrid meat poured from the interior of the store, forcing everyone to take a step back and interject their favorite expletive.

"Good Lord," Trent muttered. "What crawled all up in there and died?"

"It smells like everything in the meat cooler has spoiled," Vivian said. "This place has probably been without power for about two days now."

"Fuck it," Sherri sighed, pulling her T-shirt over her nose. "I'm starving. I don't care what it smells like—I'm getting some breakfast."

She marched through the door's dark outline in the strawberry jam of her vision.

"You gotta do what you gotta do," Bobby shrugged, pulling his own shirt over his face. "C'mon, let's go shoplifting."

Vivian stood on the front porch, looking into the shadowy darkness on the other side of the door. Although the stench of rancid meat was overpowering, all she could smell was burnt soda and spilt blood running down her chin. As her nose tingled with phantom odors, the two claw scars burned up and down her back. There was a simple pattern. Every time she went into a building something very bad happened to her.

"I … I'm not actually that hungry. It's … you know, the smell and everything," she said with affected nonchalance. "Erik, could you please just grab me something for later?"

Erik stared through the darkened doorway, paralyzed. In the unknown darkness within, he could only picture two charred corpses disintegrating into tons of collapsing parking garage. Independently reaching the same conclusion that Vivian had, he took a nervous step backward.

"Nuh-uh. No. No way," he stammered. "Forget breakfast—I wouldn't go in there for all the food in a 'Weird Al' song."

Trent shook his head, then bowed before Vivian and kissed her hand with a smarmy grin.

"*I'll* bring you something, sweet Vivi," he said. "We *real* men exist only to serve the fairer sex. I would be honored to bring you whatever tasty treats your little heart desires."

Vivian turned her eyes to the ground shamefully.

"Thanks, Trent. I'm not picky. Just bring me something that's not spoiled and has some nutritional value, please."

"Your wish is my command," Trent cooed, holding his nose and sweeping himself into the store.

"God, what a tool," Erik grumbled. "Bobby, could you grab something for me too while you're in there?"

"Ha! Do I look like I want to get into your pants?" Bobby said. "Get your own food, wussy."

"Come on, Bobby," Erik whimpered. "I don't care what it is—just grab me something, okay?"

"God, you are such a pain in the ass," Bobby grumbled.

He stepped into the store and grabbed the first thing he could reach. It was a bucket full of three-foot-long plastic straws. He stuffed it into Erik's hands.

"Thaaya. Guurly men get Pixy Stix," he bellowed in a bad Austrian accent. "Eat uup, flabby man."

Erik's face fell.

"Thanks, man. That'll ... that'll be okay. I guess."

Bobby rolled his eyes.

"Dude. Don't be so sensitive, I was just messin' with ya. Don't worry, I'll find you guys something good. But if you aren't coming in here, you have to find some way to get the gas back to the car. Deal?"

"Okay, yeah. Right!" Erik nodded. "Okay, deal. Thanks, Bobby."

Bobby took the Army backpack from Vivian and disappeared into the store. Erik pulled one of the huge Pixy Stix from the bucket and dropped heavily onto the front step. He put it to his lips and gently tipped it upward, launching a bolt of blue sugar straight down his throat. His head lurched forward with a gagging cough, spilling a mouthful of thick blue drool down his chin and through his slashed hands.

"Ow! Ow! Shit!" he choked, wiping his palms on his shirt. "That smarts!"

With each explosive cough, Vivian could see his infected scars leap against their bindings, pressing nightmarish lumps against the thin fabric.

"Erik," she ventured, "are you, you know ... okay?"

"Yeah, yeah, I'm fine," he said. "I hate these mutant-sized Pixy Stix. Every time I put one in my mouth I end up almost choking to death."

"No no," Vivian said, "I mean, are you ... *okay?*"

Erik squinted at her.

"Ohhhh, right," he nodded, looking at his torn-up palms. "Yeah, I'm okay. I just wish I'd thought of cutting a blanket out of the billboard *before* I tried to make a fire. I guess I've never really done anything more rugged than playing ColecoVision."

Vivian rolled her eyes. She couldn't tell whether Erik was intentionally dodging her question or not. Either way, she did owe him some gratitude.

"Thanks for trying to make a fire for me, and for the blanket. You didn't have to do that."

"Eh, you know. It's no big deal," Erik said shyly. "I couldn't sleep last night anyway. Let's just say that I don't exactly feel okay."

Vivian's eyes widened.

"So you *don't* feel okay?" she asked nervously. "How so?"

"Well, uh ... to put it discreetly, I feel like I haven't taken a dump since

Mork and Mindy was on the air."

Vivian closed her eyes tightly as if to shut out that imagery.

"Well, thank you," she muttered. "Just … thanks again, for everything."

"Hey, it's no problem," Erik smiled.

Vivian knew it was just from the candy, but it still bothered her that his teeth had turned a bright, glistening blue.

Bobby, Sherri, and Trent fanned out between the blue steel shelves of the tiny convenience store. Its few windows were small and ineffectively placed, allowing only a thin veil of light to intrude.

"Whoa, it's like if Rambo moved to Hazzard County," Bobby quipped. "Look at this place!"

Above the shelves of expired snack foods and warm sodas, the upper perimeter of the store was encircled with pictures torn from gun and girlie magazines. From where he was standing, Bobby could see a postcard from Stone Mountain Park ("The Mount Rushmore of the South!"), a poster of a Camaro painted up in camouflage, and half a dozen pin-ups of melon-breasted bikini models holding oversized firearms.

"Disgusting," Trent said. "Women are not objects."

With a quick glance over his shoulder, he snagged a picture of a voluptuous redhead with a flamethrower and stuffed it in his pocket.

"Hey, B-Money," he continued, "what delicacies would tickle your fine sister's discriminating palate? As her knight in shining armor, I intend to bring her back a meal that's fit for a princess, such as she is."

Bobby sighed deeply and ran his hand over his stubbly face.

"Look, Trent, I'm going to level with you here in an attempt to save us all a lot of headache. You are not going to sleep with Vivian. Ever. Trust me, I've seen her reject guys that were only *one-tenth* as disgusting as you."

Trent shrugged.

"Just you watch, dawg. Once the T turns on the charm, the ladies always—"

"Dude! Seriously," Bobby interrupted. "Give it up. It ain't gonna happen."

"Come on, B. We're pals!" Trent nudged. "Give me the inside scoop. What's it gonna take to win her over?"

Bobby blew a long breath through pursed lips and shook his head.

"Okay. How can I put this so that you can understand it? The *only way* you would even have the *slightest possibility* of a *chance* with Vivian is if *every single other guy on the planet* was *dead*. Do you get that?"

"Oh, I get it," Trent said with a smarmy grin. "But I think you underestimate me."

Bobby rubbed his eyes with his thumb and forefinger.

"It's like trying to reason with monkey testicles."

While the boys argued, Sherri turned in a slow circle, dragging her stare across the walls with a sneering squint. All she could see were four rectangles of pink light hanging in a field of darkness. The first was the door she had just come in through, followed by three windows. She held out her hand until she touched a shelf, then followed it, grasping its contents and looking them over with her blistered fingertips. Half a dozen unidentifiable cleaning products passed through her hands before thumping to the floor, rejected. She tore open a bag of Fritos only to find upon her first greedy mouthful that it was actually dry macaroni. After a second mouthful proved to be no better than the first, she dropped the bag with a clatter and continued down the shelf.

"Man, this place smells like a heavy girl on a hot day," Trent coughed. "Let's make with a little freshness in here."

He picked up two cans of aerosol deodorant, popped the caps off with his thumbs, and proceeded to spray down the fetid air with the flowery scent of shower-fresh underarms.

"Mr. Clean and the Scrubbing Bubbles working in ten-hour shifts couldn't take the stink out of this place," Bobby said, taking a can from Trent. "There is, however, still hope for my cabbagey ass."

He shoved the deodorant under his T-shirt and sprayed down his squalid armpits. He pulled the can from under his shirt, shrugged, and sprayed down the rest of his body. Trent sniffed under his own arm, winced, and followed Bobby's example.

"Whoo!" he hooted. "That B.O. has got to G.O."

He wandered into the next aisle and found Sherri, her mouth full and a trickle of thick brown saliva running down her chin.

"You schmell like vending machine tamponsh," she slurred.

Trent looked at her chomping jaw and grinned.

"So tell me, Elvira, what does a goth girl eat for breakfast?"

Sherri flashed a box of Count Chocula from under her arm.

"Typical," Trent laughed, picking up his own box of cereal and tearing off its top.

Sherri swallowed and wiped her mouth on what was left of her sleeve.

"So tell me, Preppie," she said sweetly, "what does an overcompensating closet queer eat for breakfast?"

Trent stopped in mid-chew and looked guiltily at his box of Fruity Pebbles.

"This means nothing."

"Here, take a hit of this, Stinky," Bobby interrupted, pressing a deodorant can into Sherri's free hand. "It's strong enough for a man, but it's made for an angry little woman."

Sherri dropped the can on the floor and went back to her cereal.

"Nah. I'm fine."

"Fine?" Bobby said. "Not hardly, cabbage pits. You smell like the baby that

Xavier Roberts threw away."

"I don't wear deodorant," Sherri said. "That's how the Man marks you with his scent and makes you his property. It's just like how dogs piss on trees. Every time that you wear deodorant, you're just letting the Man piss on you."

"Fine. Have it your way, Little Miss Tinfoil Hat," Bobby said, picking up the can and stuffing it into the backpack. "I'll just save it so Viv and Erik can have a spray."

"And then you'll be stanky all by your lonesome in your own little stanky club of one," Trent said. "Girl, don't you even want to *try* to be like everybody else?"

Sherri shook her head.

"You know, sometimes I can't tell if you're kidding, or if you're actually that fucking clueless."

Outside the store, Vivian and Erik had separated, each searching out a way to carry the gas back to the Rabbit.

Erik squatted on the ground to the side of the front porch, his arm shoulder-deep in its nether recesses. Its floor was held up by a series of thick, wooden beams caging a tangle of weeds and various abandoned tools. Under the porch, his fingers fumbled against the rusted handle of a watering can.

"Come on …"

His sneakers dug at the hard earth as he tried to force his arm just another centimeter closer to his prize. The can could carry at least a gallon of fuel, if he could just get his hands on it. With his cheek pressed harshly into the boards, a throbbing pressure spread across his jawbone and right eyeball.

"Come on!" he hissed. "Come on, you little bastard!"

With a final chest-deflating exhale and a thrust of his legs, he caught the handle and yanked it through the weeds. The can crashed to a halt against the support beams, sending a shockwave through his bony arm. He tried to yank the can free again and again, but it just slammed against the bars of its prison with a series of frantic clangs. It was too wide.

"But … but! Oh, come on!"

He took a deep breath and closed his eyes. When he opened them, he had gained the clarity to turn his wrist ninety degrees, aligning the tall can with the gap and easily pulling it through.

"No sweat," he sighed, wiping the sweat off of his brow.

He brushed his hands together, knocking the rust crumbles from the star-spangled maroon of his freshly bandaged palms. Climbing to his feet, he pushed aside a Confederate flag that had shrunk by several ragged inches.

"Hey Viv!" he said, holding aloft his prize. "I found something to carry the gas in!"

"Great!" Vivian said. "I found some too."

Erik stepped around the corner of the porch and froze in disbelief. In front of the pumps was Vivian, flanked by six five-gallon gas cans.

"Where did *those* come from?" he asked.

"From the Jeep junkyard," Vivian said. "They were strapped into holsters on the backs of some of them. What did you find?"

Erik looked at his hard-won watering can, noticing for the first time that it had no bottom.

"Nothing," he said bitterly. "Forget it."

He dropped the can onto the pavement, splintering off its brittle spout. With a flush of anger he kicked the can as hard as he could, shattering it against the side of the derelict pump.

"Whoa, Erik!" Vivian cringed. "Chill out."

Erik squeezed his eyes shut and shook his head as if waking from a dream.

"I'm sorry," he muttered. "I don't feel like myself today."

An icy chill ran down Vivian's spine.

"If you don't feel like yourself, then … what *do* you feel like?"

Erik glared.

"Look, I'm just beat-up and tired, okay?! Quit treating me like I'm about to claw your skull open and eat your brains! It's me, Erik. I'm cool."

Vivian tipped her eyes to the ground.

"I'm sorry. You're right. I'm just scared. I shouldn't be taking it out on you."

Erik shrugged.

"Forget it. Let's just get these tanks filled, okay?"

Vivian nodded. She stuck the nozzle of the pump into the open mouth of the first gas can and pulled the handle.

Nothing happened.

"What's wrong?" Erik asked.

"It's not working," Vivian said, pumping the trigger.

"But … but it has to work!"

Vivian shook her head with realization.

"No … it doesn't have to work. It doesn't have to work at *all*," she moaned, shoving the nozzle back onto its hook. "God, I am so *stupid*."

"What? Why are you stupid?" Erik asked desperately. "Why doesn't it work?"

"The pumps. They're machines. They need electricity, just like everything else."

"But … but this isn't how it's supposed to work!" Erik stammered. "We beat the level boss! We found the gas station! We won!"

He picked up the nozzle and clicked the trigger on and off. Not a drop of fuel fell from its tip. He dropped it into the dust and buried his head in his arms against the side of the pump, kicking it fitfully.

"This isn't right! This isn't how it's supposed to work!"

Vivian watched Erik's tantrum in silence. She felt the same frustration, but a lack of oxygen had her feeling too light-headed to express it as passionately. Turning discreetly away, she put her thumb between her squashed breasts and into the top of her corset of bandages, lifting it as far from her constricted chest as she could. Stretching the wrap in one direction only tightened it in another, but the breath that she gasped into her crushed lungs still seemed somehow fresher. She exhaled deeply and turned back to Erik, finding him with the pump nozzle in his mouth and his cheeks collapsed in suction.

"Erik!" she squeaked. "What the hell are you doing?"

Erik pulled the hose from his mouth and swallowed a lungful of air.

"Got ... to ... get ... gas," he gasped. "Only ... way ..."

He put the hose back into his mouth and continued to violently suck. Vivian yanked the nozzle from his lips, knocking his asphyxiated body backward onto the ground.

"Stop it," she said. "That's not going to work. You don't have the lung capacity to pull a column of gasoline up a hose this wide."

"Then we'll get Trent to do it."

"No, you don't understand," Vivian said. "It's impossible. The laws of physics are against you."

"No no. Physics are with me," Erik argued. "My grandpa used to suck gas out of Grandma's car to run his lawnmower. I just need to create a siphon, and physics will do all the work. It'll work!"

He grabbed the hose, but Vivian put her palm over the tip before he could shove it back into his mouth.

"It *won't* work," she said firmly. "For a siphon to work, the fluid has to be moving from a higher to a lower elevation. You can't pull gas from an underground tank that way. Not with your lungs."

"My eighty-six-year-old grandpa used to be able to do it, and you're saying I can't?"

"No. Yes. Listen," Vivian said, gesturing with her hands. "Your grandpa's siphon worked because it was going from the tank up *here* to a tank down *here*. We could *easily* get gas out of something like ... like one of those Jeeps, for example, because the gas tank is so high off the ground, you see?"

Vivian's eyes widened and blinked involuntarily, as if a very solid idea had just pounded into her brain.

Inside the store, Sherri walked with blind determination until her outstretched palms connected with something solid. With a sweep of her arms and a flutter of her bony fingers she explored the objects on its surface. Her left hand hit a small cardboard box, and her fingers scurried inside, feeling out two plastic and metal tubes.

"Oh, fuck me. I can't find a cigarette to save my life, but I can always find lipstick."

She picked up the box with the intention of throwing it at the nearest wall, but instead paused and licked her uncharacteristically pink lips. Without turning, she pulled one of the heavy tubes from the box and held it in the air.

"Hey, what color is this lipstick?" she demanded.

On the other side of the store, Bobby was thumbing through a rack of road maps. He stuffed an east coast highway map into his back pocket and squinted at Sherri in the dim light.

"Looks black," he said.

"I'll be damned," Sherri shrugged. "It's my lucky day."

"Just like a woman," Trent sighed. "You send them to get food, and they come back with makeup."

"Why don't you come here and I'll put some on you?" Sherri said. "That way you can leave a receipt when you *kiss* my *ass!*"

"Knock it off, you two," Bobby barked. "Your charming banter isn't getting us out of this stinkbox any faster."

With an unintelligible grumble, Sherri stuffed both tubes into her coat pocket and continued her groping exploration. Her left hand hit paper. She picked it up. It was a book. Not too thick. Paperback. Damp. Irrelevant. She threw it over her shoulder and heard it flutter to rest on the ground.

Her right hand brushed against a square plastic dish. She dove into its shallow bowl to find three pennies, a toothpick, and a cigarette butt. Although she couldn't see it, she knew the dish was red and it said "Take a penny. Leave a penny." She had wasted innumerable hours of her life staring into one exactly like it on her checkstand at Boltzmann's Market. From this seed of familiarity, the rest of her immediate surroundings spilled out in the darkness of her mind's eye.

Her left hand shot below the counter. Paper. Glossy. Serrated edge.

"Tabloids …"

Her right hand broke right. Square. Textured plastic. Keypad.

"Cash register …"

Both hands shot up, connecting with an expanse of smooth plastic holding a sheet of bent cardstock across its front.

"Cigarette rack!"

She turned her back toward the counter, planted her palms on its edge, and hopped her skinny behind up onto it, leaning back as far as the counterweight of her boots would allow. Both of her hands launched skyward and landed in a fully stocked rack of cigarettes, eliciting a gleeful smile from her peeling face.

"Merry fuckin' Christmas to me!"

Seconds later, Sherri was lying blissfully across the counter, sucking down lungful after ragged lungful of yellow smoke with a languid satisfaction that could have been mistaken for post-coital. Her immodest posture only added to the illusion: legs thrown apart, one boot resting on top of the register, the other swinging limply over the side of the counter. As she smoked, she noticed that the smell of decay seemed stronger here than anywhere else in the store.

"Alright, I'm done. Let's get out of here," she said. "It's like something died, but in a *bad* way."

"For real. I can't understand how this place can smell so freak nasty of food gone bad when everything in here has a longer shelf life than the Temptations," Trent said, scanning the ingredients on a bag of Texas Grill Fritos. "I realize this is just a place for weary travelers to sugar themselves up enough to get another piece down the road, but damn, homes. Vivi wants nutritional value, and this whole store has a lower vitamin content than my shampoo."

"Uber-non-perishable snacks are a good thing," Bobby said, taking the bag of Fritos and stuffing it into his backpack. "We don't have refrigeration, and we don't know how long it's gonna be before we get wherever we're going. Besides, the body doesn't need nutrients. You just need to put something inside to balance out the atmospheric pressure."

Trent patted Bobby's bulbous stomach with a condescending smile.

"And that, my friend, is why you are two seventy-five and are barely alive, and I'm a cut one-eighty and get all the ladies."

"Hah! Whatever," Bobby snorted. "I'm pushin' three bills with the mad love skills, and you're one-eighty-eight and prone to masturbate."

"Holy shit," Sherri gasped, pulling her T-shirt over her nose. "Nobody told me that Trent's bullshit mouth is contagious!"

Trent swaggered over and leaned on the counter with a grin and a salacious glance.

"I believe it's called 'infectious charm,'" he oozed. "And everyone catches it sooner or later."

"I believe it's called my skirt," Sherri growled. "And everyone who stares up it gets their eyes gouged out."

The lascivious expression fell from Trent's face as he broke eye contact with the skull and crossbones glaring back at him from the crotch of Sherri's exposed panties.

"B ... but I thought you were blind!"

"I am," Sherri said, swinging her legs off the counter and hopping down. "But you're just so fucking *predictable*."

Trent opened his mouth to reply, but then promptly lost his grasp on the English language.

"Oh m-m-my ..."

"Oh relax," Sherri said. "It's just women's underwear. You'll get used to it after you've seen it more than one time."

Bobby noticed the small booklet on the floor and picked it up, flipping through its red-flecked pages as he approached the counter.

"Hey, check this out. *Proper Cleaning and Maintenance of your Remington Firearm.* Huh. That's a weird thing to find on the floor of a—"

A gasp choked his words as he peered behind the counter.

"Holy *shit!*"

Sherri stuffed her cigarette in her mouth and crossed her arms in resignation.

"It's another killer mutant, isn't it?" she said dryly.

"M ... my ... my ... God ..." Trent stammered.

Sherri spat her smoldering butt toward the sound of his voice. The hot ember bounced off his forehead, breaking him from his trance.

"No, not a mutant," Bobby said at last. "Just a redneck who couldn't follow simple instructions."

"It's easy," Vivian said. "I'll show you how it works."

She had both hands wrapped around the empty Pixy Stix tube, which was planted into the gas tank of one of the Jeeps like a straw in an olive drab malt. Erik watched her demonstration as she continued.

"The trick is to get a column of gasoline in the tube *without* sucking it all the way into your mouth. Watch."

She wrapped her lips around the end of the tube and gave it a gentle suck, and her lungs instantly felt like they were being sat upon by a Brontosaurus. Her head began to pound, but she kept at it, sucking with all of her diminished might.

Erik watched silently. Through the translucent sides of the tube he could see a tiny percolation of fuel inching upward, then slipping back into the tank. Watching Vivian's lips work the top of the shaft reminded him of a magazine that the older kids had once shown him at summer camp, and his face flushed with embarrassment.

Vivian's vision crumbled into a mosaic of green and black distortion. With each pull she could feel the air being crushed into paper-thin sheets as it was squeezed through the rollers of her lungs. The front of her brain throbbed as if being poked with the butt end of a pool cue. She stumbled, catching herself against the side of the Jeep.

"I ... can't ... do ..." she gasped.

"It's okay; it's okay," Erik said, shifting his weight in an attempt to hide his raging erection. "I get it. I can do it. You just relax."

He took the tube in one hand and grabbed his shirt to wipe it off. Remembering everything that his filthy shirt had been through, he thought better of the idea and just put the sticky tube into his mouth as it was. He could taste the warm, rotten cabbage of Vivian's saliva, and it gave him a fluttering feeling in his stomach.

"My stomach's gonna go inside out, for real," Trent muttered. "That shit ain't right."

Sherri blinked blindly.

"What? What shit ain't right?"

She turned toward the checkout counter and squinted into a scarlet-splattered darkness. Of course, all she could see were the shadows of her own blood-soaked corneas, but had she retained her sight, the view would not have been very much different. Just over the register, a narrow wire brush was embedded in the wall, encrusted in a thin layer of dried gore. The brush pointed into the mouth of a double-barreled shotgun leaning against the front of a rocking chair. Between the end of the barrel and the brush was a gangly gas-station clerk, outfitted with gray camouflage fatigues and with a rather sizable hole that started in his chin and went clean through the back of his mullet. The wall behind the counter was covered by a huge, blood-splattered Confederate flag with the words "DIXIE MILITIA" written across it in uneven black brushstrokes.

"Congratulations, Sherri," Bobby said dryly. "You found the source of the smell."

Trent pulled an old field radio from a nail at the side of the counter. The knob was turned to the "on" position, but it was silent. He clicked it back and forth a few times but failed to bring it to life.

"Come on, speak to me," Sherri coached. "What are we looking at here, people?"

Trent returned the radio to the nail and made the sign of the cross.

"This poor bastard must have got the 411 about the bad-ass shit going down out there and decided to bust a cap in his own ass before somebody else could."

"So it's a guy who Kurt Cobained himself?" Sherri asked.

"Not a chance," Bobby said. "This wasn't suicide. This is Darwinism at work."

He flipped open the blood-sprinkled instruction manual.

"*Always make sure that your firearm is unloaded before cleaning!*" he read. "Page one, fifty-point font, bold print. He probably heard an emergency broadcast and got so excited about his chance to mow down some Yankee tourists that he lost his head. No pun intended."

Trent's stomach violently heaved, but nothing came out of his mouth but noise and bad breath. He covered his mouth with both hands, but he didn't stop looking at the body.

"Alright, show's over," Bobby muttered, dropping the manual. "Let's get the hell out of here before Trent loses a lung."

Sherri reached behind the counter and grabbed as many packs of cigarettes as her mangled pockets could hold.

"Fine by me. I got what I came for."

Before Sherri and Bobby could take two steps toward the door, Trent held out a hand for pause.

"Wait, wait," he said. "We should take it."

"What for?" Sherri said. "To give it a proper burial and a headstone that says 'Dumb Redneck Asshole - Died 1999 - Good Riddance'?"

"No, no," Trent said. "Not the body. The shotgun. Next time we run into one of Satan's fun-time freakouts, I'd like to have a little bit of phat firepower in our corner."

"You know, that's actually a good idea," Bobby nodded. "Go grab it and let's go already."

"I ain't tryin' to hear that, homes!" Trent squeaked. "I'm just the idea man here. *You* go get it."

"Nuh-uh. I'm not touching that shit," Bobby said. "It's got redneck blood all over it. I might get infected and suddenly like listening to Billy Ray Cyrus."

"Oh, come on, Big B. If I get any closer to the reek on that freak I'm going to make a big ol' pot of rerun stew—you said so yourself."

"Jesus Herman Christ," Sherri cursed. "I've been in a girls' shower room and I've never been surrounded by so many pussies. *I'll* get the fucking gun."

Feeling her way to the end of the countertop, she pushed through a saloon door labeled "Employes 'Only'!!!!" Her boots slipped on the blood-slicked linoleum behind the counter, but she stayed on her feet, sweeping her hands through the open air.

"Come on, people, hot or cold?"

"Warm," Trent said, peering over the counter. "Getting hotter … a little to the left."

"Here?"

Sherri took a step to the left and her foot came down on one of the chair's rockers. With a stiff lurch, the corpse slumped forward in the seat, forcing the cold steel barrel of the gun all the way through the hole in its skull. When the scrape of the gun shifting on the floor reached Sherri's ears, she zeroed in and grabbed its barrel with a swing of her hand.

"Got it! Now let's go!"

She turned toward the boys and took a step, but with the stock of the gun firmly anchored in the skull of its owner, it refused to move an inch.

"Oh, for fuck's sake," she said. "Hold on, it's stuck on something."

"No no! Just forget it," Bobby gagged. "Forget it! Just let it go and come on."

"I got it; I got it," Sherri spat. "Just give me a second."

With a frustrated dedication, she wrapped both hands around the barrel and started yanking it up and down against the inert human blockage like an unspeakable version of an old-fashioned butter churn. The stock banged into the floor with each thrust, throwing up crowns of drained blood that splattered against her legs. With each thunderous *bang,* the clerk's empty head slid up and down the barrel like a hairy meat yo-yo.

"God, what's this thing stuck on?" Sherri muttered. "It's like pulling teeth!"

Trent gasped, choked, and then finally released the meager contents of his stomach onto the floor. With an awkward lurch that suggested only half of his brain was in on the idea, Bobby rushed through the saloon doors to stop the inadvertent desecration.

"Sherri, stop! Just stop!"

Before Bobby's words had reached her ears, the wet gun slipped out of Sherri's hands, hammering its stock into the ground and ramming the clerk's shattered jawbone into the trigger. With an explosion that rattled the windows, the second barrel of the shotgun blasted its load into the air, eradicating the end of a hanging shop light.

Spitting out a half-realized expletive, Bobby threw his arms in front of his face just in time to catch the full brunt of the mangled fixture as it swung in a graceful arc from its one remaining chain. The torn metal sliced the backs of his arms before smashing him in the forehead. His face was already slicked with hot blood by the time his unconscious body hit the floor with a ground-shaking *thud.*

A column of cold gasoline slid halfway up the tube as Erik sucked gently upon its sugary end.

"Good, good," Vivian said. "Now put your thumb—"

Just then, the sound of the shotgun blast from inside of the store smashed through their skulls like a slaughterhouse hammer. Erik's startled diaphragm made a convulsive spasm that pulled enough gasoline into his stomach to start a moped.

The burn hit him in slow motion, like an acid fire spreading from the back of his throat, raging down his tongue and up into his sinuses. With a sputtering choke, a glut of fuel exploded from his nose, got sucked back into his gasping mouth, and rolled back down his scalded throat. He fell to the ground in a violent fit of spitting and coughing, both hands clawing at his burning face.

"Erik!" Vivian wailed. "Erik, no!"

She fell to her knees next to him and struggled to hold him upright. His eyes had turned a screaming shade of bloodshot red, and his nose leaked sugary blue petroleum. He coughed up a mass of thick, flammable goo and fell limp in her arms.

"Erik!"

She lay him down on the ground, and his eyes stared without focus into the sky.

"Erik! *Erik!* Come on, Erik!"

Vivian's mind raced. He wasn't breathing. Time seemed to both stop and accelerate simultaneously. She didn't know what to do. Her brain screamed through its medical files, but the only thing she could remember was a yellowed instructional poster from a previous food service job. A second later she had wrestled Erik to his feet and was standing behind him, arms wrapped around him, thrusting her clenched hands upward into his belly.

"Come on, Erik!" she shouted. "It's the Heimlich maneuver! Come on, breathe!"

As she repeatedly pumped her fists into Erik's midsection, dark blood squirted from around his bandages. She winced. There was no time to be gentle. She would apologize later.

"St—" Erik choked. "Sto—"

"It's working! Cough it up! Breathe!"

Erik's brain swam through a pool of fumes and burning disorientation. He didn't know what was going on. All he knew was that somebody was trying to kill him. Squeezing, squeezing, squeezing on his tortured stomach. His knees buckled, but the squeezing arms held him upright. In his stupor, he clawed at his assailant's hands but couldn't force them away.

"That's right, Erik," Vivian said, still pumping. "Hold on! You're going to be okay!"

Erik's addled brain couldn't decode the words; all it knew was the wrench of the squeezing. Squeezing, squeezing, squeezing. Squeezing him to death! The squeezing had to stop.

"Stop," he choked. "Stop it. *Stop it! Aaaaarrrrgh!*"

With a rippling strain of his abdominal muscles, Erik's bandages tore apart as his wounds exploded outward. The hardened spines of his infection burst from his scars on stalks of hairy flesh, clamping two fistfuls of gnarled fingers around Vivian's wrists!

"Aaaaaaaaaaaaaah! Aaaa! Aaaaaa! Aaaaaaaaaaaaaaaaa!"

Sherri's blighted ears were pierced by a high and frantic shrieking.

"Shut up! Shut *up!*" she screamed, clamping her hands down on the sides of her head. "Tell me what the fuck just happened!"

The shock of the gunshot coupled with the sight of Bobby's near decapitation had sent Trent over the edge. His feet were locked to the floor in sheer, primal terror, and he could do nothing but scream like a chorus of police sirens rushing to the scene of a quadruple homicide.

"Shut up!" Sherri repeated. "Trent! Shut the fuck up!"

She scrambled her hands across the floor until they hit the stock of the shotgun. The clerk's neck had wrenched all the way around, and he now lay on the floor with the barrel threading his reamed-out skull. Still oblivious to the repercussions of her actions, Sherri grabbed the gun and sprang to her feet, disconnecting the redneck's head with a pulpy *snap* of tendons that was never heard over the piercing stab of Trent's screech.

"Trent, if you don't stop screaming, I swear to God I'll blow your fucking face off!"

To drive her threat home, Sherri shouldered the weapon and swung the muzzle up toward the sound of his wail. As the barrel swished through the air, the disembodied head slid down the slick metal and launched across the room, hitting Trent in the chest with a wet and understated *thunk*.

The next thing Sherri heard was Trent's silenced body hitting the linoleum in a shock-induced faint, followed by nothing but the ringing in her own ears.

"That's better," she said, lowering the shotgun and lighting a cigarette. "Now, Bobby, could you please start at the beginning and tell me what the fuck is going on? Bobby? Trent? Helloooo?"

From outside the store, Vivian's bloodcurdling screams reached Sherri's tired ears.

"Fuck me," she muttered. "What *now?*"

Vivian screamed with such intensity that her fillings rattled in her teeth. She could feel consciousness slipping from her body as her tortured lungs filled with a cold, liquid pain. This was no hallucination. Her thrashing arms were bound by two hands, their knotted fingers dripping with ropes of thick fluid. In one powerful motion, the claws yanked her arms from Erik's waist and flung them aside. She stumbled backward, tripped over the empty gas cans, and tumbled to the ground.

Freed from Vivian's crushing embrace, Erik staggered forward with a hacking cough, wiping the sugary fuel from his lips. Vivian scrambled backward in terror. His pouchy love handles had sprouted a monstrous set of black rodent forearms. He looked down on his own body with complete incomprehension, holding his human arms out to his sides as if to protect them from their newly formed brothers.

After a second of silence that seemed to last an eon, Erik tipped his head back and released a roaring scream. In spite of herself, Vivian joined in on the scream and didn't stop screaming until Sherri kicked open the door of the convenience store with a splintery *bang*.

Sherri's bloody eyes picked out two shapes. From the scream, she knew that the one crumpled on the ground was Vivian, but even through her blasted corneas she could see that the one looming over her had two arms too many to be Erik. She brought the shotgun to her shoulder and slipped her finger into the trigger guard.

"Hey! Freakshow!" she barked, cigarette hanging from her lips. "Paws off the powderpuff!"

"Sherri!" Vivian screamed. "Wait! Don't!"

Sherri's finger squeezed the moist trigger, firing off nothing but an impotent *click*.

"Fuck!" she spat. "It's empty!"

Erik clasped his hands over his throbbing heart and turned back to Vivian.

"Oh thank Go—"

Before he could finish expressing his relief, he was silenced by the resounding *pong* of an empty five-gallon gas can hitting him square in the face.

CHAPTER EIGHT

Vivian sat in a hollow-eyed slump on the steps of the convenience store. Although she hardly moved, her breath came in a shallow, nervous pant. She held an open bag of Cheetos in her left hand, but the barely orange fingers of her right showed her lack of interest. The rocking chair had been moved from the porch to the driveway, and Vivian watched Bobby and Trent hovering busily around it.

"Yeah, I can *see* what you're doing, but I'm drawing a 'no comprende' card here, homeboy," Trent whined. "Someone's got to protect the ladies from this creature, and if you're not man enough to take action, then—"

"For once in your life, just shut up," Bobby said. "Just shut ... the hell ... up."

Trent snapped off a mouthful of beef jerky and scowled as Bobby tugged the end of an orange extension cord. In the driveway in front of the gas pumps, an unconscious Erik sat neatly bound to the chair. His ankles were tied to its wobbly legs, and his human arms were stuffed through the slats of the back and bound behind him. From there, the cable looped back around, tying his rodent limbs together in a bundle that hung limply in his lap.

Bobby knotted the end of the cord around the mutant wrists and stepped away, rubbing his own wounded arms. The blasted shop light had dug two gouges in his forearms from elbow to wrist, but his defensive posture had put the rifts relatively harmlessly up their back sides. A Dixieland medley of red, white, and blue bandages dressed his wounds, finishing off the remainder of the Confederate flag. A series of mismatched cartoon Band-Aids held together the fresh gash in his forehead. He waddled back across the driveway, grabbed a bag of chips and a can of purple soda from the backpack, and plopped down next to Vivian.

"Ahh, yes, come to Bobby," he hummed, tearing open the bag. "I think this is the longest that I've gone without Fritos in my entire life."

"No shit?" Sherri said through a mouthful of waxy chocolate cake. "You'd never know it by looking at you, fat-ass."

"Cut it out, you two!" Vivian snapped. "This is serious! What are we supposed to do about Erik?"

"He's not going anywhere," Bobby said, nudging her bag of Cheetos. "Just relax and get some calories in your system. We'll see what happens when he wakes up."

"When he wakes up?!" Trent squawked. "Listen to me, people! I'm telling you, when he wakes up, he's going to be just like that kitty cat from Hell! The last thing you're ever gonna hear is me saying 'I told you so' when that thing comes to and starts putting a fresh set of holes all up in your asses!"

"Yes, Trent. Your opinion is duly noted," Vivian sighed. "Not that I think that will stop you from continuing to voice it *over and over again.*"

Trent shoved another hunk of jerky in his mouth and grumbled to himself.

Sherri sat on the antique cooler in a cross-legged slump, perched between a half-eaten package of Hostess Sno Balls and a quart of warm beer. Two days of pollutant-riddled air had taken their toll on her blast-bleached locks, turning them from a snowy white to a grimy shade of yellow. She tilted her head back and pushed her hair out of her eyes, leaving a trail of pink coconut shavings down its length.

"I've got an idea," she said, sliding off of the cooler. "Why don't we quit screwing around and just wake him up?"

Before anyone could argue, she clomped over to Erik, stomped on the back of the rocker, and dumped half a bottle of beer over his swollen forehead.

With a wet snort that sent a whiff of petrochemical stench into the air, Erik woke up and thrashed against his bonds with a choking cough. Sherri continued to pour the bottle over his head, the peeling flesh of her face twisting into a satisfied grin.

"Up and at 'em, Sideshow. If Trent's gonna kill you, I at least want you to mess him up real bad first."

Erik floundered and choked under the dripping foam. His immobilized hands scrambled at the back of the chair, unable to come to his aid.

"Sherri, stop it!" Vivian barked.

"Okay, hold on," Sherri said, raising a finger. "Only half a bottle left."

Erik's rat arms lurched upward in a tied-together mass, yanked the bottle from Sherri's hand, and hurled it across the driveway. Trent leapt out of its way as it smashed against the pavement where he had been standing.

"Ggglglgglgg! Grr! GrrRrrrawWWwg!" Erik roared.

"Did you see that? Did you see that?" Trent squeaked, pointing at the shattered glass. "Aw shit! You went and put the rage in it now, yo!"

"Auug!" Erik choked. "Whatsaggg?"

His shoulders tugged impotently at his imprisoned human arms. He clenched his burning eyes, and his rat arms rose from his lap to swab them with the backs of their furry wrists. He blinked furiously as his eyes cleared, revealing a vision of yellow claws and matted, beer-soaked fur.

"Man," he coughed, "that stung like a son of aaaAaAaAAAaAAA!"

CHAPTER EIGHT

He kicked out in a frantic attempt to escape his own gnarled paws. With every thrust of his bound legs, he tipped the creaking chair away from the mutant hands, only for them to be shoved right back toward him on gravity's return stroke. "AAaaAaaaAaAAaa!"

"We've got to kill it!" Trent wailed. "Kill it now! Before it kills all of us!" He snatched the sword from the front porch and charged at Erik with a terrified battle cry.

"Trent, no!" Vivian screamed.

Bobby made a spastic lurch to grab Trent but missed him entirely, slipped off of the step, and crashed to the pavement. Vivian launched over her brother, and within three explosive steps she had caught up to Trent's howling stampede. She leapt onto his back, throwing them both to the ground and sending the sword skittering across the dusty blacktop. She rolled onto her back in a fit of convulsive, gasping coughs.

"Damn, Vivi!" Trent moaned, rubbing his bloody knees through fresh holes in his pants. "This is seriously not the time to be jumpin' a brotha's bones! You got to wait until *after* I slay the beast to express your gratitude!"

Vivian's exertion had left her completely breathless.

"Don't … you … touch … him!" she wheezed.

Bobby stepped behind Erik and slammed his foot down on the rocker, arresting its maddened swing.

"Erik, if you understand the words I'm saying, quit wigging out before we have to kill you!"

"*Kill* me? Kill *me?!*" Erik chirped hoarsely. "W … what the hell is going on here?!"

Bobby stepped off of the rocker and backed away, leaving Erik slowly oscillating in the dust. His rodent arms fell limp across his lap.

"We're cool. Everybody be cool now," Bobby warned.

Vivian pulled herself onto her knees and coughed violent, gravelly coughs. Trent thumped on her back with his open palm.

"Breathe, Vivi, breathe," he coached. "Don't you worry, I'm here to look out for you, girl. I'll keep you safe."

She pushed him away without looking at him and shuffled over to join Bobby and Sherri in an uneasy semicircle around the chair. Sherri held the sword slung over her shoulder.

"Dude?" Bobby ventured, leaning over Erik. "Dude. Are you okay?"

"Am I okay? Am I *okay?!* Do I look okay?! What the hell happened to me?!"

"I don't know!" Vivian yelled. "I was just trying to help you, and *this* happened!"

"Trying to *help* me?!" Erik rasped. "You were squeezing the shit out of my ripped-up stomach!"

"I was doing the Heimlich maneuver! You were choking!"

"So you were trying to dislodge the *fluid* stuck in my throat?! Very nice. You could have killed me!"

"She *should* have killed you as soon as you became one of *them*," Trent said. "But your weak-willed, so-called 'friends' decided to bind you up instead of sending you to your final reward. People, people. Why are we prolonging this wretched soul's suffering?"

"Whoa whoa!" Erik stammered. "I'm not suffering! I'm okay! Trent, you said it yourself! Humans are okay because we have souls! I have a soul!"

"Oh, I think not, Evil E," Trent said. "Heavy B had the right idea after all, yo. This ain't about souls anymore. It's about the toxic germs we breathed and the disinfectants in the blood. For real. Every one of us was drinking liquor on Judgment Day. Every one of us but *you*."

"I *was* drinking liquor!" Erik screamed. "I told you! I drank! I drank a lot! Tell him, Bobby! Right before work I had like, four Tequizas!"

"Tequiza?" Trent huffed, leaning into Erik's face. "Does that even have alcohol in it? What kind of man drinks Tequiza? That stuff is little Mexican girl piss."

Erik's face crinkled as Trent's stale, spicy meat breath rolled up his scorched nostrils.

"Look, will you just untie me? Seriously, I'm *okay*."

Trent leaned in closer to Erik, locking his bloodshot eyes in a cold stare.

"I think as long as *I'm* still in God's image, and *you're* a four-armed demon freak tied to a chair, *I'll* be the judge of who's *okay*, you abomination of—"

Erik's bundle of rat arms swung violently upward, connecting with a *crack* to the bottom of Trent's jaw. Trent staggered away, clutching his mouth as blood flowed from his freshly bitten tongue.

"Ow! Damn it! Son of a ..."

Erik's eyes widened and flicked over the shocked faces of the others.

"I didn't do that!" he squeaked. "I'm sorry, Trent! I didn't mean it! It just happened!"

"Well, that's good enough for me," Sherri shrugged. "Let him go. Anyone who wants to knock Trent on his ass can't be evil."

"I'm sorry; I'm so sorry!" Erik said. "It was an accident! I can't control them!"

"Listen to him!" Trent seethed. "He just said himself that he can't control those things! If he's not controlling them, then *who is?!*"

With a seemingly choreographed leap, he snatched the sword from Sherri's hands and thrust its tip toward Erik's chest.

"Y'all are letting your fond memories of what this thing *used* to be interfere with your duty!" he boomed. "This thing is *not* your friend!"

"I *am* your friend!" Erik screamed. "Help me!"

Bobby stepped forward and shoved Trent out of the way.

"Quit being an asshole, you asshole."

He wrestled the sword out of Trent's hands and handed it back to Sherri.

"Thanks, buddy," Erik smiled. "I knew you'd be on my side. Come on now, untie me."

Bobby looked away.

"I'm sorry," he mumbled. "You know I can't."

"You can't?!" Erik shrieked. "Why not?! You're my best friend!"

"I know. That's exactly why I can't! We both know that's exactly how this thing always plays out in the movies. Even though you're obviously all freaked up, I untie you because you're my best friend. Then when we least expect it you're jumping out of the closet with glowing red eyes and a mouthful of bloody fangs. You of all people should know this. It's your own logic. Sorry, man."

"You're sorry?!" Erik yelled. "Well, sorry doesn't cut it!"

"Don't be sorry!" Trent boiled. "Stop being sorry! Stop thinking of that thing as if it's still your friend! He's gone! We all knew that it would come to this! That's why we made a pact!"

"But I didn't make a pact!" Erik wailed.

Everyone went silent, contemplating the echo of Erik's shrieked words.

"He's right, you know," Vivian said. "He refused to be a part of our agreement."

"You see?!" Erik said. "This is *exactly* why you should never join a homicide pact! It never works out in your favor in the end!"

"Damn, woman!" Trent barked. "How can you still be on his side?! Look at him! He's a monster!"

"But what if he's *not?!*" Vivian shouted. "We don't know! We don't know anything about these creatures!"

"I'm not a creature!" Erik hissed.

"We know *something* about them," Sherri said. "We know that they glow blue once you kill them."

"Homegirl's right," Trent agreed. "Let's slice off his head so y'all can see how it shines."

"Whoa whoa," Erik said, shaking his head violently. "I can't get behind this plan."

"Oh alright, ya pussywad," Sherri conceded, raising her sword. "How about we just hack off a foot and see if *it* glows."

"No, no," Erik stammered. "I'm not on board with any plan that involves the words 'slice,' 'hack,' or 'kill.'"

"Find another way," Vivian said sternly. "This is not Salem, and it's not 1692. We're not going to have a witch trial here."

"But that's just what we're dealing with, Vivi!" Trent said. "Don't you see? The devil possesses his soul! Second book of Moses says, 'Thou shalt not suffer a witch to live.'"

"Ha! He isn't a witch," Sherri laughed. "I *know* witches, and they're way cooler than *Erik*."

"Don't get yourself all boxed in on the Lord's language, yo," Trent said. "A witch, a demon, a zombie, it's all umbrellaed under the same scripture. Thou shalt not suffer a zombie to live!"

"Stop it," Vivian snapped. "He's not a zombie!"

"Vivi, he's got *arms* growing out of his *belly!* Are you blind?! He's a freaked-up bloodthirsty zombie!"

"He's not a zombie," Vivian repeated. "He's a *mutant*."

"So *what?!*" Trent shrieked. "They're the same thing!"

"No, they're not," she said. "Zombies are nothing but rotting, reanimated corpses. All they do is shamble through the night infecting people and eating brains. A mutant *can* be evil, but it doesn't *have* to be."

Erik's lips stretched into a grin as Trent's hands fell to his sides in disbelief.

"Where on God's green Earth did you get that crazy-ass bullshit?"

Vivian gave Erik a weak smile.

"I once got lectured by someone very close to the subject."

Trent snatched the sword from Sherri and backed away angrily.

"But how do you know he's not a zombie?" he said. "It's not like you can just give him the First Response Early Zombification Test or something!"

"I can't be a zombie!" Erik volunteered. "Zombies have no thought process!"

"Put a zip-zip on your lip-lip," Trent said. "This is a discussion for normals only."

"No no," Bobby said thoughtfully. "I think he might be on to something there."

"Unbelievable!" Trent squeaked, throwing his hands in the air. "Now you're taking advice from the *zombie?!*"

"From the *mutant*," Bobby countered. "He's right. If he can still reason, then he's not a zombie. What if we give him a series of carefully worded questions and statements and monitor his response?"

"That sounds like a reasonable idea," Vivian agreed.

"Ha!" Erik snapped. "It sounds like a Voight-Kampff test! Are you trying to figure out if I'm a mutant, or if I'm a replicant, Rick Deckard?"

Bobby's lips pursed into a grin.

"Congratulations, old chum. So far you're one for one."

"Oh no," Trent said. "We must be having duck soup for dinner, because I smell something *foul*, yo. Whatever the hell homeboy just said doesn't prove anything to me. You can't go speaking your own geek language and pretend like that makes him okay."

"Trent has a point," Vivian said. "If we're going to do an interrogation, we should start with simple questions. You know, establish a credible baseline."

"Me first," Sherri squealed. "Name every country in the world!"

"Um, okay," Erik said, his eyes rolling back in concentration. "United States, Canada, Mexico, Panama, Haiti, Jamaica, Peru—"

"Wait, wait," Vivian said, rubbing her eyes. "*Simple* questions. Baseline. Like, what year is it?"

"It's 1999," Erik said. "As you can tell by the way that I'm *partying*."

"How much money do you have in your wallet?" Sherri asked.

"I don't know—about fourteen bucks?"

"Can I have it?" Sherri continued.

"Uh, I guess."

"Uh-uh. No," Trent scowled. "Don't go pullin' out the payola. Let's keep this legits, alright, E? No bribing the jury."

"I wasn't! She asked if—"

"What's it like to be a damned creature?" Trent interrupted. "What are you feeling right now?"

Erik cast his eyes downward. "I'm scared. And also really, really hungry."

"Hungry?" Trent repeated. "Hungry for what?"

"It doesn't matter. Anything."

"Anything?" Trent thundered. "Like *human flesh?!*"

"No, not human flesh," Erik smirked. "Quit putting words in my mouth!"

"I think we all know what you want in your mouth," Trent said, grasping his own arm like an oversized turkey leg and pretending to take a bite.

Bobby stepped forward and planted a palm on Trent's face, shoving him aside. He leaned down to Erik.

"On *Get Smart,*" he asked, "what was Agent 99's real name?"

"Barbara Feldon."

"Wrong! That's the actress's name! I want the character's name!"

"That's a trick question!" Erik protested. "Agent 99 had no real name!"

"He's right," Bobby nodded.

"If I asked if you liked smelling little boys' used underwear," Sherri asked, "would your answer be the same as the answer to this question?"

"No!" Erik shouted. "Er ... yes! I mean ... you're disgusting!"

"What does it feel like?" Vivian blurted.

"It's humiliating."

"No, I mean ... the arms. Do they hurt?"

"They don't. Not at all," Erik admitted. "It doesn't even feel like they're a part of me. I can't control them, but I can *feel* them."

He paused.

"When they grabbed the bottle, I could feel the glass, but ... but it was like I was feeling it in my *real* hands. They're like ... it's like they're my real arms' evil twins or something. It's ... it's weird."

Vivian stroked back the mop of Erik's beer-soaked bangs and looked into his eyes. He could feel the warmth of her breath on his cheeks and smell the old cabbage on her skin.

"You poor thing," she whispered.

Trent looked at Vivian gazing sympathetically into Erik's eyes and scowled. He stepped to the front of the rocker, gently nudging Vivian away with a protective shove of his forearm. Turning to Erik, he lightly slapped his right cheek, as if challenging him to a duel. He continued to slap the left, then the right again.

"Trent, stop it," Vivian spat.

"Yeah, knock it off, jerkbag!" Erik winced.

"Make me, *freak*," Trent smirked, slapping him again.

"I would if my arms weren't tied behind my back, you cowardly prick bastard!"

"But they're not, are they, bro?" Trent said coolly. "Not *all* of them."

Erik's mutant arms lay flaccidly across his lap like the empty sleeves of a gorilla costume.

"I just *told* you," he seethed, "I can't control them!"

"Well, *somebody's* controlling them, and I have a pretty good idea who it is," Trent said, pointing dramatically downward. "So, you can't control them, right? Well, what part are you going to lose control over next, E? Your legs? Your *brain?* Who are *they* going to attack next? Are *they* gonna be all up on me again? Or on your boy B here? Or what if *they* take a savage interest in the defenseless blind girl's fragile feminine form? Then what?"

Erik cast his eyes helplessly to the pavement.

"I ... I really don't know," he admitted.

Bobby shoved Trent aside and clapped his hands.

"*Duh-nuh nuh-nuh-nuh!* Fresh air!"

"*Duh-nuh nuh-nuh-nuh.* Times Square," Erik returned pathetically.

"Yep, this is Erik alright," Bobby said conclusively. "No self-respecting zombie would watch *Green Acres.*"

"Be serious, Bobby!" Vivian snapped. She crouched down in front of Erik and leaned in, putting her hands on his bound knees.

"Erik, do you feel like ... do you feel like you're going to hurt somebody?"

"No!" Erik pleaded. "I don't! I absolutely don't! Vivian, please! How could you even think that I could—"

The clawed fingers of his mutant hands raised ghoulishly from his lap and extended toward Vivian's soft, freckled cheeks. With a squeak of terror, she slapped them away, lost her balance, and fell on her behind.

"I'm sorry!" Erik yelled frantically. "Vivian, I'm sorry! I didn't—"

Vivian scrambled to her feet.

"I'm sorry, Erik! I didn't mean to—"

"I wasn't going to hurt you! I'd never hurt you!"

"I know, it just ... they just ... I know you wouldn't, Erik."

As Trent watched the tense affection sizzle back and forth, a new line of questioning popped into his greasy head. He nudged Vivian aside and spoke with a sudden airiness.

"Little E, have you ever been in love?"

Erik's distressed gaze broke from Vivian and landed on Trent.

"What?"

"You know. The big one. The three little words," Trent said smoothly, coming to stand in front of the rocking chair. "I'm guessing that you've never made love to a woman, but nonetheless, tell me, have you ever really, really, loved a woman?"

"What are you getting at, Bryan Adams?" Erik said defensively. "Just because I don't try to stick it in every girl I like doesn't mean that I—"

"Whoa whoa! Easy, E. So maybe you've loved a woman. Maybe you even still do," Trent said, leaning in toward Erik's face without coming into claw range. "Let me ask you this, friend. This woman that you love. Think about her. Imagine her beauty. Think about the way that her eyes glimmer in the moonlight or the way that her hair hangs across the silky skin of her neck. Think of the soft curve of her body where the small of her back melts into her perfect derrière. Are you picturing her?"

Erik glared at Trent without saying a word. Trent continued.

"Would you leave this woman you love alone and unprotected with a thing like *you?* A creature so far removed from God's great design that he can't even account for the aggressions of his *own body?* Would 'I'm sorry, I can't control them' cut it when you're standing over her laying in a pool of her own sweet blood after you've done the unthinkable? *Would it?!*"

Erik turned his head and looked at the stony faces of his friends, gathered in the driveway to his left. Tears rolled from Vivian's eyes as they darted to the ground to avoid his glance. When Erik looked his way, Bobby quickly took off his glasses and pretended to blow dust from them. Sherri was the only one who didn't look away. Her reddened eyes just stared straight through him with a kind of visual shrug that suggested neither accusation nor compassion.

"Last question, E," Trent said. "Do you realize that this is not just going to get better? Do you recognize, in your heart, that you are no longer one of us, and you never will be?"

Erik's friends didn't look at him. Erik didn't look at his friends. He didn't look at Trent or the sword in his hands. He just looked down at the hairy arms hanging impossibly from his own abdomen. They looked so harmless lying across his lap, but even he didn't know how long they, or he, would stay that way.

"I ... I can only say what I know," he stammered, his eyes welling up. "I don't know what's happened to me, but I know in my heart that I would never hurt you guys. I'll always be your friend. I just wish that I could show you all how much I—"

Erik's tearful speech was cut short by the sound of Trent's blade cutting through the air with a shrill *swish,* terminating in a muffled, organic *crack* and a guttural choke.

The red-headed twins' averted eyes shot toward the grisly noise and then seized in horror. They saw Erik in grim profile, his mouth hanging frozen in a silent scream. Trent stood before him with both hands wrapped around the hilt of the blade that was now buried in the top of Erik's wretched skull.

Vivian's icy terror melted into a scream as a wave of anguish emptied her strangled lungs and dropped her to her knees. Sherri, for once speechless, rubbed her eyes and squinted at what she was sure she had not just seen. Bobby just stood and stared in a stunned paralysis, his pasty face blossoming red with rage.

"No ... *no!*" he choked. "Trent, you savage son of a bitch!"

His trembling legs began to carry him forward as his arms prepared to perform some act of barbarism not yet fully conceived. Before Bobby laid a hand on Trent, however, Erik's jaw began to quiver at the corner of his ashen face, then came alive with a hysterical scream.

"Aaaahaaahahahahaa!" he wailed. "Shit shit! Help me! Holy shit, somebody stop this idiot! Shiiiit!"

As he screamed, Erik's tightly bound body went into spastic convulsions, thrashing the chair around in a scraping quarter-circle until it faced his friends. The new perspective revealed Trent's sword to be wedged firmly in the wood of the rocking chair, six inches from the side of Erik's intact head.

"Sit still, you freak!" Trent screamed, yanking to free his captured blade. "The power of Christ compels you, beotch!"

With a blast of dry splinters, the sword broke through the wood, freeing the blade and splitting the old chair nearly in two. Erik continued to scream and thrash, splintering the chair apart and leaving him tied to nothing but shattered debris. Bobby grabbed him by his bindings and hauled him out of the way just as Trent's blade smashed into the pavement.

"Trent, are you out of your mind?!" Bobby screamed. "Put that down, you idiot!"

"Step aside, B! I cannot allow this perversion to live! Go back to Hell, where you came from, demon!"

Trent raised his sword over his head to finish the job. With a burst of sneakers against blacktop, Vivian launched at him, throwing him off-balance with a bony shoulder to his chest, aborting his deadly swing but failing to return him to the ground.

"Trent, stop it!" she screamed, punching and clawing at his sunburnt skin.

"Stop it! Leave him alone!"

"I have to protect you! That whiny bastard is a blasphemy on legs! Ouch, shit! You're not safe with a half-breed freak like him around! None of us are! Thou shalt not suffer a mutant to live! Stand back, Vivi! I said stand *back!*"

With a fiery flash of his eyes, Trent threw out his arm, planting the heel of his palm into Vivian's bandaged chest with a powerful, resounding *thump.*

The blow hit Vivian like a shot from a cannon. Her eyes dilated as the wind was completely knocked out of her, and she felt herself suddenly drowning in open air. It was as if Trent's hand had plowed all the way through her body, pushing her organs through her back in a gooey clump.

As she stumbled back, unable to draw breath, she could feel a cold, splitting wetness pouring from her shoulders to her waist. Her corset of bandages exploded from her body as an enormous pair of bat wings erupted from her back. The black sails billowed out to her sides in a four-foot span that threw a sinister shadow over Trent's petrified body. A single flap of their leathery mass filled the air with a thrown-off mist of clotted blood and oil.

"Don't you *touch* him," she growled.

Without breaking her death glare into Trent's unbelieving eyes, Vivian inhaled a deep, full breath into her unconstricted lungs, took one shaky step, and then passed out in his arms. Her head tipped back over his thick forearm, throwing the soft warmth of her hair cascading across his skin.

Bobby, Erik, and Sherri stared at them, all motionless, all with their jaws hanging open, limp as wet laundry on a clothesline. None of them spoke. None of them even blinked.

Vivian's mutant wings hung placidly from her unconscious shoulders and draped over Trent's arm. The shredded polyester of her cocktail dress hung low across her bosom, affording him an ample view of her cleavage heaving in the newly afforded freedom of respiration.

Trent took a long, introspective look at Erik, then at Vivian's warm, soft, mutated body. Finally, he dropped the sword and clasped her tightly in his arms.

"Fine," he huffed. "Untie him."

CHAPTER NINE

The Rabbit screamed up the abandoned interstate, shattering the silence of the Carolina pine forest. Trent was gangsta leanin' in the driver's seat, with his left arm resting on the crumbling doorframe and his right hand hanging limply over the top of the wheel. In his own mind he was driving a slammed '69 Buick full of hoochies down the Sunset Strip, and nobody bothered to tell him otherwise. Vivian sat in the passenger seat, and the others were packed in behind them. As the hours ticked by, irritation had been piling up in the tiny car like sand in the bottom of an hourglass.

Erik scanned the shoulder of the road for the next installment of a running gag that had been running for hundreds of miles.

"So much *maple,* you won't want to *leaf,*" he moaned in a parody of comic delivery. "North of the Border, one hundred and thirty-two miles."

As he said the words, the car blasted past a billboard depicting the thirty-foot-tall cartoon Mountie wielding two oversized jugs of maple syrup.

"Get it? *Maple? Leaf?*" he continued. "Because he's *Canadian,* you see …"

Trent scowled into the rearview mirror.

"Seriously, y'all. I *can't* be the only one having second thoughts about not killing him."

"Give it a rest, Trent," Sherri muttered. "You're lucky we don't kill *you.* After all, *you're* the only one who's gone batshit and attacked somebody."

"Aw, now that ain't fair," Trent said. "You know I was just tryin' to protect all y'all. How was I supposed to know that Little E was okay?"

"You could have taken my word for it," Erik spat.

"God, will you two shut up already?" Bobby groaned. "Yes, we let paranoia get the best of us. Yes, it got out of control. Yes, we all screwed up. Especially Trent."

"Hey!" Trent snapped. "All I did was—"

"So let's just forget it and move on," Bobby continued. "No harm, no foul."

"No harm?" Erik squealed. "That asshole tried to put a sword in my—"

"Erik, *please,*" Bobby said, rubbing his eyes. "For the love of God …"

Erik smirked and leaned heavily on the side of the convertible. To his left, Sherri shifted her weight between his overabundance of knobby forelimbs on one side and Bobby's unforgiving girth on the other.

Though the whites of her eyes had returned to normal, her formerly blue irises were now stained a cotton candy pink. Her skin hung from her body in a feathery layer of peeling sunburn, and as the fabric of Bobby's overstuffed T-shirt rubbed against her, brittle curls of flesh flaked off her arm.

"God damn it," she said, slapping Bobby's flab with her crumbling palms. "I swear, I'm going to slice you open and let the lard pour out until you fit in a car seat like a normal person. When was the last time you got any exercise, Tubby?"

"Well, let me see," Bobby said. "If I recall correctly, I think it was this morning when I carried thirty pounds of gas up the highway for five hours while your lazy ass sat around the convenience store eating chewing tobacco."

"Hey, fuck you. While you and Trent took your sweet-ass time bringing the car back, I was kneeling next to Jeeps and sucking like the head cheerleader on prom night. You think all those gas cans in the trunk filled themselves? My lips are swollen up like an anorexic supermodel's and my breath smells like the ass end of a go-cart!"

"Yeah?" Bobby challenged. "Well, I had to spend five hours *alone* with *Trent.*"

Sherri folded her arms in a huff. "Fine. You win."

Oblivious to the constant bickering around her, Vivian sat silently in the passenger seat. She was focusing all of her energy on ignoring the pair of black wings that folded over her icy shoulders like a bony vampire cape. She scoured the side of the interstate for signs of life, but all she saw was another lonely green highway marker leaning like a tombstone.

Kickapoo - 14 miles

Baneberry - 27 miles

She glanced through the cracked windshield. Fourteen miles ahead, the sky was split by a five-mile-wide tongue of charcoal-black smoke lapping the ground on the right side of the road. Another thirteen miles beyond that, a second streak cleaved the sky from the left. With a long, mournful blink, Vivian crossed the cities of Kickapoo and Baneberry, South Carolina off of the map in her mind.

She hunkered down into her seat and petulantly yanked the thick leather of her wings around her head for warmth. As long as they were there, she may as well make the most of them, she reasoned. Although reason was now more foreign to her than ever.

There was no reason for her to have grown bat wings. It was biologically impossible. Yet there they were. And just as Twiki's mutated body had done before, these wings were growing at an alarming rate. It had only been a matter of hours since they had erupted from the ragged slashes in her dress, yet her wingspan had already expanded by at least two nightmarish feet.

From beyond the fleshy walls of her cocoon, Vivian could hear Erik attempting to assuage his road-trip boredom.

"I spy, with my little eye, something in the car."

"Is it in the front seat?" Bobby asked.

"Yes."

Sherri's pink eyes rolled up and down Vivian's bundled wingspan.

"Is it leathery?"

"I'd say so," Erik nodded.

Bobby looked at his sister's dark, shrouded form.

"Is it black?"

"Well, it thinks it is," Erik said.

"Is it Trent?" Sherri asked.

"Yes! You got it!" Erik beamed.

The back seat exploded into a round of high fives and derisive laughter.

"Oh, now, y'all are just cold," Trent sighed. "Why you gotta judge a brother by the color of his skin and not the content of his character?"

"You're not a brother!" Bobby said. "And you've got no character!"

"Always gotta be surrounded by da haters," Trent muttered.

He put a heavy hand on Vivian's chilled thigh.

"Come on now, Vivi. I know at least *you're* on my side here, girl. Come out of that shell and help the T for a spell."

Vivian's reedy hand emerged from under her sheath of wings, grasped Trent's hand, and threw it off of her lap.

"Leave me alone. I'm not coming out unless Commissioner Gordon calls for me."

"Oh, don't be like that, Vivi," Trent said. "You don't have to be self-conscious about your body! You know the T doesn't judge people by their physical appearance. It's what's on the inside that counts. Come on and show us that beautiful inside of yours, girl."

Vivian could feel Trent's warm fingertips touching her cold flesh. The sensation was indescribably weird, as if his hand had slipped under her skin and closed directly around the bones of her fingers. But as she flinched from his unwelcome touch, she realized that he wasn't holding her hand at all. He had wrapped his fingers around the bony end of her left wing and was gently peeling it upward and away from her face. As soon as the tip of the wing breached the windshield's protected air stream, the gale of their forward velocity thundered into its leathery pocket, blasting her wings open like a pair of broken storm shutters.

With a fleshy *slap*, the full span of Vivian's left wing filled up like a sail, ripping Trent's hands off the wheel and pinning him down against his seat. As the Rabbit careened madly across the empty lanes, the wind caught Vivian's right wing, blasting it open and nearly throwing her over the back of her seat.

Screaming and cursing, Bobby and Sherri clambered over each other and into a scramble of uncoordinated aid. Bobby leaned over the side of the car and grabbed the end of Vivian's left wing in both hands. With a motion like he was trying to close a stubborn sliding door, he brutally thrust the bony wing back toward his sister. Vivian wailed as a manhandled joint tried unsuccessfully to bend the wrong direction.

"Ouuuch!" she howled. "Stop it—you'll break my arm!"

"I'm not touching your arm!" Bobby screamed. "Come on, Vivian! Work with me here!"

"I can't! I can't bend it!" Vivian shrieked. "Trent! Let off the gas pedal!"

"Mmmgrrlllph!" Trent replied.

Sherri's palm shot forward and popped a hyperextended wing joint back into place, allowing Trent's scrambling hands to fold the wing down against Vivian's side. He grabbed the wheel with two shaky fists, pulling the car back under control.

Sherri clenched Vivian's collapsed left wing in a bunch between the front seats. To her right she noticed Erik sitting, flushed and silent. All four of his hands gently held strategic points on Vivian's forgotten right wing, which was neatly folded between the passenger seat and the inside of the door. Sherri raised a curious eyebrow at him and his eyes darted away from her.

"Damn, Vivi!" Trent squeaked. "Control yourself, girl! Back up off the T until the vehicle has come to a complete stop, a'ight?"

"But I didn't ... you ... *you!*" Vivian stammered, nursing the pain of a dislocated elbow that wasn't. "Just shut up, you idiot! Leave me alone. Everybody leave me alone!"

She slapped away all of the helping hands, grabbed her wings, and yanked them around her trembling shoulders like a cloak.

Bobby leaned forward and patted his sister's knotted wing.

"Don't worry, Viv. It's not that bad. You're going to be okay."

"That's easy for *you* to say! You don't look like something out of some freaky Japanese cartoon! Why is this *happening* to me?!"

"Don't sweat it, Vivi. I'm sure it's all just part of God's master plan for you," Trent said. "The Lord works in mysterious ways, yo."

"Ha!" Sherri spat. "*The Lord,* he says!"

She grabbed Erik's mutant wrist, shaking its gnarled paw in the air.

"When it was just *Erik* sporting the extra equipment, you're all fire and brimstone and Hell on Earth, but as soon as we've got a pair of wings ripping out opposite a pair of tits, it's suddenly *the Lord's* work."

"Well, I don't know what else it could be, oh ye of questionable faith," Trent said. "It's not alcohol that keeps us safe from doing the biological freakout, because Vivi was drinking, just like us."

"I was drinking too," Erik said, grabbing his paw out of Sherri's grasp and dropping its dead weight in his lap.

"And it also has nothing to do with the soul," Trent continued, "because when I look into those shimmering pools of green that are Vivi's breathtaking eyes, all I can see is miles of perfect, unblemished human soul."

"And also, *I* have a soul too," Erik growled.

"So it's got to be the Lord's plan," Trent concluded. "Ain't no other way around it."

"Uh, I hate to tear open your watertight argument," Erik said, "but there are most *certainly* ways around it."

"Like what?" Trent asked.

"Well, like that rotten pink vapor, for one thing," Erik replied. "I'm sure that stuff was toxic! It must have contaminated Twiki and Vivian and me."

"But what about the rest of us then?" Bobby said. "We were all in that shit too, and nothing's happened to us."

"Yet," Sherri added.

"Wait, hold up. Maybe it's because we were in that yellow submarine," Trent said. "That thing was as airtight as a dolphin's derrière. Maybe the mutant juice wore off the fog before we got all up in it, yo."

"Or maybe the miracle cure is frat-boy jizz," Sherri said.

"Ack. Jesus," Bobby grimaced, mopping phantom goo from his arms. "If that's the antidote, I'd rather have the extra limbs."

"Aaaugh! Knock it off!" Sherri squeaked. "You're getting your fat-boy body dandruff all over me!"

As Sherri furiously brushed Bobby's flaked-off sunburn from her leg, twice as much of her own scorched flesh crumbled through her fishnets and back onto him.

"Hey. Hey, wait a sec," Bobby pondered. "I just realized—you, me, Trent— we all got sunburned!"

"No shit," Sherri said, scraping her ragged arms. "I'm fucking molting over here."

"So listen," Bobby said, "maybe whatever is causing the mutations got in through the skin. Since our skin was all scorched on the morning after, maybe that pink shit in the air couldn't absorb through it. Maybe the burn lasted long enough to protect us, even though it's all gone now."

"Whatever," Trent muttered. "Speak for yourself, Heavy B."

He turned his collar away from the beet-red blister that still covered the back of his neck and ran down his muscular arms.

"I ain't fine at all," he continued. "This shit burns like a son of a bitch. I need to get my aloe on, for real."

Bobby shrugged and probed the clotted cut on his forehead with a stubby forefinger.

"Well, I don't know about Sherri, but fast healing has always been in my family's blood. Hey! Maybe it has something to do with the blood, or the white blood cells or something. Sunburns make all the blood come to the surface of the skin, you know? Maybe that's what made Twiki and Erik and Viv different from us!"

"What difference does it make?" Sherri sighed. "It's not like you're going to solve the puzzle and Pat Sajak is going to come out and give you the antidote and a fucking dinette set!"

"You're right," Vivian said darkly. "Figuring out the cause won't help Erik and me at this point, but at least there's still a chance we can prevent it from happening to the rest of you."

"*Prevent* it?!" Sherri squealed. "Why?! Am I the only one who thinks that this shit is dead sexy? I mean, tell me that this isn't totally bad-ass!"

She grabbed Erik's greasy black paw and thrust it between the two front seats and into the back of Trent's sunburnt arm.

"Aaah! Christ Almighty!" Trent wailed. "Hands off the T-man, Evil E! I just told you that sunburn still stings like an S.O.B! Don't go puttin' your ugly-ass mouse mitts all up on me!"

Erik grabbed his limp rat hand and thrust it back into his lap, but this time Sherri did not let go.

"Sooo, okay then, thank you," he scowled. "Leggo my Eggo."

Sherri intertwined her fingers with the claws and stroked the furry arm with fascination.

"Relax, Sievert. I'm not going to hurt you. I just think it's kinda cool, that's all."

"Whoa!" Bobby gasped. "That's the first time you've ever admitted to liking something that isn't an addictive chemical!"

"Stuff it, fat-ass," Sherri barked. "*You're* still on my shit list."

As her slender hands moved up and down the long, hairy limb lying across his lap, Erik's groin clenched nervously.

"Hey! Hey there. Watch it, you."

His cheeks burned as Sherri continued to molest his mutant arms.

"Whoa! These things are getting *really warm* all of the sudden!" she grinned. "God, I'm freezing! Gimme some of that heat!"

With a dramatic plunge, her tiny head dropped into Erik's lap. She nuzzled her frosty face into his warm fur, inadvertently rubbing her peeling nose provocatively against the fly of his pants.

"Whoa, whoa! Knock it off!" Erik squeaked, pulling her face from his groin. "If you want to snuggle up with something hairy and gross, I'll switch seats with Trent!"

"To the contrary, Furry E," Trent said. "The T is completely hairless. At least where it counts."

Sherri shuddered.

"Don't worry, Trent," she said. "I'm sure you'll hit puberty *someday*."

"Puberty is overrated, yo," Trent grinned. "Believe me. I was the last guy in my class to go through the special time, and while the rest of the pack was all pushin' out the shrubs, all the little girlies were up on Smooth T. Now I gots to bust out the lift-and-cut action, but I can still give you the simulated stimulation of gettin' jiggy with a late bloomer, girl."

Sherri shook her head with a nauseous moan.

"Trent, you are truly amazing. Just when I think that you can't *possibly* get any more disgusting, you manage to vomit up a shitbomb like that."

"Seriously!" Bobby agreed. "Dude, have any of your skanky lines ever worked on a woman, *ever?*"

"The words aren't as important as the moment," Trent shrugged. "Sometimes even the oldest line in the book will tickle a lady's fancy if the moment is just right, yo."

"For example?" Vivian asked skeptically.

Just then, the tired Rabbit began to buck against the pavement, sputtering black death from its tailpipe as the engine fell silent. When the vehicle had rolled to a complete stop, Trent put his arm around Vivian's winged shoulders with a grin.

"I'm sorry, baby, we just ran out of gas. I guess we'll just have to find a way to keep ourselves occupied until help shows up."

Vivian looked at Trent, blinked once, and got out of the car.

"Hey, come on! Give me some credit!" Trent said. "At least I didn't do 'put out or get out'!"

Though unplanned, the chance to get out of the tiny convertible was more than welcomed. Trent took two cans of gasoline from the trunk and refilled the exhausted fuel tank while Sherri stood nearby, conspicuously flicking the burning ash from her cigarette in his direction.

Erik stood with his hands on his hips, squinting at another weathered billboard. The ubiquitous cartoon Mountie held an oversized gold coin between his thumb and forefinger, and a patch of lettering screamed, *"Go loonie at North of the Border!"*

"I don't get it," he said flatly.

On the other side of the road, Vivian took long, regal steps, stretching the weariness from her long-cramped legs. Her wings hung naturally from her back, or at least as naturally as two sprawling black bat wings *could* hang from a young woman's back. They folded down neatly against themselves, their tops rising six inches above her shoulders and their bottoms hanging near her waist. She turned slowly in place, scanning a ceiling of gray sky resting on black pillars of cities that were no more.

"I can't believe we haven't found civilization yet," she said. "I thought we would have at least *seen* something by now."

Bobby nodded.

"It's hard to tell what's beyond the tree line. We might be able to actually find something if we could get a view of the whole area from the sky."

"Yeah, I suppose so," Vivian agreed.

"So why don't you just fly around for a while and see if you can spot anything."

"What … *me?*" Vivian said. "Bobby, what in the world makes you think that I can fly?"

"Well gee, Viv, because you're the only one with a pilot's license."

"Get real, Bobby," Vivian grumbled. "Just because I have these wing … like … *things,* it doesn't mean that I can magically fly. There's more to it than that."

"Oh, come on. You haven't even tried."

"No," Vivian agreed, "I have not."

"Well, what are you waiting for—a magic feather?"

"No, I'm waiting for a fundamental shift in the laws of aerodynamics! It's physically impossible! Humans aren't biologically designed for flight!"

"Yeah, and humans don't typically have *wings* either!"

"All right, all right!" Vivian snapped. "Fine! I'll show you that I can't do it!"

"That's right, think positive," Bobby said sarcastically.

Vivian bounced on the balls of her feet, squinting into the clouds and holding her arms out eagerly to her sides. If Bobby didn't know better, he might have suspected she was about to steal second base.

"Flap," she thought.

Nothing happened.

"Flap," she grumbled, clenching her teeth. "Flap! Flap flap flap!"

"Come on, Viv," Bobby moaned. "They're not even moving."

"I *know* they're not moving!"

She grabbed the ends of the wings and yanked them out to arm's length, flapping them furiously.

"And … *flap!*"

The second she let go of them, the wings fell back into their relaxed fold, bouncing to a stop against her back like a cheap Halloween costume accessory.

"There! See?! I told you it wouldn't work. They're not real wings. They don't work. I can't control them."

Before Vivian could say another word, a pair of large, muscular hands grasped her around the waist from behind.

"All you need is a little thrust, and when a woman needs thrust, the T is just the man to—"

Vivian's shoulders tensed in revulsion. This was followed immediately by the sound of flesh hitting flesh, then flesh hitting pavement. She was thrown three stumbling steps forward, but she regained her balance and spun around. Six feet away from her, Trent lay on the ground, moaning and rubbing his abruptly bloodied face.

"Trent! What the …"

Suddenly realizing why her center of gravity was so awkwardly misplaced, Vivian looked over her shoulder and saw her entire six-foot wingspan stretched out behind her. As if they had been caught at the scene of a crime, the wings guiltily dropped back into their folded position with a flutter.

"I'm sorry!" Vivian squeaked. "Are you okay?"

"I'm fine, I'm fine," Trent muttered, putting down his hands and trying to look nonchalant.

"Ugh!" Bobby gasped. "Gross!"

"Ain't nothin' but a thang," Trent said, climbing to his feet. "Forget it. S'all good."

Despite his assurances, Trent's pummeled face had already swollen into a red puffy mess. His punched-in eyes rapidly blackened as a small cut leaked more blood down his left cheek than it had any right to.

"Ha haa!" Sherri laughed. "The big man just got the shit beat out of him by a girl!"

"I said it ain't nothin' but a thang!" Trent shouted, wiping away the blood. "Just drop it, a'ight?!"

"You see, Bobby?" Vivian said angrily, tugging at her wings. "All these things are good for is getting people hurt! I can't *fly* with them! I can't even control them!"

"Enough with this 'I can't control them' shit!" Sherri snapped. "I've been watching both of you freakjobs, and those mutant parts do everything that you want them to!"

"What are you talking about?" Vivian said. "I can't control them at all!"

"Neither can I!" Erik agreed.

"Bullshit!" Sherri said. "Sievert, I saw you grab the powderpuff's wing with your rat arms in the car! And now *both* of you have thrown mutant punches at Trent's face! Tell me that *that's* not controlling them!"

"Well, I mean, I can't *control* them, as such," Erik admitted, "but sometimes they just do what I *want* them to."

"Wait, hold up!" Trent snapped. "When you punched me right in my grill you swore up and down that you didn't make them hit me!"

"I didn't *make* them hit you!" Erik said. "But I never said that I didn't *want* them to hit you."

"Man, that's a load of semantic *buuullshit*," Trent scowled.

"But what about me?" Vivian asked. "My wings don't do what I want them to at all. I couldn't even get them to flap!"

"No," Erik agreed, "but you've got to admit, they *did* just beat the shit out of Trent."

"It's just a scratch, a'ight?!" Trent snapped. "Damn!"

"Wait, I think I get it!" Sherri said. "This is just like this guy I know who got his arm ripped off in a motorcycle accident."

"How so?" Vivian asked.

"If you licked the guy's flesh stump, he could feel you licking his missing hand."

"Eww!" Erik cringed. "So what?!"

"So what?! So *this!*"

Sherri grabbed Erik's left rat paw and painted a long, wet swath of saliva up its palm with her tongue.

"Eeeaugh!" Erik gasped, wiping his human right hand on his pants. "God, you're so disgusti—whoa."

He held up his dry, untouched right hand in bewilderment.

"See? That's what I'm saying," Sherri gloated, dropping the moistened left paw. "The connections to that guy's brain got all fucked up and made him think that there were still parts there that weren't. Maybe your brain is all fucked up because there's parts there that *shouldn't be.*"

"So what does all that mean for us?" Erik asked.

"How the hell should I know?" Sherri shrugged. "I just wanted to lick your rat hand."

The cold wind licked the sides of the Rabbit as it plunged down the dusty interstate. The sky turned from a dismal, cloudy gray to an inky black as the sun set on the other side of the atomic cloud. Another blasted billboard slid into view from the darkened roadside, revealing the ever-present Mountie wearing a bib and holding a knife and fork over a plate piled high with cartoon food. Erik read the sign hungrily.

"Don't miss North of the Border's 'All *Yukon* eat buffet!'"

"Man, a buffet sounds good about now," Bobby said. "A mile of steamer trays piled high with scrambled eggs and fish sticks and greasy bacon and chicken nuggets and French toast."

"That's disgusting," Sherri said. "The buffet line is a symbol of why our whole food-based culture is bullshit. It's America sticking its big, fat, overfed middle finger right in the face of starving people all over the—"

Her tiny stomach rumbled like thunder rolling off a Category Five hurricane.

"Alright, I don't care," she admitted. "I'm fucking starving."

She leaned back in her seat and Bobby's sagging gut rolled against her peeling side like a manatee desperate for affection.

"Alright, this is fucking ridiculous," she protested, throwing an elbow. "Isn't it Lard Lad's turn to drive for a while?"

"Can't drive stick," Bobby shrugged.

"But isn't it about time you *learned?!*" Sherri hissed. "Seriously, why the fuck is Trent still driving? He can't even see where he's going!"

Trent's hideously swollen eyes peeked into the rearview mirror through a pillow of yellow-purple bruise.

"It's not like all that, yo. I can see everything I need to see to guide us safely."

"Why?" Sherri sneered. "Because God is your co-pilot? Please tell me that you weren't about to say because God is your co-pilot."

Trent's bloated eyes blinked sheepishly and returned to the road.

"Seriously," Sherri continued, "how long are we going to keep this shit up? We don't even know where we're going!"

"Maybe we don't," Vivian said. "But we do know where we've been."

She cast a poignant glance into the rearview mirror at the charred landscape behind them. She turned back to the windshield and continued.

"There's got to be better things ahead."

"Oooh, that's so inspirational!" Sherri smirked. "Get a clue, Powderpuff. There's nothing for a thousand miles in any direction but burned-up cities full of burned-up assholes. Everyone knows mankind has been trying to wipe itself out since the dawn of time. Now it finally happened, and somehow we missed the boat."

"For real," Trent agreed. "Man got too big for his britches, tried to play God, and got the atomic smackdown. Now we've got to start the whole show over again all by ourselves."

"Stop it! Both of you!" Vivian shouted. "Nothing says that we're by ourselves! Just because we haven't *found* anybody else yet doesn't mean that there *isn't* anybody else."

"Your optimism is refreshing," Bobby frowned, "but seriously, we've gone at least five hundred miles and every major city we've passed has been a *Terminator-2*-style dystopia of flame and skulls."

"Yes, major cities," Vivian said sternly. "*Major* cities. If we're dealing with the war to end all wars, and I'm beginning to think we are, of course all the *major* cities are gone. We need to find some sleepy little town with no strategic importance."

"I used to live in a town like that," Sherri said. "They bombed the living shit out of it."

"She's right," Bobby said. "Stillwater was nothing but beaches and old people, and that got nuked all to hell."

"All right, all right. You're right," Vivian sighed. "My point is that there's got to be *someplace* so insignificant and pointless that nobody in their right mind would bother destroying it. If only we had some clue where it was."

She crossed her arms and slumped in her seat as a colossal pair of wooden antlers emerged from the darkness.

Straight ahead, you can't moose it! North of the Border. Next exit.

CHAPTER TEN

The Rabbit chugged up a cracked driveway and between the blasted steel legs of a seventy-foot-tall cartoon Mountie colossus. In his hands was an enormous sign, emblazoned with a broken neon greeting: "Welcome to North of the Border!"

As if seeking safety in numbers, the convertible crunched to a stop next to the only other car in the gravel parking lot. It was a sedan from the '80s, but its heavy covering of fallout ash gave it the aura of an ancient archeological relic.

"Well, I guess we're here," Trent said skeptically.

"It's about time," Sherri grumbled. "Let me out of this crapmobile."

She stood up on the crowded back seat and hopped over the side of the car. Before her boots could hit the ground, the tangled strands of her coat caught on the broken roof hinges, yanking her out of the air mid-leap. She landed on her knees in the gravel.

"Ow, God damn it!" she seethed, climbing to her feet and rubbing her scraped knee. "I hate this piece-of-shit coat!"

She grabbed the knotted leather strands and yanked with both hands, snapping off the broken hinge with a sad little squeak of rusted metal.

"That coat is spent, for real," Trent said. "Why don't you just lose it? You'd look better without it anyway."

"Oh, sure. Okay," Sherri said, pulling the remains of her coat around her body. "I'm willing to freeze to death as long as it makes me look good to a poseur asshole with a load in his diaper."

Trent put his hands over the conspicuous lump on the back of his coarsely bandaged pelvis.

"It ain't like that. The only load here is the load of bills in my *fat wallet.*"

Sherri shook her head.

"Whatever, Mr. Poo Poo Pants."

At the far end of the parking lot, a break in the snow-flocked perimeter wall framed a leaning parody of a customs house flying a Canadian flag over a set of turnstiles. A cold breeze blew through its shattered windows, gathering papers from within and distributing them like fallen leaves. Vivian took it all in with a hopeful look straining against all logic to reach her face.

"Of course, I am not one to doubt the wisdom of the fairer sex, Vivi," Trent said, "but we drive straight on through for a million miles, and *this* is the first place you want to stop?"

"Seriously," Sherri nodded. "What a shithole."

"You're right—it is," Vivian agreed. "Exactly. That's my point! No country would bomb a place like this!"

"Canada might," Bobby said.

"Well, let's not just stand here, you *hosers*. Let's check it out, *eh?*" Erik said, as if still reading a billboard. "What do you *Saskatchewan-na* do first?"

"Let me at that buffet," Bobby said. "I hear they have four pounds of back bacon, three French toasts, two turtlenecks, and a beer."

"Hold up, Hungry B," Trent said, popping the Rabbit's trunk. "We can't just go charging in there unprotected. There might be something in there that wants to take a bite out of *us*."

He pulled out the shotgun and clapped it to his shoulder like a square-jawed hero in a bad war movie.

"Oh jeez," Bobby said. "Put that away before you hurt somebody."

"My aim is to see that *nobody* gets hurt," Trent said, offering his elbow to Vivian with a greasy smile. "May I provide secure passage to your feast, my lady?"

Vivian's wings twitched against her shoulders.

"You know, you're still bleeding from the *last* time you tried to help me."

Trent's hand shot to his face, wiping a fresh smear of blood from his cheek. Vivian crunched across the driveway and pushed through the rusted turnstile. Unfazed, Trent wiped his hand on his pants, turned, and offered it to Sherri instead.

"Alrighty then, Goldilocks. How would you like an armed guard to escort you safely to the ball?"

"I've got something to escort to your balls right here," Sherri said, clenching her hand into a fist. "That gun's not even loaded, you tool."

Trent squinted at Sherri, then at the shotgun. He cupped his hand over the end of the barrel, surreptitiously peeked inside, and shrugged. He returned the gun to the trunk, digging out his trusty old sword instead.

"I best keep it old school then," he said, turning with a swish of his blade. "Tried and true is the way to be, right, B?"

As his words fell unheard in the empty parking lot, Trent realized that he had been abandoned. He rushed to the turnstile and planted a hand on its cold steel top, leaping over it with his sword in the air like a medieval commando.

"Hold up, y'all," he shouted, rejoining the pack. "The T doesn't want to be the last one to get at those tasty ... aw, *hell* no."

Although none of them had expected much from this seedy tourist trap, North of the Border still managed to disappoint. What was once a log cabin village of stilted Canadian stereotype was now little more than a field of ravaged debris punctuated with novelty beaver pelts. Bobby read from a banner that unfurled from a faux-snowy concrete pillar.

"North of the Border: Family fun from 'Eh' to 'Zed.'"

"Who's Zed?" Trent asked.

"Zed's dead, baby," Erik said dimly. "Zed's dead."

"I don't get it," Trent said. "Who would up and bomb some skeezy interstate tourist trap, yo?"

Vivian's eyes were fixed and glassy, staring at everything and nothing at once.

"It wasn't bombed," she muttered. "There's no fire damage here."

"Well then, what happened?" Erik asked. "It looks like Godzilla stomped on this place."

Vivian turned until she saw the all too familiar silhouette against the blackening sky. A few miles away, a column of black smoke folded darkly into the night. She pointed.

"That explosion did this. A nuclear detonation causes a disc-shaped hydrodynamic front of radially expanding gases in the atmosphere."

The others looked at her skeptically. She rephrased.

"The static overpressure creates dynamic pressures."

The group continued to gaze at her blankly. She frowned.

"Bomb make big wind."

Everyone nodded and made general sounds of acknowledgment. Vivian pulled off her glasses and rubbed her eyes.

"Well, this place was a dead end," Erik said. "I guess we should get going."

"No, we might as well stay here for the night now," Vivian sighed. "It's getting too dark to drive without headlights. Maybe if we look around we can at least find some shelter."

"No way, no how," Trent said firmly. "This place got the K.O. all the day-o. I'm not letting you lay your pretty head down in some busted-ass cabin just to wake up with it smashed under a ton of logs in the morning."

Vivian took a few steps down the path, peering through the maze of shattered lumber that had once been a neighborhood of tacky shops.

"Let's just take a look around, all right?" she said, striding around a corner. "There must be *something* that we can sleep in. Maybe there's some kind of utility shed, or shuttle bus, or an—"

She stopped in her tracks.

"… igloo."

In front of Vivian was a dome of coarse cement towering fifty feet into the air. It was apparent that it had been bluish white many decades ago, but today brittle curls of paint revealed broad gray patches of poured concrete. A loose grid of dark blue lines suggested ice blocks, making the dome look like an igloo, but only to one whose familiarity with igloos did not extend beyond the realm of Chilly Willy cartoons. Although the igloo had put up a good fight, the overpressure had knocked a large crack across the apex of its dome.

"What is that thing?" Bobby asked.

"It's an igloo," Erik said. "Haven't you ever seen a Chilly Willy cartoon?"

"Well, I *know* it's an igloo," Bobby said impatiently. "But what *is* it?"

"I don't know," Vivian said, pointing to a series of sheared bolts. "The sign is missing."

An arched entryway of crudely formed cement extended twenty feet from the base of the dome, ending in a pair of broken glass doors. A sign hung from a chain in the empty doorframe.

Sorry, we're closed!

Vivian peered into the inky darkness and her stomach tightened.

"Hey, Trent," she said casually. "Why don't you go scout it out while we keep looking around out here?"

Trent shook his head.

"You know that I live to make your every wish come true, but I can't go in there and leave you here unprotected."

"Don't worry," Erik said. "I'll be here to protect her."

"What do you think I'm protecting her *from?*" Trent muttered.

"Jesus Herbert Christ," Sherri sighed. "You can all just sit out here and wait for your balls to drop—I'm going to go in there and find some food."

Sherri stepped through the broken door, carefully avoiding its teeth of shattered glass. Vivian watched the black abyss close around her friend as she slid into the shadows. In another two steps, she would vanish, and then ... who knew what?

"Sherri, wait!" Vivian called. "I'm sorry. You're right. You shouldn't go by yourself. I'll go with you."

Trent leapt to her side with a jaunty step, thrusting his sword toward the door.

"Please, allow me to accompany you," he said. "It goes against my nature to send two lovely ladies into a dark room all by themselves."

"Then I'm coming too," Bobby said. "For protection."

"But what about me?" Trent asked.

"What do you think I'm protecting them *from?*" Bobby muttered.

"Could one of you bring me back a sandwich?" Erik squeaked.

Vivian looked sympathetically into his eyes and took his hand.

"Come on, Erik," she said. "We'll be fine if we stick together. Five is better than one."

Bobby held the 5-in-1 camping lantern in front of him, in "flashlight" mode, carving a shaft of light through the igloo's entryway. As the lamp cleared the tunnel, shadows of a large, semicircular room loomed into view. The apex of the curved ceiling was indistinguishable in the darkness, save for a dull patch of gray sky representing the gaping hole in the roof.

Bobby squeezed his eyes shut and then fluttered them open, trying to accelerate their adjustment to the dim light. He slipped on the tiled floor, but grabbed Erik's arm before he could fall.

"Aaah! What?! What?!" Erik panicked, grabbing Bobby with four terrified hands.

"Nothing—nothing—jeez!" Bobby said, slapping him away. "Careful—the floor is wet. Don't fall. And don't wet yourself, spaz."

Bobby turned and held the lantern out in front of him, throwing its light over a hideous figure and forcing an uncharacteristic shriek from his lips.

"What?!" Erik chirped. "What is it?!"

"Oh! Oh, shit ... heh," Bobby chuckled.

He held the lantern up to a mannequin in a Mountie uniform saluting a flag that wasn't there. Although it seemed human in every other way, the figure's face had been paper-machéd into that of a grotesque bumblebee, and two giant wings had been bolted to its back. A signboard rested in its free hand, reading "Buzz in for a honey of a sale!"

"It's a bee," Bobby said, perplexed. "A Royal Canadian Mounted Bumblebee."

"A bee. A Mountie bee," Erik mulled. "Wait. Mountie bee? Mounteebee? Moun-T-B?"

He rubbed his chin and stared.

"No, I don't get this one either."

Bobby planted the lantern on the figure's head and pulled the shoulder strap under its chin. He clicked the switch to "lantern" mode, effectively turning the Mountie Bee into a lamppost that cast an eerie light over the room.

"What is this place?" Sherri squinted. "I can't see shit in here."

"Well, it's not the buffet—I can say that much," Bobby said.

"It's a gift shop," Vivian realized. "Or at least it was."

Vivian could imagine how the place had looked before the disaster. Rows of tall glass shelves, laden with key chains and ashtrays and personalized coffee mugs waiting to be plucked up by loud tourists in louder shirts. Many of the shelves now lay shattered on the floor, but others remained standing, untouched save for a blanket of dust that had fallen through the ceiling.

"It looks like that blast wind totally wrecked this place too," Erik said.

"Nahh." Bobby pointed to the hole in the ceiling. "I think the dome took the piss and vinegar out of that. This probably all happened when the roof caved in."

"I don't think so," Vivian said. "Look at this."

She ran a fingertip through the dust on a shelf. The flat powder swirled into a paisley of cloudy gray and rich maroon. She held up her soiled finger poignantly.

"Blood," she said. "It's all over everything."

Trent put his hand forcefully on Vivian's shoulder, raising his blade with the other.

"Another mutant attack! Don't worry, girl. I've got your back."

"Oooookay then! Nothing left to see in here," Erik said, taking a big step toward the exit. "Let's get back to the car."

"Oh, for cryin' out loud," Bobby moaned, grabbing Erik. "You said yourself that the mutations were caused by that toxic pink cloud. We've been out of that shit for three states! Relax, we're never going to see another mutant again."

Erik looked at the paws hanging from his midsection.

"Present company excluded, of course," Bobby corrected.

"I don't think it was mutants either," Vivian agreed, pushing Trent's hand off of her shoulder. "I think this blood was spilled in panic. You know how skittish tourists are. When the bomb went off, this place must have turned to complete chaos."

"Well, I don't give a flying fuck what happened in here, as long as there's some food left," Sherri said. "I'm starving."

"And when a lovely lady has a hunger at any hour or in any place, she can count on chef T to come to her aid with a fresh confectionery treat," Trent rambled, plucking up a cellophane bag. "Would a sweet girl like a sweet maple candy?"

"How the fuck should I know what a sweet girl would like?" Sherri said.

She snatched the bag, tore it open, and stuffed a soft, crumbly candy in her mouth. A second later she spit it back out with a sputtering cough.

"Bleeagh! It's like licking the floor of an IHOP!" she gagged, throwing the bag on the floor. "What else you got?"

Trent scanned the slanted shelf, reading each label aloud.

"Maple sugar, maple syrup, maple cookies, maple butter, maple cream—"

"Stop—just stop," Sherri said, shaking her head. "Do you have anything that's *not* completely disgusting?"

"Well, there's this bag of barbecue-flavored worm larvae."

Sherri grabbed the bag and tore it open.

"Now that's more like it."

"Well, this place is a total bust," Bobby said. "Unless any of you want to pick up a North of the Border T-shirt to remember this delightful experience."

"I could find a souvenir," Erik said flatly. "Just to prove the world was here."

Vivian, rubbing her frosty arms, concurred.

"We should *all* find souvenirs," she said. "Look around. There's probably some stuff we can use in here. At the very least we should all find something to wear to keep warm."

"Hell yeah," Sherri said, loosening the belt on her coat. "I call dibs on the first thing anyone finds that's black and encrusted in metal studs!"

"Fine," Bobby said. "I'll let you know if I find Dennis Rodman."

"Ba-zing!" Erik added.

The five survivors spread out through the semi-circular room. Bobby found himself in one of its two legitimate corners, formed by a wall that bisected the dome at its center. A huge section of collapsed ceiling lay heaped against this flat wall. With a grunt, he plopped down on the slab and picked up a bag of maple candies at his feet. He popped one in his mouth and managed to chew it twice before violently spitting it out.

"Blah!" he gasped, wiping his tongue. "It *is* like licking the floor of an IHOP."

He pitched the bag over his shoulder and a dull metallic thud echoed from the shadows. With a puzzled squint, he climbed to his feet to investigate. The debris was piled up against a pair of steel doors in the flat wall, barricading them shut. He wiped the dust from a small rectangular outline on the door, uncovering a plaque reading "Exit only."

"Huh. I wonder where the entrance is."

At the end of a derelict aisle elsewhere in the shop, Vivian found a large wire bin marked "Clothing Clearance!"

The first thing on the pile was an oversized wool varsity jacket, red with white sleeves. The back sported both a white Canadian maple leaf emblem and a large, unfortunate coffee stain.

She slipped her right arm into the sleeve, but when she reached back with her left she hit a wall of leathery wing. She leaned back and swung her shoulders until she managed to catch the left sleeve, but there was no way she could wrestle it on over her wings. It was like trying to put on a tube top over a camping backpack.

She pulled her arm from the sleeve and tapped her chin thoughtfully. If she couldn't go *around* them, maybe she could go *over* them. With the jacket in front of her, she slipped her arms into the sleeves and then pushed the rest over her head. It bunched up on top of her wings, yanking her shoulders to her ears and turning her into a hunchback. With a violent thrashing of her arms, she pulled the coat back over her head, leaving her hair standing in a statically charged frizz. Erik wandered into the end of the aisle with a giggle.

"Need some help there, Puffy?"

"Forget it," Vivian snapped, jerking the coat off of her arms and handing it to Erik. "Here, you take this. It'll fit *you*."

"Oh, thanks. But ... ladies first, you know? You keep it; I'll find one of my own."

"No, it's okay," Vivian sighed. "It's too small for me."

"Too small? Whatever. This thing could fit Bobby!"

Vivian thumbed over her shoulders at her wings.

"Oh," Erik said. "Right. Er … sorry."

"Hey hey, what's going on over here?" Trent interjected, sliding between Vivian and Erik. "Oh, Little E, that's disgraceful. Just disgraceful. How can you take the only coat for yourself when sweet Vivi is standing *right here,* chilled to her very bones? You are a sorry excuse for a man."

"I didn't! I mean, she—I—" Erik bumbled. "Oh, just shut up and mind your own damn business, Trent."

"Mind my own business, he says. How can I mind my own business when such a great injustice is being done to such a beautiful woman?"

Trent grabbed the jacket out of Erik's hands and returned it to Vivian. Vivian, in turn, handed the coat back to Erik.

"Knock it off, Trent. It doesn't fit me."

"Ah, you're right. It doesn't *fit* you at all," Trent winked. "I see where you're comin' from, Vivi. It would be an insult to nature to mask such a beautiful figure in such a utilitarian garment. A girl like you requires a little *style.*"

He swept a small mannequin bust from a nearby shelf, cradling it in one arm like a toddler. With a flourish he pulled a jacket from the armless torso and held it out toward Vivian.

"Here you are, my princess of discerning style. Your royal robes await."

Vivian looked skeptically at Trent's offering. It was a tiny white jacket with fluffy faux fur ringing its hem, cuffs, and hood. On its back, silver embroidery traced a crown and the words "Eskimo Princess."

"Trent," Vivian said dryly. "That is a child's size."

"So it is! That just means it's a perfect fit for my little babydoll," Trent cooed. "Ain't no man ever complained that his girlie girl's clothes were too small. Come on, Vivi. Flaunt it if you got it! You don't want people to think you're some kind of prude!"

Vivian's wings bristled against her back as her teeth ground together.

"Let me know when those black eyes go away. I'm saving another pair for you."

With that, she turned and stormed down the aisle, her wings knocking a load of curios from the shelves as they made one threatening flap behind her. Erik and Trent watched her leave and then turned on each other with mutual hostility.

"Women," Trent shrugged. "They talk tough, but they're all soft little pussycats inside."

Erik raised an eyebrow.

"You know, your face is *still* bleeding from where she beat the shit out of you."

Trent scowled and yanked the varsity jacket from Erik's hands.

"That's mine," he barked. "Go find something with more arms in it, freak boy."

On the other side of the shop, Bobby was standing behind the checkout counter. He punched a button on the old-fashioned register, and the drawer opened with a mechanical *ker-ching!* It was completely empty, bereft of even its money tray. He pushed it shut and squatted down to look under the counter. There was nothing there but a stack of mismatched coat hangers, an empty Diet Pepsi can, and a roll of tickets. They were of the generic sort that came in two halves, one ordering the bearer to "Keep this coupon," the other simply reading "Ticket."

"Tickets," he thought. *"Tickets to what?"*

He stood up, looking around the register for clues. On the back wall was a dry-erase board completely coated in dust. He slapped his palm onto the board and wiped away a streak of filth—and marker—leaving nothing but clean white lamination.

"Gah! Stupid!" he thought.

With several spittle-laden blasts of air, he blew enough dust off the board to reveal the remaining words. It was a schedule of operating hours and ticket prices. He ran his hand across his stubbly face with a grumble. It should have been obvious what the hours were for. It was written across the top of the board clear as day.

With one giant hand-streak through it.

North o ... rder

In ... gloo

B ... oo

"Ingloo boo," he thought. *"Inner igloo ... bamboo? Internet igloo broadband ... hullabaloo? Insanity igloo brain shampoo?"*

He stared at the blank spot and blinked.

"I got nothin'."

Vivian stomped down an aisle of bent steel and broken glass. She slumped against the concrete wall, sliding her winged back down its curve until she was sitting on the floor with her knees bunched up to her chest. Although she was furious at Trent, she knew that he wasn't really the problem. He was merely the drawstring on the garbage bag of horror that was enveloping her entire life.

She slipped her fingers under her glasses and wiped her pooling eyes, gazing blankly at the shelf in front of her. It was conspicuously empty. A large, opened cardboard box sat in the aisle to her side. She lifted one of the flaps and read the label.

SIX (6) - NOTB II MOUNTIE FRIENDS - #4 MORTIMER.

"NOTB II?" she thought. *"This is North of the Border two? I wonder where the original one is."*

Her mind wandered as her fingers slid over the corrugation of the cardboard flap. The tactile sensation of this box of unstocked merchandise flashed her back to the mundanity of her old job. Her old life.

She knelt down in front of the box, and noticed a small pink flip-flop in its shadow. It was typical, made of cheap foam and injected plastic. In fact, its only noteworthy feature was a splattering of telltale bloodstains. The empty shelf again caught her eye, and her lip began to quiver. She knew that this sandal had come from someone just like her. Someone who would never return to shelve this box of merchandise.

She set the flip-flop on the floor respectfully and reached into the abandoned box.

Three aisles away, Erik found a ball of gray fabric lying atop a shelf of otherwise colorful T-shirts. He picked it up and shook it, revealing a hooded sweatshirt with the words "North of" embroidered to one side of the zipper and "the Border" to the other. He slipped it on and held out his arms in appreciation. It was a good fit, and if he didn't zip it up, his extra limbs hung unmolested through its open front.

Bobby wandered up, muttering to himself.

"Inbred igloo birth taboo?"

Erik raised an eyebrow.

"What did you just say?"

"Wha? Oh, nothing …"

Sherri came up behind Bobby and growled through barbecue-scented-worm breath.

"Man, it's cold as a polar bear's ass in here. Haven't you clowns found anything I can wear yet?"

Trent swept in out of nowhere, pulling open the front of his oversized varsity jacket with a grin.

"Share the wealth, love. There's more than enough room in here for both of us."

Sherri squinted hard into the dim light, tracing Trent's coat with her weakened eyes.

"If I wanted that jock wrapper I'd have already killed you for it," she muttered. "I'd rather wear my own piece of shit coat than look like I'm fucking a high-school quarterback."

Erik pulled off his sweatshirt and handed it to her.

"Here, take this," he frowned. "You need it more than I do."

Trent snatched the hoodie from Erik's hand and threw it to the ground.

"And shroud this pretty young thing in ill-fitting cotton with mutant juju on it? Show a little bit of chivalry, Little E. For real! I can do better than your raggedy 'ol hand-me-downs."

He plucked the tiny "Eskimo Princess" jacket from the shelf, giving it a single, showy flap in the air.

"You can't deny that it's your size, my petite mademoiselle," he grinned. "And, excluding yours truly, it's got to be the warmest thing in the house!"

Sherri looked at the dainty coat hanging from Trent's hands as the cold of the sarcophagus-like room sliced through her bones. As she reached out and touched the furry cuff, the mangled sleeve of her own coat fell away from her arm, exposing its flaky surface to the frigid air. Though she could barely see the white jacket in the dim light, she could feel its quilted nylon sliding warmly between her trembling fingertips.

Her shoulders slumped with a resigned sigh.

"I'd rather freeze to death than wear that Gymboree bullshit. I'm just gonna go outside and set something on fire."

With that, she stomped to the corner of the room, planted her palms on a stainless steel push bar, and disappeared through an unknown exit. Erik squinted at the metal doors as they were pulled closed by a pair of old-fashioned pneumatic elbows.

"But the exit is ... that ... way?" he said, pointing behind him at the cement tunnel through which they had entered.

"Hey, cool!" Bobby beamed. "Sherri found the entrance door!"

"To what?"

"Damned if I know."

Vivian pulled a heavy statuette from the box and set it on the empty shelf with a sentimental gleam in her eye. The figure was an eight-inch praying mantis dressed in full Mountie regalia, cast in solid pewter. Like its bumblebee counterpart that guarded the door, the miniature Mountie stood at attention, bulbous eyes fixed on an unseen flag, clawed hand to his head in salute. Vivian saluted the figure.

"In memoriam," she whispered, "of the fallen clerks of the ..." She squinted at the text engraved on the figure's wooden base—"North of the Border ... Insect Igloo Bug Zoo?"

Before she could wonder what that meant, her focus was shattered by the sound of fists and boots pounding against steel doors.

"Shit! Shit! They're on me! They're all over me!" Sherri's muffled voice shrieked. "There's no fucking handles on this side! Open the fucking doors!"

Bobby ran to the door and slammed his palms into the release bar, and Sherri exploded into the igloo like a screeching missile.

"Fuck! Fucker fuckshit! Get 'em off! Get 'em off!"

Clinging to the strands of her coat were eight monstrous, crackling spiders, each spinning a web around its flailing prey. One the size of a basketball clung heavily to her back, slipping and clawing against the tattered leather. Another the size of a severed hand scurried nimbly around her head, wrapping it with a dense, sticky blindfold of webbing. Each bloated spider sported a horrific assortment of extra limbs that were never part of nature's blueprint.

"Do something, you fuckers!" Sherri screamed. "Help me!"

Wrapping a fist around the torso of Mortimer, the Mountie mantis, Vivian leapt to her feet.

"Sherri! Stand still!"

She bounded to Sherri's side and swung the figure's heavy wooden base through an oversized arachnid, throwing a heavy spatter of clear innards across the wall. The shattered spider fell to the ground with a piercing shriek and a heavy splash of viscera. The glistening chunks of its exoskeleton glowed a bold, ghostly blue.

"Get over here!" Vivian squeaked. "Help me!"

Erik jumped toward Sherri and raised a palm in preparation of a fierce slap. His eyes caught a spider with a row of jet-black ant legs running in an uneven row down its back, each one of them clawing against the air as if scurrying against a ground that wasn't there. He put down his trembling hand with a girlish whimper, then raised it again. Holding his breath and biting his lower lip, he slapped at the crackling spiders with his four bare hands, knocking them willy-nilly off of Sherri's body. Bobby jumped around in a kind of grotesque Irish jig, stomping on each spider that Erik knocked free. With each step, he left behind a puddle of crunched, glowing remains.

"Ack! Ack! Nasty!" he grimaced.

He could feel the slimy innards splattering over his Tevas and onto his exposed toes. Another frantic slap landed a spider the size of cantaloupe upside-down on the gooey floor. It righted itself with a surreal-looking undulation of its legs and started to scurry away.

"Oh no you don't," Bobby grunted.

As he leapt to smash the spider, his foot slipped, twisting his ankle with a *pop*. Swallowing a scream of pain, he tried to catch himself on his other leg, failed, and slammed into the remains of a shelving unit. An agonized wail tore from his throat as its shattered glass teeth sunk into his doughy abdomen. In a flash of pure reflex, Bobby slammed his palms into the shelf's metal frame, tipping it backward and extricating its blades from his gut with a sound like boots being pulled from mud. He made a move to retreat, but his greased feet went out from under him, dropping him flat on his back. He landed on the retreating spider, destroying it with a wet, splintering *crack*.

Bobby's head swam through a sea of shock and pain, but he still could see the fruits of his actions coming to bear. When he had shoved the shelf away it had rocked sharply onto its back legs, and it was now swinging forward again toward an equilibrium that it would never find. He managed to roll over and make one slippery surge against the floor before the toppling shelves slammed down on his back.

"Bobby!" Vivian wailed. "No!"

She ran to her brother's side and fell on her knees, dropping the slimy statuette. The display unit's heavy steel frame pinned Bobby to the ground, and its broken shelves sunk into the flesh of his back.

"Bobby!" Vivian sobbed. "Bobby, are you okay?"

Bobby lay with his cheek against the floor, barely moving. The blood from his back soaked through his spider-tainted shirt and mingled with the pool leaking from his perforated belly.

"It burns," he groaned. "It burns like a son of a bitch!"

Vivian looked up to find Trent struggling to close the door to the bug zoo. He had successfully shut one of the double doors, but the other was still wide open.

"I gotta close that shit up!" he screamed. "I can't close it! It won't close!"

Even in the frenzy of the moment, Vivian could see that the door's pneumatic elbow was locked open.

"Forget it!" Vivian screamed. "Get over here and help me!"

Trent scrambled to Vivian's side, his feet sliding in the pool of blood and dimly glowing spider guts that spread from beneath her brother.

"Grab the other side of the frame!" Vivian ordered, grabbing one side herself. "We've got to lift this off of him!"

Trent did as he was told, and after a quick three-count, the two began to lift the heavy shelving off of Bobby's wounded back. At that moment, Erik's continuously slapping hands batted an eleven-legged spider from Sherri's shoulder, throwing it directly onto Trent's straining chest. He immediately let go of the shelves in screaming shock.

"Aaah! Aaaaagh! Shit!"

Bobby howled as the unbalanced shelving unit slipped from Vivian's grasp and crashed back down on his back, but Trent didn't even seem to notice. His hands clawed frantically at the air in front of him, as if they were primed for action but had no idea what they were supposed to do.

"Lord Jesus Mary and Joseph!" he chattered. "Shit shit shit!"

Vivian clenched a fist around the Mountie mantis and slammed its base into Trent's chest with a spider-shattering crunch. His mouth dropped open with a gasp as she drew back her weapon, stretching out a gooey hammock of glowing innards. She threw down the statuette and returned to Bobby's side.

"Get over here and help me!" she demanded. "And don't drop it this time, you idiot!"

Trent croaked out a single, unintelligible word before slumping into a wheezing pile, the wind completely knocked out of him.

Erik slapped the last spider off of Sherri's head and stomped it dead. He grabbed her reeling shoulders, and his mutant arms reached out and gently steadied her at the waist.

"Whoa whoa!" he said. "It's okay! It's over!"

He peeled away her blindfold of webbing and swept it off her head. He tried to fling it to the floor, but it clung to his fingers.

"It's okay!" he assured her, shaking his entwined hand. "See? It's okay! We're safe! We're safe."

Sherri looked into Erik's kind eyes and fell into his four arms, squeezing him in a trembling embrace.

"I ... I ... it ..." she sobbed. "Thank you."

"Whoa. Are ... are you *crying?*"

"Shut up, Sievert," Sherri said, wiping a tear from her pink eye, "or I'll make *you* cry."

Before Erik could reply, the air was saturated with a dense, crackling buzz. His head shot up in surprise, falling upon a mannequin dressed as a bee dressed as a Mountie.

"Oh shit," he whimpered. "*Now* I get it."

"Erik!" Vivian screamed. "Behind you!"

Erik's eyes flashed over his shoulder just in time to see a swarm of swollen bumblebees burst through the door of the cursed bug zoo.

"Sherri!" he shouted. "Run!"

He turned to take a fleeing step, and stumbled into Sherri's clinging body.

"Let go!" he wailed.

"I can't!"

Sherri wrenched her arms in every direction, but her unwilling grip on Erik remained fast. The sticky spider webbing had adhered her mangled coat to his sides, effectively binding the two of them together. Their opposing steps quickly tangled their legs, dropping Sherri on her back and pulling Erik down on top of her.

"Get off! Get off!" she coughed.

"I can't," Erik shrieked. "Let go!"

"I told you I can't let go!"

Sherri and Erik flailed their limbs to no effect, like an eight-legged overturned turtle. Not only were Sherri's arms glued to Erik, but her back was now glued to the floor. She had become human flypaper.

Erik's head flipped back and forth on his shoulders as he tried to get a look at the swarming bees. His clipped glances afforded him only flashes of nightmarish deformity. A fleshy scorpion stinger sprouting from a blackened eye socket. A pair of pincers arcing from a furry thorax. Although each bee was a unique abomination of genetics, they all had one thing in common: a six-inch stinger stabbing menacingly from each backside.

The swarm turned in unison in the air, swirling toward the ceiling then diving toward Erik's vulnerable back. Sherri responded accordingly.

"Shiiiiiiiiiit!" she shrieked, screwing her eyes shut and squeezing the last breath out of Erik's bony ribcage.

The next thing the immobilized pair heard was the squeak of rubber against tile, followed by the sound of ten softballs hitting the padded wall of a batting cage. They opened their eyes to see Vivian standing astride them, her wings extended into a protective canopy. Dazed bumblebees lay on the floor all around them, struggling against their own mutated bodies to right themselves and return to the air. Vivian leapt off of them and landed heavily on a crackling bee.

"Get up, you two!" she barked, stomping another wriggling foe.

"We can't!" Erik and Sherri howled.

Vivian grabbed Erik by the shoulders and pulled him upward, but it was no use. Her friends were effectively welded to the floor, and the mutant bumblebees were quickly buzzing back into flight. One landed on Vivian's shoulder with a pinch of bristly legs. She threw a reedy fist into its face, knocking it into a broken heap on the floor.

"Trent!" she screamed. "Help me!"

Trent staggered to his feet, gasping a breath into his bashed lungs. He pulled his sword from the ground and hoisted it above his head.

"Don't worry, Vivi! I'll save you!"

With a leap like Peter Pan, Trent slashed his sword through the swarm, completely missing every one of the oversized targets. Two more prancing swings failed to connect, and a third nipped the edge of Vivian's wing.

"Ow! Give me that!" she snapped, wrenching the sword from his hands. "Make yourself useful and get those two off the floor!"

"Your wish is my command, sweet—"

"Just do it!"

Trent braced with one foot on either side of the squirming duo and clapped his hands onto Erik's shoulders.

"Up and at 'em, freak."

He threw back his head and strained upward with all of his strength, and Erik's vertebrae each popped clearly and distinctly in sequence.

"Ow—Jesus!" Erik squealed. "Stop it! You're gonna break my back!"

Trent heaved again, this time more aggressively.

Vivian clutched the sword in both hands and watched the diminished swarm as it regrouped at the ceiling. There were six bees left. She sprinted to Bobby's side and kneeled down near his head.

"Bobby, come on, Bobby. Can you move at all? Can you help me lift this?"

Bobby blinked one slow blink as his head shook negatively.

"I can't lift it by myself! I'm not strong enough!" Vivian said, grabbing his hand. "What am I supposed to do?"

"I'm cool," Bobby whispered hoarsely. "Kill the bees."

Before Vivian could protest, the swarm turned, slicing out of the air with a screaming buzz and hurtling straight toward them. She didn't take her eye off of the lead bee as she sprang to her feet and swung her sword. *Crack!* The mutant split apart upon the blade, splattering into glowing stains on the walls. The blade flashed the other direction. *Crack!* Another set of stains.

Vivian didn't hear the noise of Trent struggling with Erik and Sherri. She didn't smell the hot blood trickling from Bobby. Everything vanished beyond her arms, her blade, and her four targets. *Crack!* Three targets.

A bee with long green pincers landed on the wreckage that held her brother captive. Bobby threw a protective arm in front of his face as the sword exploded the overstuffed insect, showering him with glowing innards.

"Ugh!" he moaned. "Not cool."

Giving up hope on reaching Bobby, the remaining bees swarmed back to the ceiling and dove toward Trent's broad back instead. Without so much as a shouted warning, Vivian had bounded up behind him, sword at the ready.

With a stabbing thrust, the blade penetrated the lead bee's thorax, threading it neatly over the end of the sword. The remaining bee changed direction, and Vivian darted across the igloo in pursuit.

"Trent!" Erik sobbed. "Stop! Stop pulling! You're killing me!"

Trent released his grip on Erik's shoulders, letting him drop on top of Sherri.

"Fine, forget you then, freak!" he spat, grabbing a coffee mug off the shelf and stomping away. "I've got more important business to attend to!"

"Coffee?!" Sherri squealed. "You're leaving us stuck here for *coffee?!*"

Vivian jabbed the tip of her sword into the floor, sliding the impaled carcass from the blade with the sole of her foot. The last bee buzzed high into the vaulted ceiling, disappearing into a haze of darkness. Vivian couldn't see where it was, but she could hear its crackling buzz circling, circling, circling overhead. She followed it with her ears as she ducked behind a shelf and waited for her chance to strike.

Finally the bee made its move, screaming out of the sky at her head. She leapt from behind the shelf and bisected her foe with a clean slash of her blade. As the bee's remains dropped out of the air, their absence immediately revealed another shape, slowly turning, rapidly becoming larger. A split second later a flying coffee mug nailed Vivian square in the forehead.

The last thing that she saw was Trent, standing across the room with his pitching arm hanging out in front of him, wearing an expression that quickly changed from smarmy satisfaction to mortified guilt. Her vision dissolved into static as she dropped heavily to her knees. Trent rushed to her side, grabbing her collapsing shoulders.

"I'm sorry, Vivi! I'm so sorry!"

"You … *idiot.*"

"That was supposed to hit the bee! I didn't see you there! For real, yo!"

Trent was interrupted by the sound of tinkling glass from inside the bug zoo.

"Close the door," Vivian whispered.

"I'm not leaving you here. A man must take responsibility for his actions, and this man just—"

"Close it!" she hissed.

Trent held her barely conscious body for a long moment. Finally a loud crash inside the bug zoo roused him from his melodrama. He dropped her and sprinted to the open door, frantically pounding the locked-open mechanism with his palm.

"Close, you bitch!" he chattered. "Close! *Close!*"

With a superhuman blow, he broke the rusted elbow clean off its hinges. A mighty yank on the push bar slammed the door, but it stopped an inch short of the latch. He yanked it open and shut, but the door simply would not fit into its frame. Then suddenly—

BANG!

The explosive vibrations shook the door, traveling up Trent's arms and through his skull. Something was on the other side, and it wanted to get in.

BANG!

He yanked the door again, but it refused to close. The broken elbow lay on the floor, pinched in the doorway.

BANG!

He pulled back and braced himself against the floor, his knuckles white against the cold steel of the push bar. He clenched against the next pound from within, but it never came.

And the universe went silent.

He waited for what seemed like a lifetime, his forearms burning from grasping the awkward bar so tightly. Finally he made his move.

With a tiny push, he opened the gap wide enough to kick away the elbow, slamming the door shut and immediately retreating to Vivian's side.

"I did it, Vivi! Did you see that? I did it," he told her unconscious body. "You're safe now."

"Trent!" Erik yelped. "Trent—the door!"

"It's okay, Little E. The T saved your skinny ass. It's locked."

"It's *not* locked!" Erik screeched. "Look!"

Trent turned toward the door, which was now hanging completely open.

"It didn't latch!" Erik yelled. "You slammed it too hard! It just bounced open again!"

Trent launched toward the door, but halfway there he stumbled over his own feet as they reversed direction.

It was too late to close the door.

The entire bug zoo on its other side seemed to emit a sinister blue glow, outlining the edges of an enormous black silhouette. The shape approached the doorway. Limping. Lurching. Dragging its massive form toward Trent's pounding heart.

He scrambled away from the door and grabbed the sword in his sweating fists. His eyes flicked to Vivian, lying behind him, a thin trickle of blood running from her nose. To Bobby, no longer moving under his glass and steel prison. To Erik and Sherri, locked to the floor, watching him without words. He turned back to the door with a tremble in his blade.

"O-okay, I'm warning you," he shouted. "I already s-s-sent all your friends back to Hell, and I'll d-d-do you too, bitch!"

The creature shambled closer and closer to the door. Trent's breath caught in his throat. He wanted to run, but his paralyzed brain couldn't issue the order to his legs.

"You b-b-best not be messin' with the T! You hear me?! I'll m-mess you up!"

The creature pulled itself through the door, its form becoming clear to Trent's petrified eyes in the dingy lantern light.

"Oh ... my ... Lord."

His terror flipped inside out, turning into confusion. The figure that emerged from the darkness was not a deformed insect beast, but a young woman. She was built like an Amazon goddess: a six-foot-tall statue carved from long feminine muscle. Her short, ragged skirt and torn belly-shirt made her look like a shipwreck victim from the cover of a cheap erotic novel.

She didn't speak, but her appearance told her story as well as any words could. Her flesh and clothes were riddled with cuts, many of them crusted with dried blood, others still moist and fresh. In her bloody hand she clutched a blade of glass, glistening with slime and glowing hunks of mutated exoskeleton. A plastic nametag covered in butterfly stickers hung from her shirt.

Insect Igloo - Priscilla

She staggered through the doorway, stumbled, and fell into Trent's arms. He dropped the sword and caught her weight with an awkward, steadying step, embracing her in his muscular arms.

"Don't worry, girl, it's okay," he said, stroking her hair. "The T is here to protect you."

CHAPTER ELEVEN

A crackling campfire threw its light over a makeshift hospital ward outside the North of the Border Insect Igloo. Vivian blew a hot breath into her cupped hands. Her fingers had numbed almost beyond cooperation in the frigid night, but she was determined to finish her work. She ripped her Swiss Army Knife through the grinning face of a cartoon Mountie, turning another souvenir T-shirt into bandages.

The igloo's liberated prisoner—Priscilla, if her nametag was to be believed—lay on the cold earth, unconsciously accepting Vivian's help. Her breath was restful, but deep and hoarse, like a snore that didn't quite have the ambition to happen. Kneeling by her side, Vivian bandaged each of her cuts and scrapes, picking out shards of glass and shattered curios where necessary.

Priscilla's body was built like a Greco-Roman sculpture: solid and muscular, but distinctly feminine in shape and curve. Judging by the shortness of her skirt and the tightness of her uniform shirt, Vivian suspected that she was a believer in the maxim, "If you've got it, flaunt it."

Priscilla's brunette hair stuck in matted, dust-smeared clumps to her neck and chin. Vivian gently peeled it back with a crackle of dried blood that got lost behind her startled gasp. A gash ran across Priscilla's neck from the right corner of her jawbone all the way to her left shoulder.

"Oh, you poor thing," Vivian said. "Let's get that cleaned up."

When the wound was as clean as it was going to get, Vivian tied one last bandage snugly around Priscilla's neck, knotting it to the side like a scarf on a 1960s fashion model. She detached the sticky nametag from her patient's ample bosom, wiped it clean, and then pinned it back on.

"You just rest up, Priscilla. You're safe now. You're not alone anymore."

She put her hand on top of Priscilla's limp fist and smiled.

"None of us are."

After countless miles of ruination, they had finally found another survivor. If there was one other survivor, there would be two others. If there were two, there would be ten. Or fifty. Or a hundred. By doing nothing more than stumbling out of the darkness barely alive, Priscilla had given Vivian and the members of her oblivion society a great gift: the gift of hope.

Bobby lay asleep on the other side of the fire, slouched against a round wooden fencepost. The color had completely drained from his already pasty complexion, giving his skin the soapy pallor of a tombstone. From his hips to his armpits, his torso had been tightly wrapped in a single bandage. In its past life, this bandage had proudly proclaimed "North of the Border: Family fun from 'Eh' to 'Zed,'" but now its message was obscured with bloodstain.

Sherri sat in the dirt to Bobby's side, nervously tugging and twisting at the gentle curl of her scorched yellow hair as she watched his chest rise and fall with each struggling breath. During the melee in the igloo, the remainder of her charred skin had rubbed off, revealing a smooth, dark layer beneath. Had she stopped to think about it, she would have been mortified—her ghoulishly pale skin had been replaced with the perfect cinnamon tan of a Malibu surfer girl.

But Sherri wasn't thinking about herself at the moment. Her face had twisted into a configuration that it had never tried before, drawing out an all new, never before seen expression.

Concern.

Drool leaked from Bobby's slack jaw, spilling onto his scruffy orange goatee. Sherri gently wiped it away with the cuff of her inherited gray sweatshirt. She pushed a clump of hair out of Bobby's face and tucked it behind his ear. As her fingertips brushed his cheek, he awoke with a snort.

"Gnaagh! Wha? Whassa?"

"Oh! Um, Bobby!" Sherri stammered, yanking her hand away. "I ... uh ... hello!"

Bobby's eyes slowly focused on Sherri's face, outlined by an aura of firelight filtering through her golden hair.

"Are you an angel?" he asked dreamily.

"Am I an ... now what the fuck is that supposed to mean?"

Bobby blinked.

"You look like an angel."

Sherri looked at Bobby's vacant eyes and a tiny smile crept across her lips.

"Okay, shut up. You're just lucky that you've got one foot in the grave, or I wouldn't take that kinda shit outta you, Gray."

At the sound of her brother's croaking voice, Vivian rushed to his side, falling to her knees in the dirt. As soon as she hit the ground, her wings swung forward on her shoulders and clapped her in the back of her head.

"Ow! Bobby! You're awake!" she cried, slapping away her wings. "I was so worried! How do you feel?"

"I feel like I just got a tattoo of Charlie Brown's shirt," Bobby moaned. He tugged at the edge of his bandage. "Get this shit off; it hurts like a son of a bitch."

"Oh no you don't," Vivian said, grabbing his hands. "That bandage stays on until we're sure the bleeding has stopped. You can't afford to lose any more blood."

"Come on, Vivian. There's still broken glass stuck in there!"

"No there isn't," Vivian said.

"Don't give me that crap. I can feel it! How would *you* know if *I've* got broken glass in *my* cuts?"

"Because *I'm* the one who dug it all out."

She held up her bloodstained fingers in front of Bobby's eyes, which were immediately drained of their fighting spirit.

"Oh. Uh … right," he said guiltily. "I'm sorry. But it burns like hell, and I just thought … never mind. Thanks, Viv."

"It's okay. Forget it," Vivian said. "I picked out all the glass, but by the time that we got you out from under the shelf you were all covered in fallout ash. I cleaned you up as best as I could, but there's only so much that I can do without proper, sanitary—"

"Yeah yeah. It's cool. Thank you," Bobby said, waving his hand weakly. "Where's everybody else?"

Sherri sighed histrionically.

"The powderpuff's stomach growled *one fucking time* and then Erik and Retard-O-Dick got in a cockfight about who was going to get food for her. Now they're back inside the igloo acting like they're these big manly providers, when it's so obvious they're just trying to unlock her virgin legs."

Vivian crossed her arms tightly as her face prickled with humiliation.

"They went to find food for *all* of us. I never asked for anything."

"Well, maybe you should start," Sherri said. "I'll bet Trent could find us a four-course meal if you told him you'd flash your tits for it."

Vivian scowled.

"Can we change the subject, please?"

Bobby glanced over her shoulder.

"Hey, who's the new girl?"

Vivian and Sherri turned and looked in the direction of Bobby's gaze. On the other side of the fire, Priscilla was standing shakily on her weakened legs. Her glassy eyes seemed unable or unwilling to accept her surroundings.

"Priscilla!" Vivian beamed. "It is Priscilla, isn't it?"

She stepped briskly toward Priscilla's towering form, extending her arms in welcome. As Vivian's hands rose from her sides, her wings simultaneously extended from her back, spreading into a six-foot wall of black leather.

"I'm so glad that you're okay!" she continued. "I was so worried about you!"

As Vivian came closer, the traumatized stranger's fist instinctually raised into the air, fingers wrapped around a dagger of glass that she no longer possessed. Priscilla's eyes remained locked on the nightmarish wings as she jabbed out her fist, tagging Vivian on the nose.

"Ow! Damn it!"

As Vivian's hands shot to her face, her wings flew downward from her shoulders, fanning the fire into an explosive inferno. Priscilla's mouth opened into the shape of a scream, but her mangled throat produced only a gurgle. She turned and bolted from the demonic silhouette, half running, half limping on her crippled legs. Within two labored steps, she ran directly into another mutant emerging from the darkness.

"Hey, you guys," Erik beamed, holding aloft four shopping bags in as many hands. "Look what I fouaaaaaggh!"

Priscilla plowed into Erik's lanky body like a wounded linebacker. He dropped his bags and, in a desperate attempt at balance, grabbed her with four fumbling hands. Her skull slammed down with a heavy *thump* on his forehead, loosening his quadruple grip and knocking him to the ground.

"Whoa! Whoa!" Trent said, stepping out of the shadows. "What goes on, people?"

"Stop her!" Vivian shouted, "Before she hurts herself!"

"Herself?!" Erik moaned dizzily.

Before Trent could react, Priscilla ran into him like a frenzied bull. The fully laden Army backpack flew from his hands, but before he could fall, Priscilla was behind him, her forearm thrown around his neck as if taking him hostage.

"Aaaugh! Help!" he yelped, swinging his arms frantically. "Get this crazy beotch offa me!"

"Trent, stop!" Vivian shouted. "Stop! Don't fight her! She's just disoriented!"

Trent continued to struggle, but Priscilla's grip tightened around his neck until he was too suffocated to resist. A second later all was silent, save for a raspy, overexcited breath emanating from Priscilla's throat. All eyes were on her, waiting for her next move. After a long, tense moment, her grip loosened and she threw both arms around Trent's shoulders and pressed her face against his cheek with a sob.

"Damn girl, if you want some lovin' all you got to do is ask, yo."

Vivian stepped forward and extended her hand.

"I'm sorry if I startled you, Priscilla," she said calmly. "My name is Vivian. We're not going to hurt—"

As Vivian drew closer, Priscilla's grip tightened around Trent's chest.

"Ow ow, damn!" he squirmed. "Step back, yo! You're spooking her!"

"She's just startled," Vivian said, moving forward. "She's had a rough—"

Priscilla took a lurching step backward, squeezing her arms tighter around Trent's chest.

"I said step the back up, Batgirl!" he choked. "Your freaky physique is scaring her shitless!"

Trent's words slapped Vivian across the face, and her mouth twisted into a pout. She glanced over her shoulder and saw her wings belching from her back like a pair of gothic cemetery gates shrouded in demon hide. Her lips made shapes, trying to put her misery into words.

"But ... but ... I'm not ... I mean, *I'm okay.*"

She gestured pathetically, but Priscilla's only response was in the form of a cough squeezed accordion-like from Trent's lungs. Erik grasped Vivian's extended wings and gently folded them down to her back. He took her by the arm and led her to the opposite side of the fire, guiding her crestfallen body to the ground and kneeling in front of her.

"Look, Vivian, don't take it personally," he said. "She's been through a lot. She's in shock. She's going to need some time to get used to ... you know ... *us.*"

His right hand gestured to himself, then to Vivian. Simultaneously his left paw did the same, but in the opposite order.

Vivian frowned. "Well, she seems to like *Trent* just fine."

"I guess it's about time somebody did," Erik shrugged. "I'm not surprised. She looks like she's ... uh, you know, 'his type.'"

Priscilla's grip had loosened as soon as the wings had disappeared from her view, allowing Trent to fall out of her asphyxiating embrace. The tatters of her clothes fluttered over her bare skin with a lurid sensuality as her face melted into an expression of gratitude. Trent's own face melted into an amorous grin.

A second later he was holding the shivering girl in his arms, squeezing her tightly against his broad chest.

"You're safe now, Prissy," he said boldly. "Don't worry your pretty little head. The T-man isn't going to let any more nasty mutants hurt you."

"Hurt her?" Vivian said. "Why would I *hurt* her? *I'm* the one who dressed her wounds!"

"I'm sure he's talking about the mutant *bugs,*" Erik said, throwing Trent a condemning glare. "Just relax, Viv. We just need to take it slow and show her that not *all* mutants want to kill her. It looks like she had some rough times in there."

"Now, that's the thing that I don't get," Bobby said.

"What's not to get?" Erik shrugged. "It's pretty obvious that she was working late stocking shelves and ended up getting trapped in the zoo with all of those killer mutant bugs."

"No, I get that part, Jumpin' Jack Flashback," Bobby said. "The thing I don't understand is why there were mutant bugs *at all.* We shouldn't still be running into these things. There hasn't been any of that nasty pink fog for two states now."

"Well, maybe it's not the fog that does it," Erik said. "I mean, maybe the mutations *are* from the nuclear radiation after all."

"Oh, don't start that again," Bobby moaned. "It's just like Vivian said: Radiation doesn't just Jekyll and Hyde a bumblebee into one of those ...

Beelzebumblebees."

"That's true," Vivian said. "But just for the sake of argument, what do we know about what radiation *does* do?"

"Well, it makes 1950s novelty wristwatches glow in the dark," Erik said.

"Tanning beds use it to bronze you up all sexy-like," Trent smiled.

"Sitting too close to the TV makes you start shooting blanks," Sherri added.

"It's used to fight cancer," Bobby said, "and ironically also *causes* cancer."

"Hold on," Vivian said. "You might be on to something there."

"What—cancer?" Bobby said. "Are you serious? Those spiders didn't exactly look like the Make-A-Wish Foundation was about to take them to Disney World."

"No, but think about what cancer does to living tissue," Vivian said. "Cancer causes cells to split and grow uncontrollably. That's how tumors form."

"Oh, come on, Viv," Bobby sighed, dropping his voice two Austrian octaves. *"It's not a toomah."*

"I know I'm oversimplifying it," Vivian said. "I'm not saying that the mutations are literally caused by cancer. I'm just saying, what if the same underlying biological principles are at work? Theoretically, accelerated cell division could explain how Twiki and those insects grew to be so large."

Erik shook his head.

"But even if radiation did cause the *Honey, I Blew Up the Kid* effect, that still doesn't explain why you and me grew extra limbs. Or those bugs in the igloo for that matter."

"I have a theory on that too," Vivian nodded. "I think these mutants are infectious."

Trent's eyes popped open as he yanked his shirt up over his nose.

"Aw shit! You didn't tell me y'all were contagious! I don't want you breathin' your mutant-ass germs all up on me! For real!"

"Not *contagious*," Vivian smirked. "*Infectious*. From what we've seen, every time a mutated animal breaks the skin it causes another mutation. It's like they somehow spread their genetic pattern."

Sherri's head tilted doubtfully.

"So the bugs all stung the shit out of each other and made new bug parts. I'll buy that," she said. "But what about Erik? Rat Boy over here got fucked up by his *cat*."

Vivian raised her eyebrow and looked at Erik.

"Did he?"

Erik blinked twice as his brain untangled the facts. He remembered the last creature he had seen in the drain on the night of the blast. He remembered the weight and heft of an animal just slightly too big to be his cat … and entirely too small to be his mutant cat. He remembered that long, pointed jaw of glowing teeth.

"No, I didn't!" he realized. "It had to be a mutant sewer rat that attacked me! See! I told you I killed it!"

Bobby scratched his beard.

"That may be so, but Vivian most definitely *did* get scratched by a cat. How the hell did that give her *wings?*"

"That's the part I can't work out," Vivian admitted. "I should have had a feline mutation. Cats don't have bat DNA."

"Mine did," Erik said. "The last time I saw Twiki before she mutated she was up to her little kitty elbows in bat blood. It was probably still all over her claws when she scratched you."

Vivian smiled reluctantly.

"I guess that validates at least part of my theory," she said. "But we still don't know why animals are growing into monsters and humans aren't."

"I already told y'all the answer to that one," Trent said. "It's the soul, yo. It's God protecting his peeps from the minions of the deep. The Big Man is always lookin' out for us—isn't that right, Prissy?"

Trent was leaning against the outer wall of the igloo with his legs spread apart and Priscilla nestled between them, her back against his chest. She was wearing his varsity jacket and leaning back into his embrace as if they were two high-school sweethearts snuggling in the bleachers at the homecoming game. Despite the warmth of the crackling fire, the hair on Trent's frigid arms stood on end. But he didn't seem to notice or care. He squeezed Priscilla, and she closed her eyes and nuzzled her head into his grimy cheek without a word.

"Okay, what's *that* shit all about?" Sherri said. "Did you slip her some roofies or something?"

"Now now, don't let that little green monster get a hold of you, Goldilocks," Trent grinned. "Prissy just knows she's safe with me because I was the one who saved her from those demons in the igloo."

"You didn't save her!" Sherri spat. "If anybody saved her it was the powderpuff. All you did was stand there and piss yourself."

"We all played our own little part in her liberation," Trent said.

"And yours was pissing yourself."

"Say what you will—it's abundantly clear which one of us she feels closest to. But you don't need to be jealous, girl! The T is a two-seater! Hop in!"

Trent raised one arm in a giant scoop like a DeLorean's gull-wing door awaiting a passenger. Sherri sneered.

"I'd rather sit on the wrong end of the Kaiser's helmet."

"Damn. That's cold," Trent muttered.

"Dude, don't even talk about cold," Bobby said, rubbing his hands over his coarsely bandaged arms. "Right about now I feel like my ass should be in a plastic tube between Alexander the Grape and Little Orphan Orange."

"Oh! That reminds me!" Erik said, scampering to his feet. "I found something for you."

"If it's Otter Pops, I swear I'm going to smack you," Bobby mumbled.

Erik retrieved his shopping bags and began rummaging through them. He pulled out a bundle of lime-green terry cloth and tossed it to Bobby.

"Here you go, buddy!"

Bobby unfolded the garment and held it up in front of himself.

"A North of the Border bathrobe?" he asked skeptically. "You shouldn't have."

"It was the only thing I could find that was even close to big enough for you," Erik said. "Besides, it'll give you a certain Arthur Dentian flair."

With a series of pained grunts, and ultimately Vivian's assistance, Bobby leaned away from the fencepost and slipped into the bathrobe. It fit him well, both physically and aesthetically.

"Thanks, dude," he said. "Already I feel less panicked."

"Me next!" Sherri squealed. "This sweatshop sweatshirt is giving me a conformity rash. Gimme my coat—I don't care how fucked up it is."

Erik flinched.

"Yeah, about your coat. It's uh … you know, that spider silk was *really* sticky."

"So … *yeah?*"

"How can I put this?" Erik said nervously. "Your coat is *never* coming off that floor. Ever. I tried everything. Pulling it, pushing it, scraping at it. All I could get up was a few scraps."

Erik pulled a few pathetic strands of black leather out of the bag and handed them to Sherri.

"Well, shit," she frowned. "So that's all you got?"

"No, there's more!" Erik said in a voice like a consolation prize. "I couldn't get your coat off the floor, but I got all the stuff out of the pockets for you. I got your smokes and some change, um … some kind of bird skull, and … well, you know what you had. I put it all in here."

Erik reached into the bag and pulled out a purse made of pink plastic sewn into the shape of a ladybug. It looked like something that Hello Kitty would have rejected for being "too cute." He held it out in front of Sherri with a weak smile, looking like a suicidal zookeeper might look as he dangled a steak in front of a hungry lion.

"I'm sorry," he whimpered. "It was the only bag they had."

Sherri took the purse and ran her tiny palm over the back of Erik's mutant paw, giving it a flirty squeeze.

"Cool. Thanks, Erik. That's nice of you."

Unzipping the ladybug's back, she pulled out a pack of cigarettes and lit one up. When her pink eyes returned to her friends, she found herself surrounded by an assortment of slack jaws and raised eyebrows.

"What? Get off me," she said. "It was a thoughtful fucking gesture. So what if it's pinker than Strawberry Shortcake's snatch?"

The group breathed a collective sigh.

"Um, okay. Good," Erik said. "I'm glad you feel that way, actually."

He clenched four arms nervously over his chilled torso and continued.

"So, um … also I was wondering if … I just thought that maybe, if it wasn't too much trouble you could … um …"

Sherri exhaled a long blast of yellow smoke and rolled her eyes casually to Erik.

"Spit it out, Sievert. I'm not gonna bite you."

Erik reached into the shopping bag.

"Would you mind trading me the sweatshirt for this?"

Sherri's eyebrows knotted.

"I'm gonna fucking bite you."

Erik held the tiny white "Eskimo Princess" jacket at arm's length as he quickly rattled his defense.

"Okay, wait, I know it sucks, and I know you don't want it, but please, Sherri, be reasonable!"

"You be fucking reasonable!" Sherri screamed, hurling the ladybug at his head. "What the fuck do you think you're doing to me? I'm an individual! I'm not just going to sit here and let you cutesy me up until I match your bullshit, cookie-cutter, Delia's-catalog ideals of beauty, you brainwashed, hive-mind fuckwad!"

"Daaaamn, nice mood swing!" Trent said. "I guess it's that time of the month when somebody's getting a visit from her Aunt Flo."

"Keep that shit up and *you'll* be the one who's bleeding uncontrollably from the groin!" Sherri barked.

"Look, Sherri, I'm sorry!" Erik squeaked. "I don't want to change you! I don't care how you dress! I'd wear this stupid coat myself if it would fit me, but it doesn't."

"So why don't you just get another sweatshirt, asshole?"

"There are no other sweatshirts. It's the middle of summer; everything in there is thin and skimpy except for this leftover junk that was on clearance."

Erik's soulful blue eyes peered desperately over the top of the fluffy white hood in his trembling hands. Sherri crossed her arms and looked him up and down. He was shivering. She guessed it was partially out of fear, but mostly from the bitter cold. A cold that failed to penetrate the baggy folds of her sweatshirt but wrapped around Erik's lean body like an icy cloak.

"I know this thing's not your style," he continued, "but it's a matter of life and death."

Having lost his polo shirt to the same spider silk that had claimed Sherri's coat, Erik now wore a T-shirt with a cartoon Mountie sporting the exact same faux-age wear as the ten others in the stack from which it had been taken. Somehow his mutant arms seemed far less grotesque emerging from its two neatly cut slits than they had belching a nest of filthy polyester bandages. Nonetheless, his four bare, shuddering arms were pale with the cold.

"Please, Sherri," he said softly. "I'm freezing."

Sherri's eyes rolled back in her head as she sighed a doomed sigh.

"Fine," she grumbled. "Okay, fine, Erik. I'll wear the stupid coat if it means you won't *die*."

Erik exhaled a breath that he had been holding for nearly three minutes.

"Thank you, Sherri!" he gushed. "Thank you so much! I mean, it's not like anybody's going to see you wearing it. And we'll probably find a different coat for you tomorrow, right? Right?"

Sherri blinked distractedly.

"Oh, uh. Right."

She wasn't listening to Erik's relieved ramble. Her fingers had clasped the zipper of the sweatshirt but couldn't bring themselves to pull it down.

"What's the matter?" Erik asked. "Is the zipper stuck?"

"No," Sherri mumbled. "It's just … I … I don't want to take it off in front of Raccoon Boy over there."

"Oh, now that ain't cool," Trent said. "You *never* call a brother a 'coon, yo. That's racist and uncalled for."

"Oh, for Christ's sake," Sherri said. "I meant you've got two black eyes!"

"Damn straight they're black. Why you always gotta make it a racial issue, dawg?"

"You're not black!" Sherri snapped.

"You best learn to free your mind," Trent said. "Love is colorblind. For real."

Sherri shook her head.

"Oh, shut up and wipe the blood off your face, you fuckin' hemophiliac."

Trent's fingers darted to his cheek, wiping away a trickle of blood from his wing-related injury.

"Can we just do this later, please?" she continued. "Seriously, I don't want him watching me undress."

"What's the big deal?" Bobby shrugged. "It's not like you're naked under there, right? You're still wearing a T-shirt."

"God, can't a girl have a little privacy? You wouldn't make Vivian change in front of everybody."

"Ha!" Bobby laughed. "Are you seriously trying to get us to believe that you're *modest* all of the sudden? Seriously, what's the big deal?"

"None of your fucking business," Sherri spat, clenching her sweatshirt.

Trent's swollen eyes suddenly grew wide.

"Holy shiggedy shit," he gasped. "You got cut, didn't you?! You're hiding extra limbs under there!"

Sherri fixed her gaze on the dirt.

"I am not hiding extra limbs," she muttered. "Shut the fuck up."

Vivian's eyes ran up and down the lumpy sweatshirt, suddenly realizing that it was full of more Sherri than it should have been.

"Oh my God," she whispered. "It's happened to you too, hasn't it?"

"Nothing's happened to me!" Sherri snarled. "You shut the fuck up too!"

"Don't be ashamed!" Erik said. "It's nothing to be ashamed of! Vivian and I are both fine. You're going to be fine too!"

"I *am* fine!" Sherri screeched. "Shut the fuck up! Everybody shut the fuck up! I'm not a mutant!"

"If you're not a mutant, then what's the big deal?" Bobby said. "Seriously, stop being an attention whore and just take off the damn sweatshirt. What's the big deal?"

"*What's the big deal? What's the big deal?*" Sherri shrieked. "Fine! I'll show you the big deal!"

With a furious yank of the zipper, Sherri tore off the sweatshirt and threw it to the ground. The world fell silent except for the crackling of the fire and the imagined wail of an innuendo-laced saxophone solo.

"*These* are the big deal, alright?!"

In the cocoon of a mangled leather coat, an underdeveloped waif had metamorphosed into a shapely young woman with all the right curves in all the right places. Her bustline had grown like the Grinch's heart on Christmas Day, pressing the nipples of two perky, pink-grapefruit-sized breasts distinctly against the inside of her ragged T-shirt. Her bulging bosom distorted its form, hauling its hemline up past her navel to reveal a tanned midriff that melted salaciously into voluptuous hips. The golden curls of her hair bounced across her pointy face as her head jerked across the gaping stares of her friends.

"Sweet Jesus, Mary, and Frederick's of Hollywood," Trent prayed, making the sign of the cross. "That's a rack that would make Bullwinkle say damn! You busted right out of your bra, girl!"

"I don't wear a bra," Sherri said. "The bra is just another one of the Man's schemes to keep women uncomfortable and subservient."

"Admit it!" Trent laughed. "You just never needed one before!"

Sherri snatched the princess jacket from Erik's hands.

"Alright, show's over! This is exactly why I didn't want to take my sweatshirt off in front of you people!"

Turning her back on Trent, she rammed her arms into the sleeves and wrestled her way into the little white coat. Despite her protests, it couldn't have fit more perfectly over her narrow shoulders if it had been custom tailored. She yanked up the zipper, and the quilted nylon fabric hugged her slender form all the way up to where her now ample chest halted its forward progress. The bottom of the tiny coat left four inches of midriff exposed between its furry trim and the top of her frayed skirt.

"Oh, that's just swell," she fumed, tugging at the hem. "That's just great. What kind of retard designs a coat with no middle?"

She yanked the hood over her head and stuffed her smoldering cigarette between her lips sulkily. Vivian squinted.

"You know, this is exactly the kind of thing that we were talking about before. Sherri, your mammary tissue must be dividing at an accelerated rate."

"No shit!" Sherri said. "Why do you guys get all the bad-ass monster parts and all I get is a pair of torpedo tits full of breast cancer?"

"I don't know," Vivian admitted. "I can't explain it."

"You know, maybe you're just reading too much into this," Erik said awkwardly. "Maybe you're just, you know ... *blooming*."

"Blooming my ass!" Trent crowed. "El Pollo Loco can't cook up breasts that fast!"

Sherri crossed her arms over her chest and puffed angrily on her cigarette.

"It could be some kind of hormone imbalance," Vivian suggested, tapping her chin. "It's possible that her ovaries are what's really growing, and this is just a secondary effect."

"Jesus! Hello?" Sherri spat. "I'm right here! Please stop talking about me like I'm some pre-op transsexual fertilizing his bitch-tits with estrogen pills!"

"Wait, hold on," Bobby said. "That night. At the bar."

"So what—I was wasted," Sherri said. "We said alcohol doesn't have anything to do with it, remember?"

"No, not that," Bobby said. "In the sub. The pills."

Sherri's eyes widened as the memory sloshed back to the front of her mind.

"Shut up," she said nervously. "Just shut up."

"What pills?" Erik asked.

"Special K," Sherri said, her eyes narrowing into razor blades. "I was high on *Special K* that night. That's all."

"Isn't Special K a liquid?" Erik asked.

"What the fuck? Did you all watch a filmstrip on this or something? It comes in pill form too!"

"Come on, Sherri. You *know* this isn't a radioactive mutation," Bobby said. "It's got to be hormonal! You were popping Menoplay tablets like they were Mike and Ikes that night!"

"Shut up!" Sherri screamed. "You promised you wouldn't tell! You fucking suck!"

She threw her cigarette at Bobby's face and stomped off into the darkness, leaving behind only echoes of a humiliated sob. The others sat for a moment of silence as the new information sunk in.

"Menoplay?" Vivian said. "Like 'aisle four, women's hormone supplements'

Menoplay?"

"Yeah," Bobby nodded. "It's a long story."

"Damn," Trent said. "I guess that explains why her mood swings like the Brian Setzer Orchestra. A double dip of the lady hormones makes for one powerful rage, yo."

"Oh, shut up, Trent," Vivian scowled. "Benedictine monks have a better grasp on feminine biology than you do."

"I beg to differ," Trent grinned. "I think I've got a pretty good grasp on a fine specimen of feminine biology right here. Isn't that right, Prissy?"

He squeezed his arms around Priscilla, rousing her trancelike gaze from the crackling fire. She nuzzled against his body and stroked his chin with absent-minded affection. Swaddled in Trent's wool jacket and wrapped in his amorous arms, Priscilla looked warm, comfortable, and truly happy.

A cold breeze picked up, skating over Vivian's exposed skin, slipping though the slashes in her wrecked dress, and encircling her icy ribcage. She clenched her arms and glared grudgingly at Priscilla. As disgusting as the idea was, she found herself almost jealous of the girl being held lovingly in Trent's arms. She turned away just in time to see Erik slipping into his regained sweatshirt, and her eyes flashed covetously.

"You okay, Viv?" he asked.

"I'm fine," she said sourly. "As fine as I can be with, you know."

Her wings shivered against her back.

"Oh, Viv!" Erik said. "I'm so sorry! I just got distracted by Sherri's big—"

Vivian glared at him. He closed his eyes and shook his head.

"I just got distracted."

He reached into the last shopping bag.

"I didn't forget you," he continued. "Drum roll, please!"

With a dramatic flap, he produced the cherry-red coat of the Royal Canadian Mounted Police.

"Ta da! Sorry, horse not included."

"Oh, nice try, freak boy," Trent laughed. "How's Vampirella gonna fit her extra gear in *that?*"

Erik smiled and flipped the coat around. On the back of the Mountie Bee's former coat were two wing holes extending from its shoulders to its waist, custom tailored in a perfect double stitch. Erik's two mutant paws popped out of the holes with a showy flourish of their grizzled fingers.

"I was going to just cut some holes in this sweatshirt for you, but I think this will be a much better fit. Plus you've got to admit, it's got a lot more panache!"

"Oh wow, Erik," Vivian beamed, taking the coat and turning it over in her trembling hands. "I mean … wow. I never would have thought this."

"Well, when I was just in there, the Mountie Bee—he made me think of you," Erik said. "Er, I mean, not that you look like a humanoid bee or anything, just that ... you know, he had those big stupid wings and—not that wings are stupid! Wings are actually really cool; I just meant—"

"It's okay," Vivian blushed. "Help me put it on; I'm freezing."

Erik let out a relieved breath as he pulled the coat over Vivian's shoulders. With a bit of folding and squeezing, they worked her long, spiny wings through it until its epaulettes rested neatly upon her shoulders. She fastened its brass buttons and raised her arms to test the fit, prompting her wings to stretch out from her shoulders in a disturbing black arch.

"How do I look?" she asked.

"Like the wet dream Nell Fenwick never told anybody about," Bobby replied.

Vivian turned to Erik with warmth dancing in her eyes.

"Thank you, Erik," she said, taking his human hands in her own. "It's absolutely perfect."

Before he could reply, Sherri came stomping back to the fireside, plowing straight between them and tearing apart their tender touch. She bent down and yanked a cigarette from her new purse, stuffing it between her chattering teeth.

"Just shut up," she said preemptively. "It's too fucking cold over there."

She lit her cigarette and pulled a long, hot drag into her lungs. Her glare slid up and down Vivian as she exhaled.

"Oh, now that's just *so* unfair. I'm all faggoted up like a My Little Pony, while Vivian gets to be all Sergeant Pepper over here."

"I'm sorry," Vivian said without sounding at all like she meant it. "I don't think you realize how good you have it. I'd rather wear that stupid little coat than have these awful wings."

"And I'd rather have the wings than wear the coat," Sherri said. "Ain't irony a bitch?"

With that, she dropped into a cross-legged heap by the fire. Erik and Vivian exchanged a short, longing glance over her head before sitting down on opposite sides of her veil of cigarette smoke.

"Okay, this dress-up montage stuff is all fine and good," Bobby said, "but didn't you two bring back any *food?*"

"But of course," Trent said, grabbing the Army backpack and tossing it to Bobby. "While Little E was in there playing fashion show, Big T was bringing home the bacon."

The backpack hit Bobby in the gut with a *thump* that sent pain blistering around each side of his scarred body. He sucked air through his teeth and glared at Trent. Trent was too busy playing with Priscilla's hair to notice. Bobby set the bag down between his legs and started digging into it.

"Alright, let's see what we've got," he muttered. "Oh! What a surprise! Maple cookies!"

A unified moan went up from the empty stomachs of the hungry survivors.

"That's really all there was?" Vivian asked.

"Wait!" Bobby said, producing a brown glass bottle. "You can wash them down with maple syrup!"

"Christ," Sherri grumbled. "All we ever find to eat is sugar. I've got the diet of a fucking hummingbird."

"At this rate we're going to end up starving to death with full stomachs," Vivian agreed.

Bobby passed the tins around the fire while speaking in the exaggerated staccato of a fake Shatner.

"It's the end ... of ... the world! You ... haven't eaten anything ... but ... candy ... in three days! Your body ... is ... about to go into complete nutritional failure! This ... is a Grocery911!"

Vivian snapped a stale cookie in half with her teeth.

"This isn't *a* Grocery911," she mumbled. "This is *the* Grocery911."

"Man, what I wouldn't give for that website right about now," Bobby said. "You know what I would order if I had Grocery911.com in front of me? A frozen meat lovers pizza, two cans of refried beans, a can of jalapeños, and a jar of salsa."

"I think we'd all be thankful to share a feast like that, dawg," Trent said.

"Share? That's all for me," Bobby sighed. "I would dump all the other stuff onto the pizza and then roll it up into a burrito. How 'bout you, Erik?"

Erik wasn't listening to Bobby. He was gazing into the firelight reflected in the cracked lenses of Vivian's glasses.

"Erik?" Bobby repeated. "Hello? What would you order if you had Grocery911?"

"Oh, uh ... I think I'd order ... a box of Urkel-Os."

"Oh, come on, Erik," Bobby huffed. "Pick something else. Grocery911 doesn't sell antique cereal."

"Grocery911 doesn't sell *anything* anymore," Erik said.

Bobby shrugged.

"Fair enough."

"What the fuck is Urkel-Os?" Sherri asked.

"It was the official breakfast cereal of the wacky neighbor on *Family Matters*," Erik explained. "It had a big picture of Steve Urkel being a doofus on the front of the box."

"Oh yeah, I remember that!" Trent laughed. "One of my homeboys bought a box as a gag and it was kickin' around my crib for like, three years. That thing was hilarious, yo!"

Erik rolled his eyes.

"I'll bet you don't even know who Steve Urkel is," he sighed. "You just saw the nerd on the box and thought it was *so funny*, or *fly* or whatever. You probably never even watched that show, did you?"

"Whoa, lay off, Little E," Trent said. "So I didn't watch some lamer-ass TV show. I never actually ate the shitty cereal either. What difference does it make?"

"It's just typical of you," Erik said. "All you cared about was the packaging. You didn't even bother to look inside. I guess that's what makes us different."

"Get over it, Little E!" Trent laughed. "It was just some bullshit cereal. Don't get up in my grill like *you* didn't just buy it because it had that TV geek on the box."

Erik shook his head and looked at Vivian.

"Sure, I noticed it at first because of the package, but after the first taste I realized that the cereal was actually really, really good. Everybody else just saw the nerd on the outside, but I loved it for what it really was. I never made a big show of it, so I guess nobody really ever knew."

Vivian looked at Erik. His eyes darted to the ground as his face turned as red as her coat. After a pause, she spoke.

"I'd order a carton of milk."

"Gah! What's wrong with you two?" Bobby said. "I'm giving you a hypothetical blank check at the world's biggest online grocery store, and all you want is two-fifths of a complete breakfast? What's so great about *milk?*"

"Well, milk contains essential nutrients I need to stay healthy, of course, but it also has psychological benefits," Vivian said. "It's a comfort food. Humans subconsciously relate milk to feelings of being nurtured and cared for. At a time like this, that's arguably more important than nutrition. Even though I take it for granted, I'd be crushed if I knew that I'd never have milk again."

She turned to Erik with a tiny smile.

"Plus, milk goes great with cereal."

Her gaze caught Erik's and they shared a long, silent moment that required no further innuendo. Between them, Sherri's eyes flicked back and forth with disgust.

"Oh for fuck's sake. Hey Erik, you know what I'd order? Erik. Erik!"

Erik's eyes broke from Vivian's with an almost audible snap.

"What? Uh ... what. I don't know, Sherri. What would you order?"

"A *wiener*," she growled luridly. "A foot-long wiener."

She put her hand on Erik's knee and leaned toward him. Thousands of years of masculine instinct threw his glare down the mangled neckline of her T-shirt before he could consciously wrangle it back to her face. Her words seemed to melt like hot candle wax from her rosy pink lips.

"I want twelve inches of hot, firm meat to stick in my mouth."

Erik coughed and shifted awkwardly in the dirt, but Sherri just drew closer and grasped his inner thigh.

"Whoa, whoa, okay," he blurted. "That's no good. That's gotta stop."

"Why?" Sherri asked innocently. "Are you afraid you're going to pop another boner like you did when you were laying on top of me in the igloo?"

"I was nervous!" Erik squeaked.

"I know. You were *enormously* nervous."

Sherri turned to Vivian and held her hands ten inches apart with a knowing wink.

"Stop it!" Erik hissed. "Get your hormones under control! You're like a Vulcan with the *Pon farr!*"

"Oh, cut the Puritan bullshit," Sherri breathed, crawling into his lap. "I think it would be bitchin' to fuck a dude with four arms. You could hit all my erogenous zones at once and still hold my beer."

Erik's four hands simultaneously grabbed Sherri's body, lifted her completely out of his lap, and tossed her unceremoniously into the dirt. She seemed relatively unfazed by the setback, leaning back on one arm and taking a long, provocative drag on her cigarette.

"So uh, Trent! Trent's turn," Erik chattered, his face beet-red. "Trent, what would you order?"

Trent looked at the others, then at Priscilla with a huge toothy grin.

"The T-man wants a full-on slab of honey barbecue ribs," he declared.

"Finally," Bobby said. "Somebody who would actually order something worthwhile."

"Hellz yeah, dawg, it's more than worthwhile," Trent smiled. "I'm a man who likes to put his lips up against something with a little meat on the bones, yo. Most men can't handle the full rack, but the T delights in the biggest mouthful of hot, sweet meat that he can get. Y'all know what I'm sayin'?"

He pulled Priscilla close and gave her nose a playful nibble.

"Alright! Forget it! This game is over!" Bobby snapped, waving his hands in the air. "I don't know how you can all turn something as beautiful and innocent as a website into something so filthy and wrong!"

"Well, you're the one who thought it would be fun to talk about food with a bunch of people who are *starving to death,*" Sherri said. "Have you got any other ideas to keep us entertained, or should we just jump straight to the cannibalism now?"

"We should all just get to sleep," Vivian said. "Don't worry. I think we're going to find all the food we can eat tomorrow."

"Oh, I'm sure," Sherri smirked. "Then, after we eat all the food, maybe you can click your ruby slippers together and fly us all back to Kansas."

Vivian shook her head.

"No, I'm serious. At the rate we've been driving, we should hit Washington D.C. by tomorrow night. If we're ever going to find civilization, that's where it's going to be."

Everyone looked at Vivian, with expressions running the gamut from doubtful to outright condescending.

"Vivian, are you on crack?" Bobby said. "We're sitting here in the bombed-out remains of a two-bit roadside tourist trap, yet you somehow think the *nation's capital* is just going to be sitting there without a scratch on it?"

Vivian watched Priscilla rub her nose drowsily under Trent's chin.

"I don't think that it survived without a scratch," she said evenly. "But yesterday I also didn't think we'd ever see another living person again. Priscilla managed to survive out here in the middle of nowhere all by herself with no warning or preparation. I'd bet my life that there are fully stocked shelters the size of stadiums buried under the capital."

Sherri shook her head.

"So we're just going to roll up to an airtight underground Hilton full of crusty, old white dickheads, knock on the door and say, 'Hey, can we come in? We're cool! Less than half of us are contagious radioactive mutants!'"

Vivian frowned.

"So, do you have a better plan then?"

"Nah, your plan is cool with me," Sherri shrugged. "Let's go scare the congressional shit out of those assholes."

"That's the spirit," Vivian smiled.

"It sounds like a good plan to me too," Erik agreed. "But if we're going to drive all the way to D.C. tomorrow, we'd better get some sleep. We should try to hit the road at daylight to make sure we get there before dark."

"Any plan that involves sleep is good with me," Bobby said. "I'm beat."

A consenting chorus of grunts and yawns led into the dull activity of everyone bedding down for the night. Six minutes later, Bobby was snoring. The passing of another eight minutes found Vivian fitfully unconscious, wrapped in the blanket of her own wings. Seven minutes later Erik was blissfully dreaming, and four minutes after that, Sherri was out cold, tucked without invitation between his arms.

Trent and Priscilla were the last to remain awake. Priscilla lay face up across Trent's lap, staring into a sky as dim as her own eyes.

"Forget about them, girl," Trent said softly. "You just stick with me and everything's gonna be all right for you. I promise."

As the fire crackled nearby, he ran his forefinger around her dry lips.

"The T is going to make you forget about those nasty mutants. I'm gonna make you feel real good for a change."

He leaned down over his lap and put his lips to hers, pushing his broad, wet tongue into her unresponsive mouth.

CHAPTER TWELVE

Vivian sat on the dusty front fender of the abandoned Plymouth Reliant K that haunted the North of the Border parking lot. The morning was absolutely silent, save for the crackle of her fingers digging into a cellophane bag of maple cookies. She took a bite, and the dry crumbles scraped all the way down to her empty stomach.

She turned her sleepy eyes skyward and put her face into the golden yellow sun. Of course, the golden yellow sun was still buried behind a black mile of vaporized urban landscape hanging listlessly in the stratosphere, but just knowing that it was still out there helped to put her mind at ease. The sun was right on the other side of those clouds, just as Washington D.C. was right on the other side of a few more easy hours of driving. It wouldn't be long before this nightmare was finally over.

She slipped off of the fender and stretched her arms and legs, pulling the tightness out of her muscles. As she did so, the sails of her wings extended from her back as if trying to prove that they were part of the family too. She looked over her shoulder, and the wings dropped back into a limp bundle.

She glanced around the parking lot to ensure she was alone, then placed her feet shoulder-width apart, balled fists, and threw her arms skyward.

"Flap!" she growled. "Flap!"

The new muscles that anchored her wings to her back tensed slightly, then slackened as if ignoring a false alarm.

"Come on! Flap flap flap!"

Her wings remained motionless save for the gentle bounce that rippled from the spring of her frustrated knees. She closed her eyes and took a series of deep, cleansing breaths.

"Okay," she thought. *"I'm visualizing the flap. I can see the wings extending and falling in smooth, powerful strokes. I can see my body being pushed through the air, upwards into the sky."*

She opened her eyes and set her gaze straight through the dark clouds and into the hidden sun. Bouncing anxiously on the balls of her feet, she crouched down like a sprinter awaiting the starting gun.

"I'm visualizing the flap," she said. "Let's do this!"

With a series of explosive strides, she launched herself across the yard, kicked off the ground, and sailed into the air. The cold breeze whipped through her hair as her face cut through the sky. It continued to do so for nearly a full second before her palms and knees landed hard in the dirt, followed immediately by the rest of her battered body. As if to add insult to injury, her inanimate wings flew forward upon impact, slapping her in the back of the head and ramming her chin into the ground. When her eyes returned to focus, the first thing she saw was the license plate on the front of the Reliant.

North Carolina - First in Flight

Her face scrunched into the kind of scowl that says, *"Why I ooooughta!"*

"Vivian? Vivian, are you okay?"

Vivian sprang up onto her knees, quickly brushing the dust off of her coat.

"Oh, uh, hi, Erik! Good morning. I didn't realize anybody else was awake yet."

Erik took Vivian by the arm and helped her to her feet.

"What happened? Are you all right?"

"Oh, yeah, forget it. I just tripped," Vivian blushed. "Nobody else was awake. I didn't think you'd notice if I slipped away. I mean, you seemed to have your hands pretty full with Sherri this morning."

"Yeah, that I did," Erik muttered. "I don't know what that was all about. I just woke up and she was laying on top of me, and two of my arms were completely numb with pins and needles. Lucky for me, I still had two left!"

His left rat paw plunged into the bag of cookies on the fender, grabbing one and flicking it into the air. As it came flipping back to the earth, his right human hand caught it and stuffed it in his mouth. Vivian watched the spectacle wide-eyed.

"How did you do that?!"

"Doo wghat?" Erik chewed.

"Your hand! I mean, your *paw*," she said, pointing. "You can control it!"

"Yeah, I guess I can," Erik shrugged. "A little."

"A little? There's nothing 'a little' about it. You have complete motor control, down to the fingers! I can't even get these stupid wings to flap! I must be neurophysiologically defective."

"Oh, now that is untrue," Erik said. "There is *nothing* defective about your brain, Vivian."

"Well, it doesn't really matter either way. I don't even know why I'm trying. At the first hospital we find I'm getting these hideous things amputated. I don't want to be a freak of nature. Er … no offense."

"None taken," Erik said. "I don't think you're a freak of nature. So you've grown a pair of ornery bat wings. It's not the end of the world."

Vivian raised an eyebrow.

CHAPTER TWELVE

"Okay, so I guess technically it *is* the end of the world," he conceded. "But you've got to admit, it's not the end of *our* world! Come on, Viv. If Steve Gutenberg can survive a nuclear war, so can we!"

Vivian smiled a warm little smile.

"You're right. We could be a lot worse off, I guess."

"That's the spirit. Now let's figure out how to work those wings."

Vivian shook her head.

"Forget it. It's a lost cause. I try to visualize them flapping, but they don't do *anything*. No matter how hard I concentrate I can't even get a twitch out of them."

"Well, that's your problem right there," Erik smiled. "That's not the way they work. Don't *think* about your wings flapping, just *flap* them."

"That's a really helpful new perspective," Vivian smirked. "Thank you for that sage advice, Zen master."

"I'm serious. You need to just … how do I explain it? Okay, let me show you."

He took Vivian's hand and held it out in front of her. He pulled her fingers apart and left her standing with her open palm facing the sky.

"Close your eyes," he said. After a terse sigh, she complied. "Now visualize your hand as a fist. Picture what it looks like clenched into a fist. Imagine the way that the fingernails feel against your palm. Visualize the way that the knuckles stand away from the back of your hand. Picture your thumb wrapped over the top of your fingers. Are you picturing it?"

"I am," Vivian said.

"Open your eyes."

Vivian opened her eyes and looked at her hand, still palm up, still open.

"You didn't make a fist," Erik said.

"You didn't tell me to make a fist. You just said to visualize it."

"That's exactly what I'm saying," Erik said. "You can sit there all day and *think* about closing that hand, but it's not going to close until your brain just *does* it."

Vivian's fingers curled into a fist, straightened, and curled again. Her gaze flicked from her hand to Erik's eyes with some sense of enlightenment.

"I understand, but at the same time I don't. I mean, I understand the concept of visualizing versus actualizing, but how do you teach your brain to stop thinking and just start doing?"

"That I don't really know. My rat arms seemed to take cues from my human arms at first. Maybe you should try to train your wings by flapping your arms. Your brain knows how to make your arms move."

Vivian nodded eagerly.

"Okay, stand back."

She straightened her back and stood with her arms down at her sides.

Closing her eyes and furrowing her brow, she raised them.

"Is it working?" she asked.

"Not yet," Erik said. "Try again."

Vivian lowered her arms, cleared her mind, and raised them again. Again, nothing.

"Hmm," Erik said, scratching his chin. "I've got an idea. Lemme help."

He stepped behind Vivian and grasped the long bony ribs of her wings.

"What are you doing?" she asked.

"You just put your arms out again, and I'm going to spread your wings at the same time. Maybe we can get your brain used to the idea of your wings moving when your arms move."

"Okay," Vivian nodded. "Nice and slow. Ready? … Go."

She closed her eyes and raised her willowy arms to her sides. Simultaneously, Erik began pulling her gnarled wings apart. Their fleshy hinges were stiff and unyielding, and she began to topple forward as Erik inadvertently pushed her shoulders past her toes. His mutant paws grasped her firmly around her waist.

"Sorry," he mumbled. "Keep going."

Vivian kept raising her arms, trying to wrap her brain around the obtuse concept of moving her wings without *thinking* about it. As the stubborn sails began to extend, Erik stepped forward against her back to squeeze the last few inches of length out of his outstretched arms.

Vivian kept slowly raising her hands to her sides. She could feel Erik's body pressing against hers. She could feel his four hands holding her, his chest against her back, his stubbly face grazing her neck. Without opening her eyes, she turned her head toward him with a sly grin.

"Did you really think this was going to teach me to use my wings, or was this all just a ruse to get fresh with me?"

Erik's extra hands tensed around her waist.

"I uh … well, you see I," he stammered. "Oh man, I *so* feel like Trent right now."

A giggle escaped Vivian's lips.

"If you felt like Trent you'd be on the ground with two black eyes by now."

Erik smiled shyly as Vivian rubbed her cheek against his. She could now feel his entire body pressing a firm warmth against her back. She could feel the softness of his sweatshirt along the backs of her own bare arms.

But her arms were not bare.

"Whoa, Erik! Don't move! I feel it!"

"I'm sorry! I'm just nervous!"

"I feel my *wings*," Vivian clarified. "I can feel your arms against mine, but … but not! It's weird!"

Erik suddenly realized that his hands were no longer supporting Vivian's wings but holding them back. He released them and they spread majestically outward. They seemed larger than he had remembered, now spanning at least eight feet from end to end. His fingertips ran like soft little rakes over their leathery surface as they extended from her trembling shoulders.

"Eeesh!" Vivian giggled. "Stop it! That tickles! It's *weird!*"

She held her arms out to her sides and bared her teeth in a smile, bouncing on her toes as the ticklish feeling rained out of the air around her. The sensation was no longer coming from her arms. It had turned into a sparkling, freeform ghost that slid through her shoulders and across her back.

"How's this? Can you feel this?" Erik ran his hands in broad circular strokes over the backs of her wings. In her mind, Vivian could almost see blue sparks flying in the same spirals out of her shoulders, forming a cloudy outline of her newly awakened limbs in her subconscious. She could almost feel each individual fingertip telegraphing an impulse to her brain down a line that had never before been used.

"Oh! Right there!" she squeaked. "Yes! Yes! I can feel it! Keep touching me right there! I'm getting it! I'm getting it!"

Vivian's moment of intense physical clarity was cut short by a jarring voice.

"Oh, that's just *wrong!* My best friend and my own twin sister. Man, now I know how Luke Skywalker felt!"

The mental sparks sizzled into a numb blackness as Vivian's eyes flew open to see Bobby standing ten feet in front of her, his small, beady eyes peering from his pale face. Erik's hands slipped from her waist with a nervous cough. He took a step backward that didn't seem embarrassed as much as caught red-handed.

"Oh, uh … hi Bobby," he said, not making eye contact.

"So, now I finally see the truth," Bobby said, taking slow, deliberate steps around the mutants. "This is how it is, huh? You never really liked me at all, did you, Erik? All this time you've just been using me to get to my sister. I should have known that you liked her more than you liked me."

"That's not true!" Erik squeaked. "You know you're my best friend! You've always been my best friend! I'm not using you to get to Vivian!"

"You've got a funny way of showing it, Mr. McFeely."

Erik's four hands flexed guiltily in the air.

"I was just trying to show her how to use her wings! That's all! Nothing more! I swear!"

Bobby's accusing posture softened into his usual, easy-going slouch.

"Jeez, man. Lighten up. I was just messin' with ya. Don't get your panties all in a bunch."

Erik's expression instantly changed from "being hurt" to "wanting to hurt someone else."

"C'mere," Bobby continued, walking toward the Rabbit. "Help me with the satellite dish. Hopefully I'll have better luck at picking something up than you just did."

Erik watched Bobby's feet plodding through the parking lot, crushing the last vestiges of a lost moment into the gravel. He turned and looked at Vivian sheepishly. Her eyes were fixed on his, and her expression hung halfway between disappointment and anger.

"Viv, you know I just meant that I wasn't ... that I didn't ... I mean, I didn't mean that I don't—"

Vivian sighed and turned away.

"Just go help Bobby."

Erik nodded helplessly and crossed the driveway. When he reached Bobby's side, he punched him hard in the shoulder.

"Ow!" Bobby yelped. "What was that for?"

"Why did you have to go and do that, you big jerk?!"

"Do what? It was a joke. Get over it."

"Get over it? You just ruined our ... we were like, having a *moment* there."

"A moment? Oh please, Erik."

Bobby pulled the 5-in-1 camping lantern from the trunk and stuffed it into Erik's four hands. He pulled the cable out of the trunk and plugged one end into the lantern.

"I'm serious, Bobby. I think we just had a spark."

"A moment *and* a spark! Wow! You were practically on your way to the *warm fuzzies!*"

Bobby plugged the cable into the satellite dish and plopped into a cross-legged slump in the gravel.

"Why don't you just go after Sherri instead?" he continued, taking the lantern from Erik. "She's totally into you. And you'd get a lot farther with a lot less effort—that's for sure. I'll bet you could score with her in a second if you just asked, and I *know* you think she's hot now."

Erik crossed his arms and leaned on the fender in a huff.

"Dude! Dude, I can't believe you! What makes you think that I'd do Sherri? I'm not just gonna suddenly be interested in her just because ... okay, yes, so she's kinda cute now. But, God! Do you really think that I'm just some horny asshole looking for anyplace hot and willing to stick his—"

Bobby looked up at Erik with a sigh and a slow shake of his head.

"You're messing with me again, aren't you?" Erik said.

"I'm sorry," Bobby chuckled. "It's just so easy."

The sound of tiny feet in cloddish boots crunched stealthily into the parking lot. Sherri threw one last glance through the turnstiles and darted over to Vivian.

"Good, you're all here," she hissed confidentially. "Quick, let's get the hell out of here before Trent wakes up."

"Sherri, we're not leaving without Trent," Vivian said. "No matter how tempting the idea might be."

Sherri's eyebrows wrinkled with incomprehension.

"But if you're not ditching Trent, then what are you all doing in the parking lot?"

"We're having breakfast. Or the closest available substitute," Vivian said. "Here. Dig in."

She picked up the crinkling bag of cookies and pushed it into Sherri's hands. Sherri stuck her finger down her throat and made the universal sign for "Gag me."

"Okay, how about this," she suggested, "let's just kill Trent and eat *him*."

"Stop it, Sherri," Vivian grumbled.

"We'd be doing him a favor! He'd go a step up the social order if we turned him into shit!"

Vivian's reply was broken by a pair of tinny voices.

"Whazzat, look! That hermit has all kinds of puppets that we can use for our puppet show!"

"I don't know, Lookout. Mayor Ben says that we should never talk to strangers."

"Oh, don't be such a stick in the mud! He looks harmless enough to me!"

Vivian and Sherri stepped to Erik's side, and all three of them looked over Bobby's shoulder and at the tiny TV screen he cradled in his lap.

"What's going on?" Vivian asked.

"Well, it looks like the dumpy-ass bear wants to get some puppets from the weird, furry drifter," Bobby said, "but the kangaroo chick thinks they shouldn't be talking to—"

"I meant, what's going on with the TV," Vivian interrupted. "Did you find any new channels? Any news?"

"Nada," Bobby frowned. "Same shit, different day. Nothing but *Zoobilee Zoo* out the wazoo."

He poked the power button and the screen went black. He shifted his tightly bandaged girth awkwardly in the gravel, but he couldn't climb to his feet. He held his arm up to Vivian in surrender.

"Gimme a hand here, sis."

As Bobby's arm went up, his baggy bathrobe sleeve slipped to his shoulder, revealing slashed Confederate bandages and a row of uneven green spikes sprouting from the top of his forearm.

"Whoa!" Vivian gasped. "What the—"

Bobby held up his arm and stared at a row of bony protrusions the size of scissor blades. He flicked them with his finger—they felt like plastic.

"Well, shit," he shrugged. "Looks like I'm catching up to you guys."

Vivian grabbed Bobby's hand with both of her own, hoisting him upward with a labored grunt. When he was on his feet, she took his sleeve and pulled it back down over his arm.

"You better hide that before Priscilla wakes up," she said. "She's worked-up enough with only two of us showing mutations. If she saw this too, I don't know what she'd do."

"She'd just stand there staring like an idiot," Sherri said. "Like she always does."

Vivian turned around and saw Priscilla standing just five feet behind her. Her eyes were placid, and she stood quietly, save for the sound of air being sucked down her mangled throat.

"What's she doing here?" Bobby murmured. "I thought she was scared of you guys."

"She was," Erik agreed. "Maybe after an evening with Trent she's decided we're not so bad."

"Good morning, Priscilla," Vivian said, as if addressing a volatile child. "I'm happy to see you again. We're all happy to see you. We're your friends. Do you understand that?"

Priscilla showed no sign of acknowledgement. Her vacant glare was fixed just past Vivian's hip, on Sherri.

"Why is she looking at me like that?" Sherri said apprehensively.

Priscilla took a lumbering step toward her and raised her hand, a strangled word falling apart in her throat.

"Okay, seriously," Sherri squeaked, clutching her crackling bag of maple cookies. "Why the hell is Lurch looking at me like that? I'm going to kick her ass if she touches me. I swear to God."

Priscilla took another step forward and pointed a finger at Sherri's hands before tapping it on her lips.

"Wait, it's the cookies," Vivian said. "She wants the cookies!"

"First she wants Trent, now these shitty cookies," Sherri grumbled. "This girl is into some pretty messed-up shit."

"Priscilla, are you hungry?" Vivian offered. "We'll share with you. We're all friends here."

Vivian plucked the bag from Sherri's hands and stepped forward, and Priscilla hobbled backward with a gasp. Vivian closed her eyes and pulled back her arms, and her wings gracefully swept straight back behind her body, effectively hiding them from Priscilla.

"Nice," Erik smiled.

"It's okay," Vivian continued. "This is for you."

She set the bag on the trunk of the car and backed away slowly. When Vivian had removed herself a sufficient distance, Priscilla dug into the crinkly cellophane and stuffed a cookie in her mouth.

"Well, I'm glad to see somebody likes those things," Bobby smirked.

"We're making progress with her," Vivian smiled. "She's getting used to us. Pretty soon she won't be scared of us at all."

Erik looked at Priscilla digging her fist into the crackling bag and shoving another cookie into her mouth.

"So do you guys think she's … you know."

"Think she's what?" Vivian asked.

"You know … *special.*"

Vivian looked at Priscilla and shook her head.

"I don't think she's developmentally disabled, if that's what you mean. I think she's just got some major psychological damage that we're going to have to work through."

"How?" Erik asked.

"I don't know," Vivian admitted. "Baby steps. For starters, we just need to convince her that we don't want to hurt her. That should be easy. We've all shown her nothing but kindness and respect."

"Lookie here, lookie here! First thing in the A.M. and the T's woman is already out of bed and finding her man some breakfast. That's what I call love, yo."

Trent pushed through the turnstiles and strutted across the parking lot like a ludicrous white pimp in a blaxploitation film. He plunged his hand into the cookie bag and grabbed a handful before throwing an arm around Priscilla's waist and planting a kiss on her crumb-covered chin. His diaper of canvas bandages was gone, but its shape remained visible in the form of a clean swatch of fabric on his otherwise filthy clothes.

"Trent, what happened?" Vivian said. "Your bandages came off."

"Hellz yeah they came off. They came *all the way* off last night!"

As if to emphasize his point, Trent stepped forward and swung his hand in a high arc, preluding a dramatic zipping up of his fly.

"That girl was feisty with a capital *damn!*"

Vivian's hand flew to her mouth in horror.

"Oh my God, Trent. You didn't!"

"Didn't what?" Trent said coyly.

Vivian's eyes ticked between Trent and Priscilla's faces.

"You didn't *have sex with her!*" she hissed.

"Oh no! No, no, certainly not," Trent said, tracing finger quotes into the air. "I didn't have 'sex' with her. Not *legally,* anyway. Let's just say I didn't have 'sex' with her in exactly the same way that the president didn't have 'sex' with his intern. Aw, snap!"

The others all stared at Trent agape.

"Trent, how … how *could you?!*" Vivian stammered. "You know she's operating with a diminished capacity!"

"Says *you!*" Trent laughed. "I'd say she was operating at *full* capacity last night, if you know what I'm sayin'! Boo yah! Give the T some love!"

Trent leaned toward Erik and Bobby and threw both hands in the air in anticipation of two congratulatory high-fives. Bobby remained a statue with his arms crossed tightly. Erik just stood with his mouth hanging open in disbelief. Trent kept his hands in the air, eyes flicking back and forth between them.

"Don't leave me hangin' here, bros!"

As Trent stood waiting for accolades that would never be delivered, an overwhelming sense of guilt rose inside of Vivian. She should have known better than to leave him alone with Priscilla. This was all her fault.

She looked over Trent's shoulder at Priscilla's slack mouth, and shuddered at what it had been forced to do because of her negligence. All she could see in her mind's eye was the haunting black shadow of a shaft sliding over Priscilla's round chin and across her lips. It was so vivid that she could almost see it …

She blinked hard and gasped.

She *could* see it!

A thick black serpent twisted across Priscilla's chest. She craned her stiff neck away from it, but it continued to glide noiselessly over her chin.

"Trent!" Vivian hissed. "Step away from Priscilla. Slowly!"

She reached into the Rabbit's open trunk and wrapped her fingers around the hilt of the sword. Slowly and smoothly she raised it and held it in front of her body, preparing to strike. The serpent's undefined head bumped into Priscilla's cheek, sliding itself under her nose and across the side of her face. She twisted away from it with an annoyed grunt.

"Whoa, whoa, Vivi!" Trent said, putting his arms out to his sides in a weak position of defense. "You just step off of Prissy, a'ight? Nobody gots to get hurt over this. You don't got to be jealous of her."

"I'm not going to hurt her," Vivian growled. "Just shut up and step away, before—"

Before she could say another word, the serpent struck. In a lost fraction of a second, the creature tensed its body into a rigid arrow of muscle and rammed its head into Priscilla's nose.

"No!" Vivian wailed.

Behind Trent, Priscilla took one affronted step backward, clearly more annoyed than injured. She grabbed the snake out of the air and slammed it down on the fender of the Reliant with a resounding *bang*. Both of Trent's hands flew to his groin as he fell to the ground with a howling shriek.

"Oooowwww! Ow, shit! Shit!"

As he rolled over in agony, still clutching his crotch with both hands, his backside fell heavily toward the stupefied onlookers. From a bloodstained hole in the back of his trousers, a furry black tail thrashed back and forth in the air. The sight of it would have caused stomach-plunging hysteria only days before, but by this point the others just took it in with relief.

"Uuuuhngh," Trent moaned. "Oooww. What happened to my beaver cleaver?"

"Nothing happened to your … nothing happened to *that*," Vivian smirked.

"You're just feeling phantom pain."

"Bullshit!" Trent grunted. "This pain is too legit to quit, yo!"

"But it's not where you think it is," Erik said. "Your brain just hasn't figured out where to send the sensations for your tail yet."

Trent's eyes snapped to Erik's.

"Hold up—back up. Say what now?"

"Oh for fuck's sake, don't you even *know?*" Sherri said. "I've never met anyone as clueless as you. And I've worked at Circuit City!"

She stepped to Trent's side and grabbed his thrashing tail, thrusting it in front of his face.

"Happy birthday! You have a cat tail, idiot."

Trent's eyes followed the rope in Sherri's hand back to his own tailbone. There was a brief pause as his brain worked over the new information, followed immediately by a spasm of denial.

"No ... no!" he chattered. "It ain't like that! I'm one of the chosen ones! It ain't like that! It ain't like that!"

He scrambled to his feet and took one fleeing step before Sherri yanked his tail like the starter on a lawnmower. With another wailing clutch at his groin, Trent returned to the ground.

"Ha haaa!" Sherri grinned. "This is more fun than Whack-A-Mole!"

"Ooooouuugghhh," Trent moaned.

"It looks like Twiki got a piece of you after all," Vivian said. "Serves you right for what you did to Priscilla last night, you creep."

Trent sat up and pulled his tail around his front. He glared at the greasy appendage with horrified fury.

"This ain't right, y'all. This wasn't supposed to happen to me. I'm trippin'. I'm straight trippin'! I'm not one of you freaks! I'm chosen! I'm one of His chosen ones!"

"Knock it off, Trent," Vivian said. "It's just biology. God hasn't forsaken you."

"Yeah, quit being so melodramatic," Bobby agreed. "On the one hand, you've got a grotesque physical deformity brought on by exposure to deadly doses of ionizing radiation, but on the other, Jesus loves you!"

"I can't have this," Trent said sternly. "It's got to come off."

"It will, very soon," Vivian said. "All of us will have these things amputated just as soon as we get to Washington D.C."

"No," Trent said. "Now. This thing has gotta come off now. I can't live like this, yo. It ain't natural. It ain't part of His plan."

"Trent, we can't just cut it off," Vivian said. "We don't have the proper tools."

"Bullshit!" Sherri yelled gleefully.

She snatched Vivian's purse from the front seat of the Rabbit and yanked out the Swiss Army Knife.

"We've got all the tools we need right here. Let's cut off some of Trent!"

She dropped to her knees by Trent's side and grabbed his tail, pulling it taut and flicking open the blade with a sinister *click*. Trent could feel her fingernails digging into a sensitive shaft that she was not actually holding, and his hands again slapped over his groin.

"Wait! Hold up, girl! I changed my mind. Stop!"

Sherri slashed the blade through the air in a savage arc. Halfway to Trent's tail, her arm came to an abrupt stop with a sharp slap of flesh against flesh. The knife dropped into the gravel as her tiny forearm was crushed in Priscilla's fist. Before she could even look at her assailant, Sherri had been yanked to her feet.

"Aaaaagh! Shit! Let go of me, warrior princess!"

She planted an oversized boot into Priscilla's kneecap. Priscilla threw her to the ground her and stumbled backward, clutching her crushed knee.

"Oh my God, Sherri!" Vivian gasped.

Vivian rushed to Priscilla's side and put a supportive hand on her shoulder.

"I'm sorry, Priscilla! I'm sorry," she soothed. "Sherri didn't mean to hurt you. You just startled her. She didn't mean to hurt you. We're not going to hurt you."

Sherri sat up and knocked the gravel out of her hair.

"It's okay, I'm fine. Feel free to kiss Gigantor's ass."

"I'm sorry, Sherri," Vivian said. "If we want her to trust us, you're going to have to be a little less aggressive. Especially toward Trent. For some unfathomable reason he seems to be her favorite."

"But … but he told me to!" Sherri argued. "He actually *told* me to cut him! Didn't you, Trent?"

Trent snatched his bristling tail and held it protectively.

"Vivi's right," he said. "We best just wait until we get to a hospital."

Sherri's face collapsed in disappointment.

"But you'll go to Hell if I don't cut it off, right? You don't want to go to Hell, do you?"

"I'm not keeping it," Trent said. "But we gotta wait until we can see an M.D., for real. If we just chop it off I'll still be griddled up with mutant DNA, right? I want a biopsy on that shit so I know it ain't comin' back, yo."

Bobby twisted his head back and then threw it forward, rubbing his eyes in an exaggerated double take.

"What?! *What?!* Did Trent just dismiss biblical mumbo jumbo in favor of a valid scientific theory? Holy shit, we should have started threatening his penis from day one!"

Vivian shook her head and looked at the brightening cloud cover.

"All right, cut it out, you guys. If we're going to be to Washington D.C. by tonight, we need to get on the road."

"We still need to grab all of our stuff," Bobby said.

"It's taken care of," Vivian replied, returning the camping lantern to the trunk. "I packed up everything before you guys woke up. We're ready to go."

"Well, somebody's a little eager beaver," Trent said. "I'm surprised you didn't just leave without us."

"I second that," Sherri growled.

"I'm just excited," Vivian said. "In just a few hours we'll be back in civilization. Or a reasonable facsimile thereof."

"For real," Trent agreed. "Let's all hop in that little car and get us to a hospital, stat."

"I call shotgun!" Sherri screamed.

"Sherri," Vivian said. "You know that you're the smallest and you need to be in the back—"

"Not listening!" Sherri said, planting her palms over her ears. "Not *even* listening."

Vivian turned away with a sigh.

"That's fine with me, yo," Trent said. "Me and Prissy are going to take the back seat with you, Vivi."

"She can't ride the back seat," Vivian said. "Her legs are too long."

"What if she sits on my lap?" Trent said.

"That doesn't actually make her legs shorter, does it?"

"I'll ride in the back seat if I can sit on *Erik's* lap," Sherri grinned.

"Veto!" Erik chirped. "I veto that!"

"This looks like it's gonna take a while," Bobby said. He plodded over to the Reliant and plopped down on the hood, exercising the shocks.

"What if I sit in the back and Vivi sits on my lap?" Trent said innocently.

"Or even better, what if *I* sit in the back, and she sits on *my* lap?" Erik bristled.

"I can't sit on *anybody's* lap!" Vivian snapped. "Hello? Eight-foot wingspan here!"

"Okay, alright," Trent said. "I drive. My girl Prissy is the tallest—she rides shotgun. Vivi needs someplace to put her extra gear, so we stick her in the center of the back seat with her wings all stuck out over the back. Goldilocks and Lil' E stick their scrawny butts in on either side. Is that copacetic with y'all?"

"Sounds great ... except for one little thing," Bobby said. "What am I supposed to do, ride in the trunk with Spritle and Chim-Chim?"

"That's no good," Erik said. "You won't fit in there either."

"This is like the losing end of a game of *Tetris*," Bobby scowled. "It's physically impossible for all of us to fit into that car."

"You're right," Vivian agreed. "We'll have to take both of them."

Everyone looked skeptically at the derelict Reliant.

"It's a good idea, but how are we supposed to start it?" Erik asked.

"We can push start it, just like the Rabbit," Vivian said. "It's just another bucket of bolts from the '80s. It shouldn't have any complex circuitry that would have been damaged by the EMP."

"Well, yeah, I agree with you there," Erik nodded. "But the thing is we can't even push start it unless one of us knows how to hot-wire a car."

Four pairs of eyes turned simultaneously to Sherri.

"What are you looking at?" she snapped. "Just because I'm the only one of you white-bread pantywaists who has ever stolen anything it doesn't mean that I've got grand theft auto under my belt. I'm not your one-stop larceny shop, for fuck's sake."

The others looked at the ground guiltily. Sherri continued.

"Why don't you just get the Gorgeous Lady of Wrestling here to give you the keys?"

"Wait—you think Prissy has the keys?" Trent said. "What makes you think that?"

"Christ, I feel stupider just standing next to you," Sherri moaned. "When they bombed the shit out of this place there was *one* car in the parking lot and *one* person still inside. Come on, people, let's have a little deductive fuckin' reasoning here."

"She's right," Erik said. "This has to be Priscilla's car! Check her pockets!"

"With pleasure!" Trent grinned.

He reached out for the hip pocket of Priscilla's skirt, but Vivian slapped his hand before it got there.

"Ow!" he winced. "Okay, ladies first."

"Please excuse the intrusion, Priscilla," Vivian said.

She slipped her fingers into Priscilla's pocket and came back with a set of car keys attached to a pink rabbit's foot.

"Looks like our luck is changing for the better," she smiled.

Ten minutes later the gang had dusted off and push started the butter-colored relic with Sherri's negligible weight behind the wheel. As soon as the engine sputtered to life, she did a donut that showered the others with gravel. She pulled up alongside them and rolled down the window.

"Alright, losers, I am out of here. See you in D.C."

"Sherri, you can't take that whole car all by yourself," Erik said.

"You're right," Sherri agreed. "Get your sexy mutant ass in here."

"You also can't drive stick."

"You know, you are really starting to get on my nerves, Sievert."

"Come on, Sherri," Vivian said. "You can ride shotgun in my car."

"Fuck that. Your car is colder than Santa's sack. I'm staying in the car with a roof."

CHAPTER TWELVE

"I'm with her," Bobby said. "It'll be nice to go somewhere without my snot freezing to my mustache for a change."

"You can all ride in Priscilla's car," Vivian said. "But there's not enough room in there for me. My wings alone would take up the space of two people. I'll follow you in my car."

"Nobody should be all alone," Erik said. "You know—the buddy system. I'll ride with you. I'll even drive if you want."

"You do realize it's going to be cold if you ride with me," Vivian warned.

"Will it?" Erik asked.

Vivian looked into his apologetic eyes with a tiny smile.

"We'll see."

The Reliant followed the Rabbit in a caravan of two through the cold, smoky ruins of northern Virginia. Erik and Vivian led the way in the convertible, while the rest of the group followed in the relative comfort of the sedan.

Trent sat crushed behind the steering wheel of the Reliant with his knees pressed against the underside of the dashboard. Priscilla was by his side in the properly adjusted passenger seat, stroking his tail as if it were a soft baby bunny. A broad, toothy grin was plastered on Trent's face, and his eyelids hung in a semi-orgasmic slouch.

"That's right, Prissy," he moaned. "Pet the snake. Pet it like you mean it."

"Um, hello?" Bobby called from the back seat. "There's other people in the car here, you know. Could you please not get a tail job right in front of us?"

"Seriously," Sherri spat. "You're so disgusting. You were scared shitless of God smiting you over that thing until you realized that it's the big hairy manpole your late-blooming ass never had. Now you're in love with it!"

"Well, it's like it says in the first book of Corinthians," Trent said. "'We shall not all sleep, but we shall all be changed, in a moment, in the twinkling of an eye at the last trumpet.'"

"You're unbelievable!" Sherri said. "When Erik mutated, you said he was the son of Satan, but now that it's happened to you it's actually *written in the Bible?!*"

"Greater theologians than I have misinterpreted His divine word at first," Trent shrugged.

"In other words, the Bible always says what suits your needs, even when you change your mind," Bobby said.

"My faith is strong enough not to get hung up on the Lord's words, but to just trust the gist of it."

Priscilla closed her eyes and rubbed the end of Trent's tail over her tongue.

"Oh yeah, Prissy, that feels good," he groaned. "Baby, don't stop. Mmm, don't stop."

The tip of Trent's tail disappeared into Priscilla's mouth, but before he could

231

appreciate it, her teeth slammed shut like a nutcracker.

"Yeeeeaaaaaghhh!" Trent wailed.

His whole body recoiled, slamming his knees into the bottom of the dashboard and sending the car careening back and forth across the dusty highway. He quickly regained his composure, pulling the car back into its lane and yanking his tail away from Priscilla.

"Bad girl!" Trent shouted, rubbing his crotch. "Bad! How many times do I got to tell you! Lips and tongue! No teeth!"

"Trent!" Bobby barked. "For Christ's sake, she's a human being! If you don't start treating her with respect I'm gonna start smacking you around!"

"She's the one who's down on a brother like the jaws of life, and you're telling *me* to treat *her* with respect? I think that shit just busted my kneecaps, yo!"

"Well, why don't you just move the seat back, you retard?" Sherri asked.

"I tried, Strawberry Shortlegs. It doesn't move. You got it all jammed up here when you did the push start."

"Oh, I didn't do shit to your stupid seat," Sherri said. "Maybe it's all just *a sign from God* that you should pull over and let somebody else drive for a while? Did you think of that?"

"Like who?" Trent asked. "Last time I checked, Vivi and Little E were in the other car, and none of you other jokers can drive stick. Excluding Prissy of course, but I don't think that she's in any condition to drive in her diminished capacity."

"Oh, *now* she's got a diminished capacity!" Sherri laughed mirthlessly. "Now that it's *beneficial* for *you*, suddenly she's got a diminished capacity. Tell me, Trent, how did you get so detached from reality? I want to smoke some too!"

"You can spin it any way you like," Trent said, "but the simple truth is this: The T is always going down that righteous path, yo. Isn't that right, Prissy?"

He put his hand high on Priscilla's thigh and gave it a lecherous squeeze.

"Jesus, give it a rest, Trent!" Bobby spat. "You're not even touching me and I still have this image in my head of Webster telling me to say no, go, and tell someone I trust."

Trent threw a glance at Bobby in the rearview mirror.

"It's important to give your girl constant physical contact, dawg. I know somebody like *you* wouldn't be familiar with how to treat a lady, but I call that the first T."

"The first T?" Bobby said. "What the hell is that supposed to mean?"

"It's the T's three Ts," Trent grinned. "If you can successfully execute the three Ts on a woman, it's a fast lane, all-access pass to her heart."

"Oh please, good sir," Bobby said sarcastically. "Please educate my poor pathetic soul on the matter of these three Ts of which you speak, so that I too may find true love as you so obviously have."

Trent slipped his hand off the wheel and ran his knuckles gently across Priscilla's cheek. She leaned into his touch and closed her eyes.

"The first T is touch," he said. "If a girlie ain't gonna let you touch her, then there's no point in even continuing the application process, yo."

In the passenger seat of the open convertible, Vivian struggled to hold down a road map against the raging turbulence of the wind.

"Here, let me help with that," Erik said.

Leaving his two left hands on the wheel, he reached over with both of his right and grasped the corners of the map. His human hand inadvertently landed on top of Vivian's. It lingered there for a pronounced beat before letting go and catching the fluttering corner.

"Thanks," she said.

She held the map's other two corners with her own hands, securing it well enough to read it. The wind whistled through a long, otherwise silent pause before Erik spoke.

"I'm sorry. I didn't mean it."

"Don't worry about it," Vivian said. "It was just a little touch."

"No, not for that. I'm sorry about before in the parking lot. The thing with Bobby."

Bobby shook his head disgustedly.

"Alright, I'll humor you," he said. "So in the unlikely event that you can touch a girl without her immediately vomiting or knocking you unconscious, then what?"

"The second T stands for 'tell,'" Trent said. "If the lady is interested in your tender touch, then she almost certainly is in the market for something more. Just tell her whatever she wants to hear."

"So let me make sure I've got the steps straight," Bobby said. "It's manhandle first, and *then* lie?"

"I didn't say lie—I said *tell her what she wants to hear*," Trent corrected. "The second T works even better when it's true blue and from the heart, yo."

Vivian tipped her head down toward the map.

"That did hurt my feelings a little. When Bobby showed up you practically knocked me over trying to deny what was going on."

The cold wind blew straight through Erik's chest and into his stomach.

"So ... what *was* going on, exactly?"

"You were helping me with my wings and we, you know ... we kind of had a *moment.*"

"We *were* having a moment!" Erik smiled. "Bobby thought that I was on crack when I said that."

"Well, you shouldn't care so much about what Bobby says. You know that he just says things to get a reaction out of you. He does it to everybody. It's his thing."

"I know that," Erik said. "But the thing is, this time he was actually ... well, he was sort of right."

Vivian looked at him with surprise.

"He was *right?*"

"Sort of right!" Erik backpedaled. "Don't get me wrong, he *is* the best friend that I ever had in my life, and I love your brother like he's my own, but ... well, let's just say that I've been a lot more eager to come and hang out with him ever since he moved in with you."

Vivian's cheeks flushed until they matched her hair.

"But ... but in all the time we've known each other you've barely even spoken to me other than to regale me with pop culture trivia."

Erik's face began sprinting toward its own shade of red.

"Well, I'm ... I was too intimidated to really talk to you."

"What?!" Vivian laughed. "Why in the world would I intimidate you? You do realize that I was just a minimum-wage-earning peon at Boltzmann's Market, right?"

"Well, yeah. That's how everybody *else* sees you. To me, you were always like some kind of super heroine. The befuddled stock clerk was just your mild-mannered secret identity. Then, by night, you turn into the savvy intellectual who clears *Jeopardy!* boards without even trying. *That's* the real Vivian Gray. That's the one that kept me from ever listening when you told me to go home. That's the one that I always wanted to spend a lot more time with."

He gave her a shrugging little smile and continued.

"I guess that wish came true in a big way, huh?"

A fuzzy pink warmth spread outward from Vivian's chest and poured into her face like a hot cup of tea.

"And the third T?" Bobby said with only the most marginal interest.

"The third T is for 'take,'" Trent said. "Take her on her dream date. It doesn't matter if she wants you to fly her sweet ass to the *moon*—you take her wherever she wants to go. If you've got through 'touch' and 'tell' and the girl is still all into you, then 'take' will get you into the boudoir every time, guaranteed or your money back."

"Well, it looks like you're almost there," Vivian smiled.

She pulled her finger over her map, tracing the line of Interstate 67 straight into Washington D.C.

"I've always wanted to go to the capital and experience it all," she said dreamily. "The Lincoln Memorial, the Washington Monument, the Smithsonian.

I hope at least some of it is still standing."

"We'll have a chance to see everything there is," Erik said. "D.C. is gonna be our new home."

Vivian put her hand on top of his and gave it a squeeze.

"Go home, Erik," she smiled. "And take me with you."

She shifted in her seat but Erik's eyes stayed on the road, squinting into the distance. She leaned in toward him and whispered in his ear.

"Erik, what would you say if I told you that I was about to kiss you?"

Erik's eyes flew wide open.

"Oh shit!"

Before Vivian could respond, Erik had slammed the clutch and brake pedals to the floor, locking the Rabbit's tires in a squealing scream. He grabbed her with his two right arms and held her tightly as the speeding car began to fishtail.

"Hold on!" he screamed, wrestling the wheel. "I've got it under control!"

With two hands on the wheel, Erik managed to keep the front tires pointed straight ahead through his sheer will to survive. For the briefest second, Erik did indeed have the situation under control.

But only for the briefest second.

For days on end the Rabbit's temporary spare tire had shown admirable grace under fire, far outperforming its specifications for speed and endurance without complaint. To force this little trooper into an unexpected stop at seventy miles per hour, however, was simply asking too much. After leaving a suicide note of black skid mark down one hundred feet of pavement, the donut blew, peeling off of its narrow rim like an exhausted roll of tape.

The driver's-side corner of the Rabbit dropped onto the bare rim, snapping its axle and slamming its front end into the pavement. A fountain of hot white sparks flew from the frame as it scraped across the interstate. Despite Erik's efforts, the forces of physics threw the car into a leftward arc, forcing the rear tire of the passenger side to take the lead.

Behind the grinding shower of sparks, the dragging front fender wrenched free from the Rabbit's body. It bounced off the pavement and turned end over end in the air until it crashed down in a blast of beaded safety glass on the windshield of the Reliant.

One second later, friction had ground the Rabbit to a stop, but it wasn't until three seconds later that Trent pressed his brake pedal. Able to see nothing but a gray fender slammed lengthwise across his windshield, he plowed the Reliant into the front of the spun-out Rabbit, silencing the roar of both utterly devastated engines.

The momentum of the collision carried both cars across the scorched pavement until they scraped to an eerily silent stop at the lip of a ten-mile-wide atomic crater that had once been Washington D.C.

CHAPTER THIRTEEN

Washington D.C. was not destroyed.

It was not in ruins.

It was simply *gone*.

Interstate 67 had literally become a road to nowhere, crumbling into an abyss where the nation's capital had once stood.

At the edge of the crater, Vivian's Rabbit lay in a posthumous slouch on its broken axle. The Reliant was smashed against it, its hood thrown open, its engine hissing steam and dripping fluids.

Vivian pushed herself off of the dashboard as her brain waded through various depths of consciousness. Her ear wrapped around a sound, which resolved into a voice.

"Oooouch," it groaned. "Vivian, you okay? Viv?"

She pushed her glasses onto her nose and surveyed the damage. To her left was the steaming ruin of the Reliant; to her right, a mile-deep crater; to the front, an Archimedean screw of wrecked satellite dish thrown thirty feet from the road.

"Ooowww, shit," Erik hissed. "Viv, are you hurt?"

"No. I'm fine."

It was a lie. She wasn't injured, but she was certainly not fine. They had lost everything. Again. They had lost their transportation. They had lost their only cursory link to the rest of the world. They had even lost their *destination*. But what bothered her most was what remained.

A rusty green overpass soared above her head. It left the ground a hundred feet to her left and extended over the void, terminating in the empty sky. The sight of it ripped a memory from the back of her mind.

On that first terrible morning, she had been introduced to the apocalypse by the remains of the Skyshine Causeway bridge. Now here she was, on the other side of countless days and miles, facing an identical vaporized bridge. To her it was more than just another piece of urban wreckage. It was the start of a tragic film loop coming back through the projector of her life a second time. It was a stinging reminder that no matter how long or far she ran, she would never reach the end of this merciless atomic wasteland. The sight of it made her do something that she had managed to keep from doing for this entire hellish journey.

It made her break down and cry.

"I'm so sorry, Viv," Erik whispered. "Come on, don't give up. We're gonna be okay."

Vivian ran her hand along the ruined dashboard of her car.

"It's over," she said.

"It ain't over till it's over."

"Erik, it's over!" Vivian sobbed. "We're screwed! There's nowhere else to go! I give up! I just give up."

She buried her head in Erik's chest, weeping with an intensity that boiled her sinuses. Her last reservoir of hope had been shattered, releasing a deluge of pent-up emotion. She cried so hard her tears turned to blood.

Her eyes shot open. Blood?

She suddenly realized that the driver's seat was saturated in it. The Reliant had rammed into Erik's side of the car, buckling his door into a jaw of serrated steel that bit deep into his thigh.

"Oh my God, Erik! You're hurt! Why didn't you say something?"

Erik shrugged tightly.

"You didn't sound like you could take any more bad news right now."

The whole time that Erik had been trying to convince her that she would be okay, he had been quietly bleeding out into her seat cushions.

"Erik, I'm so sorry! I didn't know!"

"Don't worry. I'm gonna be fine," he hissed. "*I'm* not giving up."

"But Erik, I—"

The cold air was sliced open by a scream from inside the Reliant. Vivian's eyes flicked toward it, then back to Erik.

"Go help them," he nodded. "I'm fine."

"You're not fine—you're hurt!"

"I'm fine! Go!"

He gave Vivian a firm shove, and she leapt out of her car and sprinted to the other. She yanked open the back door and leaned inside. Bobby and Sherri were sprawled across the seat, looking dazed but unharmed.

"Are you guys okay?" Vivian asked.

"Can't complain," Bobby moaned.

"Aaaaaauggh!" Trent screamed. "Shit! Get it off!"

"Hold on!" Vivian shouted.

She pried open the driver's-side door, and it fell off its hinges and smashed to the ground. Her heart leapt up and stuck in her throat. there was just so … much … *blood*. Blood dripped from the steering wheel and leaked from the seats. Blood spattered over Trent's silk shirt. Blood collected in pools in the floor.

"Get it off!" Trent wailed. "Oh Lord, get it off!"

The collapsed dashboard had become a rake of jagged steel and plastic stabbing into his thighs and pinning him to the seat. Priscilla struggled to lift it, and the shattered instruments dug into her palms, drizzling her blood into the hot puddle in Trent's lap. She didn't speak, but her eyes screamed for help.

"Bobby! Sherri!" Vivian snapped. "Get over here and help me!"

The two back-seat passengers scrambled dizzily out of the car and rushed to her side. Vivian curled her fingers under the rounded plastic edge of the dashboard.

"Okay, Priscilla! Lift!"

With a groaning flex of muscle, the two girls raised the shattered dashboard from Trent's lap. He shrieked an unholy shriek as the gnarled blades pulled from his flesh.

"Bobby!" Vivian grunted. "Grab him!"

Bobby reached into the car, threw Trent's arm around his shoulders, and hauled him out of his seat. With uncharacteristic compassion, Sherri squirmed under Trent's other arm and helped Bobby lay him down in the road.

Vivian and Priscilla dropped the heavy dashboard with a crackle of snapping steel and plastic. Priscilla began to crawl toward the driver's-side door, but a pike of twisted automotive steel sunk into her leg. Her face contorted, but her eyes remained fixed on Trent, convulsing on the cold pavement beyond. With a stuttering breath, she pushed herself forward, digging the wreckage deeper into her calf. Vivian planted her palms on Priscilla's broad shoulders and shoved her back.

"Priscilla, stop!"

Priscilla's face clenched with agony as her feet pushed against the side of the car, forcing her inches closer to the door and driving the steel deeper into her leg. Tears streaked from her eyes, but she never looked away from Trent's body lying in the street.

"Priscilla, stop!" Vivian wailed. "What's the matter with you?! Stop!"

The passenger-side door flew open and Erik leaned into the car.

"What's going on?" he chirped.

"Erik, stop her!" Vivian screamed. "Her leg!"

Erik grabbed Priscilla's ankles with two hands each. Despite her struggle, he quickly pulled her off of the glistening spike and out the door. Vivian bounded to the passenger side and helped Erik wrestle her to the ground, all the while cooing reassurances that she showed no signs of comprehending.

"It's okay, just relax, just relax. It's okay," Vivian chattered.

"Oh my God," Erik gasped. "She's hurt bad!"

"No, she's not. Most of this blood is Trent's. She's okay."

"No, she's not! Look!"

The bandage around Priscilla's scarred neck was saturated with an oozing crimson. She coughed, and a wave of blood spilled from her mouth and down her chin.

"Oh no. No no no no," Erik panicked. "This isn't happening. What do we do?"

Vivian just stared as blood ran down Priscilla's neck and dripped onto her chest. Blood ran from her slashed leg and pooled in the dirt. Blood gushed from Erik's torn thigh. All Vivian could see was blood.

"Vivian!" Erik screamed. "What are we going to do?!"

Vivian's mind went totally blank. The overload of gore had tripped its circuit breaker, leaving her in a total mental darkness.

"Vivian, what do we do?!"

"I don't know!" Vivian screamed. "I don't know, Erik!"

"Don't you have a first-aid kit or something?!"

"Yes, Erik!" she said sarcastically. "Yes, I've had a first-aid kit in my trunk all this time, but I've been saving it for your birthday!"

"Well, check *her* trunk then!"

Vivian yanked the keys from the Reliant's ignition and unlocked its trunk with a *pop* that was barely audible over Trent's continued wail.

"Aaaaagh! You're killin' me B!"

"I'm sorry!" Bobby yelped. "This is gonna hurt even more!"

Bobby grabbed the hem of his bathrobe and threw it across Trent's lap. He planted one of his palms on each of Trent's thighs and leaned into them, compressing the wounds under his massive body weight. Trent shot upright from the waist and slapped him wildly about the chest and face.

"Ow! Ow! You asshole!" he shrieked. "Get off! Get off!"

"I'm sorry," Bobby growled, turning his face away from the blows. "We need to put pressure on it to stop the bleeding!"

"*You're* going to be bleeding in about two seconds if you don't get offa me, bitch!"

"Sherri!" Bobby barked. "We need bandages! Take off some clothes!"

"Screw you! I'm not getting naked for this jackoff!"

Bobby threw his eyes at Trent.

"I meant take off *his* clothes."

Sherri blinked.

"I don't see how that's any better!"

Vivian pushed open the trunk lid, throwing dull gray light over a pile of random junk within. A pink sweater. A gas can. A half-empty bottle of cola. She dug into the mess, frantically searching for a little white box with a red cross. She pushed aside a Chemistry 101 textbook, revealing a card made of pink and red construction paper.

Happy Valentine's Day, Prissy. I love you to the ends of the Earth. —Lee

She threw the card aside and dug deeper into the trunk.

"AaaaAAAAaAAggh!" Trent screeched.
"Shut up! Shut *up!*" Sherri snapped. "Stop being such a pussy!"
Bobby kneeled on the blacktop with Trent leaned back against him. Trent thrashed and squirmed, but Bobby held him tightly against his own body.
"Aaaaghh!" Trent seethed. "Get your bitch ass off of me, B! I told you I don't swing that way!"
"Sit still!" Bobby grumbled. "I don't like it any more than you do! Now be a man and let Sherri finish!"
Sherri straddled Trent's left knee and wrapped a strip of his own torn rockabilly shirt tightly around his thigh.
"Just one more knot," she said.
"Make it tight enough to stop the bleeding," Bobby ordered, "but be gentle, alright?"
Sherri nodded, then yanked the two loose ends of her knot as hard as she could.

At the sound of Trent's tormented scream, Priscilla lurched bolt upright with a fire in her eyes. Erik took her by the shoulders and gently pushed her back toward the ground.
"It's okay," he said. "Don't worry; they're taking good care of him over there. Now stay still!"
Priscilla's mouth moved silently as a huge, glistening teardrop rolled out of the corner of her eye. She struggled to stand up, forcing a renewed gush from her throat. Erik shouted over his shoulder.
"Um, Vivian. We need some help over here. Like, *now!*"
At the very bottom of the trunk, Vivian unearthed a shoebox and yanked it from the debris.
"Be first aid," she pleaded. "Please be first aid!"
She tore off the lid with a desperate optimism, revealing a box of photographs.
"Damn it!"
She pitched the box back into the trunk, scattering its contents. As her mind raced, her eyes lit on one of the photos. It was Priscilla wearing an oversized flannel shirt. Unremarkable, except for one thing. She was smiling. Her eyes were sharp and alive, glistening with a vivacious spirit that Vivian had never seen.
She turned, passing her eyes over a Polaroid of Priscilla at a fast-food restaurant, laughing. An unfocused rose loomed in front of the lens, presumably being held by the photographer. A bubbly cursive caption scrawled in blue ink read "Lee = Mr. Romance! Valentine's Day '97."

Vivian shook her head and reached up to close the trunk, but a photo sticking out of the shoebox seized her attention.

"Alright, just one more," Bobby said.

"Come on, Goldie," Trent pleaded. "Easy this time, a'ight? Please. Please?"

Sherri slipped the silk bandage under Trent's leg and crossed it over the top.

"Alright," she said, glancing up at Bobby. "Give the crybaby something to bite on."

"Oh no. No, girl, come on. No. No. Come on, girl—"

"Stay with me, here," Bobby muttered, giving Trent's shoulders a manly shake. "Sherri, count of five. Ready? One, two ..."

Vivian pulled the folded photo from the shoebox. It was of Priscilla standing in an athletic field, towering over a band geek with a battered trombone. She hunched over him with her arms wrapped around his shoulders and her cheek pressed lovingly against his. The trombone player's face sent a shock through Vivian.

It was Trent.

She scrutinized the picture in the dull light. No. It wasn't Trent at all. This boy had the same haircut as Trent, and the same gigantic toothed smile—even his nose was similar—but his eyes were entirely different. They were large, bright blue, and totally innocent. Vivian flipped the picture over and unfolded it, revealing the curly inscription on the back.

Priscilla + Lee 4 ever!

A myriad of open questions slammed shut in her mind.

"Oh my God. She thinks Trent is her boyfriend!"

She turned the unfolded picture back over, revealing another terrible secret.

Lee was standing on the grass. Priscilla was standing on the team bench.

She couldn't have been more than five feet tall.

"Five!" Bobby shouted.

Sherri yanked the bandage, cinching a knot of silk around Trent's thigh and forcing a pealing scream from the very bottom of his being. On the other side of the Reliant, his cry burrowed into Priscilla's ear. She shoved Erik away and lurched to her feet.

"Priscilla, no! Lay down! Lay down! How many times do I have to tell you not to get—"

Erik was silenced by a fist thumping into his stomach. He took one gasping breath and fell to his knees, clawing at Priscilla's jacket for support. It slipped off her broad shoulders as she limped away, dropping Erik into a gasping pile.

Vivian looked up from the photograph of the petite girl just in time to see the seven-foot giant rounding the rear fender. The bandages on Priscilla's arms had torn away, revealing dozens of oversized insect legs sprouting from her flesh. Vivian took a step back and threw out her hand, thrusting the photograph in front of Priscilla's face.

"Priscilla, stop! Listen to me! Trent is not Lee! He's not your boyfriend! He's a creep!"

Priscilla didn't take her eyes off of Trent as she grabbed Vivian's outstretched hand and wrenched it around, throwing her to the ground.

"Bobby! Sherri!" she screamed. "Get away from Trent! Now!"

Bobby and Trent were both facing Priscilla as she came around the corner of the car, but from her reversed perch on Trent's knee, Sherri never saw her coming. A swollen palm smashed into her shoulder like a wrecking ball, and her tiny blond head hit the blacktop with an explosion of fireworks that only she could see.

"Aaaagh! Shit!"

A fresh scrape on her forehead poured blood down her face as she slowly pulled herself to safety. Before Priscilla could attack Bobby, he was already on his feet and shoving her away from his crippled patient.

"Get back!" he snarled, slamming his palms into her shoulders. "I know Trent's been a dirtbag to you, but you don't have to kill him!"

"She's *protecting* him!" Vivian shouted. "She thinks she loves him!"

Bobby's eyebrows arched.

"Say *what?*"

In Bobby's instant of distraction, Priscilla threw her mutated arms around him. She turned her back on Trent and lifted his perceived attacker off the ground in a bone-crunching bear hug.

"Uggh!" Bobby gasped. "Can't … *breathe!*"

He struggled madly. A lucky kick connected with the fresh gash in Priscilla's leg, and she dropped him with a sucking wince. He hit the ground with a limp, wet *slap*. The rigid insect limbs that sprouted from her arms had pierced his doughy flesh and broken off inside his body. Before he could even form a scream, an explosive crackle ripped from her throat, showering him with blood and tissue.

Having dispatched his assailants, Priscilla turned back to Trent and happily dropped to her knees in front of him. Her top lip smiled with relief, but her bottom lip hung lifelessly from a detached jawbone swinging from the side of her head by a single strip of intact skin. In the place where her tongue had once been, an eighteen-inch beetle mandible curved in a serrated hook. An identical mandible arced out of her left shoulder, clicking arrhythmically against its mate like a pair of unholy wind chimes.

She put her enormous hand on Trent's leg and leaned in lovingly, prompting him to release a louder, more bone-curdling scream than he had ever screamed before. He crab-walked backward, a terrified sense of self-preservation overriding the pain blasting from his legs.

"Get back! Get back offa me, you freak! Freak! You fugly demon *freak!*"

Priscilla raised a hand toward him, and he kicked it away. Her remaining lip began to quiver, and her dull eyes filled with complete and utter heartbreak. A single tear rolled down her cheek, over her lip, and down the curve of her newly formed mandible.

The air sizzled with a crack of wood against flesh, and Priscilla fell forward on her knees. Behind her, Sherri stood with her hands wrapped around the barrels of the shotgun, its walnut stock already swinging back for another beating.

"Don't you *ever* hit me when I'm not looking, bitch! I'll kick your bloated fucking ass!"

Sherri delivered another savage blow to the monster's back, but outside of a gentle sway, Priscilla did not react. She just kept looking at Trent, pleading with her eyes.

"Sherri! Stop! Don't hurt her!" Vivian shouted, clambering to her feet. "She's confused! She doesn't understand!"

"Well, let's see if she understands this!"

Sherri wound up and took a third swing, but her attack ended in a *slap* against an outstretched palm. Priscilla yanked the shotgun from her hands and threw it aside as she climbed to her feet. The mutant towered over her petite attacker, a foul ichor dripping from her glistening mouthpieces. Sherri's pink eyes narrowed into a defiant glare.

"Come on, bitch!" she said, spreading her arms. "You want a piece of me? Come get some!"

Priscilla charged forward, throwing her arms around Sherri and clasping her tightly against her chest.

"Put me down!" Sherri wailed, kicking and clawing. "Put me the fuck down!"

Her boots scraped over Priscilla's legs, tearing off her bandages and releasing another sprawl of mismatched insect limbs. They scrambled madly against the air, like a swarm of enormous bugs clawing their way out of Priscilla's body.

"Sherri! Stop fighting! Don't fight her!" Vivian screamed. "Priscilla! Look at me! *Look at me right now!*"

Sherri fell momentarily silent as Priscilla turned to see Vivian standing before her with the sword drawn menacingly in front of her body.

"Priscilla, I don't want to hurt you. I've *never* wanted to hurt you. But if you don't put Sherri down, I promise, I *will* hurt you. Do you understand me?"

Priscilla's bulbous eyes glared right through her.

"You're just confused," Vivian continued. "That guy is not your Lee. Lee is dea—" She bit her lip. "Trent doesn't love you like Lee does. Look at how he runs away from you. That's not love."

Priscilla looked at Trent, and her eyes filled with heartbreak as they absorbed his horror and revulsion. She quickly turned away from him with a tortured sob and an unexpected *crack*.

As her head turned, the mandible curling from her jaw closed against the one fixed to her shoulder, clamping down on Sherri's skull like a giant pair of scissors. Sherri lurched into a brief spasm before falling limp in Priscilla's arms, fresh blood gushing through her hair.

"Sherri, *no!*" Vivian screamed.

She rushed forward, swinging back to deliver a disabling strike to Priscilla's legs. Priscilla retreated from the blade, lumbering backward until she was pressed against a concrete pylon. Vivian lowered her sword with a final plea.

"Just put her down. Please, just put her down and I promise I won't hurt you."

Priscilla pressed her back against the smooth concrete slab and swung out her free arm, desperately clawing at the wall for an escape route. To her surprise, the highly adapted insect legs dotting her flesh gripped the cement, holding fast. Her scrambling human legs affixed themselves in the same way, and with a few lurching thrusts, she was six feet up the side of the pylon.

"No!" Vivian gasped. "You'll drop her! Stop! Please, stop!"

She threw down her sword and rushed forward, but it was too late. In a motion like a clumsy, one-armed backstroke, Priscilla raced up the side of the support and adhered herself to the bottom of the overpass. She hung there with her back to the steel girders, facing downward, with Sherri dangling over her forearm.

Vivian jumped against the pylon, planting her rubber toes into its smooth face again and again, only to slide back down with tiny squeaks of failure. She whirled on her heels and looked up at Sherri's inert body dripping blood onto the two cars below her.

"No, no, no," Vivian sobbed. "Priscilla, come down here! *Please!*"

There was no way Priscilla was coming down, and no way Vivian could climb up. There was simply no way to reach Sherri. Vivian turned her back to the pylon and slumped against it, her massive wings cushioning the impact.

Her drizzling eyes popped open as a new plan suddenly became clear.

She stepped away from the wall and flexed her knees, springing up and down in anticipation. She didn't think about moving her wings, she just moved them. In perfect synchronization, her four-foot-long wings unfurled from her back and came down in a powerful flap. She opened her eyes, backed away from the bridge, and fixed her sights on Sherri.

"Vivian Gray," she said through gritted teeth, "you are cleared for take-off."

A sprint burned through her legs. She could feel the muscles of her wings pulling all the way through her back as their fleshy sails forced two massive scoops of air into the dirt. She flapped again, and her feet left the ground, not coming back to earth for a good two yards. A feeling of weightlessness tugged at her as she continued to run and flap, run and flap. She flapped as hard and as fast as she could, but all she was doing was increasing the length and height of her strides. She could cheat the law of gravity, but she just couldn't break it. Her efforts quickly exhausted her malnourished body, and she slumped into a lightheaded heap.

"I'm … sorry … Sherri," she gasped.

Erik and Trent kneeled by Bobby's side and carefully plucked the shattered insect legs out of his belly.

"Oh God, Bobby, oh God," Erik chattered. "You're gonna be okay! Stay with me! Push through the pain!"

Bobby's face was ghostly, and he spoke in a thin rattle.

"It doesn't hurt."

"Well, hold on to that happy thought, dawg," Trent said, "'cause this is gonna hurt like a son of a bitch."

He grabbed onto a barbed beetle leg and yanked it free of Bobby's flabby side. Its jagged edge snagged his bandage, tearing it open. Freed of its constricting girdle, Bobby's gut ballooned outward, unleashing a pair of gigantic spider legs. Their blunt, hairy tips pounded into Trent, bowling him over. By the time that he had righted himself, Bobby's waist was encircled by five enormous, auburn-red tarantula legs: two in front, one on each side, and one in the back.

"Ho-leeeeeee shit," he said reverently.

"Oh my God!" Erik squeaked. "Are you okay?"

"I'm better than okay!" Bobby grinned. "Dude, I'm *Spider-Man!*"

He struggled onto his sandaled feet, and the spider legs sprawled out in an awkward, arm's-length circle around him, their tips lying sideways against the ground like giant stuffed socks. His gut hung over the top knuckles of the two that branched from his front, and his bathrobe hung in shredded ribbons over the rest.

Vivian rushed to Bobby's side and grabbed his hand.

"Are you okay?" she cried. "Does it hurt?"

"No, it doesn't hurt!" Bobby snapped. "Come on, people, you *know* it doesn't hurt! It's not like this has never happened to you before!"

His three mutated friends looked at each other and nodded in acknowledgment. A shrill scream ripped from the overpass above. All eyes snapped to Sherri, who was surprised to be regaining consciousness fifty feet from the ground. She clamped onto Priscilla's arm as they hung together in the center of the wrecked span.

"Oh shit!" Erik gasped. "We need to get up there and help her!"

"We can't climb it! It's too slick!" Vivian said. "Priscilla could only climb it because she's got those clingy insect legs!"

She looked at Erik, and in turn both of them looked at Bobby. Bobby wiggled his eyebrows and grinned.

"Whenever there's a hang-up, you call the Spider-Man."

He grabbed the spider leg slouching on the ground in front of him and set it upright on its furry tip. His friends righted the rest of his sagging legs, setting them like flying buttresses around his waist.

"Okay, now what?" Bobby asked.

"Now go get her!" Vivian cried.

"Wow! Great idea!" Bobby barked. "I mean, how do I make them work?!"

"Oh God, there's no time for this!" Erik moaned. "Okay, crash course in mutant limbs—ready?"

"Ready!"

"First, do they work with your real legs? Stand on your toes!"

Bobby stood up on his toes, and his spider legs all rose in the air like a Can-can dancer's skirt.

"They bend when you stretch out. It's a mirror!" Erik said. "Try bending your legs instead!"

Bobby started to kneel down, and as his human knees bent, each spider joint extended. When his butt was halfway to the ground, his arachnid legs landed and his body was lifted on their flex. Inside the cage of spider legs, his human legs bunched beneath him in the air, the backs of his heels pressed against his behind.

"That worked!" Bobby beamed. "Now what?!"

"Now *go!*" Erik screamed.

Bobby's folded legs swung in an abbreviated shuffle against his belly, and his spider legs launched into action, running backwards across the road.

"No no! They're *mirroring* your real legs!" Erik yelled. "Run *backwards!*"

"Get offa me! I'm new at this!" Bobby growled.

He stopped and reversed direction. This time his spider legs danced forward, racing him to the concrete pylon and straight up its side. He reached the top and charged onto the steel, hanging upside-down from the bottom of the overpass. His ponytail and bathrobe hung toward the ground like Spanish moss as the little blood he had remaining flowed to his head.

"Whoa, shit," he muttered, pounding his palms into his forehead. "Dude, head rush."

Priscilla saw the human spider creeping across the bottom of the bridge, and she turned on him with a shrieking hiss. Sherri's purse slipped from her shoulder and plummeted to the blacktop, exploding on impact in a blast of split plastic seams.

"Whoa whoa! Alright lady, take it easy," Bobby said. "You know you don't really want Sherri. She's a royal pain in the ass."

"Fuck you too," Sherri muttered.

"And she speaks with such vulgar language," Bobby continued. "So why don't you just let me take her off your hands, okay?"

He took a clumsy step forward and held out his arms.

"Okay? Priscilla? Hello?"

Looking into Priscilla's eyes, he saw nothing but fear and confusion. He could see his own horrifying reflection in her glistening irises, and it sent a chill up his spine. His spider legs sprawled out of his bloodied midsection like the fingers of a gigantic, gnarled hand tearing him apart from the inside out. From her upside-down perspective, his mangled clothes seemed to stand straight up in an intimidating display of dominance. He realized that from her perspective he was just another mutant demon come to kill her.

For all of these reasons, he was not surprised when Priscilla pitched forward in a misguided attempt at self-defense.

He was surprised, however, when she unceremoniously dropped Sherri.

"Sherri, no!"

He took a skittering step forward and threw out his arm, but he was too far away. Sherri's shapely body slid through the air past his outstretched fingertips in a tragic slow motion. In a blink, he was looking at the top of her quickly shrinking head, her golden hair waving goodbye as she plummeted to her death.

He could not reach her. She was gone.

"No!" he screamed.

In that moment, every fiber of Bobby's body chose to ignore reason and continue to stretch out toward the lost cause. He could feel the muscles in his arm striving to bridge that gap of inches. Though it had gone strangely numb, his forearm seemed to swell and burst with the strain of its extension.

And that's exactly what it did.

The sleeve of Bobby's bathrobe exploded as the mohawk of knobby green teeth tore from his forearm. Three gigantic segments of green exoskeleton swung outward from his elbow, forming the double-hinged span of a praying mantis foreleg.

With an extraordinary precision that strained plausibility, his claw hooked into the back of Sherri's hood, tearing to a stop at the ruffle of synthetic fur lining its edge. Her fall arrested, she swung in a broad arc from the end of a four-foot pendulum anchored to Bobby's shoulder. She raised her head dizzily.

"Thanks, Bobby."

Bobby opened his mouth to reply, but was interrupted by a fist hammering him in the jaw. A flash of light and color swirled before his eyes as he stumbled backward. His rear leg darted upward to find a girder, but caught nothing but the open air beyond the bridge's edge. The unexpected misstep threw him into an off-kilter swing, but his hanging weight quickly found equilibrium on his four other legs. He pounded his palm into the top of Priscilla's head and shoved her away, and she retreated toward the bridge's center by two skittering backstrokes.

Erik and Vivian stood petrified next to Trent's injured body sprawled on the pavement. Their eyes were fixed unflinchingly on the struggle above.

"She's going to kill them!" Erik said. "Oh my God, she's going to kill them! We have to stop her! We have to help them!"

"We can't stop her," Vivian said. "There's no way to get up there. No way."

"Yes, there is!" Erik pleaded. "Come on! We can go up the ramp!"

He turned and furiously limped toward the end of the ramp in the distance. Vivian could see thin splatters of blood flick out of his leg every time it hit the ground. She could hear the determination in the agonized grunts choked back in his throat.

Inspiration boiled through her resignation. For Erik, just getting to the ramp would be an agonizing marathon. And even when he was on top of the bridge, there was no way that he could reach his friends hanging from its bottom, let alone pull them to safety. It was a hopeless, pointless endeavor. Yet there he was, charging through his pain, completely unwilling to give up hope.

"Erik, stop," she called. "You can't help them."

"But I have to!"

Vivian's eyes were fixed on the bottom of the bridge in fevered calculation.

"No," she said. "*I* have to."

With a single, billowing *snap* of her wings, she turned away from the bridge and sprinted away down the interstate, leaping over the scattered remains of Sherri's purse. A small bird skull and seventy cents worth of change stared back at Erik, slowly drawing a memory to the front of his mind.

"Whoa, wait a second. I *can* help!"

He hobbled over, dropped to his knees, and pawed through the debris with all four hands.

"What the hell are you doing, E?" Trent said. "There's nothing in a lady's purse that's gonna save our peeps from that freaky freak!"

"Yes, there is. It was in Sherri's coat when I emptied her pockets! ... There!"

He grabbed it and ran off, leaving Trent baffled.

"Black lipstick?"

Bobby looked down the extended green shaft of his arm at Sherri.

"Grab my arm," he ordered, "er ... hook!"

Sherri raised her hands, and her thin body immediately slipped through the slick nylon lining of her jacket. With a gasped expletive, she bent her elbows and wrapped her arms over her head, catching herself before she could completely slide free of her makeshift harness.

"Aaagh! Shit!" she snarled, clutching her coat. "I can't reach you!"

As Sherri struggled, Bobby could see the fur trim ripping away from her hood, detaching stitch by stitch like a sudden death countdown.

"Oh, for Christ's sake," he groaned.

He could hear Erik screaming at him from the ground below.

"Bobby, move! Get away from Priscilla, now!"

Before Bobby could respond, a pinching, tearing pain sailed up his human leg. His head whirled around, throwing out a scream in a broad arc of sound. Priscilla was in front of him with her head pressed against her shoulder and a severed spider leg twitching between her plier-like mandibles. From his inverted perspective, a drizzle of blood fell upward toward the ground from the stump sticking out of his belly.

"Aaaaaghh!" he gasped. "I am not your enemy, goddamn it! Leave me the hell alone!"

Priscilla spat a sharp hiss, and Bobby's remaining legs took a staggering step backward, plunging a second hairy foot over the edge and toward the charcoal clouds above. The bristles of his two remaining spider feet grasped the steel, suspending him from his sides like a playground swing. As they slowly lost their grip, a strange sensation tingled across the bottoms of his human feet. It felt like the sound of Velcro being pulled apart.

"Ah shit," he growled. "Now what? Think, Bobby, think …"

He looked back over his shoulder at the edge of the overpass, then down at Sherri hanging helplessly from his mantis arm, then back up at the bridge.

"Well," he sighed. "Here goes nothin'."

With a mighty flex of his bicep, he swung Sherri up in a long, graceful arc beneath the bridge. When she had reached the top of her backswing, he yanked in the opposite direction, sending her whistling through the air beneath him, all the way around the edge of the bridge. Her legs swung over its top, folding her in half at the waist and hanging her safely over the railing like a wet towel.

The wrenching force of Bobby's swing completely detached his last two spider legs from the girder. His pudgy body dropped, and his spine made a crunching *pop* as he came to a swinging rest, his mantis arm hooked over the concrete edge of the bridge.

As his full weight hung by one narrow hook of mutated chitin, Bobby could suddenly feel every cheeseburger he had ever eaten sitting in his enormous gut. He could feel every Big Gulp and every all-you-can-eat barbecue session yanking at the burning tendons of his shoulder. He could feel every corn chip and pork rind jabbing like salty knives through the sweating meat of his strained back.

A heavy drop of black goo splashed against his cheek. He looked up to see Priscilla stuck to the steel above him, closing her pincers around his mutant arm.

"Oh no. No! No, Priscilla, no!"

"Bobby! Move!" Erik wailed. "Get your fat ass away from her, God damn it!"

"What do you think I've been trying to do?!" Bobby screamed.

Going against all of the advice he had ever heard about dealing with heights, Bobby looked down. The first thing he saw was not Erik, but Vivian, sprinting at full speed up the long, straight runway of the abandoned interstate, wings fully extended and flapping in gigantic, powerful strokes.

Her legs threw her body forward, harder and harder past the blur of the dotted center line. With each flap of her wings, her strides got longer and longer, faster and faster. The wind seemed to be embracing her, guiding her, pulling her forward.

"Hold on, Bobby," she growled. "I'm coming."

She closed her eyes and threw her arms out like a diver, launching herself into the sky.

One and a half flaps of her wings later she was ten feet away, face down in a battered heap on the cold, hard blacktop. A searing collection of fresh road burns bleeding from her palms, knees, and elbows reminded her that human beings were not designed for flight. She pounded her bloody fist into the ground.

"No! Damn it!"

She looked up at the bottom of the bridge just in time to see Priscilla's head swing down against her shoulder, bisecting Bobby's brittle mantis arm with a splash of clear viscera and hard green splinters. There was a complete and deafening silence as he plummeted fifty feet through the cold air, landing with a fleshy bass note as he caved in the roof of the Reliant.

"No!" Vivian shrieked.

A fraction of a second later the air over her head ignited in a burst of noise and fire. Before her blasted eardrums had registered the sound, she saw Priscilla's chest tear apart in an explosion of bone and blood. She slammed into the bottom of the overpass and then peeled off, sailing through the air with a tragic grace and landing in a broken heap on the ground.

Vivian turned with a deafened, heart-pounding lurch to see Erik standing behind her, holding the shotgun in his trembling hands. He tipped it to the ground, clicking open the breech and ejecting a spent, lipstick-shaped shell. His eyes dilated as he stared at the carnage.

"I tried to ... to stop her, b-but ... I ... he ... he just kept getting in the way. He wouldn't get out of the way ..."

He began to convulse in heaving sobs until he finally fell to his hands and knees and violently threw up. Trent just stared at the two bodies, his face as white as his teeth.

Vivian clambered to her feet, launched herself onto the roof of the Reliant, and collapsed on her knees at Bobby's side. His glasses had been lost in the fall, but his eyes still had a flickering spark. She clenched his hand and squeezed it hard, as if trying to force the life back into his broken body.

"You're going to be okay," she said. "You hear me? We're going to get you to a hospital. There is still time, brother."

Bobby shook his head and coughed.

"I know there isn't. I don't need you blowin' sunshine up my skirt."

Vivian bit her lip.

"I'm so sorry, Bobby! This is all my fault! I tried so hard to fly, but the aerodynamics are all wrong! But I thought ... I thought if I just *believed* in myself that I could do it!"

Bobby shook his head.

"That's just *Full House* monologue bullshit, and you know it. Believing in yourself doesn't change the laws of physics."

Vivian's lips quivered. Bobby tugged gently on the edge of her wing and continued.

"You're never going to fly with these ..."

He tapped her forehead.

"... unless you fly with this first."

Vivian squeezed her brother's hand as tears streaked down her grimy face.

"You're going to be okay, you hear me?" she choked. "I'm not leaving without you!"

Bobby shook his head weakly.

"Knock it off. The rest of those dumb-asses will never survive without you. Promise me you won't ever stop fighting until you're all safe."

"But—but I can't—"

"Don't argue with me, Vivian! I'm dying here!"

Vivian's eyes clenched and her head tipped into a frantic little nod.

"I promise."

Bobby blinked a long, slow blink before he spoke again.

"Good. Now promise me one more thing."

"Yes, Bobby. Anything."

"Don't let Trent pick up any more chicks."

He smiled, squeezed Vivian's hand, and closed his eyes for the last time.

CHAPTER FOURTEEN

Two lifeless bodies lay with their hands crossed over their chests in tranquil repose near the shoulder of Interstate 67. A scraped Volkswagen fender and the few clods of rock-hard dirt it had chipped from the ground symbolized a foiled attempt at burial.

On the other side of the road, Vivian knelt next to a small patch of wilted purple wildflowers. Trails of tears ran from the corners of her sober eyes. She could see the others hovering around the bodies, each paying their respects.

Trent stood at the head of the above-ground graves with his eyes closed, muttering some piece of scripture that he found relevant for all the wrong reasons. He was wearing the bloodstained varsity jacket and holding himself upright on his wounded legs using the shotgun as a crutch.

Erik stood to the side of Priscilla, brooding sulkily. He held the last remaining shotgun shell, turning it over and over again in his fingers. The sleeves of the pink sweater discovered in Priscilla's trunk now bandaged the gash in his thigh. Its remainder was wrapped in a tight bonnet over Sherri's slashed scalp, tied in a bow under her chin. She was kneeling at Bobby's side with her head buried in her arms over his bloated belly, sobbing uncontrollably.

Vivian picked a handful of the dismal flowers and noticed something in the tall grass beyond. She pushed aside the withered foliage and found Bobby's glasses. A sniffle launched out of her throat and lodged itself somewhere behind her nose.

For a set of twins, Bobby and Vivian shared very little common physiology, but their eyeglasses were absolutely identical: the same style, the same frames, even the same prescription. She picked them up and looked at them through her own cracked lenses. From the bold black outline of his frames, she could almost see Bobby's face ripple outward, the split of her left lens bisecting the phantom into two vertical slices.

"I should give these back to him," she thought. *"He would want them."*

She knew that Bobby couldn't see without his glasses any better than she could, which was not very well at all. Returning them seemed like the right thing to do. As she crossed the street, however, the ghost image of Bobby rolled his eyes.

"You're such a sentimental wiener," it seemed to say. "What the hell am I supposed to do with glasses now? I'm all dead and shit."

"But what if you ... you know ... need them?"

"What, in the afterlife? Give me a break, Vivian. I think Valhalla will have an optometrist. How are you supposed to get these chumps to safety if you can't even see where you're going? Be reasonable; don't be superstitious."

Vivian pulled her own glasses off of her face and replaced them with the unbroken pair. The plastic was cold against her skin but quickly warmed as her vision adjusted to the clarity of the intact lenses.

"Okay, logic over sentimentality. That's what you would have wanted," she said. "But how about we compromise?"

She knelt down by her brother's head and placed her own broken glasses on his cold nose. She could see Trent's reflection in the split lens as he limped to her side. He put his heavy hand on her shoulder with a long, lingering rub.

"You okay, Vivi?"

"I've said my goodbyes," she nodded. "We should get away from this terrible place before it gets dark. There's nothing else we can do here."

"But ... but what about *them?*" Erik mumbled, gesturing to the bodies. "We can't just take off and leave them here by the side of the interstate like roadkill, can we? It just seems so ... *wrong.*"

Vivian stood up and shook her head.

"I'm sorry. We can't take them with us, and we can't bury them. I don't know what else to do."

"No, Little E's right," Trent said. "If we can't give them a burial we can at least hook them up with a proper funeral to guide their souls to the pearly gates."

"All right," Vivian nodded. "If nothing else, it might give us some sense of closure. Go ahead."

Trent cleared his throat and boomed. "Almighty God, we commit these bodies to the ground: earth to earth, ashes to ashes, dust to dust. The Lord bless them and keep them, the Lord make his face to shine upon them ..."

Vivian's mind drifted sharply away as Trent's stony oratory dredged up the celluloid memories of every funeral that she had ever seen in the movies. In her mind, the four of them were now standing in the rain amid a crowd of mourners dressed in sharp black suits and veils, each holding an identical black umbrella. Most of them were content to stand with pensive looks on their faces, but there was that one woman wailing uncontrollably. Wailing, wailing. Vivian opened her eyes not to a grieving widow, but to Sherri, hot tears streaming down her reddened face.

"Uh, Trent," Vivian interrupted, "I ... we all appreciate the sentiment of what you're saying, but ... you know, Bobby was never sentimental. He wouldn't want to go out with us all weeping over him like this. Don't you know another passage that's more, I don't know, uplifting?"

Trent thought for a moment, then cleared his throat and spoke with a metered passion.

"Dearly beloved … we are gathered here today to get through this thing called life. Electric word, life. It means forever, and that's a mighty long time."

Erik shook his head.

"Okay, do you know anything that's uplifting and *isn't* from a Prince song?"

"This is pointless," Vivian muttered. "Look, if you want to say goodbye to Bobby and Priscilla, just do it. Just speak from your heart, okay?"

Sherri nodded and stood up, drawing a long, wet breath before finally speaking.

"Bobby Gray was a stupid motherfucker."

"Sherri!" Vivian snapped.

"Well, it was from the heart—you've got to give her that," Erik shrugged.

"You'd be alive right now if you didn't come after me, you stupid asshole! Why did you get yourself killed to save me? What were you thinking?! I never did a goddamn thing for you! I never did a goddamn thing for anybody! I didn't ask for this, you asshole! You stupid … *asshole!*"

Sherri's eulogy collapsed under the weight of a gratitude that she was ill-equipped to express, degenerating into a shuddering sob. She didn't protest when Trent offered his conciliatory embrace, but actually returned it, rubbing a cheek full of tear-activated grime across his shoulder. Without a hint of subtlety, Trent's cat tail stood as upright as a flagpole.

"It's okay, girl. It's all right. You know that God has a plan for all of us. Maybe Big B's purpose was to protect you, because you have the most important purpose of all."

"Important purpose? I don't have *any* purpose! I've *never* had a purpose besides giving assholes somebody to point at when they make their itty-bitty-titty-committee jokes. Now I don't even have *that* going anymore."

Trent put his fingers under Sherri's chin and pushed her head upward until her wet pink eyes met his own dull brown smolder.

"I know, Goldie. It's all part of His plan," he smiled. "And I'm here to help you serve your divine purpose."

He leaned in and pressed his chapped lips against Sherri's, probing his tongue into her mouth and flooding her palate with the taste of neglected oral hygiene. Almost before his advance had begun, it was ended by a fishnetted knee delivered swiftly to his groin. As Trent staggered back with a seething groan, Sherri leapt away from him, frantically wiping her tongue with her fingers. She drew a massive wad of contaminated spit into the back of her throat and deposited it with a wet *thump* on Trent's chest.

"You horny asshole cockbag dipshit motherfucker!" she spat. "What the fuck are you doing?!"

"Isn't it obvious?! It's your purpose!" Trent moaned. "You just said it yourself! You spend your whole life built like a carpenter's dream, and then just when we need to repopulate the earth, you suddenly bust out all over like some kind of freaky tiki fertility idol! How can you not see what you're supposed to do next?!"

"What? *What?!* What the fuck, Trent?! Just because some asshole conned me into overdosing on old-lady hormones it doesn't make me your goddamn baby oven!"

"Aww, that's bullshit and you know it! If there was a magic pill that just slapped on hips and tits like a Beverly Hills surgeon, don't you think that every sixteen-year-old girl in the country would be all hopped up on that shit? This isn't a side effect of bad drugs, girl! This is the work of a higher power! It's time to accept and carry out your purpose. You're the new Eve. You're going to be the new mother of mankind!"

Sherri crossed her arms over her swollen chest and glared at him.

"That is *the* most desperate and clumsy attempt at getting a girl into the sack that I have ever heard in my entire life. Did you ever stop and think that if God was so gung-ho about the survival of the human race that maybe he wouldn't have *killed everybody on Earth?!*"

Trent shook his head.

"It worked out okay for Noah. Look, I know you think I'm some kind of superfly slick playa, but I'm being honest with you here. For real. With Prissy gone, you and Vivi are the only ones left who can carry on the human race. Why can't you see that, girl? Even Prissy understood what we needed to do if we didn't want to be the last bookend on God's mighty shelf."

"Um, I don't mean to speak ill of your noble attempt to propagate the species," Erik interrupted, "but to put it delicately, if you were trying to reproduce with Priscilla you were using the wrong end."

"Damn, E! The T doesn't steal home on the first date! There is still such a thing as chivalry, you know!"

A high, mirthless laugh clucked out of Sherri's throat.

"What the *fuck* is the *matter* with you?! Listen to yourself! You're trying to write off date raping a retard as fulfilling a biblical mandate! She didn't want to fuck you any more than the rest of us do, but she was just too goddamn stupid to say so!"

"To say so?" Trent said. "You know she couldn't talk! She had a gash in her throat the size of the San Fernando Valley!"

"Even if she could talk, I'll bet she wouldn't have said *shit*," Sherri argued. "I've seen guys passed out under pool tables with better communication skills than her!"

"Stop it!" Vivian screamed. "All of you stop it! You're unbelievable! This is supposed to be a funeral! Do you think that Priscilla would have wanted her eulogy to be a bunch of strangers arguing about her sex life?"

The others hung their heads in disgrace.

"Well, what the hell are we supposed to say about her then?" Sherri growled. "She was a giant evil bug bitch who murdered your brother. End of story."

"That's not the end of the story," Vivian said. "She wasn't always like this."

She pulled the old photograph of Priscilla and Lee from her coat pocket and looked at the smiling face of a girl who no longer existed. She held the picture up to the others and continued.

"Don't demonize her, Sherri. This creature lying in front of us isn't Priscilla—I mean, the *real* Priscilla. The real Priscilla was just an average girl, just like you. Just like me. She lived in an average little tourist town. She worked an average job selling average junk to average people. And just like us, I'm sure that she dreamed of something better than that average life. The real Priscilla wasn't an atomic monster, Sherri. She was just an average girl. Just like us."

The group observed a moment of silence as Vivian's words slowly sank in. Finally Sherri grabbed the hood of pink bandage on her head and threw it to the ground with a growl.

"What are you doing?" Vivian said. "Your cuts are going to get infected."

"So what?" Sherri spat. "A few germs aren't going to make any difference once I turn into a giant fucking ogre, are they? Somebody just kill me right now before I change into a freak like her."

"Change? You're not going to change!" Vivian said. "Just because this happened to her doesn't mean that it's going to happen to us!"

"Not going to happen to us my ass!" Sherri roared. "You just said like, ten times that she was just like us before all of this atomic shit went down! But by the time we met her all she understood was 'eat,' 'fuck,' and 'don't die.' I don't want to live with the brains of a fucking cockroach!"

A stuttering of rebuttal tumbled from Vivian's lips, but fell apart before it could form.

"You're right," she said. "She *was* just like a cockroach."

"Oh, that's great, Vivi. That's real nice," Trent said. "You complain that we're doing a bad job eulogizing Prissy's memory, and then you step up here and start calling her a cockroach."

"No no, I'm not saying that Priscilla was a cockroach," Vivian said. "I'm just saying that's what she had been reduced to in the end. The mind of a cockroach. I mean, I saw her drive an eight-inch metal spike into her leg just because she lacked the simple cognitive skills to pull it back out. It was like the evolved parts of her mind had been shut off, leaving her with nothing but the most basic fragments of human instinct."

"Well, yeah," Erik said. "Getting stuck in that igloo with all of those killer bugs broke her brain."

"That might have had something to do with it," Vivian conceded. "But I don't think that's what really happened to her."

Her eyes flickered as thoughts worked themselves into logical clusters in her mind.

"I have a theory," she continued. "We think that Priscilla's cells multiplied so rapidly because her DNA was damaged by the radiation, right? Well, if her body absorbed that much radiation, imagine the damage it must have done to her brain! It would have been like getting a hundred skull x-rays at once."

"But she couldn't have lived without a brain," Erik said.

"No, you're right," Vivian said. "But she could have lived with only *part* of one. What if the radiation only damaged the lobes of the brain that handle reason and cognizance, leaving nothing but motor function and basic instinctual behavior?"

"Damn, Vivi, that's a whole heapin' helpin' of the what-ifs," Trent said. "If all that brain-damage jive is true, then why didn't the exact same thing happen to anybody but Prissy?"

"It did," Vivian said. "It hasn't happened to any of us, but it's consistent with all of the other mutants we've come across. Think about it. Those bugs in the igloo seemed to be attacking us, but what did they do, really? The bees were defending their hive, and the spiders were capturing prey. That's what bees and spiders do! Erik, what about the rat that scratched you in the storm drain? Did it chase you down and attack you?"

"No, I picked it up," Erik said. "It didn't claw me until I tried to … uh … hug it."

"You see? It was probably just acting in self-defense. What if all this time we've been mistaking animal instinct for aggression?"

"But what about the cat?" Sherri said. "That bitch was definitely out for blood."

"She was," Erik agreed. "But Twiki *always* tried to kill anything that moved. She had some serious aggression issues."

"It all makes some kind of sense now," Vivian said. "What if none of those mutants was evil, but just brain damaged?"

Erik's glance drifted to the thin tangle of wildflowers that failed to camouflage a hole bored deep into Priscilla's chest.

"Oh my God," he whispered. "I executed a retarded girl. With a shotgun! I'm worse than the governor of Texas!"

As the words came out of his mouth the sentiment behind them became concrete, and Erik broke down in horrified tears.

"I … I didn't know!" he wailed. "I didn't realize that she was just brain damaged! I thought she was some kind of monster!"

"But she *was* a monster! That's what I'm trying to say!" Vivian said. "I'm not talking about the Special Olympics here—I'm talking about a walking brain stem! Her personality and humanity were completely destroyed! That thing that you killed was not a retarded girl, Erik. It was just a mindless shell. It was a ... it was a *zombie*."

"She was *not* a zombie!" Erik sobbed. "Zombies are the walking undead who kill people and eat their brains! She did not come back from the dead, Vivian!"

"Didn't she?" Vivian shouted.

She held up the creased photograph and planted her forefinger on Priscilla's tiny smile.

"*This* girl was dead long before we ever met her."

Her finger slashed downward to Priscilla's mutated body.

"*That* girl was a bundle of burned-up neurons parading around in a human body! She may not be an according-to-Romero zombie, but the *person* who was once Priscilla died, and this *creature* was born. The *real* Priscilla was already dead before you shot this body, Erik. You are not a murderer. She was no different from any of the other monsters that we've had to defend ourselves against."

Erik tipped his head to the ground in pained resignation.

"You're wrong. She's not like the other atomic monsters at all."

"How can you say that?" Vivian asked irritably. "Every single fact that we have says that she was *exactly* like them!"

"No, it doesn't," Erik muttered. "All of the other mutants started glowing as soon as we killed them. Look at her, Vivian."

All eyes turned to Priscilla's inert form. The grotesque black mandibles still jutted from her fractured jaw and shoulder, and dozens of horrible legs stuck out of her body like a mad entomologist's pincushion. A lot of words could be used to describe how unnatural she looked, but "glowing" was not one of them.

"She's not glowing, and neither is Bobby," Erik continued. "She may have been mentally handicapped, but she wasn't some kind of undead atomic freak. She was still a human. Just a mutated human. Just like Bobby. Just like us."

"But ... but that's just one little incongruity!" Vivian stammered. "Whether or not she glows is irrelevant in the face of all of the other evidence! Priscilla suffered gigantism, just like the others. She acted on instinct, just like the others. All she had left in her head was fight or flight, eat or starve, live or die."

Erik threw a finger toward Trent.

"Well, if she didn't have any higher thought, then why did she try so hard to defend this idiot that she thought was her boyfriend?!"

Vivian's eyebrows knitted and she spoke with a trembling clarity.

"Because the only human instinct stronger than survival is love."

Erik gazed into Vivian's eyes for a long moment before he spoke.

"I want to join the pact."

"What?"

"Your homicide pact. I've changed my mind. Growing extra limbs is one thing, but if I go brain-dead like Priscilla, I want you to kill me."

"Damn it, Erik! You *won't* go brain-dead!" Vivian shouted. "None of us will!

Just the fact that we're able to *have* this discussion proves that we're going to be okay! There's something different about us!"

"No, there's not," Sherri said. "There's not jack shit that makes us different from Priscilla."

"There's *so much* that's different!" Vivian argued. "What about ... what about that pink vapor back in Stillwater? Every one of us breathed it except for Priscilla! What if there was something in that cloud that's protecting us?"

"It's no good, Viv," Erik said, shaking his head. "Both the rat and Twiki were exposed to the fog too, and they both went brain-dead in a matter of hours."

"Yes, a matter of hours," Vivian said desperately. "Both of them turned into zombies in a *matter of hours*. We don't know how long it took Priscilla, but she was changed by the time we got to her. It's a quick process! If it was going to happen to any of us, it would have happened by now!"

"I'd like to believe you. I really would," Erik said. "But biology doesn't follow a neat and orderly time table. I mean, look at us. Bobby's cuts got splattered with spider goo and he grew legs the next afternoon. Twiki cut Trent and he didn't grow a tail for *days*. Things affect everyone's body differently. We're not machines, you know. We're not going to fall over in rows."

"But we're all going to fall over eventually," Sherri mumbled.

Erik stared at the shotgun shell as he turned it over in his fingers.

"I've already committed one murder out of ignorance," he said. "I don't ever want to do it again. When I lose my mind, I want you to take this last shell and blow my brain-dead head off. I deserve it. Will you do that for me, Vivian?"

"No!" Vivian screamed. "Cut that out!"

Erik's hypnotic stare was broken as Vivian snatched the shell out of his hand and stuffed it into her coat pocket.

"Nobody is going to be blowing anybody's head off! Do you understand me? We're all going to get through this! We're all going to survive!"

"I'd rather put a gun in my mouth right now than survive riding the short bus to Hell," Sherri grumbled.

Vivian turned on Sherri with a fire raging in her eyes.

"Sherri, just a few minutes ago you were furious because Bobby sacrificed himself to save you! He thought your life was important enough to die saving, and now you just want to throw it away?"

Sherri lowered her gaze.

"I've been throwing it away for years," she whimpered. "If he thought that saving me was worth killing himself over, then *he* was brain damaged."

Her jaw broke into a quiver that quickly burst into a sobbing cough.

"Bobby, you idiot! Never waste your heroics saving a smoker!"

Vivian stepped forward and put her arm around Sherri. Sherri pressed her head against her chest and wept.

"We're doomed. It's just a matter of time now," Erik said. "It doesn't matter how far we go—we can't outrun biology."

Vivian closed her eyes and took a deep, steadying breath. She knew that they weren't going to turn into mindless zombies. She knew that there was a safe haven waiting for them somewhere. She just knew it. But somehow she had to make the others know it too.

"Do you know what the last thing Bobby said to me was?"

"If I know Bobby, he ended on a joke," Erik said.

Vivian slipped her hand under her glasses and rubbed her eyes.

"Okay, do you know what the *second-to-last* thing Bobby said to me was? He made me promise to never stop fighting. As he was lying there bleeding to death, just as sure as he knew that he wasn't going to make it, he knew that the rest of us *were*. That's what separates him and us from Priscilla and those creatures. Hope. We have the mental capacity to transcend this moment of desperation and see a point in the near future when we're all clean, and fed, and safe. If you give up hope, then you may as well just lie down and die right here, because without hope, you're no better than a brain-dead zombie."

"But, Vivian," Erik pleaded, "hope doesn't keep gamma radiation from destroying brain tissue! We're still going to lose our minds, one by one, and have to be put out of our misery! When the time comes, you'll have to respect our final wishes."

Vivian let go of Sherri and took a sharp step toward Erik, flicking out a finger at his face.

"Okay, fine, Erik. Fine. You want to change your mind about the homicide pact? Fine. Because you know what? I change my mind too. I'm out. I'm out because I know it's pointless. I'm absolutely certain that there are *two* kinds of survivors out here in this atomic wasteland, and Priscilla and Bobby prove it. There's the kind of survivor that devolves into a brain-dead zombie, and then there's the kind that evolves into a hero."

She looked down at the bodies and continued.

"I loved Bobby with all my heart, but let's be honest here. Before the bombs dropped, Bobby Gray was a lazy, self-centered jerk. But today, when he sacrificed his own life to save Sherri's, Bobby Gray became Atomic Bob, post-apocalyptic mutant hero."

Sherri wiped the wet streaks from her face and nodded in agreement. Erik shuffled his feet noncommittally while Trent just stared at the dirt as if afraid to let out whatever demons were haunting his mind.

"So what's it going to be, people?" Vivian demanded. "Are you going to just sit around and wait to see if your brains collapse, or are you going to suck it up and be heroes like Atomic Bob? I've made my choice. From now on I'm going to be Vivian Oblivion, and I can't get through this without an Erik the Barbaric, and a Scary Sherri, and a … and … well, Trent."

She winced, and then continued.

"My point is, we're not zombies now, and we never will be. You just have to have faith in that fact and … uh … believe in yourselves."

After a tense pause that seemed much longer than it actually was, Trent broke the silence with a slow, insincere clap.

"Oh, that speech was aces all the way, Vivi. For real. But all the motivational speaking in the world isn't going to make any difference when our brains turn into Jell-O pudding. You can pull Biology 101 guesstimates out of your derrière all day long, but you just don't have any *proof.*"

Vivian's mouth fell open. She blurted out the start of a word, then started another word, then just cackled in disbelief.

"Proof?! You want *proof?!* The *one time* I ask for you to have faith, and Mr. Bible-Knows-Best wants proof! Okay, you know what—fine! If every piece of logic and reason that I can knit together into solid scientific hypotheses aren't good enough to make you believe me, then it's up to God."

She raised her arms and shouted into the sky.

"Excuse me, God? Science isn't cutting it down here—could you please give us some heavenly sign that we're going to be okay?!"

A drop of ashy black water streaked down her new glasses. Then another, and another. The tar-black clouds above tore themselves open, dropping the char of a thousand burnt cities in a grimy deluge. Trent silently screamed, "I told you so" with one raised eyebrow before shaking his head and shambling off toward the cover of the overpass. Erik and Sherri followed him without a word.

Vivian did not take cover. She just stood like a crumbling statue in the black rain, letting its cold embrace her. As the dirty water ran across her skin and over her wings it streaked away layer upon layer of blood and grime. She dropped to her knees at Bobby's side.

"I'm sorry, Bobby. I tried. But how am I supposed to keep fighting if nobody else will? I used my brain. I used logic. I even resorted to telling them to believe in themselves! But nothing worked. I *know* that she's different from the rest of us, but I just can't make the pieces fit together. Even God is against me!"

She closed her eyes and rocked back on her heels, taking a deep, wet breath. The heavy drops pounded a drum solo from the remains of the satellite dish nearby. She remembered the looping episode of *Zoobilee Zoo* and wished that they had taken its advice about not talking to strangers.

"Why don't you glow, Priscilla? What's the missing piece?"

She opened her eyes and looked at Priscilla's dead body in a desperate, foolish hope that it would somehow give her the answer to her question.

Which was exactly what it did.

Through the dark sheets of rain, Priscilla's twin mandibles glowed with a more intense blue than a temporary price reduction at the Smurf Village K-Mart.

The teeth jutting from her shattered jaw all emitted the same blue glow, as did the insect legs that hung from her mangled flesh.

"You ... you're glowing!" Vivian gasped. "Why are you ..."

The answer ran down her body in cold, wet streaks.

"The rain! It's the water!"

Her mental filing system flipped through the memories of each zombie they had encountered. Erik said that the rat's teeth started to glow after he threw it into the puddle of street runoff. She remembered Twiki's remains glowing from the Port Manatee fountain. None of the bugs in the igloo had glowed until they had been smashed open, splashing their fractured exoskeletons with their own clear, wet viscera.

"That's it! That's the missing piece!" Vivian shouted. "It's not *dead* zombies that glow! It's *wet* zombies!"

She looked at Bobby and reached out for his face, flinched, and then leaned back in with a muttered apology.

"I'm sorry. I have to know."

She took his stiffened lips and peeled them back. As the cloudy rainwater splashed into his mouth, his teeth retained their non-illuminated yellow stain.

"I knew it! We *are* different! Only the *glowing* mutants grow and lose their minds! I have a test!"

She turned her head to the sky and bared her teeth in self-examination, but she could see nothing but her own cheeks. Without thinking, she turned her head to the ground and tried it again, as if that would make any difference. Finally she scrambled to her feet and sprinted off toward the remains of the overpass. When she got there she did not enter its umbrella, but yelled to those huddled within.

"Look at my teeth!" she grinned, hopping up and down with her chin thrust forward. "Look at them! Look at my teeth! Look at my teeth!"

"Knock it off!" Sherri barked. "You're freaking me out!"

Vivian stopped dancing, barely containing herself. "My teeth," she said again, pointing to her manic grin with both hands. "Are they glowing?"

"What, you mean like a Crest kid?" Erik asked.

"No, I mean like a wet zombie! Look! Priscilla is glowing! The zombies' teeth and bones glow when they're wet!"

The landscape was obscured behind the curtain of rain, but everyone could see two distinct, curved blades of blue light shining from the darkness like an angel's hedge clippers.

"Wait, I've heard of this," Erik said. "When highly radioactive particles move faster than light, they glow blue! They call it Cerenkov radiation. I read all about it in a *Lost in Space* fanzine!"

"That's unbelievable!" Sherri cried.

"It's true!" Erik said. "I mean, it's impossible for anything to move faster than light in a vacuum, but it can happen in something dense like water!"

"No, I mean a *Lost in Space* fanzine? You seriously read that shit?"

"Hey! Look at me!" Vivian interrupted. "Are my teeth glowing with Cerenkov radiation or not?!"

"No!" Erik beamed. "They're not! They're not glowing! You're okay!"

"That's what I've been trying to tell you!"

The heavy blanket of despair whipped off of Sherri like a magician's tablecloth as she sprang to her feet and out into the splashing rain.

"What about me?" she snarled through bared teeth. "Anything but nicotine stains?"

Vivian grabbed Sherri by her cheeks and turned her face into the rain. The drops pelted off of her teeth without a hint of glow.

"You're good!" Vivian cheered. "You see?! No need to kill yourself!"

Trent hobbled out of the shelter of the bridge, and the rain ran in rivers down his face as he grinned his huge, toothy grin into the clouds.

"Ooo, what about Trent?" Sherri said. "Can we kill Trent?"

Vivian took Trent's chin and glared into his mouth. Despite his holiday from toothpaste, his teeth remained perfect squares of unblemished, non-glowing white.

"Sorry, no such luck," she smiled. "Trent is okay."

Lost in the moment, she leaned in and gave Trent a congratulatory hug around his neck, which he reciprocated with a two-handed squeeze of her behind. Vivian leapt backward and wagged a shameful finger at him, but even Trent's hornball antics couldn't take the wind out of her sails.

"Come on, Erik," she called. "Let's see those pearly whites!"

Erik stepped slowly into the rain, but he did not open his mouth.

"I'm scared," he said. "What if I'm the only one who glows?"

"You're not going to glow!"

"But what if I do? Do you promise that you'll honor the pact?"

"Oh come on, Erik," Vivian groaned. "Stop being so melodramatic. Yes, if your teeth glow, which they *won't*, I promise I'll blow your zombie head off. Okay?"

Erik nodded.

"Okay."

He slowly leaned his head back and bared his teeth to the heavens, allowing the water to pool up between his lips.

"You see!" Vivian said. "Your teeth are—oh."

"*Oh?!*" Erik spluttered. "Why 'oh'? What 'oh'?!"

"Nothing," Vivian mumbled. "I'm sure it's nothing."

She pulled the last shotgun shell from her pocket and held her hand out to Trent, whispering out of the corner of her mouth.

"Ivegay me the otgunshay."

"Oh my God!" Erik wailed. "Oh my God, I'm one of them! I knew it! I'm one of them, aren't I?"

Vivian dropped the shell back into her pocket with an explosive burst of laughter.

"Erik, you're fine! Lighten up—I was just messin' with ya."

Erik blinked, waiting to feel his heart beat again. His lips pulled back from his non-glowing teeth into a fierce grin. He rushed forward in the rain and threw his human hands under Vivian's arms, grasping her around the waist with his mutant paws and lifting her off the ground for a joyous orbit around his twirling body.

"Your brother must have left you his sick sense of humor."

"Sorry, I couldn't resist. You know that somewhere out there he's watching this and laughing his head off," Vivian smiled. "*Now* do you believe we're going to be okay?"

"I'll never doubt you again," Erik blushed. "You're right. We *are* different from the others. But I still don't understand *why*."

"There's only one answer," Trent said, saluting the sky. "We *are* the chosen ones after all."

Sherri groaned.

"You know what? At this point I'm willing to accept that answer if it means that I'm not going to get so fucked-up that I think blowing you is a good idea."

"Okay, okay," Erik conceded. "Vivian, you may not have all the answers, but you sure have enough to let me sleep at night."

With a shy smile, he leaned in and gave her a tiny kiss on her lips. When he backed away, Vivian grabbed his ears and pulled him in for a big wet kiss of her own.

"Damn, E, don't bogart our heroine!" Trent said, wiping his dirty mouth on his sleeve. "The T is cookin' up a big batch of congratulatory action for you too, Vivi girl!"

He leaned in toward Vivian's face with puckered lips, which she deflected with a gentle push of her open palm.

"All right, settle down, you. If we're going to survive, we're not going to do it by standing around here. I say we wait out the storm under this bridge and then keep moving first thing in the morning. All right?"

"Moving toward what?" Erik asked. "Washington is gone. We don't have any idea where to go from here."

The rain seemed to pelt down harder on the heels of Erik's words, driving a calypsonian beat from the steel drum of the wrecked satellite dish.

"We're going to Pennsylvania," Vivian said.

The others looked at her quizzically.

"The satellite broadcast," she explained. "It was coming from a PBS station out of Liberty Valley, Pennsylvania. It's not much, but it's the closest thing we've had to making contact with other survivors."

"Pennsylvania?" Sherri said. "How in the hell are we supposed to get to Pennsylvania without a car?"

Vivian looked into the distance with hope in her eyes.

"Get a good night's sleep. We've got an awfully long walk ahead of us."

CHAPTER FIFTEEN

It rained.

It rained a rain so thick and black that it was like the very night was melting.

It had been like this for weeks.

Billions of sooty drops pounded relentlessly against the pavement of a forgotten country road somewhere in Maryland. Tiny slivers of moonlight sliced through the ashy clouds, lightly sketching out four figures staggering single-file through the deluge.

"Are we there yet?" Erik moaned.

"Are we *where* yet?" Vivian asked.

"Anywhere."

Vivian shook her head.

"No."

The water pelted against the flattened copper curtain of her hair, flowing over her face and through her drenched Mountie coat. Her wings hung limply from her shoulders, dragging on the ground behind her like a pair of drowned animals. Wet grime ran over her dress and through the red fur that covered her bare, unshaven legs. But the filth and the rain weren't as bad as the hunger clawing at her stomach.

Erik sloshed along behind her. The gash in his thigh had long since resolved into a ragged scar, but its pink bandages still hung loosely around his leg. Thin as a skeleton, with a few weeks' worth of beard sprouting from his face and the 5-in-1 camping lantern hanging dimly in his mutant hand, Erik was beginning to look like a prop from a cheap Halloween hayride.

Sherri dragged herself along behind Erik. Her blond curls lay in waterlogged clumps over her heavily lidded eyes. Her princess jacket was stained with long vertical streaks of soot, giving her the appearance of a crumbling smokestack looming over some abandoned Victorian factory. Behind her, through the continuous, deafening clatter of the rain, an uneven rhythm repeated itself in an erratic loop.

Zip. Clunk. Zip. Zip. Clunk. Zip. Clunk.

Trent hobbled upon the scraped barrels of his shotgun crutch, clunking it heavily into the ground with every other step. In an attempt to keep the filthy rain out of his wounds, his legs were now wrapped in scavenged tarpaulin and bound with twine. With each step that he took, his thickened legs rubbed together like the thighs of a husky boy in corduroy pants.

Zip. Zip. Clunk. Zip. Clunk. Zip. Zip.

Trent's peripheral vision had been lost to the overstuffed pillows of his black eyes, and the narrow corridor of his forward gaze was fixed firmly between Vivian's wings and upon her soaked behind. Like a carrot on a string in front of a cartoon mule, her skirted bottom seemed to be all that kept him moving through his famished delirium.

Zip. Clunk. Zip. Zip. Zip. Splash!

Through the roar of the rain and the cloud of their own starvation, it took the others a full ten seconds before they realized that Trent was no longer following them. Vivian and Erik stopped, but Sherri just kept walking.

"What happened?" Erik muttered.

"Trent ate pavement," Sherri said. "Just keep going."

Despite Sherri's suggestion, the others turned to find Trent lying face-down in the road. With a great physical effort, Vivian returned to him, squatting by his side on her wobbly legs.

"You okay?" she mumbled.

Trent grabbed onto her coat and laboriously pulled himself upright, leaning against her and pressing his stubbled cheek into her chest.

"I can't keep going. I ain't gonna make it, yo."

"You are going to make it," Vivian said. "We'll find Liberty Valley."

Trent pressed his face tighter against her bosom and moaned.

"We ain't never gonna get to no Liberty Valley without a ride! It just ain't gonna happen!"

"We don't need a car," Vivian said. "We can do this. We just need to stay strong and keep moving."

"Girl, you out yo mind! How's a brother supposed to keep moving his busted ass without any food in his belly? I'm done, Vivi! I'm spent! For real!"

Vivian pulled off her glasses and slicked her overgrown bangs over her forehead with her palm. She impotently rubbed the lenses with her pruny thumbs as she stalled for a rebuttal. Trent was right. If they were ever going to get to Pennsylvania they needed at least one of two things: a car, or a reliable source of food. But she wasn't about to give up.

"We don't need a car," she repeated, slipping her glasses back onto her nose. "When pushed to its limits the human body can adapt to even the most punishing conditions. We can make it. All we need is—"

"A car!" Erik yelped.

"I just said we don't need a car!" Vivian snapped.

"No," Erik squeaked. "A car!"

Vivian turned to Erik, then to where he was pointing with three excited hands. Barely visible through the rain was a heavy-duty pickup truck, shimmering in a moonlit silhouette of ricocheted droplets.

"A car!" Vivian gasped.

Sherri turned and bolted toward the truck, leaving one shouted word hanging in the air.

"Shotgun!"

Vivian and Erik tucked themselves under Trent's arms and took off in a dizzy, lightheaded trot toward the vehicle.

"We're saved!" Trent grinned. "We gonna drive all up out of this bitch, yo!"

"You see!" Vivian said. "I told you we'd be okay!"

"Girl, you said we could get there *without* a car!"

"I lied," Vivian admitted. "There's no way we could have made it to Liberty Valley on foot. Not without food. Not in this rain. No way. But now we don't have to worry about it."

They stumbled to the truck to find Sherri already standing before it with a scowl hanging on her face. A wave of emotion overtook them all, but Sherri managed to encapsulate everything they were feeling in a single word.

"Fuck."

The truck looked like a toy that had been hit with a lawnmower. Each tire was flat and turned upward at the axle. The body was bent at a shallow angle, touching the center of the vehicle to the pavement. This truck had clearly taken a flight for which it had been totally unprepared.

Under the weight of her disappointment, and Trent, Vivian's head went into a spin that threatened to relieve her of consciousness.

"What do we do now?" Erik whimpered.

"We'll be fine," Vivian backpedaled. "Like I said, we just need to find food and we'll be fine."

"Food my ass!" Trent said. "Unless the Lord starts servin' up a heapin' helpin' of chocolate manna, we are done and done, girl! For real!"

They stood in the pouring rain and stared at the broken truck, but in reality, they were staring at a broken charade. The charade that they could actually walk all the way from Washington D.C. to the mountains of northern Pennsylvania. The charade that they were going to find safety. The charade that they were going to be all right in the end.

The doomed survivors were speechless for a long, wet moment before Sherri finally broke the tension with a shrug.

"Fuck it, dude," she said. "Let's go bowling."

Without another word, she stomped away across what the others suddenly realized was a small parking lot. As the boiling clouds shifted, a patch of moonlight fell across a sign depicting a sassy-looking cowgirl with breasts as large and round as the bowling ball she held in her weathered steel hands.

Beneath her was a western lasso scrawl spelling out the words "Calamity Lanes."

Vivian and Erik followed Sherri, dragging Trent between them. As they moved closer, the sheets of black rain revealed a small bowling alley at the edge of the parking lot. Its face had been slapped off by the hand of a distant atomic overpressure, creating a life-sized shoebox diorama of blue-collar recreation.

They climbed over the low debris field and through the massive hole in the side of the building. Finally sheltered from the driving rain, their skin tingled eerily as phantom drops continued to pelt their overstimulated nerve endings. Erik's rodent paws clicked on the lantern's flashlight and swept its beam across the darkened interior.

In life, Calamity Lanes had been an intimate sort of place, sporting only four oiled pine lanes. The smooth, dull sheen of ancient chrome and linoleum dominated the interior surfaces, curving over benches and swooping through the spoon-shaped arcs of jet-age ball returns. Even with a hole blown in its side, the place was still quaint and inviting, but its current visitors were not interested in being charmed by the décor.

Vivian smudged her lenses clean, and this time they actually managed to stay that way. Even in her excitement, her eyelids barely managed to get above half-mast as they scoured her surroundings.

"Look!" she said breathily. "There!"

Erik swung the flashlight's beam in the direction of Vivian's pointing finger, revealing a modest cocktail bar built into the far end of the room—so modest, in fact, that it didn't even have shelves of liquor bottles behind it. Or beer taps. What it did have, as Vivian's hungry eyes had spotted, was an art-deco refrigerator straight out of a Tex Avery cartoon.

"Food!" she gasped.

Sherri's head throbbed with starvation as she took off across the bowling alley, leaping over the loose balls that had fallen from their chrome racks. The others pursued with a gait like a three-legged race times two, and a moment later they had regrouped behind the bar. The smooth white face of the monolithic refrigerator was blemished only by a smattering of magnets in the shapes of ambulances. Each one bore the same message.

Buy groceries online @ Grocery911.com

"It's like I tried to tell you," Vivian said. "We'll be fine, as long as we have food."

"I should have never doubted you, Vivi girl," Trent smiled.

"Let's eat already!" Erik groaned. "Before I black out!"

Sherri swung the refrigerator door wide open on its hinges, revealing an interior full of absolutely nothing.

"Well. That's just swell," she murmured.

As the last held breath of chilled air escaped the refrigerator, the last dregs of strength escaped the survivors, dropping them into an exhausted, waterlogged heap on the floor.

A film of dried ash crumbled from Erik's eyelids as they slowly pulled themselves apart. He found himself lying with his cheek pressed into the rubber floor mat, staring between several sealed cardboard beer crates. He slowly rolled over to see Sherri standing over him, guzzling a longneck bottle of cheap domestic beer.

"Get up, Waffleface," she said. "It's happy hour."

Erik pulled himself upright and dragged his fingers across the sunken red gridlines on his face. Regaining his bearings, he noticed one of the beer crates had been opened and half of the bottles were missing.

"How long was I out?" Erik muttered.

"Six hours? Ten hours?" Sherri shrugged. "How should I know? I just woke up too."

She thrust a bottle toward him with a smile.

"Here—breakfast is served."

Erik wrinkled his nose.

"I don't drink beer for breakfast."

"Fine. Think of it as a toast soda."

Erik climbed nauseously to his feet and plunked down on the stool behind the bar. On the other side of the bowling alley he could see a small fire crackling from the end of lane three. Its broad chrome ball return had been filled with debris and turned into a makeshift fire ring, throwing out a warm yellow light and wafting smoke across the building's slanted ceiling and through its blasted-open front. Vivian and Trent sat on a semicircle of creamsicle benches near the fire, each holding their hands to the flame and drinking bottles of warm beer. A Mountie coat, a varsity jacket, and a nylon parka hung on chairs, slowly drying. A clammy chill gripped Erik as he peeled off his own drenched sweatshirt and hung it over the steel push bar of the back door.

"What is there to eat in this place besides beer?" he asked.

"That's it," Sherri said. "The fridge is empty. This shitty bar doesn't even have any hard stuff. Just a coupla cases of beer on the floor. Not that I'm complaining."

She held up her half-empty bottle with a toasting waggle of her eyebrows before downing the remainder. She punctuated her achievement with a thunderous belch and a wipe of a tanned forearm across pouty pink lips. Erik twisted the cap off of his bottle.

"Well, I guess this is better than nothing," he said. "At least my stomach will have something in it for a change."

"It's best to drink on an empty stomach," Sherri nodded. "You get shitfaced twice as fast. Every scumbag who ever tried to get a girl drunk knows that."

"You drink up on that beer, Vivi," Trent said. "You haven't had any food, so those fluids will do your body good, yo."

"Actually, it won't," Vivian said. "Alcohol is a diuretic. Drinking beer will only accelerate my dehydration."

She held her bottle up to the crackling firelight and sighed.

"But at this point, I can't bring myself to care."

She put the bottle to her lips and took a long swig. Whether it was good for her or not was irrelevant. She relished having a taste in her mouth besides her own cruciferous saliva. Her tired eyes blinked without synchronization as she stared at the fluttering ash that rose hypnotically on the fire's hot updrafts.

"I just hope they have something a little more nutritious than beer waiting for us in Liberty Valley," she said.

Trent smiled at her long, weary body. With her coat, shoes, and socks drying by the fire, she wore only her brutalized cocktail dress, giving her a wild, untamed sort of allure. He slid across the bench and put his hand on her damp arm. Vivian's nose wrinkled against the musk of body odor that poured off of him.

"You need to quit foolin' yourself, Vivi," he said. "This Liberty Valley is just a fairy tale. For real." He smiled his huge white smile and winked. "Give it up, girl. You don't need to go chasing rainbows when the pot of gold is right in front of you."

Vivian ignored that last remark, taking a sip of her beer.

"You're wrong. Liberty Valley is real," she said firmly. "All of the available evidence suggests that there are still reasoning people there. If WOPR is still broadcasting, that shows that there's an operational TV studio and a satellite dish still capable of putting out a signal. That also means that they still have electricity. Most power plants would have been wiped out in the disaster, and with the unbalanced load the power grid would have collapsed without intelligent human supervision. Occam's Razor says that we'll find some kind of civilization in Liberty Valley."

Trent chuckled condescendingly.

"That's some pretty convoluted shit for Occam's Razor to prove, isn't it?"

Vivian shrugged, then stared into space.

"It's better than believing the alternative."

Trent put his hand on Vivian's furry thigh with a smile.

"If you're so keen to apply Occam's Razor to something, maybe you ought to hit these bushy stems of yours, girl. The T ain't down with that Parisian flair."

Vivian's cheeks burned as she threw Trent's hand off of her lap and stormed away without a word.

"Hey, give me some credit, Vivi!" Trent laughed. "It's not like I told you to apply a razor to liberty valley!"

"Seriously, Erik," Sherri said. "Don't you think this Liberty Valley thing is total bullshit?"

Erik leaned back on his stool and finished his second bottle of beer.

"No, I really believe there's something there," he said. "Don't you remember *Woops!?*"

"Now, what in the hell is *Woops!?*"

"It was a short-lived sitcom. It was about an accidental atomic disaster that destroyed the entire world."

"No wonder I don't remember it," Sherri said. "Any comedy about a nuclear apocalypse is guaranteed to suck."

"It did suck," Erik continued. "The show was a really shitty *Gilligan's Island* rip-off where six unlikely survivors found this farmhouse that was the last livable place on Earth."

"So?"

"So the farm was in a deep valley that protected it from the war. I think Liberty Valley must have survived the same way."

Sherri blinked.

"You seriously believe that lame sitcom bullshit?"

Erik shrugged and stared into space.

"It's better than believing the alternative."

Sherri shook her head and opened another beer.

"Well, it doesn't really matter if there's anything there or not. We're never going to get there without a car anyway."

Vivian stood at the edge of the blasted wall and peered at the wrecked pickup truck in the parking lot. The license plate read "LV2BOWL." She could hear Trent's clanking shotgun crutch over the crackle of the rain on the tarpaper roof as he approached her from behind.

"It's another abandoned building with a single car in the parking lot," Vivian muttered. "After Boltzmann's and the igloo, I see this as a very bad sign."

Just as the words came out of her mouth, two large hands grabbed her around the waist from behind.

"Forget about the bad sign, girl," Trent cooed. "It'll be a lot more fun if we obey the good one."

He pulled her against his body, grinding her backside into his swollen groin. Vivian's shoulders clenched as she lurched away, clapping her wings together like a pair of giant hands swatting a fly. Trent tumbled dazedly from between them and fell onto the puddled floor. Vivian whirled around furiously.

"Trent, what's the matter with you?! What the hell do you think you're

CHAPTER FIFTEEN

doing?!"

Trent shook his head and pointed at the splintered front door lying on the ground to his side.

"Damn, Vivi! I was obeying the sign! It was just a joke, girl! You need to lighten up! For real!"

Vivian's narrowed eyes shifted toward a small plaque on the door, reading "Make all deliveries in the rear."

"Oh, ha ha. *Very* funny," she smirked. "Seriously, Trent, can't you ever stop thinking about sex for five seconds?"

Trent slowly climbed to his feet, shaking his head with an unsettling crackle of displaced vertebrae. He leaned on his crutch with a rakish grin.

"Oh, quit frontin', Vivi. You make it out like knockin' da boots is some kind of dirty sin. It ain't like that. The good Lord made sex feel good for a reason, yo. It's just natural instinct for a man and woman to want to get their groove on. It ain't nothin' but a beautiful natural high, girl."

"Well, it's a lot more than that to me," Vivian scowled. "Most girls don't have such a cavalier attitude toward sex as you do, Trent."

Sherri lay on her belly across the length of the bar, knees bent, feet playfully swaying in the air. She leaned on her elbows, arching her back and framing her ample cleavage between two slender arms. As her pointed tongue suggestively circled the neck of her beer bottle, her seductive pink eyes smoldered at Erik. Erik didn't notice. His attention was focused on a dead laptop computer sitting on the far end of the bar.

"Hey Four-Arms," Sherri growled. "What do you say you quit poking around with that laptop and start poking around with mine?"

Erik rubbed his chin.

"It's kind of weird, isn't it?" he said.

"What's weird about it? You get a hot, busty blond girl; I get a guy with two grotesque rat arms. I think we'd both get our money's worth out of the deal."

Erik shook his head and tapped on the fried computer.

"No, I mean the laptop. It seems out of place here, doesn't it?"

Sherri's eyebrows knitted.

"Yeah, it's all wrong. Let's do something about it."

She slapped the computer off of the bar, knocking it to the floor with a clatter of displaced keys. Erik's eyes finally landed on her as she leapt off of the bar, landing with a *crunch* of heavy boots on delicate electronics.

"There," she said sweetly. "Now that I have your undivided attention."

Sherri grabbed Erik by the collar of his T-shirt and pulled his face down into hers. He felt her smooth lips pressing against his own cracked mouth. He could taste the tang of old cabbage and cigarettes being brushed over his tongue by her passionate counterpart. He could feel a pair of hands grabbing his mutated

273

limbs and pulling them around a hot, fleshy hourglass of perfect feminine curves.

It was, in short, the most erotic thing that had ever happened to him in his entire pathetic life.

Yet as Sherri began to fumble with the fly of his jeans, all four of Erik's hands took hold of her body and gently pushed her away.

"No," he said softly. "Don't. I can't do this."

Sherri smiled a dirty little smile.

"Yeah? Well, I think your little friend disagrees!"

Her tiny bronze hand swung forward, grabbing a generous fistful of Erik's groin. The look of surprise that snapped onto Erik's face was eclipsed only by the one that snapped onto hers. She let go of her flaccid handful and spoke with soft astonishment.

"Your little friend *doesn't* disagree. What the hell, Erik? Are you queer or something?"

Erik bowed his head and blushed.

"I am *not* queer. It's just I ... I just don't like you that way."

"What do you mean, *that way?*" Sherri asked incredulously. "I've turned into the Playboy Princess of Candyland and you *still* won't fuck me? What's your fucking problem?"

Erik scowled with humiliation.

"Most guys don't have such a cavalier attitude toward sex as you do, Sherri."

"Bullshit!" Sherri spat. "Like you've never just gone out and fucked some girl before!"

Erik's already reddened cheeks turned a brighter shade of crimson. Sherri shook her head in disbelief.

"Holy shit, you've never fucked a girl before. Please tell me that you have some kind of medical condition, and you're not just 'saving yourself for that one special girl.'"

"So what if I am? What do you care?! You don't even like me! The only reason you want to do me at all is because of these!"

He raised his rodent arms and wiggled their gnarled fingers. Sherri pursed her lips in acknowledgment.

"Well, it wouldn't matter if you had *ten* arms now," she sighed. "Your dumb virgin ass wouldn't know what to do with them once you got my panties off anyway."

Erik nodded in a weak sort of agreement. Sherri leapt back up on the bar and lit a post-coital cigarette that wasn't.

"So, we're cool then?" Erik said.

"No. *I'm* cool," Sherri corrected. "*You're* pretty fucking far from cool. I don't fuck virgins. I'm not some kind of remedial sex-ed class for losers."

Erik smiled with relief.

CHAPTER FIFTEEN

"Thanks for understanding," he said, extending a friendly hand. "Still friends?"

Sherri just shook her head.

"Get lost, Sievert. Christ, I can't believe I almost fucked an Afterschool Special."

"What's the T got to do to show you that you're his special girl, Vivi?"

Vivian sighed.

"Trent, if I really was your 'special girl,' you wouldn't have to ask. Just give it up, all right? I'm sure you'll find somebody out there who's a better fit for you than I am. There's plenty of other fish in the sea, you know."

"Are there?" Trent asked.

Vivian nodded optimistically.

"I'm sure of it," she said. "There's got to be at least one."

Trent looked across the bowling alley at Sherri's perfect behind perched on the bar.

"You're right," he grinned. "And what a fine piece of tail it is!"

"Look, Sherri, Trent's been throwing out bait for you since day one," Erik said. "If you're just looking for a meaningless quickie, maybe you should just bite already."

Sherri's eyebrows lowered with disgust.

"Fuck you. I'd rather die than be teamed up with that douchebag."

"Fuck me! Why do I have to be teamed up with this douchebag?"

"It's all good, Goldilocccks," Trent slurred. "Don't worry, girl. This one has 'shtrike' written all over it, cho. This is th' good one."

Leaning heavily on his crutch, he hobbled to the line and drunkenly hurled a bowling ball down the dusty lane. Five feet later it dropped with a pathetic *bang* into the gutter, rolling agonizingly slowly past ten standing pins.

"You suck, Trent," Sherri snarled. "Fuck this schit. I wanna new teammate."

Erik slouched behind a score table littered with two dozen empty beer bottles. His hand moved with all of the delicate subtlety of an arcade claw machine as he marked down Trent's final gutter ball on the worst score sheet in bowling history.

"Iss not like it rilly matters which one of us is on your team, Sherri," he said. "We're in the tenth frame and nobody's hit a damn thing yet."

"At least it saves us from havin' ta reset the pins," Vivian shrugged.

Erik pointed at her with the nub of his chewed-up pencil.

"You're up, Viv. Make it count. Thissiz our team's last chance to hit some pins."

275

Vivian pushed herself to her feet and a wave of disorientation swirled around the inside of her brainpan. She leaned against the score table with a clumsy giggle.

"Hit some pins?" she laughed. "I'll be lucky if I can hit the lane!"

"Come on, Viv," Erik smiled. "I know you can do it."

He picked up a stray bowling ball and slipped it into her hands, standing up and guiding her wobbling steps to the foot of the alley. Vivian's bloodshot eyes blinked heavily, but she could not stop the pins from swirling. She stood for a long, swaying moment.

"Are you all right?" Erik asked.

"I'm just waiting for the kaleidoscope to stop turning."

"Come on, now, you can do it," Erik smiled. "Here, I'll coach you through it."

Vivian suddenly felt a creeping warmth sliding over her cold skin. She looked to her right to find Erik holding her gently oscillating body with four steadying hands. One of his rodent paws rested on the small of her back, the other on her sloshing belly. His left human hand tenderly deflected her wings away as he leaned in and took her right hand in his own. Together they lifted the ball to her chest, and he pressed his cheek against hers as they stared down the lane.

"Just keep your eye on the pins, swing straight, and follow through," he coached.

As he spoke, he slowly guided Vivian's hand backward and forward, practicing the swing with a sloppy sort of coordination. Although they both stumbled with a drunken giggle, somehow their bodies seemed better balanced together than they had been on their own. As their arms swung as one, the world slipped away, leaving nothing in Vivian's clouded mind but the warmth and stability of Erik's hands.

"You ready?" he said.

"I am," Vivian nodded.

Erik's hands slipped from her body, but before he stepped back he took her face in his human hands, tipped her head forward, and gave her a tiny kiss on the forehead.

"For luck," he smiled.

Vivian blushed as Erik stepped away. Her eyes narrowed in concentration as she took two steps, drew her arm back, and swung it forward in a graceful arc. The ball hit the boards with the tiniest knock, sliding at a picturesque angle all the way to the pins. Although beautifully thrown, the ball only managed to pick off one pin before dropping into the gutter.

"I did it!" Vivian cheered. "I did it! I hit one!"

She jumped up and down in excitement, nearly pounding the consciousness out of her own head. Erik rushed forward and grabbed her in a four-armed embrace.

"You're awesome!" he laughed. "I knew you could do it!"

"I couldn't have done it without you, coach."

"Alright, alright, break it up," Trent said. "Y'all didn't win yet. My girl still has one more chance to school your lame asses."

Vivian and Erik exchanged a twinkling glance as they returned to their seats. Trent stuffed a neon-pink ball into Sherri's hands and gave her a slap on the behind.

"Hey, watch it, dickbag," she growled.

"You can do this, girl," he grinned. "You just need a little coaching from Pro T."

"Fuck off," Sherri spat. "I don't need any help from you."

She stepped onto the lane and held the ball before her narrowed pink eyes. The nine remaining pins echoed outward in an infinite picket fence, but she saw them with a certain clarity born of years of drunk driving. She targeted the headpin and threw her arm backward in anticipation of her pitch.

"That's right, girl. Slow and *uungh!*"

Before Sherri could complete her swing, the ball thudded to an abrupt stop behind her. Her unbalanced feet pivoted on the floor, turning around to see Trent doubled over with the ball buried in his groin.

"You wanged up my swing!" she snapped. "What the fuck are you doing?!"

"Just ... coaching ..." Trent gasped.

He stumbled forward and grabbed Sherri clumsily by her shoulders.

"Trent, what the fuck?! Get off!"

"For ... luck!" he wheezed.

He grabbed the sides of Sherri's head and leaned in to deposit a kiss. Sherri dropped the ball and took a lurching step backward as his stench burned her nose.

"Fuck no! Hey! Get off of me, you shitbomb!"

She pounded her hands into Trent's broad chest, but he grabbed two fistfuls of her hair and pulled her closer. As his stubbly lips connected with her forehead, Sherri planted her palms on his shoulders and shoved him away with a tearing *rip* of uprooted hair.

"Owwww! Jesus Hyman FuckGillicuddy!"

She took two reeling steps and slapped her hands to her scalp. Trent looked at his hands in shock. Two clumps of blond hair clung to his sweaty fingers, but he hardly noticed them. All he saw were the crumbling streaks of dry, dirty blood.

"I'm sorry, girl! I'm so sorry! I was just tryin' to give y'all some luck! You didn't have to get all hostile! Damn!"

"Owww, shit fuck motherfucker," Sherri seethed. "You tore open my scabs, you shitbasket!"

As she raked the hair away from her reopened wounds, Sherri felt the strangest sensation. It didn't hurt, but it felt like a paper cut happening inside-out, all around her scalp. She fell silent as her trembling fingertips bumped up against what felt like a wide-brimmed beach hat.

"What ... what the hell is that?" she stammered.

The others didn't answer. They simply stared in disbelief. Sherri's eyes darted across them with an increasing uneasiness as their mouths began to curl into smiles.

"Holy shit, I just mutated, didn't I?" she gasped. "What is it?! What did I get?!"

Vivian opened her mouth to speak, but all that came out was a barely squelched giggle, which Erik and Trent were soon echoing.

"Alright, you assholes! What is it?! What's so goddamn funny?!"

She wiped her palm across the dusty chrome of the ball return and looked into its mirrored surface. An expression of unadulterated horror slowly flushed through her face.

"Oh no. Shit no. No no no. Why?! Why *me*?!"

Her voice trailed into a whimper as she gently ran her fingers around the soft edges of two butterfly wings the size of dinner plates that blossomed from the sides of her head. They were colored in a palette of pastel blues and yellows so resplendent with spring cheer that one could imagine the Easter Bunny choosing them to redecorate his bathroom.

"What the fuck?!" Sherri shouted. "How come you guys all turned into something out of a Hieronymus Bosch painting and I turned into a fucking Lisa Frank?!"

She grabbed the frilly wings in her fists, crumpling them like two old magazines. The second they began to bend, she squealed sharply and released them, pressing her palms over her eyelids and rubbing out a phantom pain.

"Ow! God damn it!"

She stretched out her face and gave her eyes two exaggerated blinks. As her eyes opened and closed, her wings moved up and down in a sweet little flutter.

"Oh, that is *so* messed up," she muttered. "Why butterfly wings? Why me?"

"Seriously, what gives, yo?" Trent asked. "Girlfriend didn't get bit up by no giant butterfly!"

"It was Priscilla," Erik said. "She must have passed her infected DNA on to Sherri when she pinched her!"

"Priscilla's DNA?" Sherri spat. "That bitch was a hard-ass monster! She didn't have Shirley Temple's DNA!"

"No, it makes sense," Erik said, scratching his scruffy beard. "You saw the crazy way she mutated. Every bug in that zoo must have taken a stab at her while she was trapped in there. Her bloodstream probably carried more bug juice than the bottom of an exterminator's shoe!"

Sherri shook her head in furious denial.

"This is so unfair!" she cried. "That freak drools a jawful of mutant bug slobber all over me, and I grow *this shit?!* Why?! Why not claws?! Why not stingers?!"

"I don't know! It's not like I'm not an expert on this!" Erik squeaked. "What do you think, Vivian?"

Vivian raised her heavy eyes and looked at the absurd mutation with a shallow shake of her head.

"I think I need another drink."

The world slowly blurred past Vivian's boozed-up eyes as she knelt behind the bar and pulled the last warm beer from the last sliced-open crate. She stood up and turned toward the door, bumping into a wall of arms and hair.

"Ack! Oh. Erik," she blushed. "What are you doing back here?"

Erik held the score sheet in his two rodent hands and pointed to Sherri's tenth frame with his bony index finger.

"Ol' gutter mouth just threw her last gutter ball. We won!"

"With just one pin?" Vivian laughed.

"Hey, what can I say?" Erik nodded. "We make an unbeatable team. I'm entering this massacre into the hall of fame for future generations to marvel over."

He reached across Vivian's body and used all four hands to slap the score sheet onto the fridge and affix it with Grocery911 magnets. Vivian leaned languidly against the icebox door and squinted at the single-digit victory.

"That's a pretty pathetic score we racked up."

"Yeah, but at least we had fun," Erik shrugged. "After all, there's more important things in life than scoring."

Vivian's eyes rolled to Erik in a slow, coy arc.

"Even so, it's nice to score when you have the right teammate."

She threw her arms around Erik's shoulders and planted an awkward kiss on his surprised lips. Erik managed to catch her, but her reeling weight sent them stumbling backward, slapping his back against the wall. His lips returned her clumsy affection, but she was distracted by a length of cable knotted around her bare ankle.

"I can't believe this is actually happening," Erik whispered. "Vivian, I … I … from the moment I met you I've wanted to take you in my arms and hold you against my—"

"Laptop?"

"Well, no. But I admit, this time it's not just because I'm nervous."

Vivian bent down, untangled the phone cable from her leg, and held it up in front of her. The broken clamshell of the computer hung from the cord like a dead possum.

"Oh, right. *That* laptop," Erik blushed. "I just meant to say ... I mean my 'laptop' is, er ... you mean so much more to me than just a quick ... I mean, don't get me wrong, I'd sure like to ..."

He closed his eyes and took a deep, cleansing breath.

"What I'm trying to say is that I ... I love you, Vivian. And I'm sorry that I had to drink a whole shipment of beer to get up the nerve to finally say it."

The shattered laptop lowered to the floor as Erik's confession seeped into Vivian's inebriated gray matter. Somewhere behind the haze in her eyes, the words seemed to ignite a pile of dry kindling that had been awaiting a spark.

"You're right. A whole shipment of beer," she repeated distantly. "Erik, we drank an *entire shipment* of beer that hadn't even been put in the refrigerator."

"I know; I know," Erik said. "But I promise it's not just the booze talking. Vivian, if you'd have me, I promise you that I'd—"

"Make all deliveries in the rear!"

Erik's eyes widened, narrowed, and then shrugged.

"Well, I was going to say 'be true to you forever,' but I'm open-minded."

Vivian shook her head and pushed herself away from Erik distractedly.

"The unopened beer crates! They were all stacked up right next to the back door!"

Vivian's point planted itself behind Erik's cloudy eyes.

"Wait! The computer! The magnets!" he gasped. "Vivian, you don't think that—"

"I do!"

Vivian stumbled to the back door and squished her palms into the soggy sweatshirt hanging over its push bar, knocking it wide open.

"Just minutes before the bombs dropped, this place must have taken a delivery from ..."

They tumbled through the door and into the pouring rain of the back alley, putting them face to face with the hulk of a Grocery911.com ambulance glistening in the sharp white moonlight.

"Oh my God, you found it!" Erik said. "You found us a ride out of here!"

"*I* didn't find it," Vivian said. "*We* found it. Together."

The warmth of Erik's smile cut through the chill of the pounding water.

"It's like I said. We make an unbeatable team."

The black water flew from Vivian's hair as she turned to Erik and held out her hand with a beaming grin.

"Come on! Let's check it out!"

In their excitement, Vivian and Erik completely failed to notice two waterlogged corpses and an unsigned invoice lying in the shadows behind the Dumpsters as they scampered across the pavement and climbed through the unlocked driver's-side door of the ambulance. Erik tumbled into the passenger seat as Vivian slipped behind the wheel and slammed the door. The rain clattered like thousands of tiny fingernails over the vehicle's steel shell as they giddily caught their breath.

"This is awesome!" Erik grinned. "Do you think we can actually push start this thing?"

Vivian shook her head as she examined the faux-wood and yellow plastic of a dashboard that should never have left the 1970s. Between the rolled odometer and the eight-track player, one little word caught her eye and spread a smile across her lips.

"We shouldn't even have to push it. It's a diesel," she said, tapping on the labeled fuel gauge. "No electric ignition. No spark plugs. I'll bet this old tank would start on her own if we could just find the … keys?"

Her eyes fluttered in disbelief as they landed on a set of keys hanging from the steering column.

"What the? What kind of person just leaves the key in the ignition?"

Erik shook his head with a knowing smile.

"A stupid person," he said. "And I once heard that the only people at Grocery911 stupider than the drivers were the suits."

Vivian wrapped her fingers around the key without any further argument.

"I never thought I'd say this, but thank God for the stupid people."

She closed her eyes and gave the key a hopeful crank, awakening the beast under the hood with a blast of black smoke from the twin tailpipes. She pumped the accelerator and the engine roared like a grizzled old pack animal ready to carry its next load.

"It works!" Erik cried. "Let's go get the others and get out of here!"

Vivian turned to him with a conspiratorial glint in her eyes. She put her long hands on his thigh and tossed her head toward the small door leading to the back of the ambulance.

"Hey, what's the big rush, teammate?" she said silkily. "Wouldn't you rather spend a little time alone in the back of the ambulance first?"

Erik's eyes widened as a smile poured across his face.

"You … you mean …"

"That's right," Vivian said. "We get first dibs on all the food!"

CHAPTER SIXTEEN

The gray blanket of the doomsday cloud spread itself thin over the yellowing sky, filtering a web of afternoon sunlight over the rolling wheat fields of Turnstone, Pennsylvania.

After a marathon of driving, the weary heap of the Grocery911.com ambulance enjoyed a steaming reprieve. It slouched on its bowed axles next to a mailbox at the mouth of a long, dirt driveway leading straight down a gentle slope into the heart of a small family farmstead.

The driveway ended in front of a barn that sagged so drearily it made Andrew Wyeth paintings look cheerful by comparison. Between the ambulance and the barn a smaller driveway crossed the main run, terminating in a drab, colonial-style farmhouse on one end and the sixty-foot tower of a Dutch windmill on the other. Although the farm didn't look abandoned, its decaying buildings seemed to remain standing due to little more than a stubborn refusal to collapse. A collection of derelict cars set up on cement blocks populated the lawn, giving the farm that quaint redneck flavor that nothing else but derelict cars set up on cement blocks can.

Sherri drew in a hot, smoky breath as she lit the last of her cigarettes. The Grocery911 ambulance had offered a smorgasbord of canned foods to fill her hungry belly, but it had offered nothing for her blackened lungs. She let a cloud of smoke trickle from her nostrils, and then fanned it away with her butterfly wings.

"Well, I guess I quit," she said, tossing the empty pack on the ground.

She sat down on the steps of the farmhouse and leaned back on her elbows, looking around the yard at her bustling companions. To her right, Erik ran down the driveway and toward the ambulance in the distance. Its back door let out a rusty squeak as he yanked it open and climbed inside.

She took a savoring drag on her cigarette and turned to her left. Next to the steps, a tiny shack was built on to the front of the farmhouse. To even call it a shack was generous. In reality, the waist-high, shingled wooden box was nothing more than an enclosure designed to protect a single piece of machinery from the elements. Vivian had followed a thick bundle of electrical cables across the front of the house and into the box, and now its low front door hung wide open, belching out two long black wings.

Trent struggled toward the farmhouse on his clanking shotgun crutch. The endless cycles of wet and dry had taken their toll on his varsity jacket, and his broad forearms stuck out of its shrunken sleeves like an idiot who accepted hand-me-downs from his younger siblings. He was heading directly, and somewhat unsurprisingly, toward Vivian's squatting buttocks.

Vivian could barely see inside the box's cramped interior, but her eagerness to repair the machine within outweighed her patience for Erik to return with the lantern. A bead of sweat rose from her forehead as she pushed all of her weight into the handle of her Swiss Army Knife. The tip of its Phillips head screwdriver bucked out of the last rusted screw in the faceplate of a diesel-powered electric generator.

"Come on, work with me here," she grumbled. "How am I going to fix you if you won't open up?"

With a grunting flex of her forearm, she finally broke through the oxidation and twirled the screw out of its hole. The access plate dropped to the ground, revealing a gutful of rusted wheels and crumbling belts. A dizzying haze of diesel fumes wafted from the machine and into the claustrophobic chamber.

"Okay, diesel repair. How hard can this be?"

The smell of fuel in the air was suddenly overpowered by a rancid stench of body odor. Vivian's nose wrinkled as her sliver of sunlight was completely eclipsed.

"Hey. Move it, Trent. You're in my light."

The next thing she knew, Trent was kneeling on the ground beside her, squeezing his shoulders into the box like a size-10 foot into a size-6 shoe. The weathered, brittle wood crackled violently as Vivian was crushed against the doorframe.

"Aaagh! Trent! What are you doing?! Get out of here!"

"You can't hide from me, Vivi," Trent grinned. "I need to be with you."

"No, you need to be *outside*," Vivian said, shoving him away. "Get lost, Casan*odor*."

Trent struggled to turn his body toward Vivian's in the cramped space.

"Quit playin'. You know you want me all up in your box, girl."

Trent's breath blasted into Vivian's face like a spray of fetid oil. The smell included a comprehensive selection of ghastly odors, but regurgitated beer was obviously leading the charge.

"Gah!" Vivian winced. "Trent, what's *wrong* with you? Go bother Sherri for a while!"

"Screw that! Every time a brother tries to hit that he ends up getting his nuts busted in. You got the sweetness, Vivi. For real."

Trent's head suddenly flew forward and whacked against the iron casing of the generator with a hollow *clang*. Before Vivian could question why, he was yanked backward out of the box and dropped dazedly to the ground.

"Jesus. Sit down and give the girl some space, you drunk-ass, stank-ass, horny-ass bastard," Sherri spat. "What's your fucking problem?"

Vivian barely had a chance to regain her balance before Sherri leaned inside the door, blowing a cloud of tobacco smoke into the box.

"You okay, Powderpuff?"

"I'm fine," Vivian coughed, fanning her nose. "Jeez, Sherri, do you mind?"

"Oh, well you're so fucking welcome," Sherri sneered, swinging her cigarette hand out of the box. "What are you doing in here anyway?"

"I'm trying to get this old generator running. The water pump and heater in this farmhouse are both electric. If I can fix this, we all get hot showers."

"It's about time," Sherri moaned. "For the past week Trent's smelled like a dead homeless guy's jock strap."

"We all could use some freshening up," Vivian agreed. "As soon as I get my hands on some soap and water I'm going to start scrubbing, and I'm going to scrub, and I'm going to keep scrubbing until I smell absolutely nothing like cabbage."

"I hear that," Sherri agreed. "I smell like the green smears on Peter Cottontail's toilet paper."

"Oh, that's pleasant," Vivian smirked. "Get out of here. I can't fix anything with you blocking the light."

"Alright, alright, keep your skirt on," Sherri muttered. "I got you covered."

Vivian heard a sparking scrape, and the vapor-filled enclosure was suddenly bathed in firelight lapping from Sherri's lighter.

"Sherri, no!"

With a clumsy, frantic snatch, Vivian plucked the lighter out of Sherri's hand and lurched backward out of the doorway. She stood up, snapped the lighter shut, and stuffed it safely in her coat pocket.

"Important safety tip," she scowled. "Diesel fuel and open flame are not charming bedfellows. Let's just wait for the lantern, okay? I don't want to blow anything up today."

Sherri took a long drag on her cigarette and shrugged.

"You've got some major gratitude issues, you know that?"

Erik jogged up the driveway, hopping over Trent's sprawled body without interest or query.

"Here you go," he beamed, holding out the lantern.

"Thanks. Could you please hold it for me?" Vivian asked sweetly. "I'm going to need both hands to work on this."

"Anything for you, Viv," Erik smiled.

"Barf," Sherri said under her breath. "And I thought I'd totally lost my gag reflex …"

Vivian squatted down and squeezed back into the generator enclosure. Erik tucked the lantern's flashlight nose into the gap between her shoulder and the top of the doorframe and clicked the power switch.

"It's time for the big puppet show! I'm so excited, Talkatoo!"

As the voice screamed in her ear, Vivian jumped, slamming the back of her head against the wooden ceiling with a rattling *thump*. She tumbled backward out of the shed, trying to rub the flashing stars from her vision.

"Aaagh! Damn it, Erik!" she growled.

"I'm sorry! I'm so sorry! I thought it was set to flashlight! I didn't know it was on TV mode!"

Vivian's eyes popped open through the haze of her head trauma.

"Wait!" She leapt up and grabbed the lantern. "Let me see that!"

"Brkwaaak! You and Whazzat have worked so hard, Lookout! I'm sure the puppet show will be a huge success! Brkwaaaak!"

"Jesus! Turn that shit off!" Sherri growled, covering her ears. "I thought losing the satellite dish meant I'd never have to hear that bird bitch's voice again!"

"It did!" Erik said. "This is impossible! We can't get a satellite feed without a dish!"

Vivian reached around the back of the lantern and yanked out half a yard of telescoping antenna. The distortion fell out of the signal, revealing a crystal-clear image of a girl kangaroo with a sock puppet on her hand.

"We're within broadcast range!" she said. "We must be getting close!"

"And someone in Liberty Valley is still calling us home," Erik beamed.

"Bkrwaaaak! You have to work hard to make your dreams come true! Bkwraaak-waaak-waaaaaak!"

"Alright, alright," Sherri barked, grabbing the lantern. "Christ! I can't stand that fucking chicken lady!"

"She's not a chicken," Erik corrected. "She's a cockatoo."

"I don't care what she is! She's fucking annoying!"

"Bkwraaaak!"

Sherri jabbed the power switch, and the screen went blank.

"Ahh, that's better. Christ, if I hear another—"

"Bkwraaaaak!"

Sherri's shoulders leapt to her ears as the squawk pierced her skull. Vivian and Erik fell into startled silence, and Sherri whirled around to see what they were looking at. Three chickens were standing there looking at her.

Looking *down* at her.

"Holy shit," she murmured. "It's Colonel Sanders's wet dream!"

She took a slow step backward toward the house as the ostrich-sized chickens scratched their talons menacingly in the dirt. Two of them were fat, awkward-looking hens, the third a lean red rooster. With undersized feathers clustered unevenly over their six-foot bodies, the chickens looked like an arts and crafts project suffering from inadequate supplies. Their heads cocked nervously from side to side as their black eyes sized up Trent's body lying in the grass.

"Damn," he muttered airily. "I ain't seen a cock that big since last time I took a piss, yo."

"Trent!" Vivian hissed. "Get up, you idiot!"

She grabbed him by his undersized coat and hauled him to his feet. He threw his arms around her waist and held her body tightly against his own.

"Don't worry, Vivi girl. I'll protect you."

Vivian wrestled herself free and shoved him against the side of the farmhouse.

"Nobody needs to be protected from anything," she whispered. "Chickens don't attack people. They're just curious. Watch."

She leapt forward and threw out her arms and wings with a shout. The two hens exploded into the air in a blast of feathers and dirt before scampering away down the driveway. The rooster also leapt backward at the noise, but did not flee. He spread his massive wings as the undersized feathers of his neck puffed out with a threatening crackle.

"Go on!" Vivian yelled, waving her arms. "Get out of here! Scram!"

The rooster rose up on his toes and thrashed his wings with an earsplitting crow. His beak whistled through the air, stabbing into the ground inches from Vivian's toes. She leapt back against the farmhouse next to her three companions.

"What's it doing?!" Erik squeaked. "I thought chickens didn't attack people!"

"They don't!" Vivian agreed. "Maybe zombies don't act on instinct after all!"

"Make up your mind!" Sherri barked. "This is not the time to be making new shit up!"

The rooster made another lunge at Vivian's feet, and she pressed herself against the wall. As she forced her back to the shingles, her wings squashed out from her shoulders. The rooster spread his own wings with a retaliatory cluck.

"Wait! The wings—the red coat!" Vivian said. "It thinks I'm another rooster!"

"So it's trying to kill you?!" Sherri chirped.

"No! It's just trying to be dominant! It's trying to establish a pecking order!"

"So what do we do?" Erik squeaked.

Vivian grabbed a stick and spread out her intimidating twelve-foot wingspan.

"We put ourselves at the top of the pecking order."

Vivian leapt forward and poked the rooster in the chest with her stick. The mutant made a motion to counterattack, but Vivian rapped it on the beak, and it stumbled backward with a frightened squawk. As she forced the rooster away, her friends peeled off of the wall of the farmhouse and followed her.

"What's the matter, rooster?" Vivian jeered. *"Chicken?"*

"Ouch," Erik winced. "That was a cock-a-doodle-*don't*."

"If you ask me," Sherri said, "you've both got *fowl* mouths."

She slapped her palms over her mouth and gasped.

"Oh shit! What have you lame-asses done to me?!"

Vivian kept jabbing the rooster, but he just hopped back and forth, refusing to abandon his machismo. Vivian threw out her wings, forming a black wall of intimidation.

"Go on—get out of here!" she shouted.

The rooster jumped back and hit the ground with a *thud* that sent a quake rumbling up Vivian's legs.

"What the …"

A second tremor rattled through her knees, and the rooster turned and fled across the yard. As it ducked behind the windmill, a gigantic black hoof stomped out from behind the barn, rattling the earth.

"What the hell was that?" Erik squeaked.

Vivian whispered in awe.

"It's the top of the pecking order."

Her shoulders slumped as her arms fell to her sides, dropping her wings and revealing the creature to the others.

It was a bull. A bull the size of a cement truck.

The monster took a pounding step and blasted steaming air from its cavernous nostrils. Two impossibly large horns jutted from its skull in angry yellow arcs as it slowly raised its head with the thunderous crackle of an old-growth forest being shoved to the ground.

Even in a world of hideously mutated beasts, the bull stood out as being particularly gruesome. In its unchecked orgy of growth, bone had outstripped flesh, pushing a wet, glowing skeleton through its mangled skin. Yet even with its internal organs hanging like hammocks from its sides, the bull didn't look like it was suffering.

It just looked angry.

"Its instinct is to chase," Vivian whispered. "Whatever you do, *don't* … *run.* Okay? Guys?"

She glanced over her shoulder to see the others racing off in different directions as fast as their legs could carry them. In the bull's black, empty eyes the farm became a Lilliputian Pamplona. It opened its throat and bellowed a bassnote that shattered the windows of the farmhouse. Before Vivian's skull had stopped ringing, the bull dropped its head and charged across the farm.

Vivian took three bounding strides, pounding her wings desperately against the air. Gravity held fast, granting her only a single enhanced leap over the hood of a derelict pickup truck. She landed awkwardly, twisting her ankle with a loud *pop.*

"Aaagh! Damn it!" she hissed.

She tumbled against the fender and rubbed her wrenched bones as Trent hobbled up to her side. His face twisted into a lusty grin as he threw his arms around her and pulled her close.

"That's right, girl. You're safe here with the T."

"I know I'm safe!" Vivian spat, slapping Trent away. "It wasn't chasing *me!* Look!"

Far across the yard, Sherri's boots clipped the ground in a blur of speed. Her butterfly wings flapped frantically against her skull, begging for the power to lift her to safety. But even at her almost superhuman velocity, the tip of a bloodstained horn was overtaking her on either side.

"Sherri, run!" Vivian screamed. *"Run!"*

The bull's hot, rancid breath enveloped Sherri as she flung out her arms and kicked her feet off the ground, sailing like an arrow through the open rear door of the Grocery911 ambulance. Before she even hit the floor, the bull's skull smashed into the vehicle, crushing it like a beer can against a biker's forehead. The impact threw the ambulance into a squealing spin, flinging a fan-tailed wake of food across the driveway.

The bull staggered backward and shook its monstrous skull, an enormous gash in its forehead surging blood. With a bellowing wail, it charged the ambulance again, collapsing the passenger side. From inside the vehicle, a blue streak of screamed profanity proved that Sherri was still among the living, if only for a limited time. Vivian watched helplessly from behind the swooping green buttock of the truck's fender.

"Think, Vivian! Think!" she pleaded, pounding her forehead. "You've got to do something!"

Trent's oily hands slid around her waist.

"Why so tense, girl? Come here and let the T soothe some relaxation into your tight little body."

"Stop it, Trent!" Vivian screamed, wrenching his hands away. "Sherri's going to *die* if we don't *do* something!"

She pounded her fists into the truck, sending a tremor through three bottles sitting on a fender riddled with small-caliber bullet holes.

"Target practice?"

Inspiration struck as she patted the last shotgun shell in her coat pocket. She hoped she was a better marksman than whoever had been shooting at these unbroken bottles. If she was going to save Sherri, she was literally only going to get one shot at it.

"Quick, give me the shotgun!" she ordered, throwing out her hand. "Before it kills her!"

Trent grabbed Vivian around the wrist and yanked her body toward his, slapping her chest against his own.

"Let it kill her!" he growled. "I ain't interested in dat skank ass! I want you, Vivi!"

"Trent, have you lost your mi—"

Vivian's question broke in half as Trent shoved her against the side of the truck, forcing her wings through its broken window. He pressed his body heavily against hers, pinning her down. His stench burned her eyes as his hands slid clumsily up her skirt.

"Stop it!" Vivian choked. "What are you doing?!"

"Don't play like you don't know," Trent snarled. "You know I been ready to pop for weeks! This 'hard to get' shit ain't cute anymore, girl!"

"Stop it! Trent, stop it!" Vivian shrieked. *"Stop it!"*

Her foot launched from the ground, driving her knee into Trent's crotch like a sledgehammer into a railroad spike. The impact was so solid that it made an audible *pop* and sent a tingle of pins and needles down her calf, but Trent barely even seemed to notice it. The air squeezed out of her chest as he leaned harder against her, dragging his ragged fingernails against her skin as he attempted to liberate her from her underpants.

"Trent! Stop! Get off of me!"

She clawed at the sides of the truck as a cold breeze blew through her stretched-out panties, tingling across the exposed warmth of her chaste flesh. Her fingertips connected with something solid, and in a blind lunge she grabbed it and swung into the side of Trent's head. The butt of a tall orange bottle connected with a heavy *crack* and exploded into shards. Trent stumbled away from her with a yelp, clutching his face with his hands.

Vivian pried her wings from the window frame and hobbled away on her twisted ankle, thrusting out her shattered bottle like an unarmed cowboy in a spaghetti western bar brawl.

"Stop it! What's the matter with you?!"

Trent lowered his bloodied hands and turned on Vivian with a savage snarl. He spit out a wet mouthful of blood and drool, and a displaced front tooth bounced across the dirt to Vivian's feet. Its cap was an unblemished white, but its root glowed a hot radioactive blue.

"Oww, shit," he moaned, rubbing his jaw. "You busted up my grill! I just got that enhanced, bitch!"

Knocked from the safety of his gums, Trent's tooth betrayed the secret to his perfect smile: a shroud of dental-grade porcelain, recently installed by Ben Affleck's Stillwater dentist.

Vivian thrust her bottle toward Trent, glaring into his blood-slicked maw.

"You … you glow! You're one of *them!* But *how?!*"

The clouds shifted, throwing a slice of sunlight through the orange prism of her broken bottle. The reflected glare etched her corneas with a spongy sort of molecule and five extreme words.

Fusion Fuel - Load and lock!

Vivian's face took on the expression of one who had just finished the last page of an Agatha Christie novel.

"That's *it!*" she shouted. "*That's* the key! Now I get it!"

"Girl, you're about to get it," Trent roared. "And you're gonna get it good, yo!"

He leaned on his crutch and fumbled with his fly. A dark stain spread across the front of his trousers as his tail went into a stiff, spastic convulsion.

"No! Stop! Listen to me!" Vivian pleaded. "Fight it, Trent! You're better than this! You're better than your animal instincts!"

Trent finished wrenching down his zipper as his crotch erupted in a volcano of pus and torn flesh. Horror saturated Vivian's psyche so completely that she didn't even scream. She just froze with cold comprehension as three words clicked together in her mind.

Priscilla's infectious saliva.

Between Trent's bandaged legs stood a fleshy white scorpion tail the size of a bodybuilder's arm. A scrap of urine-dappled underwear hung impaled on an eight-inch black stinger slicing from its tip. Trent leaned back on his crutch and flexed his rippling member with a look of Christmas-morning awe. More horrifying than the fact that Trent's genitalia had been obliterated was the fact that he didn't even seem to realize it.

"How you like me now, Vivi? I'm hung like Godzilla, yo!"

Vivian went pale as Trent turned his nightmare phallus on her.

"Are you woman enough to take on Long Dong Trent?"

"I'm not!" Vivian screamed. "*Nobody* is! You can't possibly have sex with that ... *thing!* It's a physical impossibility!"

Trent's blackened eyes showed no trace of understanding as he plodded forward. Vivian hurled her bottle at his face, but his throbbing stinger swatted it harmlessly out of the air.

She limped away from the truck, her twisted ankle sending rockets of agony up her leg with each step. When she reached the center of the driveway, her concentration momentarily shifted away from Trent's stinger. At the end of the driveway, the bull nudged the wrecked ambulance with its enormous head. The wrecked, blood-slicked ambulance was silent as a tomb.

"Oh no," Vivian whimpered. "Sherri!"

The bull's ears pricked up at the sound of her squeaky voice. Colossal ropes of muscle pulled through its neck as it turned to lock eyes with its new prey. Vivian sucked a sharp breath and stood completely and utterly still in the shelterless driveway. After what seemed like hours, the bull turned away and continued prodding the side of the destroyed ambulance.

With a tight sigh of relief, Vivian turned and began to run, nearly impaling herself on Trent's mutated phallus. Its onyx stinger whistled up through the air, slashing her coat from waist to shoulder. She toppled over backward, sprawling across the ground and grabbing the blood-soaked gouge in her chest.

But there was no blood. No gouge.

She pulled her hands apart to find her coat and cocktail dress slashed open, revealing the pale skin of her completely intact midsection. Before she could release her clenched breath, the spear slammed down between her knees, stabbing through her skirt and into the ground. With a simultaneous kick of her legs and flap of her wings, she threw herself backward, pulling the blade through the worn polyester with a high, peeling *rrriip*.

"Sit still, girl!" Trent yelped. "I ain't gonna hurt you! I'm gonna make you feel good!"

Vivian was already on her feet and limping desperately across the driveway. Her ankle felt like it was being crushed in a vice with each agonizing step. There was no way that she could outrun Trent. She had to find shelter. Hopping and flapping her wings like a wounded bird, she made her way to the creaking hulk of the Dutch windmill.

She grabbed the handles of the barn-style double doors and yanked with all of her strength, but they failed to open. A pair of U-shaped steel brackets sprouted from them, bound together with a combination lock.

"Damn it!"

Her eyes flashed over her shoulder. The bull had abandoned the ambulance in favor of some grazing, but Trent was not so easily distracted. His bandaged legs hobbled ever closer to his carnal reward with a sinister *zip, zip, zip*.

"Y'all act like it's unnatural!" he screamed. "You can't fight nature, girl!"

"Shhhh!" Vivian hissed, glancing at the bull. "Trent, shut up!"

She turned back to the door and took a deep, calming breath.

"Use your logic," she breathed. "Find a way."

She picked up the combination lock.

"Only three tumblers," she mumbled. "Ten digits each."

She blew a blast of air into her bangs.

"Only a thousand possible combinations," she grimaced, slamming the lock against the door. "You've got a better chance of unlocking the *brackets*."

The brackets! She lifted the lock, revealing two large, exposed mounting screws.

"Yes! That's the way!"

She flicked her Swiss Army Knife from her pocket, rammed its screwdriver into the top screw, and cranked as fast as her fingers could maneuver.

"Come on, baby, come on, come on," she begged.

She twisted and twisted, but the screw just got longer and longer. Sweat beaded on her forehead as she looked back over her shoulder to see Trent, still limping forward in a mad delirium. The screw finally wobbled in its setting and fell from the door.

"One more!" she grunted.

"Saddle up and spread 'em, girl!" Trent bellowed. "Cowboy T's gonna ride you like a rodeo!"

In the distance, the bull's blood-caked eyes squinted at Trent. Vivian could see it draw up to its full, barn-like height in her peripheral vision as she frantically cranked away at the second screw. The bull took a few pounding steps toward them and stopped, tilting its head curiously.

"Work the screw; don't look at the bull; work the screw," Vivian chattered.

With a rumble like a space shuttle reentry, the bull released its bellowing moo, lowered its horns, and charged the windmill. Vivian's pupils dilated as she faced fifty tons of beef bearing down on her. Her eyes snapped back to the screw and her hands worked with increased vigor.

"You looked at the bull. Don't look at the bull; work the screw!"

Vivian saw Trent's long shadow slide between her legs and up the front of the windmill. She took small comfort in knowing that when the bull stampeded her, forcing her internal organs out of the openings at both ends of her digestive tract, the same thing would also be happening to Trent.

Her eyes bounced in their sockets as they turned to her right and were filled with black fur and flying drool. She had always heard that you're supposed to see your life flash before your eyes just before you die, but all she saw was chickens. Three gigantic chickens bolting out from behind the windmill and cutting a direct perpendicular to the rampaging bull's path.

"Go on! Go!" Erik screamed. "Move your McNuggets!"

Like a rancher from some bizarro universe, Erik ran behind a flock of super-sized chickens, swinging a rusty pitchfork at their giant backsides. As soon as the overstuffed poultry crossed the bull's eye line, their thrashing wings and terrified squawks immediately captured its full attention, drawing it away from Vivian and Trent as if they had never existed. Erik peeled away from the flock and pressed himself against the side of the windmill.

A monstrous hoof slammed down on the rooster, exploding it like a rotten, meaty grapefruit. The senseless carnage energized the two remaining hens, pushing them far ahead of the bull as the trio disappeared around the side of the barn.

Erik scampered up to Vivian's side and threw his arms around her. She shoved him away with a scowl.

"Not now, Erik!"

"Are you okay?!"

"Yes I'm okay!" Vivian barked, throwing out a finger. "*He's* the one who's not okay!"

Erik turned toward Trent's claw-like phallus swinging in a crackling metronome two meters away.

"Oh shit!" Erik yelped. "What the—"

"He's a zombie!"

"But his tee—"

"Porcelain veneers!"

"But why did it take such a long—"

"Late bloomer!"

"But how come—"

"Fusion Fuel! That's why he doesn't smell like cabbage!"

"What?!"

"There's no time for this, Erik!" Vivian snapped. "We'll be safe in here! Just hold him back for two seconds!"

She planted her miniature screwdriver and continued twisting. Erik's brain throbbed with non-information, but he understood one thing: He had to stop Trent. He retrieved his pitchfork and pounced in between Trent's bladed shaft and Vivian's unprotected rear end.

"Get back, Ginsu dick!" he screamed, brandishing his pitchfork. "Get away from her!"

Trent lurched backward, stumbling several clumsy steps before righting himself on his crutch.

"Stand back, little boy," he said, flexing his stinger. "Vivi wants to get with a real man!"

"A real man?" Erik laughed. "Big talk from a guy whose testicles are lying in the driveway!"

Trent's stinger flew out toward Erik's face, and he swung the pitchfork into a defensive position. Trent's mouth dropped open in a wailing scream as the force of his own swing impaled his mutant shaft on the rusted prongs.

"Now that I've got your attention," Erik snarled, "I'd like to raise a few points."

A hot trickle of blood spiraled down Trent's white shaft like a barber pole as Erik lifted the fork, intensifying the pitch of his impossibly high scream. Erik leaned in and spoke through clenched teeth.

"Number one: I'm not going to kill you unless you make me, alright? So be cool!"

Trent's swollen eyes did not look at his pierced stinger. They didn't look at Erik. His sweat-soaked gaze was fixed on Vivian as she yanked the last screw out of the lock bracket. Erik noticed this lusty glare.

"Number two," he snarled, twisting the fork. "If you ever so much as *think* about having sex with Vivian Gray ever again, I'm going to Bobbitt your hobbit! You got that?!"

Trent's anguished face turned on his captor with a flash of rage.

"Get offa my jock, you pussy-ass bitch!"

Trent's weight wobbled on his toes as his arm swung from his side. The last thing Erik heard was a scrape of steel against dirt and a cold swish before two shotgun barrels connected with the side of his head. He was unconscious before he hit the ground.

Vivian clawed the bracket out of the massive door and grabbed its handle, pulling it open on creaking hinges.

"Erik, I got it!" she screamed, turning toward him. "Come on! Get insi—"

The scene unfolding in front of her squeezed Vivian's throat into silence. Erik lay flat on his back, spread-eagled and unconscious in a growing pool of blood drizzling through his wild hair. Trent stood in a striking silhouette against the yellow sky, holding the bloody pitchfork in both hands, prongs down, ready to drive it through Erik's groin.

"I'll show you who's the real man around here, bitch!"

"Trent, no!" Vivian shrieked. *"Stop!"*

With a grunting heave, Trent hoisted the fork over his head in a momentum-building upswing. Vivian staggered across the driveway, but she knew that she would not reach Erik in time to save him.

She had to find another way.

"Oh God, I'm so *horny!*" she moaned breathlessly. "Trent! I need a big man to sex me up, and I need it *right now!*"

Her eyes clenched shut as if she had just been slapped in the face with a jellyfish. She had one chance to save Erik, and *that* was the best dirty talk she could come up with? It was pathetic. Yet the tensed muscles in Trent's arms slackened as he turned toward her. Vivian didn't waste the moment.

"Yeah you, big sexy sex, uh … man," she growled, bending over and pulling her palms gawkily up her inner thighs. "I'm all hot and bothered and, um … ready for some big stud to make sweet animal love to me all night long!"

To supplement her awkwardly slung innuendo, Vivian whipped off her glasses, pouted her lips, and struck a pose like something out of a Gil Elvgren painting. Trent's eyes widened as his dull gaze flicked back and forth between Erik's loins and Vivian's provocatively arched body.

"That's right, forget about him," Vivian cooed. "I've got what you want right over here, hot stuff!"

She pushed aside the slashed halves of her coat and cupped her hands around her polyester-clad breasts, jiggling her modest endowment as her face flushed in utter humiliation. A red, runny grin spread across Trent's face as he tossed the pitchfork to the side and dragged himself toward her with a lusty sort of limp. Vivian slapped her glasses back onto her face and backed away toward the mill, not taking her eyes off his crackling stinger.

Now what was she supposed to do? She could make it to the windmill, but locking herself inside would leave Erik in danger. She had to stop Trent, but the pitchfork was behind him and his shotgun crutch was under his arm. She couldn't remember the last time she had seen the sword. She was desperate, unarmed, and out of ideas.

At the far end of the driveway, the scraping stroke of a diesel engine grinding to life pounded through the still air. Vivian's eyes snapped toward the sound, picking out a blond head behind the wheel of the nearly totaled ambulance.

"Sherri!" she gasped.

In the distance, Sherri's filthy sleeve mopped a trickle of blood from under her nose as her boot revved the engine. She thrust a finger at Vivian that screamed, *"You!"* followed by a crank of her thumb that said, *"Get the fuck away from him!"*

Vivian stumbled backward as the ambulance launched forward on its bald tires, clattering loose gravel against its wheel wells. Trent gazed dimly at its approaching bumper. His scorched brain obviously hadn't worked out all of the details, but Vivian could tell that he knew something very bad was about to happen to him.

"Hey, Boner McGee!" she yelped, waving her palms. "I'm all hot and sexy and ready for action over here! Come get a hot piece of this hot girl meat!"

She twisted on the balls of her feet and thrust out her backside, giving it a sharp, sassy slap and squeaking with naughty delight. Her posturing captured Trent's full attention, and he turned and dragged himself toward her soft, slender body.

Vivian could hear the scream of the engine growing louder and louder, but she did not break her gaze from Trent's face. His expression was filled with primal lust, yet his swollen eyes were hollow and empty.

The ear-ripping howl of the engine grew deafeningly close as Vivian backed across the open driveway. She could almost hear each exploding piston as they drove the snarled grille toward Trent's hobbling legs. He lunged at her and she jumped backward, throwing herself into the air with a flap of her wings. She landed on one leg in the open door of the windmill, leaving her attacker alone in the path of the screaming ambulance.

"Uh-oh, Trent," she yelled. "It looks like *you're* having a Grocery911!"

Trent's head snapped to the side in horror, but in completely the wrong direction. Two enormous, terrified chickens thundered past him with the bull in hot pursuit, its slashed forehead leading ten thousand pounds of mutated beef on a collision course for the ambulance.

"Look out!" Vivian wailed. "Sherri, stop!"

Behind the cracked windshield, Sherri's teeth were bared in defiance. As the chickens darted around the sides of her thundering chariot, her eyes filled end to end with a field of black fur, broken only by the tiny dot of Trent in its center.

"One of us better be wrong about the afterlife, Trent," she said stoically. "'Cause I don't want to see you in Hell!"

The next few seconds drizzled through Vivian's eyes in a grisly slow motion, as if too many horrible things were happening at once for time to keep up.

Trent bent into a stiff crouch as he attempted to jump clear of the approaching flesh and steel closing in around him. His feet twisted outward … and just kept twisting, all the way around to the back. His bandaged legs flashed black with blood before exploding into sticky shreds, revealing a pair of colossal grasshopper legs.

Vivian stood dumbfounded as Trent's new limbs pounded into the dirt, launching him straight toward her. His shoulder rammed her chest, throwing her into a tumble across the floor of the windmill. In the fraction of a second before she hit the ground, a single memory flashed through her mind: Priscilla's contaminated blood spilling down a wrecked dashboard and into Trent's wounded lap.

The thought was obliterated by the steel-and-flesh cacophony of an ambulance crushing itself to death against a bovine skull. The wail of the silenced diesel engine was replaced by the bull's thousand-decibel scream. It staggered backward on its butcher-block hooves, shaking its crushed skull in a slow, drooling denial. With a final snort of atomized blood it keeled over dead, dropping its five-ton body to the ground.

Vivian saw it fall against the windmill's door, slamming it closed and buttressing it with its collapsing weight. A rattling creak echoed through the tower, dropping a sepulchral sprinkling of dust from the shadows of its rafters.

With the door permanently closed, the octagonal room was lit only by a shaft of sunlight falling from an open vent in the roof, sixty feet above. Shadows chewed at the walls as the light filtered through a series of massive wooden gears, still driven to work by the lazily turning blades outside.

Trent ground the shotgun into the floor and pushed himself up onto the stiff cradle of his new legs. Their human counterparts had been obliterated, leaving nothing but a few ropes of glistening meat dangling from his pelvis. His grasshopper legs cut in swift angles from his hips, angling at the knees behind his back before reaching the ground beneath him.

Vivian scrambled to her feet and turned in a quick circle. She was surrounded by eight stone walls with a few twenty-foot-tall aluminum storage silos tucked into their obtuse corners. Trent's towering, blade-phallused form stood in front of the solitary exit, which was now barricaded by enough beef to feed an army.

"Well, that could have gone somewhat better," Vivian muttered.

Trent rocked back and forth as his damaged brain seamlessly mistook the grasshopper legs for his own. He dropped his shotgun crutch next to the door and took a pounding step forward. Vivian fingered the shell in her pocket as she eyed the gun longingly.

"You don't have to keep up the good-girl act anymore," Trent said. "We're all alone now, girl. Just you and me. It's time to get *freaky*."

His clawed toes dug into the floor as he leapt into the air, landing with a *crack* in front of Vivian. She made a move to dart around his right side, but he cut her off. She made a clumsy break for his left, but another swift leap threw him between her and the shotgun. Vivian suddenly realized that Trent now had the upper hand in size, strength, *and* agility.

"Find another way," she thought.

She backed away, but for every three steps she retreated, Trent closed the gap with one clomping stride. As he moved into the sunbeam, the gold cross hanging from his neck glimmered, catching Vivian's eye.

"Trent, what would the Bible say about this? What kind of Christian assaults helpless girls?! What would God say if he saw you trying to rape me to death?!"

"Forget God," Trent said, flexing his hulking shaft. "I'm bigger than God now."

Vivian jumped back as the stinger howled past her chest, clipping the torn flags of her jacket. She stumbled backward until the tips of her wings bumped against a barrier of solid wood. With a quick glance over her shoulder, she threw up her wings in surrender.

"Oh please, Trent, oh please," she sobbed. "Don't hurt me, Trent!"

"I'm not gonna hurt you, girl," he growled. "But I am gonna make you scream."

He grinned lasciviously as he slid his stalk across Vivian's cheek, over the hammer of her heart, and down the inside of her thigh.

"I give up, Trent! I'll kiss you. I'll touch you. I'll do anything you want. Anything! Just please, *please* keep that stinger out from between my legs!"

Ignoring her pleas—or perhaps driven to new heights of arousal by them—Trent leaned back and stabbed his bayoneted phallus between her thighs. But instead of an embrace of warm flesh, his thrusting assault was rewarded with grinding agony. The pathetic expression on Vivian's face curled into a mischievous grin.

"Aww, Trent," she cooed. "I'm so sorry to disappoint you after you got all geared up!"

She dropped the curtain of her wings with a gigantic flap, launching herself off of Trent's arrested stinger and revealing a pair of enormous vertical gears. A scream tore out of Trent's throat as two sets of wooden teeth rotated upward, drawing his distended member into their crushing bite.

Vivian's battered ankles collapsed as she hit the floor, sending her tumbling toward the door. She grabbed the shotgun, fed the last shell into its chamber, and snapped it shut. Planting the battered stock against her shoulder, she squinted down the barrel and into the back of Trent's skull.

"You are not bigger than God," she growled, slipping her finger into the trigger guard. "But I'll let Him explain that to you in person."

The shotgun sent a teeth-rattling punch through her shoulder as a load of red-hot lead flew from its muzzle. But a sliver of a second earlier, the gears had already pushed Trent's abused shaft from the top of their rotating snarl. He kicked out his legs, and the buckshot flew past his nose and punched a fist-sized hole in a silo, releasing a thin, mocking spout of milled grain.

He landed with a clatter of chitinous feet, and a roar gushed through his teeth. He spun around to face Vivian, his mangled phallus now split like an overcooked hot dog, dripping toxic blood from its glowing stinger.

"Aaaagh! You cocktease *whore!* You'll pay for that with your ass, bitch!"

Vivian dropped the shotgun and snapped her wings together, blasting out of Trent's reach. She landed on her knees, and Trent's long legs threw him effortlessly over her head. She spun around just in time to lurch clear of his swinging blade, but instead of hitting the hard plank floor, she landed flat on her back in a heap of flour.

The jagged teeth of the silo's puncture wound were being forced farther and farther apart by the pressure of the escaping grain, turning the original trickle into a surging fantail of flour. Vivian coughed as the stream beat down upon her, filling the sails of her wings and pinning her to the ground. She thrashed her anchored shoulders against the floor as Trent bent over her.

"I can do anything I want to your virgin ass now," he hissed. "Girl, you're gonna get your cherry popped by a real man."

"Thanks for the offer," Vivian groaned, "but I can de-flour myself!"

She threw her wings forward in a mighty snap, launching twelve cubic feet of blinding white powder into Trent's face. He scrabbled at his burning eyes and stumbled backward as Vivian leapt to her feet. She pounded her wings against the waterfall of flour again and again, beating it into a stifling cloud.

She could hear Trent gagging and thrashing through the thick, silty haze as she pulled her coat over her face and retreated to the perimeter of the windmill. She crouched behind the aluminum belly of a silo and thought very, very hard.

It was ironic. Trent had been reduced to the basest level of human instinct, yet *she* was the one with her options reduced to fight or flight.

The cloud of drifting flour obfuscated all details of the windmill's interior, except for a single beam of sunlight. Vivian's palm settled on a lump in her coat pocket as she saw her only option for survival.

Fight *and* flight.

On the other side of a mountain of unprocessed hamburger, two six-foot hens pecked at the driveway.

"Scram! Get outta here! Go write a love letter to Gonzo!"

The hens retreated in a cloud of feathers as Erik stumbled between them. He thumped dizzily against the wrecked ambulance and wrenched open the door.

"Sherri? You okay?"

Sherri lay hunched over the bent steering wheel with her arms hanging flaccidly at her sides. Erik took her gently by the shoulders and leaned her back against the seat.

"Oh God, oh no," he gasped. "Oh God, Sherri, no!"

The torn neckline of Sherri's T-shirt plunged in a horrific décolletage, showcasing a contiguous field of black and purple bruise covering her chest and wrapping around her neck. Erik leaned in for a closer look, and Sherri's head rolled over on the seat.

"I'm not dead," she rattled. "Quit staring at my tits."

"You're alive!"

"Yeah, thanks, for the second opinion, Dr. Genius."

Wincing and sucking air between her teeth, Sherri pulled her head forward onto her shoulders. Her bent wings fluttered pathetically as she blinked her eyes into focus over the blood-streaked hood.

"Did I hit Trent?" she asked.

"I don't know," Erik admitted. "It doesn't look like it."

"Damn it!"

Through the hole where the windshield had once been she could see the bull lying dead against the windmill.

"Well, at least I killed that mad-cow megafreak."

"Forget about what you killed!" Erik yelped. "How are *you* still alive?!"

Sherri's thumbs thrust weakly toward her enhanced bosom.

"Dual airbags, motherfucker."

Inside the windmill, Vivian clawed her way up the corrugated steel ribs that encircled the silo like a ladder. She drew a breath of fresh air as she hoisted herself out of the dust cloud and onto the container's top. She could see Trent's dark form stalking furiously through the haze below, stirring the cloud with every slash of his stinger.

"You can't hide from me, you dirty whore!" he roared. "Where are you?!"

"Way above your head," Vivian said. "As usual."

Trent looked up through the chalky fog to see Vivian click open Sherri's Zippo lighter with a flick of her thumb. His palms slapped the floor as his grasshopper legs folded into a preparatory crouch.

"You're goin' down, bitch!"

Vivian sparked a tall flame out of the lighter.

"To the contrary," she said. "I'm goin' up."

She bent her knees and leapt into the air, spreading her twelve-foot wingspan like a leathery hang glider. Trent's powerful legs simultaneously launched him off the ground toward her soft, lean body. As they sailed toward each other, Vivian tossed the lighter between the goalposts of Trent's extended arms and into the folding swirls of airborne flour.

In a flash too fast for the human eye to see, the yellow-blue flame ignited a single flour particle, instantly wrapping fire around its combustible surface bathed in the oxygen-rich air. The fire spread to another suspended particle, and another, and another, slicing a millisecond-long cone of flame through the dust. Before the lighter had even hit the floor, every flying particle in the enclosed windmill had near-simultaneously caught fire, pushing a thunderous explosion against its cobblestone walls.

For the briefest of seconds, Vivian saw the fire wrap around Trent, incinerating his mutated body into a red and yellow torch. His mouth opened to scream, but only a forked tongue of fire and smoke rolled from his throat as the unforgiving hand of gravity pulled him back into the depths of the hellish blaze.

Before Vivian could plummet to the same horrible fate, a blast of heated air punched into the sails of her outstretched wings like an invisible fist. The explosive updraft had already thrown her thirty feet into the air before she gave her wings a single, majestic flap, launching herself further skyward. As she sailed toward the roof, she folded her wings straight back toward her toes, and her willowy body shot through the open vent like a bullet from a rifle.

Fresh air whistled over Vivian's face as the thrust of her launch fell away, slowing her ascent to a gentle standstill a hundred feet from the ground. Without panic, she bent in half at the waist and pointed her fingers to the ground like an Olympic high diver. As she fell toward the earth she unfolded her powder-covered wings, feeling out the currents in the air and carrying herself gracefully across the sky.

Vivian was flying.

With instinctual adjustments of her wings, she swooped in a wide, smooth circle around the crumbling farm. She could see Erik and Sherri far below, their faces punctuated with tiny black dots representing their gaping mouths.

The flapping of her shredded clothes was like a drum circle of seraphim heralding her arrival to the skies as she sailed over the farmhouse, and the air rushing down her neck and whipping across her wings sent euphoria sizzling through her body. She had done it. She had put it all together. And for once, she had actually come out on top. For the first time in her life, Vivian Gray had actually succeeded at something. And it felt *good*.

Flour trickled from her hair as she approached the broad, mossy roof of the slouching red barn. With a grand flap of her wings, she flung herself over its eaves, dropping to her feet in a landing so gracefully light that it barely disturbed her swollen ankle.

Perhaps it was the sudden rush of oxygen, or victory, or both, but as Vivian stood on the peak of that crumbling barn, she felt as if she was standing on top of the world. She gave the squeaky weathervane a playful spin and took two long strides toward the edge of the roof in preparation for launch. But before she could return to the air, a rotten, wet crackling thundered from beneath her feet. She dropped like a stone through the decayed shingles and into the darkness of the barn.

The tips of her wings hadn't yet cleared the hole when her feet hit a tall, sloping haystack leaning up against the wall. She rolled head over heels down its gentle grade until her backside landed with a dusty *slap* on the dirt floor. Bits of straw stuck to her hair and clothes as her head wobbled in a slow, dizzy orbit of her neck.

Five seconds later her vision was filled with the beaming, chattering faces of Erik and Sherri.

"Holy shitbombs! You blew the ever-living fuck out of that windmill!" Sherri cheered. "Please, Powderpuff, *please* tell me that you actually killed Trent."

Vivian nodded and Sherri stomped her boots in delight.

"Fuckin' A! You're officially my best friend. You're so fucking bad-ass!"

Erik dropped into the hay by Vivian's side and grasped her hand.

"You flew! Vivian, you actually *flew!* That was incredible! You were amazing!"

He planted a kiss on her lips, but she just continued to stare forward in a dreamlike trance.

"Vivian? Viv, are you okay? What is it?"

Erik's puzzled eyes met Sherri's, then they both turned to see what had Vivian so captivated.

A beam of bright white sunlight sliced through the fresh hole in the roof, landing on the gleaming yellow fenders of a fully restored 1953 Cadillac Eldorado convertible. A committee of tool chests and rusted-out parts cars looked on from the shadows as if waiting for their humble gift to be accepted. Vivian smiled knowingly.

"That's the kind of car you drive to paradise."

Several euphoric hours later, the pristine chrome of the Cadillac's grille whistled melodically through the Pennsylvania mountain air. Its V-8 hummed an elegant bass note as Vivian guided it through the curves and past a reflective road sign.

Liberty Valley - 1 mile

Vivian's clean, vivacious red hair danced in the breeze under the brim of a straw cowboy hat. Just as she had suspected, the repaired generator had yielded a round of much-deserved long, hot showers to herself and her friends, peeling weeks of apocalyptic filth from their bodies and out of their souls. The farmhouse had been equally hospitable with clothing, offering up rural fashion for every sex, style, and freakish mutation.

A slender pair of bib overalls covered Vivian's freshly shaven legs, crossing its denim straps between her wings. A modified sweater hung over her mutated limbs, its accommodating slashes tied off in two sassy knots beneath them. Erik sat in the passenger seat, his face looking clean and sharp atop a secondhand tweed suit.

Vivian's seat was reclined flat to make room for her wings, but the back seat still had plenty of room for Sherri to sprawl out in. She wore a black leather jacket embroidered with the words "Classic Caddy Club." Its immodestly zipped neckline displayed the dark purple orbs of her bruised cleavage like a trophy of heroism. A pair of cut-off "Daisy Dukes" spilled her shapely bronze legs into her battered combat boots.

She leaned on the back of Vivian's seat and twisted her platinum-blond hair around her finger. Lost in her own world, she pouted her tiny pink lips into the rearview mirror with a coy flap of her butterfly wings. Vivian glanced into the mirror and Sherri's pink eyes dropped to the floor.

"It feels good to finally be clean and feminine again, eh Sherri?"

"Hey, I'm not *that* clean," Sherri smirked. "I scrubbed myself raw, and I *still* smell like the ass end of a cabbage."

"Me too," Vivian agreed. "We all do, and we should be thankful for it."

"This is obviously some strange usage of the word 'thankful' that I wasn't previously aware of," Erik said.

"That cabbage smell is what separates us from the zombies," Vivian explained. "By process of elimination, it *has* to be. It all makes sense now. That pink fog that we breathed back in Stillwater was vaporized bay water. It must have been infused with red tide bacteria."

"So what?" Sherri asked.

"The radio said the bacteria was resistant to radiation," Vivian said. "What if it made *us* resistant to radiation once it got into our bodies?"

"But what about the rat and Twiki?" Erik asked. "What about Trent? They all breathed the fog too. How could that be the secret?"

"It's the Smilex factor," Vivian said. "I don't think the vapor could absorb into living tissue on its own. It needed Fusion Fuel to serve as a catalyst."

"Fusion Fuel?" Erik said incredulously. "The energy drink? Are you saying that all that 'Load and lock' marketing hype was actually *true*?"

"Apparently so," Vivian shrugged. "That would also explain how an overdose of estrogen tablets could turn Sherri from a skinny waif into a voluptuous little powderpuff."

Sherri's eyes flashed.

"I am not a powderpuff. I am an individual."

"All right, all right," Vivian smiled. "Save it for the people in Liberty Valley."

Sherri leaned back in her seat and frowned.

"But what if there is no Liberty Valley? Or what if all we find there is more saber-dicked zombies?"

The gentle hum of the whitewall tires changed in pitch as they bumped onto the pavement of a bridge spanning between two rolling mountain peaks. Tons of smooth, white concrete held aloft a long, straight shelf of green steel. Six seconds later, the wheels returned to their original pitch on the other side of the bridge.

"I have a feeling that everything is going to be okay from now on," Vivian said.

The truth was, Vivian didn't know what they would find in Liberty Valley. But it didn't matter. She just knew that everything would be okay from now on.

The purr of engine intensified as it pulled the Cadillac toward the final rise before the road dipped into the valley ahead. A large wooden sign slid silently up the shoulder. It was painted in red, white, and blue, spelling out a message in tall, serif letters.

Welcome to Liberty Valley - An Historic Past, A Bright Future

Vivian glanced at Erik to find him smiling back with unflinching optimism. He put his left hand on her thigh and gave it an excited squeeze. Vivian put her hand on top of his and smiled as the Cadillac's bumper crested the top of the hill.

Marcus Alexander Hart is the author of *Caster's Blog: A Geek Love Story,* the tale of one improbable year told as an online journal; and *Walkin' on Sunshine,* a quantum physics sex farce. He was the editor and movie critic for the comedy website *misinformer.com,* and is a writer for *Geek Monthly* magazine.

Marcus is also an award-winning digital animator. His resume includes over ten published video-game titles, including *Scan Command: Jurassic Park* and *American Idol.* His short film *A Narrow Martian of Error* has been screened in festivals around the world.

Marcus actually drinks Tequiza. And likes it.

To find out more about Marcus, visit his website at MarcusAlexanderHart.com.

ISBN: 978-0-9789707-0-3

PLAGUE OF THE DEAD
BY Z A RECHT

A worldwide viral outbreak brings the dead to life. On one side of the globe, a battle-hardened General surveys the remnants of his command: a young medic, a veteran photographer, a brash Private, and dozens of refugees, all are his responsibility. Back in the United States, an Army Colonel discovers the darker side of the virus and begins to collaborate with a well-known journalist to leak the information to the public...

DYING TO LIVE
a novel of life among the undead
BY KIM PAFFENROTH

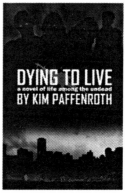

After wandering for months in a zombie-infested world, Jonah Caine discovers a group of survivors. Living in a museum-turned-compound, they are led by an ever-practical and efficient military man, and a mysterious, quizzical prophet who holds a strange power over the living dead. But Jonah's newfound peace is shattered when a clash with another group of survivors reminds them that the undead are not the only—nor the most grotesque—horrors they must face.

ISBN: 978-0-9789707-3-4

ISBN: 978-0-9789707-2-7

DOWN the ROAD
on THE LAST DAY
by Bowie Ibarra

In a small south Texas town, the mayor has rallied his citizens against the living dead and secured their borders. When two strangers from San Antonio stumble into town, they bring news of a global peacekeeping force sweeping toward the city. Led by a ruthless commander, the force is determined to secure the republic of Texas on its own terms, and establish a new, harsh government for the plague-ravaged nation.

MORE DETAILS, EXCERPTS, AND PURCHASE INFORMATION AT
www.permutedpress.com

Lightning Source UK Ltd.
Milton Keynes UK
UKOW021614300112

186334UK00012B/129/A